A Man Without Guilt

# A Man Without Guilt

Bob Marshall-Andrews

Methuen

Published by Methuen 2002

1 3 5 7 9 10 8 6 4 2

This edition published in Great Britain in 2002 by
Methuen Publishing Ltd
215 Vauxhall Bridge Rd, London SW1V 1EJ

Copyright © 2002 by Bob Marshall-Andrews
The right of Bob Marshall-Andrews to be identified as author of this work
has been asserted by him in accordance with the Copyright, Designs and Patents Act 1988

Methuen Publishing Ltd. Reg. 3543167

A CIP catalogue record for this book is available from the British Library

ISBN 0 413 77196 2

Printed and bound in Great Britain by
Creative Print and Design Ltd (Wales), Ebbw Vale

'Plaider le faux pour savoir le vrai'

*'Allege that which is false to discover that which is true'*

For Tony Bevins

# Contents

# Part I

---

# CRIME

# Prologue

## July 1986

The car, motionless and apparently empty, occupied the greater part of the country road. Tall hedges on either side prevented the passing of larger vehicles in either direction. It was watched by two groups of men. Both were armed and suspected the invisible presence of the other. Nothing had passed along the road for several hours and the surrounding countryside of Armagh, wooded and old as conflict, was totally still in the afternoon sun. The car was a Volkswagen, recently stolen in West Belfast. Now it sat, hunched like a watchful, unblinking toad, awaiting action and the assumption of risk. Captain Thomas Aylen inspected the visible surfaces through the telescopic sight of his rifle. Full details had been obtained of its last known legitimate condition from which some deduction was possible. The front boot had not been forced. The true owner at the end of a field telephone had systematically explained observed dents. Ephemera lying on the rear seat, a jacket, two books and a spectacle case, had likewise been confirmed innocent. Inside the car the front and rear foot wells could not be seen. Direct viewing of these areas would have required movement on to higher, open ground or on to the road itself. Decisions had been taken and orders given to Captain Aylen. The road had been sealed by roadblock a mile distant in both directions. Observation was to be continued for a further two hours in the hope of ambush. Thereafter the car would be destroyed by missile, wire-guided from helicopter. The silence of a summer afternoon lay across the valley in natural suspension. Behind him Aylen heard the tiny thud which indicated the operational use of the field transmitter. A moment later the blackened face of his Marine corporal appeared directly next to his own. 'There is a bus on the road.'

'A bus?'

'Evans has seen it from the top of the hill. Half a mile west. It is full.'

'The road is blocked.'

'Evans says he thinks there's a branch road to Ballanoch. They're not on these bloody maps.'

'It must be stopped. We must get in front of it.'

3

The corporal parted undergrowth to this right-hand side. 'Couldn't make it across that country. Woodland and hedges, far too slow.'

'We can do it on the road.'

The corporal looked directly at his officer. 'We would have to pass the car.'

In the short silence that followed Aylen heard himself say, 'I'll go.'

'We can't give you any close cover from here. I will come. Chambers too. He can see in the dark.'

Aylen paused, then nodded once and jerked his head to the left. Without more conversation the three men retreated twenty yards on to a farm track which ran beside a tall hedgerow. Descending along it, they came to a gate beyond which was the tarmac of the road. Fifty yards to the right was the car. Beyond it on a hill in the middle distance Aylen saw the momentary flash of sunlight on glass; a windscreen beyond doubt. Without instruction the men fell into a practised routine. At a fast crouching trot they moved in triangular formation. Aylen went first, scanning ahead of him left and right. Behind him the corporal moved forwards on the left. Beside him Chambers ran backwards, scanning to the rear. Precisely every twenty paces the role of those following was reversed. The capacity to run backwards in body armour is limited.

The front of the car drew towards them. Aylen calculated speed and distance. Assuming constant movement they should be well round the following bend before they met the coach. Deliberately he controlled his momentum. Safety lay in the routine. As he drew alongside the car he allowed himself one glance at the wells of the seats. They were empty. The books on the back seat, he noticed, were mathematical textbooks, just as the owner had said. Oddly comforted, he continued past, his eyes raking the hedgerows and hearing the regular footfalls behind him.

When the car was equidistant between them the explosion occurred. Five hundred yards away the bus came to a shuddering halt, throwing its passengers across the interior. Some remained, shaken and frightened, in the position of their fall. Others watched in silent horror as the fireball extended into the sky and falling debris beat a discord on the roof. In ten minutes the helicopters arrived. One showing a Red Cross contained a doctor and two nurses. The charred remains of two bodies lay in opposite hedges that were still burning. The third Marine, an officer, was found only after searches of the fields beyond. He was alive and, amazingly, conscious, although incapable of communication. His right side had suffered massive injury and burning but was complete save the lower right arm, which was never found.

# Chapter 1

## 21 October 1988

Mr Justice Elias Golding received the news of his daughter's kidnap and abduction while discussing French farce over dinner with an elderly barrister who also wrote novels. That statement is strictly true but an illusion. True, he received, from the doorman of the Garrick Club, the handwritten envelope containing a single sheet of paper on which the message was written. Communication itself was delayed. He gave curt acknowledgement and thrust the envelope unopened into his jacket pocket. Observing the gesture, the club doorman bent to the judge's ear. The envelope, he whispered, had been brought to the desk by an 'unpleasant-looking' man who had stated, on enquiry, that it was urgent and concerned the judge's daughter, Melanie. This increased Elias Golding's sense of irritation. Disapproval of his daughter had, for a considerable time, been exceeded only by disapproval of her many friends, particularly the men. Most of them, in his view, looked unpleasant in some way. He was enjoying his dinner and, despite his relative ignorance of Molière and Racine, he considered he had kept his end up rather well. His contributions, though short, had been respectfully received without appearing to advance the general conversation among his companions. He therefore raised one hand in brief response and continued his potted shrimps and the discussion.

It was not until two and a half hours later, when the judge retrieved his coat from the cloakroom, that he remembered the unopened letter. Even then he did not read it. He had removed it from his jacket and discarded the envelope to a waste bin at the entrance when the arrival of his taxi was announced. In order to avoid further delay, he replaced the paper in the same pocket and hurried across the pavement into the rear seat. He directed the driver to his address in the Temple and was then reluctantly drawn into a conversation about the relative merits of two London football teams, a subject about which he was even less well informed than seventeenth-century French theatre. He disposed of the taxi in King's Bench Walk, carefully checked the change and made his way to his fourth-floor flat. This was a fine residence with extensive river views. He had occupied it for several years by reason of his position as a High Court judge and his ability, well renowned, to cultivate the good opinion of those upon which such privilege depended.

On entering the flat he discovered a quantity of unopened mail. This was not unusual, as it was his habit on Fridays to work late in his rooms in the Strand before going straight to the Garrick. He settled at the study desk and inspected the post. He carefully divided out the junk circulars and requests for charitable assistance, which he thrust straight into the bin, reflecting as he did so on the unnecessary waste of effort and material. He then opened two bills and a bank statement which he placed on a neat pile of documents for later attention. Finally he disposed of a circular from a firm of publishers seeking to sell him a copy of *Who's Who in the Law*. This caused a brief struggle between vanity which desired possession of this work (in which he had a prominent mention) and parsimony which balked at the massive cost. Unable to decide, he placed the circular on the same pile for future consideration. The time was now 11.15 p.m.

The judge's last chore concerned the perusal of five written applications to appeal against sentences passed in the Crown Court. After peremptory consideration, he rejected them all, made himself a cup of cocoa, performed his ablutions and went to bed. Only after he had switched out his bedside lamp and assumed his normal right-sided foetal position did he recollect the existence of the document, apparently concerning his daughter, lying in his jacket which hung on the Corby trouser press at the foot of his bed. In the darkness he gave a sigh of exasperation. He was comfortable, warm and close to sleep. Melanie rarely wrote letters. Manifestos, yes, essays and articles by the ton, but letters to her father were rare and they usually contained spontaneous and random polemics on the shortcomings of the judiciary, the welfare state, foreign policy and the world economic order. Indeed almost everything that Mr Justice Golding regarded as essential for a civilised life was subjected by his daughter to vigorous literary assault. Certainly it was literate stuff and even amusing in a pyrotechnic way but not (the judge briefly opened his eyes to the luminous dial of the alarm clock) at 12.30 a.m. on a Saturday. Tomorrow would be soon enough. Before he drifted into unconsciousness he reflected on the method of delivery. Certainly unusual but not in any way surprising. His daughter possessed a seemingly vast and eclectic range of friends and admirers. It would not be the first time she had prevailed upon one of them, no doubt at great personal inconvenience, to deliver her works. Her lifestyle presupposed a near-perpetual absence of stamps and she would have assumed his presence at the Garrick on the basis of long experience. With that thought, Mr Justice Golding relaxed into a calm, self-satisfied oblivion, which was destined to be his last for many months to come.

The flat in which Golding slept occupied one half of the top floor of a staircase. The adjacent flat was leased by Lord Justice James Stoker and his wife Mary. In the last months of World War Two, Jim Stoker, then a captain in the Green Jackets, was involved in the final assault on Hamburg. During this battle he had been hit by twenty bullets from a machine gun, fired, it later transpired, by a boy of thirteen in full SS uniform. Having expended the last clip of his ammunition, the youth climbed above a ruined wall, gave the Nazi salute and blew himself apart with a stick grenade. Jim Stoker suffered the loss of his left leg below the knee and a lifetime of nagging pain and sleeplessness caused by the phantom aching of his missing leg and visions of the tiny, fearless zealot who had died in defence of, and total dedication to, political infamy. This insomnia caused him to rise early, a circumstance shared as a matter of duty by his wife. At 6.45 on the morning of 22 October 1988, the Stokers were standing together eating their halves of the same grapefruit and looking from their window at the flat sweep of the Temple lawns as they disappeared into the morning mist of the Thames. They were silent, contemplating a perfect autumn day. As they did so, the brass knocker on their front door began a violent and urgent banging. Despite practised use of his false leg Jim Stoker was slower than his wife, who opened the door beyond which their neighbour, Golding, could be seen in pyjamas, dressing gown and high agitation.

'I am sorry,' he said, 'to come to you in this way but I have just received an extraordinary letter. I am not entirely sure what to do.' So saying, he held out a piece of plain writing paper which Mary Stoker took from him as she led him to a chair in the dining room.

'Stay there,' she commanded, 'while I get you some coffee and then we can talk about it. Just calm down. You are obviously in a state.'

In the short time that his wife was in the kitchen, Jim Stoker observed his neighbour with a set smile concealing both curiosity and distaste. The Stokers did not like Elias Golding. Their animosity towards their fellow lawyer (Mary Stoker had also been at the Bar) sprang from a period many years before when Mr Justice Golding, then plain Elias Golding, had obtained a tenancy in Jim Stoker's Chambers. The tenancy had been brief and unhappy, culminating in Golding leaving to form his own set. The parting of ways had been entirely predictable. The two men could not have been more dissimilar in every facet of their characters. Jim Stoker was physically recklessly brave and had won a Military Cross, rescuing a wounded Marine sergeant under heavy fire on the Normandy beaches. During the same war, Elias Golding had been on permanent placing in a staff college near Esher due, it was unkindly said, to the creative endeavours of his family doctor. This, in itself, would not have earned the displeasure of the Stokers, whose natural generosity would have disposed them to disbelief. There were many other distinctions. Whilst the Stokers were funny and noisy (frequently rather excessively so), Golding was an acerbic bore in the company of any save those that he perceived were able to advance his own station. As a result of their jolly living and frequent imprudent charity, the Stokers were invariably broke. Golding, during his career at the Bar, had amassed a very considerable personal fortune by methods wherein lay the greatest distinction between the two men. Whereas Jim Stoker had operated his legal practice on a cheerful Robin Hood basis, frequently forgoing his fee to the exasperation of his otherwise handsome-spirited clerk, Golding, a formidable (if dull) court performer, charged all comers to the hilt. Also, from the simplest cases he would produce a staggering quantity of written advices and opinions, all of which con-cluded with an exhortation to his solicitors to carry out further, invariably useless, investigations and, having done so, to return the papers for yet another advice. By this simple expedient the most straightforward litigations were transformed into cases of Byzantine complexity, incorporating monumental heaps of paper which stood at every corner of his room like the monoliths of Mammon. It is an unhappy fact that all professions, however honourable, have their bounders and Elias Golding was one of them.

In all these circumstances it was scarcely surprising that a profound animosity grew between the two men. Stoker regarded Golding as a rogue and Golding, with substantially less justification, regarded Stoker as a fool. None of this would have been apparent to the casual observer. Before Stoker's elevation to the Court of Appeal they had, of course, been brought into close contact as judges and on a number of occasions had shared Lodgings. When they did so the only indication of their feelings for each other was the excessive and elaborate courtesy which attended every gesture of their relationship. The differences were further illustrated and compounded by their behaviour on the Bench. Stoker was a popular judge, combining an aversion to excessive detail and an attachment to wider justice. In criminal cases his summations to the jury were fair and reasonable and when conviction resulted his sentences generally erred on the side of leniency. Golding was a querulous, nit-picking, caustic tribunal, whose obvious bias frequently led to unlikely acquittals from stubborn and unbiddable juries. His sentencing was always heavy and became progressively harsher as a reflection of the increasing bitterness in his private life.

Despite his considerable aversion to his neighbour, two things had always caused Stoker to seek to reassess his opinion. The first was that Mr Justice Golding was Jewish and the second was Golding's daughter. Unlike many of his generation and class, Stoker loathed anti-Semitism, an instinct rendered the more powerful by his presence at the liberation of Belsen concentration camp. He was aware that Golding's reputation was well-known at the Bar and it troubled him to think that the odium reserved justly for the man was, in some cases, extended to the race. All in all he would have preferred Mr Justice Golding to be Welsh. The principal reason for his tolerance, however, was Melanie Golding, the judge's daughter. Golding's marriage had, for a while, been the wonder of the London Bar. At the age of forty-five he had married a dancer from the Sadler's Wells Ballet, a Jewish Italian from a refugee family and one of her profession's acknowledged beauties. The marriage subsisted long enough for her to provide Golding (then a wealthy QC) with a baby daughter. The dancer was then inevitably driven into the arms of a famous and impecunious actor by the mean-spirited dullness of her husband. How she had failed to comprehend these deficiencies prior to her marriage was a matter of universal astonishment. The child, known as Mel, was thus brought up in a strange mixture of houses, the bohemian and the boring. The Stokers themselves had no children, a misfortune which was incurable (firing blanks, as the ex-soldier freely admitted). However, due to the proximity of their London flats and the crushing dullness of her father's home, Melanie Golding was a frequent visitor in the Stokers' living room. They, for their part, swiftly perceived that the child was rare and enchanting to a degree inexplicable by any study of genetics. Indeed as she grew order it was widely rumoured that her true father was 'the judge next door'. This was untrue but possessed a compelling logic. She had an untidy, dashing beauty and a generosity of spirit which was as warm as sunshine in May. Imperfection, if it may be, was provided by excessive laughter which flowed ceaselessly across her features, bringing to her dark, broad face lines and creases premature for her twenty-five years. Inevitably the Stokers became her honorary godparents and, indeed, in the course of time became frequent visitors to Melanie's flat overlooking Hackney Marshes, from which she pursued a frenetic and disorderly life imperfectly disciplined by her post-graduate studies of nineteenth-century philosophy at King's College,

London. As coincidence had it, on that very weekend, the Stokers had been asked to Sunday lunch, an event which they relished with happy anticipation.

When Mary Stoker returned from the kitchen she carried a tray on which was a coffee jug, three mugs and the folded paper she had been handed on Golding's arrival. She put down the coffee, distributed the mugs and in a gesture of politeness offered the letter to her guest who rejected it with the palm of his hand.

'No, please, I would like you to read it. You know Melanie well and I would welcome your views.'

Mary Stoker unfolded the paper and beckoned to her husband who sat beside her. Both in rapt silence read the text. The handwriting, they noticed immediately, had a backwards slant and childlike construction, though whether this resulted from incompetence or a desire to conceal its identity was, of course, impossible to tell.

This is what they read.

Golding,
By the time you receive this letter your daughter will be our prisoner. She will discover what many have unjustly experienced at your hands, the total loss of liberty and freedom. Do not be under any illusions. This is not an ordinary kidnap carried out by the weak. We do not seek your money, filthy-rich though you are. You and your disgusting kind must learn that there are those, unlike yourself, who are above the instincts of the herd. There are those who can act as they wish, as they please, as we have done in the execution of our Self Fulfilment. You may now await such news as we may give you which will be provided, or not, as we decide. The fate of your daughter is entirely in our hands. Understand that we recognise no moral constraints or categorical imperatives. If you inform the police or other authorities be confident that we will know and will consider it to be a token of your own weakness, the spiteful excesses of which has caused misery to so many. The consequences may or may not be fatal. That is all.
Elan Vital

Having completed the letter somewhat faster than her husband, Lady Stoker transferred an incredulous gaze to her neighbour and opened her mouth to speak but in the event said nothing. At her side the Lord Justice read the document a second time. Finally he placed the document on the table.

'Is it possible,' he said, 'that this is a joke?'

On the other side of the table, Golding shook his head. 'That's what I thought, a mad hoax in appalling taste. Melanie has some very odd friends. Of course I tried immediately to telephone Melanie's flat. The phone was engaged, which it usually is, but not at this hour on Saturday morning. I have tried several times.'

In the silence that followed the letter box of the flat opened and the morning post was delivered to the mat.

Jim Stoker looked sharply at his visitor. 'When did you get this?'

Avoiding his eyes, Golding replied, 'It was last night by a messenger at the Garrick.'

'Last night?'

'I am afraid so. Yes, I know, I know. I should have read it but I did not as I was in the middle of dinner. It didn't seem important.'

'But *after* dinner?'

'I don't know. I just forgot it. It was in my jacket pocket. I was tired. I had work to do. It was only this morning that I remembered and looked at it, then I came here.'

Observing the crumpled figure before him, Jim Stoker was moved to sympathy. 'Don't distress yourself. You did not know this was about Melanie.'

Golding appeared to sink further into his chair. 'Well, I'm afraid I did.'

'*What?*'

'The doorman who gave me the envelope. He said something about Melanie.'

Mary Stoker stood up. 'Let us get this straight. You knew it concerned Melanie?'

'So I was told.'

'And you did nothing?'

'No, I am afraid not.'

'Why not?'

'I just don't know.'

Jim Stoker intervened to deflect his wife's anger and did precisely the reverse. 'Where is the envelope? It may give some clue.'

There is a moment when a witness collapses under questioning. Placing both hands before his face, Golding spoke through his fingers. 'I haven't got it. It's at the Garrick.'

The Stokers spoke together: 'At the Garrick? You opened it?'

'I opened it but I did not read it. I got a taxi. The light didn't work. I forgot it, that's all.' Removing his hands he stared helplessly at his neighbours. 'I just forgot it. I'm only human, for God's sake. And we still don't know that it isn't some ghastly joke. Melanie can be very odd sometimes. We have never really seen eye to eye, you know. And she has got some pretty funny friends. Also there is all this mumbo-jumbo about "categorical imperatives" which I am sure is some reference to some crackpot philosopher.'

'Hegel,' said Mary Stoker quietly.

'Oh yes, Hegel. I had forgotten you know all about this kind of thing. And then there is this whole Marxist business she is involved in. I am not sure she isn't still.'

'I can see no Marx,' said Lady Stoker evenly; 'insofar as I can discern anything, it is a hopelessly confused mishmash of Hegel, Nietzsche and possibly Freud. Melanie could not have written this if she tried.'

There followed a heavy silence in the Stokers' living room as though all three occupants stood on the very verge of statements too wounding to express. Finally, Jim Stoker said, 'Have you told the police?'

'No.'

'Then we must do so at once.'

'But if this is Melanie's idea of a joke, for God's sake, it could cause the most frightful scandal. Also I am in court on Monday morning and so are you.'

Jim Stoker leaned forward and took hold of the arm of Golding's dressing gown. 'Your daughter and our friend may be in terrible danger. She may be dead or wounded. Your court or my court will wait for as long as is necessary. Go and put on your clothes. Do not touch the letter, none of us must touch it again. Mary will go with you and phone the police from your flat. I will inform the Lord Chief Justice and the Listing Office that there has been a family crisis, unspecified, which means neither of us can sit on Monday. Then we will face this out together.'

As he watched the judge's retreating back and reached for his own phone, Jim Stoker found himself tapping his false leg against the chair, a familiar gesture of frustration and anger. 'The letter got it right,' he thought. 'That man is as weak as water. And he is not telling us the truth.'

# Chapter 2

Before the telephone rang at his Enfield home, Superintendent Eddie Cole, Head of the Serious Crime Squad, was a worried and unhappy man. He had just thought to himself that everything that could go wrong was going wrong. Having answered the phone and conducted a short semi-hysterical conversation with his sergeant at Scotland Yard, Eddie Cole felt infinitely worse. Shaking his bald head, he lay back on his study carpet, raised his dimpled legs straight into the air before him and, with a grimace of pain, resumed the exercises which the telephone had interrupted. As he did so the door opened and Janet Cole entered with tea, newspapers and a well-practised air of weary resignation. She placed the tray on the desk, negotiated her husband's flailing feet and began to remove the pillows and duvet from the sofa on which he had slept.

'You were in very late. I heard you, four a.m. Has there been a crime wave?'

From the floor Eddie Cole spoke through grunts of exertion. 'Needed some information. Entertaining my best snout. Feel terrible. Now there's another bloody mess. Got to go back in.'

'What was the call?'

'Brendan O'Hara. A judge's daughter has gone missing. Sounds like a hoax but the Commissioner is panicking. Says it's got to be me, personally.' Pulling himself into a sitting position, the policeman took a cup and stared gloomily into the liquid. 'As if I haven't got enough to panic about.'

The account that Eddie Cole gave his wife concerning his night's activities was only partly untrue. He had spent the night in bed with Anita Flynn. This lady, in addition to performing admirably as the mistress of the Head of the Serious Crime Squad, was London's most successful brothel keeper and general procurer for the City's elite. She was also a surprisingly consistent and accurate police informer. Eddie Cole had spent the previous night at her premises, partly to satisfy his declining libido and partly to pursue information as to the doings and whereabouts of Roddy Nailor.

Eddie Cole's interest in this particular gentleman was both personal and professional. Roddy Nailor was, according to his own self-description, 'a typical East End Rough Diamond' or 'one of Nature's Gentlemen'. In fact he was an extremely dangerous and powerful gangster and a profound, intractable and incurable psychopath. He was the elder of the infamous Nailor brothers. Whether this was, indeed, their family name, or whether it related to some of their more unpleasant characteristics, was a celebrated mystery. The younger brother was called Willie. Their mother, Mrs Nailor, was a formidable woman of Scottish extraction. According to her own self-assessment she was 'one of the Salt of the Earth Cockneys'. This reputation, together with the undoubted fact that she had succeeded in producing from her loins two of the country's pre-eminent sadists and thugs, was later to bring her to the attention of anthropologists driven by the increasing shortage of primitive tribes in the Amazon Basin to pursue their studies in the Mile End Road. She was indeed a fascinating object of academic interest, since her kindly maternal nature, warmth and personality, endless small charitable deeds in the community, not to mention her ample bosom and twinkling eyes, gave no clue whatsoever to the undoubted fact that she carried within her genes the capacity to produce monsters.

The Nailor brothers themselves were, by common consent, fond of children, assuming of course that they were white. Indeed, it was well-known that they contributed lavishly to the local Boys' Clubs and children's charities a not insubstantial fraction of the monies which they obtained by extortion, menaces and fraud. The Nailors' commercial activities had begun shortly after they left school at the ages respectively of fourteen and fifteen. Like all commercial empires, the original idea from which it was based was entirely straightforward. It began with a simple demand for the payment of money. Refusal to pay led immediately to Grievous Bodily Harm. This type of activity was, of course, not unknown in the East End. What was impressive about the Nailors was the scale of the operation, the rates of growth and their total indifference not only to the law (which was common enough) but to every other form of social restraint, restriction, mores, value, precept or regard for the public weal, the study of which has engrossed philosophers from Socrates to Sartre. Nor should it be thought that the philosophical consequences of this behaviour were lost on the inhabitants of Stepney and Bow, who have for generations learned to replace the study of philosophy (which was denied to them by circumstances) by an infinitely greater wisdom, namely the immediate recognition of raw atavistic power. As the Nailors' reputation grew and widened, so also did the public realisation (without conscious deliberation) that the Nailor brothers and their acolytes represented something far greater than a mere criminal nuisance. They represented in its most elemental form the desire of man to be Free. They did as they pleased, to whom they pleased, whenever they wished. Their business methods also changed. Whilst the principle remained similar the enterprise became more sophisticated. Personal intimidation gave way to professional extortion. Stealing became hijacking, widespread fiddling became long-term fraud. And so they prospered.

This activity, of course, did not go unnoticed by the police. Initially, indeed, attempts were made to control and curtail the activities of the Nailor family. All came to naught. Two cases of demanding money with menaces were actually brought to court, neither of which was successful. On the first occasion the principal witness refused even to open his mouth once called to the witness box and thus suffered, in addition to his previous injuries, three months' imprisonment for contempt of court. In the second trial the main witness simply disappeared without trace. After these early attempts, however, an uneasy truce was established. The power of the Nailors now extended throughout the East End and Home Counties, including under its aegis the pleasant and deeply dishonest County of Essex. As a result crime was at least tidy. Theft, of any consequence, was committed only on the basis of license from the Nailor family. Unlicensed, wildcat thieving was punished by them either by the infliction of serious injury or, more subtly, by exposure, together with all the necessary fabricated and perjured evidence, to the police. Thus the conviction rates remained reasonably high and serious criminal activity assumed an orderly and measured flow. Good discipline was kept by sporadic acts of extreme violence invariably involving nailing some part of the victim to the floor or some other convenient wooden structure. All the while Mrs Nailor was daily to be found wheeling her wicker trolley between the local supermarket and the council flat from which she refused to be moved.

This state of affairs would, no doubt, have lasted indefinitely had it not been for the arrival of the Won-Ki family from Hong Kong. Apart from the fact that they were Chinese and members of the Triads, the Won-Kis bore a clear resemblance to the Nailors. The family consisted of a mother and two sons, Lin and Chian. Prior to their arrival in England the Won-Ki family had run a successful extortion and prosti-tution racket in Hong Kong. Indeed, so successful had they become that even the prosecuting authorities in the Colony determined upon their downfall and it was only by dint of skilful bribery that they were able to escape to the United Kingdom. Here they established themselves within the Chinese community and industriously embarked upon their own profession. Their chosen method of intimidation was that frequently associated with the Triads, namely the summary removal of any specified part of the anatomy. Save for this one, scarcely important, distinction, their operations and those of their swiftly assembled gang were, as already observed, near identical to those of the Nailor family. Inevitably, therefore, rivalry swiftly degenerated into conflict. This process was hastened by the increasing exasperation of the victims themselves. The commercial *raison d'être* of a protection racket is, of course, that no protection is required, save from those who are providing the service. Before long large numbers of publicans, costermongers, car salesmen and market traders who had been threatened with dismemberment by the Won-Kis were applying to the Nailors to provide the service for which they were, in a sense, contractually bound. Furthermore, whilst most East Enders will endure, for the sake of community life, the danger of being nailed to a floor, few relished the prospect of losing the very body parts necessary for this purpose. In short the whole thing was getting, as the incomparable vernacular has it, Out of Order.

Things deteriorated rapidly, and when the landlord of the Nailors' own pub was divested of his index finger and right eye following a confrontation with the Won-Kis and their friends, the Nailors decided to move in. The action they took was spectacular, if unimaginative. Lin Won-Ki was ambushed when leaving his favourite nightclub, after which Roddy Nailor personally supervised the nailing of both the Triad's feet to the floor of a disused warehouse close to St Catherine's dock. This was, as it transpired, a serious mistake for two reasons. First, it invited immediate retaliation (some would say over-reaction) from the Triads and three days later Willie Nailor disappeared. Most of him, indeed, was never found again. Only his head reappeared in his mother's supermarket trolley, a meat cleaver firmly embedded between his close-set eyes. Secondly and of infinitely more long-term significance for Roddy Nailor, the choice of warehouse was unfortunate. It was one of three such buildings then undergoing extensive refurbishment and reconstruction for what would become known, ten years later, as Young Upwardly-Mobile People. The developers were funding the project by selling the flats, before conversion, on the basis of existing specifications and demonstration units. In their haste (and in the dark of night) Nailor and his henchmen had unwittingly nailed Lin Won-Ki to the floor immediately outside the show flat on the night before its grand opening, to which several hundred enthusiastic would-be purchasers had been invited. As the unhappy developers discovered, there is nothing so deadening to the get-up-and-go yuppie spirit than the sight of someone with his feet nailed to the floor, notwithstanding that he is a Chinese gangster. The news spread swiftly. The warehouses achieved an unsavoury reputation and remained unconverted for ten years. The developers went bust. This was not, in itself, very important since they were a subsidiary company of a large and influential multinational. However, it is invariably the case that where a profit is denied to the Great and Good, public outrage, suitably stimulated by the media, is seldom far behind. Thus it was that the popular press (owned by interests not wholly dissimilar to those of the developers themselves) embarked upon a crusade against organised crime in the East End. Inevitably it was not long before dark suspicions were being raised about the acquiescence or connivance of the police. Questions were asked in the House. Names were named, prominent among which were those of Roddy Nailor and his deceased brother Willie, whose head had been accorded a full gangster funeral at St Mary Magdalene's in the Bow Road.

It soon became obvious, even to the highest echelons of the Metropolitan Police, that urgent action was necessary to restore a modicum of public confidence. A team of detectives was appointed specifically to deal with organised crime under the leadership of Detective Inspector Eddie Cole. It was said that Eddie Cole was good at three things – locking up villains, knocking up other people's wives and knocking back pints of beer. Most of this was true. He also possessed furious energy, a capacity for self-righteousness and, until the whisky got him, an insatiable libido. As to convicting criminals, his success rate was the highest in the capital. Whether or not he was an 'honest copper' depended entirely on the definition of that interesting term. Certainly he was incorruptible, and indeed in his private life he rarely told a lie save, of course, to his wife. In his professional life things were a little more complicated. Like many gifted policemen Eddie Cole had very little difficulty catching criminals. Catching them was easy. Putting them in prison – 'banging them up' – was a quite different, tedious and irritating matter. Tedious and irritating because it required the provision of evidence. On occasions, he was the first to admit, some evidence was necessary, for instance in cases where a sensible person would perceive the possibility of innocence. What annoyed Eddie Cole was that it was equally necessary in cases where the accused was patently and obviously guilty. Guilty of what, exactly, was a matter of little consequence. In the case of Roddy Nailor 'almost everything' would have been a fair answer.

The whole thing was compounded by yet another unhappy fact in a policeman's life. Eddie Cole had learned very early that the more serious, widespread, persistent and dangerous the crime and the more serious, professional, dangerous and organised the criminal, the less likelihood there was of obtaining a shred of evidence. Quite apart from the obvious administrative advantages employed by the professional criminal and the sophisticated nature of the equipment used both to commit the crime and to avoid detection, there existed a near-immunity from incriminating witnesses. 'Confucius he say,' thought Eddie Cole bitterly, 'man with meat cleaver in head make very bad witness. Man who contemplate meat cleaver in head, even worse.' However, when Eddie Cole was placed in charge of breaking organised crime ('Buster Cole', the press called him) something had to be done and done quickly. On the very day of his appointment the country's largest-selling tabloid had carried the headlines POLICE PACT WITH ORGANISED CROOKS. There followed a story about a left-wing London MP reporting to the House a conversation with an unnamed constituent who claimed to have overheard a conversation in a pub between a notorious local gangster and a detective sergeant from the Fraud Squad. 'So what,' thought Eddie Cole, 'where was the evidence? An anonymous constituent. Confucius he say, anonymous constituent make very silent witness.'

In the event Eddie Cole solved the problem in the way that he had always done. Roddy Nailor's fingerprints were found on a hammer discovered by no fewer than three police officers in the immediate vicinity of Lin Won-Ki's firmly secured foot. Furthermore, it was proved by a plethora of forensic examination that the striations on the head of the nails matched exactly with the irregularities of the hammer. Thus a conviction was ensured without putting Lin Won-Ki in the witness box. Putting him into that position would, in any event, have been quite useless for two reasons. First, Lin Won-Ki did not believe in co-operating with the police, and second, he was himself on trial. His fingerprints had been found on the meat cleaver embedded in the head of Willie Nailor. In the event both men were found guilty. Roddy Nailor, convicted of Wounding with Intent to Do Grievous Bodily Harm, was sentenced by Mr Justice Golding (newly appointed to the Bench) to a term of fifteen years. At the same time in an adjacent court, Mr Justice Stoker was passing a sentence of fifteen years upon Lin Won-Ki, who had been duly convicted of the manslaughter of Willie Nailor.

The contrasting reactions of Roddy Nailor and Lin Won-Ki to their identical sentences, both obtained on the basis of entirely concocted evidence, would have formed, had it been common knowledge, a fascinating reflection on the cultural and political divisions between East and West. Lin Won-Ki received his sentence with polite composure. Guilty he most certainly was, since he had pinioned Nailor's arms at the time that the blow was struck. That his fingerprints could not have been on the cleaver was equally certain since the murder weapon had been obtained and wielded by his brother Chian. The reaction of Roddy Nailor could not have been more different. Since his role had simply been to direct where the nails were to be inserted in Lin's feet and, afterwards, to give his victim a friendly push, his fingerprints likewise could not have been upon the hammer. Indeed, the hammer that was in fact used now safely rested at the bottom of the Thames in Tilbury. Knowing this to be the case, he was grasped by a sense of manic injustice. In this state he demonstrated a well-known and peculiar truth, namely that there is no man with a more profound and nobler sense of forensic fair play than the English psychopath. In no other hearts than those belonging to the professional and English villain do the immortal words of John Curran carve themselves with greater depth: 'The condition of liberty,' as Roddy Nailor knew full well, 'is eternal vigilance.' Vigilant he had been, but of his liberty he had been robbed and in his heart and brain there grew a massive torrential storming against the injustice of it all. In a mind flattened and debased by the psychopathy which was his birthmark there grew an awful, grinding, consuming desire for revenge. Revenge on Eddie Cole whose perfidy had brought him low. Revenge on Mr Justice Golding whose summing up to the jury had sealed his doom and who had sent him down. Revenge against Society itself, the Herd from whom the bone-headed jurors had been culled in order to judge and reject Him, the Free Spirit. Him, to whom the Collective Will, the Social Contract, the Governance of Reason, the ghastly utilitarian moral dilemmas, balances, codes and codices, precepts and prerogatives were mere scorched earth and chaff.

# Chapter 3

All these things preyed on the mind of Eddie Cole as he was driven to Scotland Yard. It was all so long ago. Nearly ten years and he had been worried, if he was honest with himself, the whole time. The origins of the disquiet troubled him as much as the anxiety itself. His conscience was, after all, entirely clear. Justice had been done. Not the pettifogging, mean-minded nit-picking justice which proceeded from the endless minute sifting of ephemeral evidence. Not the tedious observations of Codes of Practice, Rules of Interrogating, Rights of Access, so dear to the hearts of civil libertarians who had never seen a man with his foot impaled on a stake. Real justice had been done. The guilty had been punished, the innocent had been protected. He, Eddie Cole, had done it. In the place of small wrong he had created, yes created, a greater truth.

He shifted angrily across the back seat of the car, a characteristic movement as though to release some form of nervous pain.

What did they know about it? The judges and the Home Office mandarins from their fat schools, the tight-lipped ladies from the Liberty Council with their tiresome platitudes and scarcely-veiled political ambitions or, for that matter, the modern breed of police super-intendents, high fliers fresh from their university courses and token weeks in the back of a panda car driven no doubt by another graduate sociologist from Brighton? Did they think that their wretched rules protected the innocent? The Code of Practice for Police Officers designed to fetter and chain every minute of the copper's life. 'Rubbish,' thought Eddie Cole. For ninety-nine per cent of the criminal classes it didn't matter. Get them in the nick, obey all the rules, sit them in a cell for a couple of hours, bang the doors, then let them look at Eddie Cole's face, creased and lined and wounded with the anger and pity of it all. Sometimes you couldn't even get the caution out before they started to bring it all up. So who did they protect, these forty-two pages of rules and regulations, appendices and schedules and clauses? The one per cent, that's who they protected. The Nailors and the Won-Kis who sat with their smiles and their lizard-skin solicitors from Stepney and Bow.

That's who they protected. It didn't work. Not with Eddie Cole, the creator of his own truth. In the back of his car Eddie Cole smiled.

But he was troubled. It wasn't his conscience. What was it? He shifted across the seat. Like a neurotic recently informed of the symptoms of some dreaded disease he searched his body, burrowing after tiny reactions, prey simultaneously to apprehension and the morbid certainty of doom. He could not avoid it. It was Fear. But nothing frightened Eddie Cole. Two things made him untouchable. The first was his rank. Superintendents in the Serious Crime Squad are as inviolate as Medici princes. Secondly, he held them in contempt. The underworld with all its ghastly inhabitants. There was no threat that had not been made to Eddie Cole by those he pursued. There was no pain or torture which human ingenuity could perceive at the wildest extremity of malice that had not been wished upon him. Sometimes indeed it was wished upon his whole extended family, his wife, his children, his parents, his second cousins, not forgetting his dog, Truncheon. Sometimes they spat in his face, threats and warnings delivered with the manic power and articulation of the damned. Sometimes they were contained in letters, illiteracy failing to curb the hyperbolic flow of language designed to crush the spirit by the awfulness of its imaginings and the depths of its crude malevolence. Burning, boiling, buggering, impaling, gouging, dismembering, spiking, disfiguring, scalping, all found their part in a restless imagery of agony and revenge sufficient to render Thomas Torquemada spellbound with admiration. Yet for it all he gave not a fig. He knew them for what they were and, knowing what they were, he regarded them not. Where others saw gangsters, saturnine power and legendary influence, he saw damaged, vainglorious, strutting men full of glare and menace and signifying nothing. Most of all he despised them for their dependence. They *needed* him, needed the Old Bill and Flying Squad, the police and the parking wardens, the East End and the West End, the banks and the building societies, the licensed bookmakers and the licensed clubs, the dole queue and the Stock Exchange, the privileged and the deprived, the whole social corporate structure. They needed it. Without it they were nothing. Without the structure they would be lost like fleas without a dog. As they broke the rules so they revered them; as they kicked against the pricks they abhorred their removal. For this reason of course they were Conservatives to a man, petty bourgeois in their hearts. They longed to belong. And so Eddie Cole despised them. They were not Free. They lived in the high-security prison of social dependence and aspiration. And as he despised them he regarded them not. Yet Nailor was different.

In his case there were no threats or hysterics, but the man had burned with a terrible intensity. Even the judge, Golding, appeared quite shocked by it. It was all ten years ago and now Nailor was out. The Free Man was free.

Nailor's release had apparently been preceded by a period of two years at Grafton Hall Open Prison near Bournemouth. This Institution, which consisted of a Manor House and a motley assortment of Nissen huts, prefabs and workshops, had originally passed into public hands in the mid-1930s and had since that date been used as a hospital, Approved School, training camp, art college, lunatic asylum and, finally, an open prison, in which capacity it played host to an interesting collection of stockbrokers, shipping merchants, solicitors, publishers, systems analysts, clergymen, gangsters and mass murderers, the latter two categories enjoying short periods of semi-confinement at the end of their sentences deemed to be essential for their return to the waiting world. Because of the nature of its inmates and, let it be admitted, the indulgence of its regime, it was known to the local inhabitants and the wider criminal fraternity as 'the Country Club'. Among the numerous facilities it offered to broaden, improve and rehabilitate its guests were courses in sociology, anthropology and philosophy at Bournemouth College. These courses were always heavily oversubscribed, thereby proving that middle-class convicts of substance will endure almost anything for a daily trip to the seaside. Indeed on Tuesday, Wednesday and Thursday afternoons many of the gentlemen to be found solicitously assisting the elderly across the Bournemouth promenade were swindlers or serial rapists enjoying a brief respite from their studies of the Age of Enlightenment or the marriage rites of Borneo headhunters. Also available as an adjunct to these academic pursuits were courses in basic business administration, shorthand and typing.

During his two years at Grafton Hall Roddy Nailor had been an enthusiastic participant in these intellectual pursuits, achieving diplomas in Anthropology, Nineteenth-Century Philosophy and elementary Business Studies. Not content with this academic distinction, Roddy Nailor, with the active encouragement of his well-meaning tutors, succeeded in contributing an article to the national press on the subject of Radical Subjectivism and the Principle of Universality. Publication of this article was not motivated on the part of the *Evening News* by any intention to illuminate the works of Hegel, Nietzsche or Kant. Rather the reverse. Upon receipt of the typescript, which arrived on his desk in a plain brown prison envelope, the features editor read it twice. Thereafter he took the precaution of consulting his chief editor and inviting him to read the article without knowledge of its author. The chief editor, who had once unsuccessfully read philosophy at Balliol, flipped through the pages with an expression of steadily mounting delight. 'Who wrote this garbage?' he said. 'The man's as mad as a hatter.'

'Make a guess.'

'God knows. I haven't read anything like it since *Mein Kampf.* All this Superman stuff. Not being bound by Moral Imperatives, the necessity to rise above the Common Herd, the Slave Mentality. Look at the prose. Who can write stuff like that?'

'Roddy Nailor.'

'Roddy Nailor?'

'The same.'

'What, *the* Roddy Nailor?'

'That's it. Nail-em-down Nailor. The man with a hammer and tacks. Anyway, do we run it?'

'Run it? Of course we run it. This is wonderful. Make it the first feature. Also,' the chief editor added after a moment's reflection, 'knock out a short leader. Heavy stuff, you know, "Published only after serious and lengthy consideration – does not signify approval of the views expressed ... – a fascinating insight into the criminal mind", et cetera, et cetera. That sort of thing. God, he must think he's Napoleon.'

'It's worse than that, I think,' said the features editor as he closed the door.

And so the words of Roddy Nailor were published in the quality press. At the time they caused a minor stir in the letters column, but were swiftly forgotten. Roddy Nailor sent a copy to his former persecutor, Eddie Cole, a gesture which was destined to affect both of their lives profoundly as future events unfolded. Curiously enough, the article had the effect of delaying Roddy Nailor's release. The prison psychiatrist formed the clear view that the article revealed Nailor to be in a state of advanced and dangerous paranoia. It was determined that he should be retained in prison until the very last moment of his sentence. Thus an early release date in February was deferred until June, when Roddy Nailor finally walked through the gates of his prison and into a waiting Rolls Royce. With him was released his friend, Harry 'Bonkers' Bedser, club owner, bank robber, pederast and recent anthropologist. Both men subsequently attended a large party at a pub in the Mile End Road, organised by Mrs Nailor who had, during her son's absence, run the family business from her council flat between visits to the supermarket with her trolley.

What worried Eddie Cole was the absence of any information

following Nailor's release. The man had gone to ground. All that Anita Flynn could tell him was that Nailor was thought to be living above a garage in Bow, one of the family's dubious assets. It was also thought that Bonkers Bedser was living with him. This last piece of information caused Eddie Cole even more anxiety. It was well known that Bonkers was unable to return to Manchester. Lacking a mother, or indeed any near kin, psychopathic or otherwise, his influence and power had waned in his absence. Gentlemen of even greater criminal propensities had been swift to appropriate his considerable assets shortly after his incarceration for bank robbery ten years before. 'Hence,' thought Eddie Cole irritably, 'Bonkers' residence in London.' Bonkers' sobriquet represented two separate sides of his character and activities. The first was his capacity to go suddenly and wildly berserk for no apparent reason. The second related to his own chosen method of retribution which consisted of repeatedly striking his enemies (and on occasions regrettably even his friends) on the head with a sledgehammer. Whether his course in anthropology had done anything to cure these character defects was, of course, as yet unknown. Eddie Cole doubted it. He doubted it very much indeed. What concerned him most, however, was that Bonkers, unlike most professional criminals, also had previous convictions for serious sexual assault, a fact which would normally have earned persecution from his fellow prisoners were it not for his immense size, his colossal strength and the character defects previously recorded.

It was, thought Eddie Cole, as his car turned into the entrance to Scotland Yard, just about as nasty a mix as one could ask for. And now, just when he could do without it, the daughter of some bloody judge got herself kidnapped. 'Me,' thought Eddie Cole as he stepped into the building, 'why is it always fucking *me*?'

# Chapter 4

Lord Justice Stoker, Lady Stoker and Mr Justice Golding were all waiting, with impatience, in the office of the head of the Serious Crime Squad when Eddie Cole entered. Despite the nature of the occasion and the anxieties which possessed her, Mary Stoker was immediately struck by the appearance of the man who now sat before her. At first she took him to be mildly deformed. She swiftly realised, however, that the damage was self-inflicted. Eddie Cole was short (barely five foot six, she calculated before he reached the chair behind the desk). The width was disproportionate, giving the impression of a moving cube. In the girth area a thin imitation lizard-skin belt and nylon waistband strained visibly against a mountainous gut. From the forehead the face fell in festoons oddly reminiscent of a Christmas tree decorated by a drunk. Bags were everywhere. Under eyes and chins, ears and bottom lip they trembled in remote sympathy with facial contours now almost eroded. Across the head what little hair remained was pasted over a wide expanse of flesh gleaming with the sweat of exertion. The policeman did not speak until he had crossed the floor and arranged himself behind his own desk, a gesture that, deliberately or not, implied an indifference to the status of those who now invaded his room.

When he spoke the flat North London vowels formed a strange counterpoint to the formality of the address. 'Good morning Lord Justice, Lady Stoker, and Judge. I have been told,' he continued, 'the outlines of the story. I wonder if you would give me the details. It is, I think, your daughter that is involved.'

From this invitation Golding began his narrative. When he reached receipt of the letter he produced it from his pocket and laid it upon Eddie Cole's desk. With elaborate care the policeman pulled it towards him touching only the extreme edges of the paper. Squinting against the reflected neon light, he read slowly without comment, his head bowed and his pendulous flesh suspended barely a foot from the face of the paper. Having read it, he read it again. As he did so the creases on his face deepened and his tongue began to protrude like an escaping mollusc from between his fleshy lips. He was conscious that his bald head was the subject of scrutiny by the three other occupants of the room. Finally he pushed the document carefully to one side, readjusted his face, looked up and said, 'Go on.'

The judge continued his account. When he finished there was silence. Eddie Cole transferred his gaze to the framed photograph of a sailing boat which hung upon his wall. 'Do I understand,' he said, 'that you think this may be a joke?'

Golding paused, then said, 'I think it is . . . possibly no more than that.'

Lady Stoker could contain herself no longer. 'Superintendent, I am sorry to interrupt but we have known Melanie for many years. Since she was born. We are strongly of the view that she would never dream of doing such a thing. Nor could she conceivably have written that letter.'

'Ah, yes,' said Eddie Cole uncomfortably, 'the letter.'

James Stoker spoke. 'What do you make of it, Superintendent? The letter, I mean?'

'Well,' said Eddie Cole cautiously, 'much of it means nothing at all to me. I have never heard of a categorical imperative.'

'I think it's Hegel,' said Lady Stoker. 'Or Kant.'

'I am afraid that doesn't get me much further.'

Elias Golding shrugged with impatience. 'I can't see that it matters much but Mary read philosophy at Oxford and can explain some of it.'

'I think I need all the help I can get. If you could keep it simple I would be grateful.'

'I will try,' said Mary Stoker. 'Kant and Hegel were both nineteenth-century moral philosophers. As to categorical imperatives, Kant believed that if one was unable as a rational being to *will* that any maxim should be a universal law, one which should be adopted by all rational beings, then it cannot be accepted as a moral rule. It follows, of course, that if a rational human being can will any maxim to be a universal law, then it will become so. Furthermore he maintains that there is, indeed, a single set of such conditions upon which we may base the essential concept of morality.'

'Ah, said Eddie Cole, 'of course,' and then with gathering confidence, 'this chap is obviously barking mad.'

'That is precisely what worries me,' said Mary Stoker. 'But there is something much more sinister and much simpler. I hope you don't mind if I say so?' Eddie Cole shook his head. 'It is possible to piece together some further references to nineteenth-century philosophy. You note that he (or she) mentions the herd instinct and Self Fulfilment. You see what I mean?'

'Not really,' said Eddie Cole cautiously, 'but please go on.'

26

'Well. This is plainly a reference to Nietzsche.'

'Ah,' said Eddie Cole. 'Explain please.'

'Nietzsche rejected all forms of common morality, all forms of general values. He believed that the strong should be able to get on with things, to live life to the very pitch of their own needs and the weak should, if necessary, be allowed to go to the wall. But what is most alarming,' continued Mary Stoker, 'is that he believed there were "Supermen" to whom no law applied, who were above the common herd and the slave mentality of the majority of mankind. People who literally made their own rules. That is what worries me about this letter, mad gibberish though it is.'

'What you mean,' said Eddie Cole slowly, 'is this man may be a dangerous madman.'

Lady Stoker shook her head. 'Worse than that, this is a dangerous madman who believes whatever he does is right.'

Eddie Cole drew in his breath. The time, he thought, had come for some conventional policing. He had already formed the strong view that Mr Justice Golding was probably right. This was likely to be a joke. Throughout his career as a police officer few kidnapping cases had found their way across his desk. Kidnapping for money was not a British crime. Professional criminals despised it; petty criminals had neither the means to commit the crime nor the audacity to risk its consequences. Generally speaking, British kidnapping involved the abduction of spoilt children by over-indulgent parents. Otherwise the motives were invariably political, involving diplomats and factions from the Middle East who, in the mind of Eddie Cole, were welcome to kidnap each other as much as they liked providing it was not within the Metropolitan Police area. It was, thought Eddie Cole, just possible that some dangerous nutcase might break the rules, but in his experience dangerous nutcases did not possess knowledge of Hegel and Kant, however rudimentary. Had the father been anything other than a High Court judge he would have given the matter scant attention, if any attention at all. However, in this case it was at least necessary to go through the motions, and so, removing a yellow report pad from the desk drawer, he recorded upon instructions the details of Melanie Golding's short, happy and chaotic life. What he learned provided the final confirmation that he was dealing with an elaborate spoof designed to discomfit her father.

According to the judge's candid account Melanie had always been a 'difficult child', wilful and disobedient to a degree which exasperated her father and placed in permanent jeopardy the expensive boarding-school education to which she was consigned at an early age. Indeed, her expulsion from St Augusta's Ladies College at the age of seventeen came as no surprise to even her most devoted admirers. That she had survived at that establishment for so long was due only to the erratic brilliance of her academic record, her fanatical and ill-co-ordinated bravery at lacrosse and the fact that her father was an eminent lawyer. Shortly after Melanie's seventeenth birthday Mr Justice Golding had been summoned to the school. On arrival he had been shown into the head-mistress's study, an impressively elegant room overlooking the hockey pitches. The headmistress, Emily Thompson, was a large-boned spinster of misogynist disposition, who could speak without apparent movement of the lips. She came straight to the point. 'I'm afraid,' she said, 'that there have been a series of incidents as a result of which we must ask you to take Melanie away.' Encouraged by the judge's silence she continued. 'Things came to a head last week when she called the Head Girl a "silly bourgeois twerp" and said something rather unpleasant about her joining the Household Cavalry. Not,' she added quickly, observing the widening of Golding's eyes, 'that I would consider such a thing, in itself, as warranting expulsion. I in fact ordered her to be confined to her room for two days, but she flatly refuses to stay there.'

'Is it not possible,' the judge asked evenly, 'to lock her in?'

'Well, that's it,' replied the headmistress unhappily, gazing at a hockey post, 'we can't find the door.'

'Can't find the door?'

'Yes, I'm afraid she's taken it off its hinges and hidden it. Short of physically removing her to the sanatorium there's nothing we can do.'

'But surely . . .'

'Any more serious punishment is, I am afraid, out of the question. She has unfortunately become very popular with the Lower School. Some of the girls are quite infatuated with her. Before half term she taught Jessica Matthews in 1B to recite extracts from the Communist Manifesto. It caused a lot of trouble. Her father's an estate agent. He lives in Esher. Then there was the business of the shotguns.'

'The shotguns?'

'Yes, I'm afraid we are rather overrun with squirrels. Last week two of them got into the chapel and ate the Communion biscuits. So I contacted a local farmer with a view to having them eradicated. Naturally, there was a certain sentimental opposition from some of the girls, including your daughter. The farmer sent two of his farm hands, but before they could get to the chapel your daughter and a friend of hers lured them into the gym. They're rather simple boys, I'm afraid.

While they were in there someone stole their shotguns. This caused a lot of bother. The police have been here. Frankly, I am very worried about the publicity if it became known. We have quite enough difficulty filling our places without people thinking that there were shotguns loose in the fifth form. I have offered a general amnesty to anyone who hands them in but nothing has happened. I am worried that they could get into the wrong hands. I am not suggesting of course that Melanie would shoot anyone, but there are some girls in the school . . .' The headmistress shuddered as she transferred her gaze once more to the far goalposts. 'I am not suggesting,' she continued, 'that Melanie is not a charming girl. Of course she is. Indeed, as I say, she is really very popular but that, of course, is half the trouble. I have considered the matter carefully with my senior staff and we are all of the view, I am afraid, that we must ask her to leave. I will, of course, arrange a suitable refund of the term's fees.'

Following upon her expulsion Melanie was admitted with some difficulty and protest to the sixth form of Hags Martin public school in Northumberland, a suitably remote and monastic establishment, anxious at the time to recruit girls into its sixth form in order both to appear generally progressive and to diminish its reputation for sodomy. This arrangement was a partial success and in due course Melanie Golding achieved the highest qualification in the school, having, it was reliably rumoured, conducted a passionate affair with the arts master. On leaving Hags Martin she accepted a place at the University of London and rented a flat in Hackney.

'What's she studying now then?' asked Eddie Cole.

'I'm not really sure . . .' said her father, before Lady Stoker interrupted: 'I can tell you that, Superintendent. She is studying nineteenth-century philosophy, concentrating on Schopenhauer and Kierkegaard.'

'I see,' said Eddie Cole. 'This,' he thought, 'looks increasingly like a very bad joke.' Aloud he said, 'I don't suppose you have a photograph of her?'

'I have, indeed,' said Mr Justice Golding. 'I thought you might need one.'

Eddie Cole took the framed portrait and inspected it. The face he observed was, indeed, beautiful. Untidy but radiant. Dark Tuscan eyes looked evenly into the camera, the eyebrows arched in faint irony, while the mouth, too large and generous for perfection, smiled as though in happy surprise.

'Nice photograph,' said Eddie Cole. 'Is it recent?'

'I took it last summer,' said Lord Justice Stoker, 'in the Temple Gardens.'

Eddie Cole looked at him. 'You know her well?'

'I have known her all my life, as a neighbour and friend.'

In the pause that followed Eddie Cole said, 'Well, let us hope that this is a joke.' He held up a hand against the Stokers' incipient objection. 'But we will proceed certainly as though it is not. I will have a permanent watch placed upon her flat and will have the Scenes of Crime Officer inspect immediately. I will get this letter to Forensic first thing tomorrow.'

'Tomorrow . . .' began Lord Justice Stoker.

'I am afraid,' said Eddie Cole, 'our Forensic Department does not work on Saturday unless there has been a murder.' This pronouncement was greeted with yet another uncomfortable pause before Mr Justice Golding said, 'Is there anything more, Superintendent, that we can do?'

'Not at the moment,' replied the policeman, 'but please let me know if anything unusual happens, however small. I will give you my own number where you can reach me.'

After the three lawyers had left his office in the company of Sergeant Brendan O'Hara, Eddie Cole stood looking at the incessant rain. What a waste of time. He'd lay a month's salary to a whore's knickers that the girl would be back tonight. That mad bloody letter. It had hoax written all over it. Returning to his desk he picked up the document and placed it in a clear, polythene envelope that had at one corner a white adhesive label. On this he wrote 'Golding, Melanie, EC 1'. He replaced the envelope on his blotter and walked to the window. Here his thoughts returned to his principal preoccupation. Nailor. Nailor and Bedser. What a pair. Still, thought Eddie Cole, he may have become a different man. They said he'd got some education inside. Written to the press. Still watching the weather Eddie Cole transformed his mouth into a sneer of derision. Become a half-baked philosopher. He had read the article. Roddy Nailor had actually sent him one from prison. On an impulse he returned to his desk, opened the bottom left-hand drawer and extracted a file, from which he drew a copy of the *Evening News* dated several months earlier. The front page contained the information that Roddy Nailor, the most infamous gangster in Britain, had contributed an article on nineteenth-century philosophy. Also on that front page it was revealed that the Nailor article was the subject of a leader column. Eddie Cole smiled. 'Taking them for a ride.' He turned to the leader column and began to read '. . . most remarkable insight into one of Britain's most notorious gangsters . . . interesting form of prison education . . . does it justify the cost? . . . what practical benefit to have knowledge of Kant and Hegel . . .' Eddie Cole's face set like a rock. An awful possibility passed across the back of his brain. 'Christ,' he said in the silence of his room, 'Christ, I don't believe it.' Turning on his heels he snatched up the transparent envelope. Through the distorting film he read and re-read the letter, his eyes darting from line to line as though following a game played at immense speed. 'Crackpot philosophy . . . the Common Herd . . . Hegel . . . Superman.'

Suddenly he had the telephone in his hand and was hammering on the keys that controlled the internal network. Seconds later Brendan O'Hara's voice was heard in the receiver. Eddie Cole interrupted the first word. 'Brendan, get in here now. I've got it, I've bloody got it.'

Within a minute Brendan O'Hara's head appeared round the door. 'What's the . . . ?'

'Come in for Christ's sake. Listen. It's Nailor.'

'Nailor?'

'Fucking Nailor. Nailor's got her. Nailor kidnapped her. Golding put him down. All this philosophy. This is his new trick. It's that Neechy, Nasty bloke. The bloody Hun philosopher. He's bought it. Nailor. He's bought it. He think he's God. Jesus.'

A frown was set across the features of Brendan O'Hara. Small movements of his head indicated disbelief.

'Don't you see, *it all fits*. Golding sent him down. He's just got out. Why would he want Bonkers Bedser? The man's a dangerous nutcase. He's a sex maniac.'

The frown cleared. 'You don't think . . .'

'Don't even say it. Christ, we've wasted so much bloody time. Right, get Team Beta One. Whatever they're doing get them off it. Send two of them round to her flat *now*. Get the best SOCO you can. Get Parsons now. I want it checked for everything, but everything. Then I want half a dozen round at that garage in the Mile End Road. You know, the one Nailor's bloody mother bought from Fats Walker. Nailor and Bedser are living there. Turn it upside down. Fuck the warrant. Just do it. Send someone to that fucking club, the Garlic, or whatever it's called. There is an envelope there. Search every waste-paper basket and dustbin. Take it to Forensic, and this.' He picked up the letter from the table.' I want it taken apart *now*. Get the bastards in. Whatever they are doing get them in. I want it tested *now*. Jesus Christ, why is it always fucking *me*?'

When Sergeant O'Hara left him, the light of urgency burning across his Irish face, Eddie Cole phoned the Temple. No reply. Mr Justice Golding had not yet returned home. Five minutes later he tried again. This time after a short while the telephone was answered and the breathless voice of the judge could be heard reciting his number at the other end of the line.

'Judge,' said Eddie Cole, 'It's Superintendent Cole. I think we have something. If I am right it is much more serious than we thought. I am taking a number of immediate steps including sending two men to guard your flat.'

The judge's voice sounded, shrill with apprehension, 'But what is the . . . ?'

'I am afraid I cannot tell you on the telephone. I am taking a number of immediate steps and will let you know. Please stay close to the phone.'

For the remainder of the day Superintendent Eddie Cole, head of the Serious Crime Squad, spun his web. From London suburbs complaining men assembled to do his will. Nailor's garage was found and searched. No one was there. Furthermore, according to Brendan O'Hara who had personally supervised the operation, there was no sign of habitation in the past several days. At Mrs Nailor's flat two members of the Serious Crime Squad refused repeated offers of tea and biscuits and ascertained that she and only she was present. Scrupulous searching of the Garrick's waste-paper baskets revealed a cheap brown envelope marked 'Golding – urgent', and this, together with the letter it had once contained, was delivered to a Forensic Department full of sullen scientists untimely called from their Saturday pursuits. Anton Penello, the best of hand-writing experts, was the last to arrive, his silk shirt coruscating in the neon light. Until he had taken his photographs for enlargement and minute dissection, the business of fingerprinting and analysis could not begin. So they worked for Eddie Cole. By four o'clock it was clear that there were no incriminating fingerprints to be found on either document. The paper was that of a common manufacturer. Melanie Golding's flat was searched under the meticulous and expert guidance of Alan Parsons, the best SOCO of them all. What was found was alarming. There were clear signs of a violent struggle. Working papers were widely scattered, furniture had been displaced. Blood was found. In the single bedroom a broken alarm clock was discovered by the bed, its face ground into the carpet. The time stood at 9.08. Leading from the bed-room a first-floor balcony overlooked a garden and marshland beyond. The balcony doors were open. Below the balcony a ladder lay across two flowerbeds. Extensive fingerprinting of surfaces and windows revealed no traces of known or convicted criminals. Most moveable items were seized for subsequent analysis. The garden, marshland and surrounding areas were searched. Melanie Golding was not found.

The handwriting remained. At 8 p.m. Eddie Cole was sitting opposite Anton Penello. Also present were Brendan O'Hara and two members of

Team Beta One of the Serious Crime Squad. Before the expert lay photographic copies of the kidnap letter, some enlarged and some bearing the marks of minute measurement and dissection. Other documents lay before him in piles. Closer inspection revealed them to be a diverse collection of letters, written statements, signatures and photocopied scraps of ephemeral writings. On each pile was an index card at the top of which was a single name. 'Nailor R' and 'Bedser H' were two of them. Anyone with knowledge of serious criminals in the Metropolitan Area would have recognised the remainder. All this was part of the unknown, unrecorded treasury of detection, a sleuth's lexicon. The documents represented the painstaking harvest of previous arrests, searches, trials and investigations. Operations long ago concluded, some in successful prosecution, some in failure, some aborted. All delivered up an apparently irrelevant hoard of documents bearing the writings of defendants and suspects, targets, accomplices and known villains. Most of the originals had long since been returned with no hint or acknowledgement of the fact that they had been copied, indexed and stored for the very purpose for which they were now employed.

Conscious of the tension about him, Penello leant forward and picked up the original letter which he held above the table. His elegant and manicured fingers gripped only the extremity of the document. As he moved a delicate scent reached Eddie Cole who wrinkled his nostrils in faint disgust before he asked, 'What have we got?'

Penello frowned. 'We have,' he said, 'everything and nothing. First you can completely exclude Nailor and Bedser. That may disappoint you but it is unavoidable. Neither of them wrote this letter. Their fingerprints are not on it and the handwriting is certainly not theirs, despite the obvious and bizarre aspects of the calligraphy.'

Eddie Cole lent forward and picked up a copy of the letter. 'Bizarre? Why is it bizarre?'

Anton Penello sifted through the photocopies before him and selected one upon which three words had been magnified by a factor of ten. He pushed it across the table until it lay directly below the face of the policeman, who stared down at the paper from which the magnetic gloss shone faintly under the lamp which Penello now trained upon it. Eddie Cole gazed intently. The process never failed to excite him. The vastly enlarged strokes of the original pen now appeared like painted trees and branches. A hand had moved across this landscape leaving the still, exact evidence of guilt and intention. The thickness of the strokes and the crude imperfections of line, now expanded and revealed, would have been invisible and unknown to the man that made them. This was the power of pursuit. The adrenalin was unmistakeable. This was the surge of the hunter, the tracker, the pursuing instrument of wrath. As primitive men read the minute signs which showed the passing of the hunted beast, so Eddie Cole and his experts read the tiny variations of line and punctuation left by the object which they sought.

On to the face of the document Penello placed the needle-sharp point of a mathematical pencil. It moved steadily along the downward curve of a letter 't'.

'What do you see?'

'Tell me,' said Eddie Cole.

'No, you tell me, if you can see it the jury will see it too.'

Eddie Cole's wide forehead furrowed with concentration. 'The height of the letters is uneven.'

'Just so. Is it only the height?'

Helpfully, the point of the pencil moved to the branch of the 't'.

'No. It is also the branches. The horizontal strokes are at different levels.'

'That is right. Similar imperfections appear in the other letters requiring two strokes of the pen. Look at the "k".'

Eddie Cole looked up at his expert. 'What does this tell us?'

'You tell me.'

'It looks like the writing of a child.'

'Well done. These are the classic hallmarks of a juvenile hand.'

'What age?'

'Difficult to say. It does vary enormously. More likely to be primary than secondary education. Ten or eleven perhaps.'

Eddie Cole's eyes narrowed with disbelief. 'Would it be possible to simulate? To fake it?'

'Possible but unlikely, very unlikely. It would be near impossible to achieve a regular pattern of error: consistency in inconsistency if you follow me. The other characteristics of your own natural hand would become apparent. This has all the hallmarks of a genuine juvenile hand but there are other problems.'

'Surprise me,' said Eddie Cole.

'Observe the slope of the letters. What do you see?'

Again the graphite tip of the pencil traced the line of the downward strokes.

'They slope backwards.'

'Indeed they do. Like these.' Penello took another written sheet of paper and placed it before the superintendent's gaze. 'This is not the same hand but you see precisely the same common characteristic.'

'Who wrote this?'

'Sergeant O'Hara.'

Eddie Cole looked at his sergeant. 'When did you do this?'

'This afternoon. Anton told me to copy out the letter. I didn't ask why.'

Eddie Cole turned to Penello. 'What's the point?'

'It is very simple. Sergeant O'Hara is left-handed, a characteristic he shares with twenty per cent of the population. To write left-handed it is necessary to push rather than pull the pen. In many cases, the majority in fact, the result is this characteristic backward slope. Any other possibility can really be excluded.'

Eddie Cole drew a deep breath. 'So you are telling me that the author of this document is a left-handed child?'

'Not exactly.'

'Not *exactly*?'

'No, I am afraid it is more complex.'

'Surprise me,' said Eddie Cole.

'Look for a moment at Brendan's writing. For this purpose I have enlarged part of his offering to a size similar to the enlarged letter. Put the two together. What do you see? Take my magnifying glass if it helps.'

Silence ensued as the bald head of the Superintendent tracked back and forward across the two photographic images, his eyes barely six inches from the paper and a large magnifying glass suspended between. Finally he spoke. 'They are written by a different pen.'

'No, or rather not in any way that matters. I can tell you from long experience that the original was written by a common black biro, medium point. This is precisely the same kind of pen that I provided to Sergeant O'Hara. But your conclusion is entirely understandable. It *appears* to be a different pen because the strokes themselves appear to be of different widths. In fact, they are not. The difference is more subtle. The width of the strokes made by Brendan is even and constant. The writings on the kidnap note are clearly uneven and broken, indicating varied pressure on the pen and/or the pen changing angle as it passes over the paper.'

'What does that mean?'

'I think it is really quite simple on one level and incomprehensible on another. Sergeant O'Hara's writing is even because it is fluent. It is fluent because he has written with his left hand since infancy, literally since he started to write. Furthermore, this pattern, this evenness, would have occurred very early and certainly would normally be evident in a case of any child old enough and educated enough to be able to write or copy (never mind construct) a letter of this length with words of this complexity.'

'So what do we deduce from this?'

'The inevitable deduction is that the person responsible for this letter was not naturally left-handed, whether he or she be adult or child. Equally and as importantly, we can deduce that this could not be the work of someone naturally *right*-handed, simply attempting to produce normal calligraphy. The writing is far too consistent for that, just as it is far too uneven for the other.' Anton Penello paused and looked squarely into the eyes of Eddie Cole who sighed with impatience.

'So given all that, what do we conclude? Give me a target, however wide.'

'I can't. I simply can't. All that I can conclude is that something very strange has happened to this person to enable or require him to write in this way. What it is I just do not know. In twenty-five years I have never seen anything like it.'

'So we have absolutely nothing?'

'Not quite. While it is impossible to conclude, it is possible to exclude. I have here,' the expert moved his hands across the piles, 'the documents and writings of those known in the past to have been criminal associates of Nailor, including incidentally his mother. These identities we were able to obtain from the Criminal Intelligence Service. I have handwriting samples of all known associates, save three. That is of no consequence since two are dead and one has been in prison in Italy for the last five years. Of all the remainder it is possible to be categoric. Applying any of the normal tests, none of them could have written this letter.'

Eddie Cole intervened. 'Nailor has been in prison for ten years. We need to know whether he had known associates inside prison.'

Anton Penello looked at Brendan O'Hara, who nodded his head. 'It's been done already, guv. Excluding the early stuff, remands and such like, Nailor was in three nicks. Wandsworth, Parkhurst and Grafton Hall. Any close associations that he formed would have been reported to the Governor, should have come back through Intelligence. There are none except Bedser. We are checking the prison record anyway, where they exist and we can get to them. Should take a couple of days. If there *is* anything, I can get samples of handwriting to Anton immediately.'

Penello lifted a hand. 'Before we go on, I think I should make it very clear that I see little chance of success for these enquiries. I know they must be made but I would pin no hopes on this line. What we have here is something very odd. A mutant. An aberration. I know the answer is in there, that letter, but I will need time to consider it.'

'That,' said Eddie Cole, 'is precisely what we do not have. I have not got a shred of proof but I know that Nailor has her, whoever or whatever is involved. If I am right, her life expectancy is about as long as a hooked fish.' The policeman shook his head and allowed his eyes to fall on the photocopies and the original letter behind them. For a reason which disturbed him, he shuddered. 'Pursue it, Anton. Hunt him down. There is something evil at work here. I can feel it. Now I must go to the Temple. I have a judge to see.'

An hour later, Eddie Cole was sitting at the dining table in Elias Golding's flat. On the opposite side, Lord Justice Stoker, Lady Stoker and Mr Justice Golding looked at him with identical expressions of alarm.

'*Nailor?*' said Mr Justice Golding, his voice high with apprehension. 'Roddy Nailor?'

'I'm afraid so.'

'How long has he been free?'

'Not long, a matter of weeks. We have reason to believe that he is with another released criminal, called Bedser.'

'Have you been . . . following or monitoring him?'

'We have tried, but I am afraid my intelligence is very limited. In fact, at the moment, it is non-existent.'

'So what connects him with this apart from the fact that I sentenced him?'

'The philosophy stuff. That is all. He did a diploma in philosophy at Bournemouth College before he was released. He wrote an article in the *Evening News*. I've got a copy. I have had it photocopied for you.'

Eddie Cole distributed three photographs of a page of the *Evening News*. While it was read, he took a large draught of the whisky that he had accepted on his arrival.

'This is gibberish,' said Mary Stoker, 'absolute rubbish.'

'Precisely,' said Eddie Cole. 'Like the ransom note.'

'Is that all?' Elias Golding's voice was close to petulance. 'Is that *all* that we have?'

'At present, that is all. There is nothing else to connect Nailor with this crime. All the forensic work excludes him. The handwriting analysis in particular poses serious problems.' Briefly the policeman rehearsed his conversation with Anton Penello.

'Can Nailor be connected with any left-handed children?' Jim Stoker sounded incredulous. 'Is this possible?'

'Nailor has no children. Nor does Bedser. It is possible, of course, that they could have employed a child but very unlikely since it would be much too risky. I am afraid we simply do not know. At present we are carrying out every investigation which is open to us. In my view it is essential, absolutely *essential*, that there is no publicity. If I am right that it is Nailor (and pray God I am not right) then the first publicity will, I am afraid, place your daughter at the greatest possible risk. You will excuse me if I leave you. I have an informant to see who may be able to assist. It is the best informant that I have.'

Having obtained a taxi in High Holborn, Eddie Cole gave the address of Anita Flynn's premises and sat back to watch the London streets.

'It's him,' he said softly. 'I can feel it in my bones.'

# Chapter 5

When Eddie Cole arrived at Scotland Yard at 7.30 on Monday morning Anton Penello was already there, sitting in Eddie Cole's office radiating the joy of discovery. 'I think,' he said, 'that I have cracked it. I have been through all my books and specimens and spoken to a number of my colleagues. I think I've found it.'

On the other side of the desk Eddie Cole's head jerked forward. 'Who wrote it?'

'I cannot tell you that yet, but I believe I can tell you how we can get there.'

Through the veil of his hangover a familiar sensation spread through the battered body of Eddie Cole. Adrenalin, testosterone perhaps; the unmistakable surge of the hunter. 'Tell me the secret.'

Anton Penello opened his briefcase with two emphatic metal snaps. From it he obtained further enlarged copies of the kidnap note. Placing them on the desk, he laid the tip of his pencil upon the thickened strokes and began to trace the edges, pausing to illustrate the discovery he had made. 'You will remember the previous analysis and the problems it caused. The writing has many of the characteristics of a juvenile hand but equally there are elements which virtually exclude the efforts of a child. The lines of the vertical strokes strongly suggest the use of the left hand but there is no fluency. The movement of the pen is hesitant, causing breaks in the line, as here, and here and here again.' The expert's pencil glided along the trunks, pausing to make sharp lateral movements across the spines into gaps which the enlargement revealed like valleys on a mountain map. 'This writer is not naturally left-handed. The dominant side is right, but, again, this is not a crude attempt at disguise. The use of this hand is not aberrant. It is practised. It is repetitive. It is *trained*.' The expert paused. The eyes of Eddie Cole and Brendan O'Hara fixed upon him.

'Trained?'

'Precisely. This also accounts for our first error. The writings of a child reveal not only imperfection but also the labour of tuition. That is what we both saw as a matter of instinct and experience. It was a false trail.'

'So,' said Eddie Cole with a hint of impatience, 'where does this leave us?'

'Think about it,' said Anton Penello. 'If you can see it so will the jury.'

Eddie Cole's voice became quiet with concentration. 'Why should anyone be trained to use their left hand when their dominant hand is right? What requires someone to become ambidextrous? A sportsman perhaps. Is that it? What sport requires this ability?'

Penello shook his head. 'Possible, but unlikely, is it not? Even if there is such a demand, why should it extend to writing? Calligraphy is not part of any game that I am aware of and I would know if it were. No, Superintendent, I think the answer is much simpler, more obvious.'

Brendan O'Hara's eyes widened with discovery. 'He's lost it. He's lost his right hand!'

'Precisely. Or, to be more precise still, has lost the use of it for the purpose of writing. He, or she, has been on a training course to develop skills with the left hand.'

'Where can you get this training?' Eddie Cole already had the telephone receiver in his hand. His index finger punched out numbers on the internal board.

'I have done some research through my professional association. A number of my colleagues are involved in this work. As far as I can gather there are twenty-six hospitals and rehabilitation centres that have such specialist units in England and Wales. There will be more in the rest of the UK but this is a start. Here is the list.'

Eddie Cole took the document and looked at his expert. 'Thank you, Anton.'

'Not at all. My own way of life precludes my having daughters, which does not affect my desire to see this one returned.'

Eddie Cole spoke into the receiver. 'Paul, I need a team assembled now. Ten, no, twelve. This is top priority. Very top. Get them off anything else. Brendan will brief you in fifteen minutes. Do it now. Thank you.' Turning to his sergeant, he continued. 'Find him, Brendan. Get handwriting samples of everyone they have trained in the last year. Use every fax machine we have got. If necessary get the local plod involved. Get warrants if necessary. It shouldn't be. Give Anton his own room, anything else he wants, anything at all, give it to him. Find him, Brendan. We are close to this bastard now. Hunt him down. Hunt him down.'

For the remainder of the day eight men and four women worked the will of Eddie Cole. Telephones wedged between shoulders and flattened ears they announced and enquired, cajoled, requested and threatened.

'No, I cannot tell you why . . . No, tomorrow will not do I am afraid . . . Can't you get him out of the meeting? . . . Yes, it is very urgent . . . Yes, it *is* a matter of life and death . . . Phone my sergeant back and he will confirm . . . Yes, sir, *the* Serious Crime Squad . . . No, the hospital is not being investigated . . . Yes, I can arrange for your local police to come round . . . yes, we will get a warrant if you require one. It can be issued in half an hour.'

In the event no warrants were necessary. Documents cascaded from fax machines. Police cars, pressed into service across Southern England at reckless speed with screaming sirens, carried the files and packages that contained the cautious writings of the injured, the disabled and the recently maimed. In his room Anton Penello and two assistants sat below angled lamps. Many documents were discarded rapidly on to growing piles. Others required minute dissection, magnifying glasses, rulers, protractors and compasses ceaselessly employed in the geometry of proof and pursuit. Repeatedly throughout the day the door opened to reveal the pendulous face of Eddie Cole, eyebrows raised in hopeful enquiry, before Anton Penello shook his head.

At five o'clock Anton Penello opened the last file and softly groaned. Ten minutes later he sat in the office of Eddie Cole. Gloom prevailed. Brendan O'Hara poured whisky into three glasses.

'You are sure?' said Eddie Cole.

'Quite certain. In the event it was simpler than I thought. We have examined over three hundred specimens. The vast majority can be rejected outright. Frequently, of course, the left hand has also been disabled due to injury or disease but is a little better than the right. In these circumstances the trained writing is still very poor, unlike that of our man. This makes me think that we are almost certainly dealing with a right-sided *injury*, possibly the loss of one arm while the left side is intact and operates near normally. This is much more likely than a condition such as arthritis that tends to affect both hands to varying degrees. We are beginning to picture our target but the man himself eludes us. It is very frustrating. Cheers.'

'Cheers,' said Eddie Cole. 'Are we sure we have got all the material?'

'There is still Scotland, which has five centres. Their material is coming tomorrow but I have had details of the subjects and their disabilities. They are all disease cases except four. Three are children and the fourth is a long-term mental patient. I think we have lost it.'

'There are no other hospitals or institutions?'

'We have checked every establishment in the public and private sector that is known to provide this training. I am sorry.'

41

Eddie Cole raised his whisky glass and held it between them. 'We did our best. It's a battle lost. The war is still to be won. What's the matter, Brendan? What have I said?'

' "War, battle." We have only checked civilian hospitals.'

'Civilian?'

Anton Penello leaned forward across the desk. 'Of course, that's it. That has got to be it. A military unit. The most obvious place for an amputation.'

'Do these units exist in military hospitals?'

Anton Penello was already on his feet. 'I don't know now but I will.'

Three hours later a further collection of files was placed before the expert, whose eyes were red with tiredness and alight with anticipation. Half an hour later he entered the office of Eddie Cole. Without speaking he placed a file on the desk under the policeman's gaze. Then he said, 'It's in there. That's what you're hunting.'

Eddie Cole drew the file towards him and studied the cover, which he then opened. Silently he sifted through documents, then suddenly closed his eyes and exhaled. 'Jesus wept,' he said, 'Holy Jesus wept.'

At nine o'clock the telephone rang in Elias Golding's flat. The judge answered it before the second tone and heard the voice of Eddie Cole. 'Judge, I would be grateful if you could come into my office at eight o'clock tomorrow morning. I have information and I am still making enquiries. I cannot say more on the phone.'

The judge's voice was shrill with anticipation. 'Do you know who we are looking for?'

'I believe so.'

'Is it . . . who you thought?'

'In part. In part it is much worse.'

# Chapter 6

At eight o'clock the following morning those most interested in the disappearance of Melanie Golding were re-assembled in the office of Eddie Cole. Lord Justice Stoker, Lady Stoker and Mr Justice Golding occupied chairs at one side of the battered and untidy desk. Opposite sat Superintendent Eddie Cole, Sergeant Brendan O'Hara and Anton Penello. The last was busy assembling newly-created files that revealed enlarged photographs of handwriting. Several magnifying glasses and lenses lay beside them. Closer to Eddie Cole was a thick, ragged manilla file, the cover of which bore a regimental crest, identifying labels and manuscript annotations.

The superintendent began. 'This,' he said, indicating Penello, 'is Anton Penello, our handwriting expert who has, we believe, identified the person responsible for this crime.'

'You know it's a crime?'

'Yes, Lady Stoker, we now have no serious doubt about that.'

Turning to Penello, Eddie Cole continued, 'If you would like to explain.'

The handwriting expert leaned elegantly across the desk and distributed three identical files. 'You have,' he said, 'magnifying glasses if they are necessary, but I think they are not. Please look at page one, where you will see on the right-hand side photographic enlargements of the handwriting discovered on the kidnap letter. The first thing that we notice is that the downward strokes of the handwriting slope backwards. This is a common characteristic of left-handed people who must, of course, push rather than pull the pen, moving from left to right. That, of course, tells us little since one in five of the population is left-handed. There is, however, another important characteristic which tells us much more about this gentleman.' Penello smiled into Lady Stoker's raised eyes. 'Yes, it *is* a gentleman. What is peculiar can be seen clearly in each of the bottom curved strokes of the "e", the "a" and the "t". In each there is a significant pause represented either by a gap or by a definite thickening of the line before it enters the upward stroke. This movement represents a natural obstacle when the pen is being pushed and not pulled, but,' Penello paused in order to achieve the full attention of his audience, 'anyone naturally left-handed will have overcome this difficulty while learning to write in childhood.'

'So this would indicate,' said Elias Golding, 'that this is a right-handed person using his left hand.'

The expert frowned slightly and continued. 'Precisely, but that in itself again tells us very little. Any right-handed person may seek to disguise their hand by the expedient of using their left. There is, however, a further and more important matter.' Again came the significant pause. 'The handwriting is quite even. Where there is an attempt to use the non-dominant hand there is always a tendency for the writing to become uneven.' Extracting a pencil from his lapel pocket, Penello passed it to Golding. 'Try it,' he said. 'Write "a matter of conscience" on this paper, using your left hand.'

With a little reluctance the judge scratched the required rubric across a page of lined exercise book provided. The unevenness of script was immediately apparent.

'So what do we deduce from this?' asked Lady Stoker, her voice filled with impatience.

'What we deduce,' continued Penello, 'is a right-handed person, writing with their left hand, who has been trained as an adult to write with that hand.'

Three pairs of eyes settled upon the expert, all wide with enquiry.

'Yes, trained,' said Eddie Cole. 'Let us put it all together. What we have here is a man, naturally right-handed, who has, for some reason, been trained to write with his left hand within the recent past. Had he become used to the practice then these imperfections would have gone. It occurred to us that this person could recently have become disabled, lost the use of their right hand and been trained to write with the left. There are, we discovered, a limited number of rehabilitation centres where such training takes place in the United Kingdom, about thirty in all. In the last twenty-four hours we have received from them faxed lists of handwriting exercises carried out in the past twelve months by every patient disabled in their right hand and taught to write with the left. As a result, Mr Penello has been able to identify with certainty the author of this document.'

In the silence Eddie Cole reached for another file, opened it and laid upon the table a number of paper sheets bearing lines of manuscript. 'This is his writing, carried out during the course of exercises at the Ardingley Rehabilitation Unit.'

Lord Justice Stoker leaned forward. 'Ardingley is a military hospital.'

'Indeed it is. This is a military gentleman.'

'A soldier?'

'A Marine officer.'

'Who is he?'

'His name is Thomas Aylen. He was a captain in the Marine Commandos. In 1986 he was blown up on special duties in South Armagh. The whole of his right side was torn apart and he was lucky to survive. He was patched up pretty well. After two years in hospital the main physical disabilities other than disfigurement were the loss of his right arm and his right eye and shortening of the right leg.' Eddie Cole paused again. 'He also has a serious mental condition. What is it?' Eddie Cole anticipated the question about to be spoken by Lady Stoker. 'It is called Menkies' Syndrome. The effect of it? I do not know. I have a police psychiatrist arriving within the hour.'

'What else do we know about him?' Lord Justice Stoker was looking intently at the military file.

'It's all in here. His whole history including one alarming fact.' Eddie Cole paused again as though considering the weight of his disclosure. 'It's very important that this, above all else, is not revealed. If this information became public knowledge his position could be even more dangerous than it is.' He paused again, and continued. 'After his *physical* rehabilitation he was sent to college to learn elementary clerical and secretarial skills with a view to some form of employment. He went to the nearest college, which is in Bournemouth.' The police officer paused. 'Roddy Nailor was at the same college.'

'Oh no.' The eyes of Mr Justice Golding fixed helplessly on the policeman.

'Together with an associate of his called Bedser.' Eddie Cole spread his hands across the desk. 'We don't *know*, but it does seem to fit. Nailor was doing some kind of diploma course. They taught him all about Hegel and Kant and the other bloke.'

'Nietzsche.' Lord Justice Stoker spoke evenly, with effort. 'Do you know where they are now?'

'No, but we are looking as hard as we can.'

Lady Stoker spoke next. 'This Marine officer . . . Thomas Aylen . . . do we know what he looks like?'

Eddie Cole moved towards him the Army file, slipped the cover and removed a number of loose sheets. From these he selected two documents both bearing photographic images.

'In the bombing he was very badly disfigured. This was taken when he began his commission.' An upturned photograph was pushed towards

Lady Stoker. The classic blood-line of Hampshire stock stared upwards from the page. A uniform set on straight shoulders. Features which spoke of tennis and Ypres and Waterloo.

A further photograph was pushed across the desk. 'That's how he looks now.'

'Oh God,' said Lady Stoker. 'Oh my God.'

# Chapter 7

Superintendent Eddie Cole stood in front of his superior, Chief Superintendent George Watson, attempting to maintain an expression of amiable simplicity. He did this for two reasons. First to conceal the dislike and contempt, and second, because he knew it was an expression which infuriated George Watson to the limits of endurance.

George Watson was a Fast Track Police Officer. Everything about him said so. George Watson was a sprinter. At St Hugh's, Oxford he read philosophy, graduated with an Upper Second and played cricket and fives for the University. On graduation in 1975 he had entered the police force under the Fast Track provisions. These were designed to provide meteoric promotion for those with high academic attainments and a marked disinclination to indulge in such matters as violent arrests, thief-taking, endless form-filling, chain-smoking, expenses-fiddling, bottom-pinching, fast-food-eating and monumental, chronic liver-splitting boozing, which is the modern policeman's lot and through which a greasy pole extends to an uncertain future. A chief superintendent at thirty-seven, George Watson was a full fifteen years younger than his immediate inferior now regarding him with an infuriating, conde-scending smirk.

'I hope you realise, Eddie,' he said firmly, 'just how serious this is.'

This man, thought Eddie Cole, is a cretin.

'I think so, sir.'

'This man, Nailsford . . .'

'Nailor.'

'Yes, quite, Nailor, is a very nasty piece of work.'

'I know that, sir, I banged him up.'

'Yes, yes, I see. Section Eighteen wounding, wasn't it? Nailed a Chinaman's hand to a door.'

'Foot to the floor, actually.'

'Right. Unprovoked attack, was it?'

'The Chinaman had cut his local publican's finger off and gouged out his eye.'

'Right, I see. Well, I haven't had very long to read the papers.'

This man, thought Eddie Cole, is a moron.

'No, sir, of course.'

George Watson thought for a moment. 'It certainly seems to me that this chap Nailor is pretty unbalanced.'

He looked at Eddie Cole and thought, 'Why does he look at me like that?' Then he thought, 'God, he's an ugly specimen.' He said, 'I think, Eddie, that we might contemplate getting in a police psychiatrist.'

'Yes, sir.'

'What do you think?'

'He's on his way, sir.'

'Oh well, Great Minds, eh? How are the, er, judges taking it?'

'Very well, sir, I think. They are in my room. I've ordered them some coffee. The police psychiatrist will be here soon, and the doctor who dealt with Aylen during his rehabilitation.'

'Excellent, excellent, good. I think I ought to speak to Golding.'

'I think that the Stokers are rather more useful on this, sir.'

'Oh well, then I will see all of them. Could you arrange for them to come up? No, no, on second thoughts, you stay here, I'll go and bring them up personally.'

Eddie Cole watched his superior's retreating back and thought of the wide open green landscape of Salisbury Plain, laced and patterned with spring flowers and undulating from time to time into a false topography created by the burial mounds of the Great.

# Chapter 8

Those interested in the disappearance of Melanie Golding reassembled in the larger offices of Chief Superintendent George Watson. Anton Penello, his task successfully performed, had disappeared back to his laboratory. Newcomers had arrived and the group was now sitting in a variety of chairs around a substantial desk. It comprised George Watson himself, Superintendent Eddie Cole, Lord Justice Stoker and Lady Stoker, Mr Justice Golding, Sergeant Brendan O'Hara and a police stenographer drafted in by Eddie Cole to maintain a verbatim record of proceedings. In prime position and ready to hold forth was Alan Barlow, Consultant Police Psychiatrist.

Alan Barlow was enormous. In addition he radiated colour, mainly different shades of red. That part of his face which was visible was tomato, substantially interlaced with vivid purple streaks which found their source in a vast nose, itself almost entirely purple and cratered like the moon. Much of his face was obscured by a beard obviously once red but now streaked with grey. Like Eddie Cole, he was nearly bald and, also like the superintendent, had pasted thin strands of hair, in his case orange, across a glowing and freckled skull. His clothes appeared to have fallen upon him in some form of unkind and violent ambush. Each garment seemed to be in conflict with his body, the slightest movement creating violent related activity over the entire surface. Creases and valleys of dirty flannel and nylon appeared to move like primeval faults on a primitive landscape.

Finally Lady Stoker noticed his eyes, which, she supposed, had peered for many years into the pits of human depravity and which now swam like grey oysters in a soft milk of alcoholic tears.

Sitting beside Alan Barlow, Superintendent Eddie Cole regarded his expert with undisguised affection and admiration. In the mind of Eddie Cole, Alan Barlow had every conceivable attribute of a psychiatrist. These included a second-class degree from Swansea, an unquenchable capacity to drink every known form of liquor, and a profound scepticism as to the effect (or indeed the existence) of most forms of mental illness.

Many years earlier Alan Barlow had worked with Eddie Cole (then Inspector Cole) on the case of Ivan Lurcher, a German/Polish immigrant charged with the rape and murder of four women. The hallmark of Mr Lurcher's crimes was his preference for coating his victims in petrol after their sexual ordeals and burning them conscious and alive. The defence, supported by three eminent psychiatrists, was that Mr Lurcher was mad and thus guilty only of manslaughter. The premise was advanced that he was deeply psychotic and, in carrying out his odious crimes, was obeying the voice of God which spoke to him uniquely, directly and persuasively from a glass dog bearing the legend 'A Present from Lyme Regis'. This object had belonged to Mr Lurcher's mother until her death as a result of alcoholic poisoning. The case had achieved a gratifying level of publicity for Eddie Cole, not least as a result of Alan Barlow's performance under cross-examination. When it was suggested to him by leading counsel that Mr Lurcher was suffering from 'a psychotic state resulting in compulsive behaviour devoid of coherent motivation', the police psychiatrist had murmured quite audibly, 'Bollocks'. Following an admonition from the judge, he had amplified his reply thus: 'You may take it from me as a psychiatrist of many years' standing, who has observed the worst and most evil men in the world, that burning someone alive is a calculated act devoid only of humanity.' Lurcher was convicted of four murders and, shortly thereafter, hanged himself (with some possible assistance) in his cell at Strangeways. This was widely regarded (particularly by Eddie Cole) as being an entirely satisfactory outcome to the case and due, in no small measure, to Alan Barlow. Whatever his manifest deficiencies as a scientist, there was no doubt that juries loved him, judges secretly admired him and convictions of those he examined were virtually guaranteed.

Whenever Eddie Cole needed a police psychiatrist, this was the man. Thus it was that Alan Barlow now cleared his throat and addressed those before him. When he began to speak, Lady Stoker experienced another sense of astonishment. From the depths of the human wreck that she observed before her there emerged a Welsh tenor voice of quite extraordinary clarity and mellifluence. ('It was,' she said later, 'like lifting a manhole cover and hearing Beethoven.')

'Ladies and gentlemen,' said Alan Barlow, 'I have, as you know, had these papers only for a short period of time. However, I have been provided with all the background material which I need and have been able to form strong views in respect of all four people whom I have been asked to consider.'

'Four?'

'Yes, Judge', said Alan Barlow, turning towards Elias Golding, 'four people: Bedser, Nailor, Aylen and your daughter, Melanie.'

'Why is she being investigated?'

'If, as we believe, she has been kidnapped by this group of men, then it is important to establish how she will react to each of them and to any ... indignities which she may suffer. It is important when considering her safety and the actions which we should take in trying to help her.'

In the silence which followed Lady Stoker slowly nodded her head. 'You think she may be ... ill-treated?'

'It depends very much what they want but it has to be a strong probability. First may I take the simplest proposition, namely, Bedser? Bedser is a classic of his kind; low IQ, easily led, capable of acts of extreme violence or cruelty. In part this is induced by frustration both intellectual and physical. Perversely he may be capable of acts of apparent kindness and compassion, particularly, for instance, towards animals. This stems from his extremely low level of self-esteem and an almost complete lack of insight. When carrying out such benign acts he is, literally, attempting to impress himself. From the point of view of a victim it is essential that these acts are reciprocated and appreciated. If they are rejected then Bedser will swiftly become morose, by turns self-destructive and explosively violent. Particularly at such times he is prone to excessive, 'binge' drinking which also triggers, during and after, periods of extreme, uncontrollable violence. Unusually for such a criminal he has a background of sexual delinquency against women. This is very unusual and worrying. It indicates a high degree of probability that Bedser is homosexual. He, of course, does not know this and subordinates his feelings, which, in turn, fuel the general sense of frustration which leads to violence. For precisely this reason he is liable to be fanatically *anti* homosexuals and homosexual behaviour. He is, if you like, the classic SS bully. His prison record reveals him to be a violent racist and particularly anti-Semitic. Another alarming fact in this case.'

Jim Stoker intervened to ask, 'Is he mentally ill?'

Alan Barlow scratched his ear. 'I do not entirely understand the meaning of that expression when applied to an animal like Bedser.' He continued, 'I now come to the famous Roddy Nailor. To those people who employ such terms and purport to know what they mean, Roddy Nailor is a classic psychopath. He is, according to all his assessments during his period in prison and prior to his last sentence, substantially above average intelligence, scoring between 110 and 120 in IQ tests. He is emotionally almost completely blunted. In this respect he is quite different from Bedser. Bedser craves affection to the point of desperate impatience. As I have said, this leads rapidly to frustration and violence. Nailor, if he considered emotion at all, would regard it with contempt. It is weakness and, worse still, extends down the difficult road towards guilt. Guilt is unknown to him both as feeling and concept. Partly because of this and partly as a result he has no *empathy*. No sympathy with or understanding of the suffering of others. This defect of character (some would say deficit) is balanced by a manic sense of personal injustice and, very often, a festering, implacable desire for personal vengeance. Like Bedser, he also may seem capable of kindness, decency and generosity. Typically gangsters of his type will support local charities, particularly those that cater for the young. However, in his case, such acts are a crude calculation. Reputation is important, as it is the handmaiden to power. Finally in the case of Nailor there is one serious and dangerous complicating factor, namely his exposure to nineteenth-century philosophy and, in particular, the works of Friedrich Nietzsche, courtesy of the Bournemouth Polytechnic College Day Release Course Number Fourteen. The philosophical works of Nietzsche could have been written for a world of psychopaths. Nietzsche teaches that among human beings there is a superior species, literally Supermen. This species has one essential primary characteristic. They are free from guilt. Because they have no guilt it also follows that they obey no rules. They are free spirits devoid of the petty consciences of liberal democracy, *noblesse oblige*, the social contract, the whole wet pluralist consensus between governing and governed.

'The fatal relationship between this ghastly philosophy and the psychopathic mind is now well known. The classic example is provided by the Leopold and Loeb trial in America. In that case two wealthy young men, saturated by Nietzschean philosophy, kidnapped and murdered a young boy known to both them and their parents. The unimaginable crime committed under the crude doctrine of some Godlike gift. In the case of Mr Nailor I am afraid that the Bournemouth Polytechnic has taken a monster and given us a supermonster. Are there any questions?'

'What is he likely to do?' asked Lady Stoker quietly.

'He is *capable* of almost anything. But it is important to avoid direct provocation of any kind. In those circumstances, in my view, it is absolutely essential that there should be no widespread press publicity and certainly none that identifies Nailor himself as a suspect or a man who is sought by the police. Such mass attention will simply fuel his present state of paranoia. If he has Miss Golding in his power it could well be fatal.' After a moment's silence the psychiatrist continued, 'I now come to Thomas Aylen and an obvious and bitter irony. Insofar as we identify Olympian characteristics Aylen had them. It is quite clear from the photographs taken before his accident that he was a strikingly beautiful boy. There was no sport at which he did not excel and no intellectual activity that he could not master. At Cambridge, apparently, he was a legend. Double Blue, cricket and rugby, Double First in Greats, with a major voluntary dissertation on Greek philosophy. In addition to these small achievements he was Chairman of Footlights, by all accounts wrote the funniest revue that the University has produced and chaired the University Labour Club. Given his left-wing credentials, he surprised everyone by accepting a short service commission in the Marines and was, as we know, on tour in Northern Ireland when the accident occurred which destroyed him. You have seen the photographs of the physical damage. Facially he is grotesque. Much of his right side is affected by intermittent palsy, though he can walk with considerable pain and has the use of his right upper arm. The lower arm was amputated following the accident and he has a metal prosthesis providing, I understand, some dexterity and a finger-grip of considerable power. That is the physical state of affairs. The mental condition is, if anything, worse. The bomb blast destroyed much of the right frontal lobe of his brain. This has left two major impediments. The first affects his speech. According to the reports he has a pronounced and incurable defect. The second consequence, known as Menkies' Syndrome, is rare and bizarre. It has a number of unpleasant effects but most important is a significant loss of free will.'

'In what sense?' Lady Stoker's intervention cut across that of her husband.

'In both the clinical and, if you will, the theological sense. The right frontal lobe of the brain controls a number of its functions, but the most important is that which governs judgement or choice. Without it human beings become suggestible, lacking in individual judgement, and ultimately, of course, susceptible to any form of manipulation.'

Alan Barlow ceased talking and an uncomfortable silence filled the room. George Watson eventually ended it. 'Are you saying that this . . . man, Aylen, is now under the influence of Nailor?'

'I am afraid that is not my province. I can only tell you what the boffins say. It also appears from the last clinical notes made up when Aylen was at the Bournemouth College that he began to behave strangely. That he became quiet and would not communicate with his therapist. The note on the file actually says, "Secretive. Has become withdrawn and almost hostile. Will not react to questioning. Feel there is something very wrong. Sinister almost."'

'My God,' said Lady Stoker, 'this is terrible.'

'I am afraid,' said Alan Barlow, 'that it may be. Shall I go on to Melanie Golding?' No one replied and the psychiatrist continued, 'Melanie Golding is well known to the three of you so I need not go into her background. She is obviously an extremely attractive woman with a mind of her own.'

'She is also,' said Jim Stoker evenly, 'possessed of considerable physical and mental courage.'

'Just so, and therein lies the potential danger. Kidnapping is, of course, an ultimate manifestation of power. So is the infliction of physical injury. There is now abundant evidence to confirm one's instinctive feelings that this necessity and longing for power is stimulated and provoked by resistance. I am afraid that the old aphorism that bullies are cowards at heart and deterred by confrontation has caused a great deal of physical injury and pain.'

'I think we should stop talking about this,' said Lady Stoker.

'I do not wish to distress you, but it is likely within hours or days that further contact will be made, possibly with Melanie herself. This may be with one of you. It is absolutely essential for her safety that she is told to co-operate and not to confront.'

In the renewed silence Elias Golding spoke. 'I know that this is not, technically, "in your province" but could you, nonetheless, give us your opinion based upon your view of these men? What do you think has happened?'

Alan Barlow looked squarely at the judge. 'My honest view is this. I believe that Nailor has used this poor man to kidnap your daughter. He has done it not for money but for revenge and to feed his own madness. If this is right then Aylen is acting so contrary to his previous character that the influence, demonic though it is, must be very strong. He will do to her what he is told. True, he is disabled, but the reports all indicate that he is still possessed of considerable strength, so her position is very dangerous indeed. However, I do not think that Nailor would simply order her death or disappearance without his own intervention. I think at some stage he will become personally involved, perhaps Bedser as well. There may, of course, be others whose identity we do not know. The Nailors are still an important and wealthy criminal family capable of widespread enlistment. Certainly they were linked to international criminal circuits. Whether they still are is doubtful.'

Having reached the realms of pure police work, Alan Barlow held out a large and misshapen hand to Eddie Cole, who leaned forward and spoke rapidly, counting, as he did so, on the points of his fingers.

'Let me tell you what I have done and then I suggest that you should go home and leave everything to us. I am in the process of assembling a large and dedicated squad. Five men each from One, Two, Four and Five Regional Crime Squads, and ten of my own. Surprisingly we stand more chance of avoiding publicity by creating a separate new group without existing hierarchy. Special Branch and the Security Services have been informed. What they will do God knows. At present they are leaving this to us. Nailor and Bedser have been put top of the national Most Wanted list under the pretence that they have committed a serious armed robbery. Scenes of Crime Officers and Forensic have examined most of Miss Golding's house and the street outside with a magnifying glass, but I do not anticipate anything of substance. The identity of these criminals is now well known. Their whereabouts is the only question. I will keep you informed by the hour.'

At this signalled end all rose from their chairs and George Watson delivered the valediction. 'I have,' he said, 'every confidence that Superintendent Cole will make the necessary efforts. He is an excellent officer.' Turning to Eddie Cole he thought, 'Why does he look at me like that?'

# Chapter 9

Superintendent Eddie Cole lay unhappily in the bed of his mistress, confidante and principal informant Mrs Anita Flynn. With both hands behind his almost invisible neck, Superintendent Cole gazed morosely at the plaster on the ceiling and discoursed on the impenetrable difficulties of modern policing. Whether his views were of interest or assistance to Mrs Flynn was difficult to ascertain since she lay in a foetal position, her back firmly towards her lover, and appeared, to all intents and purposes, to be asleep.

'You should see the state of the incident room. It looks like a council tip. Every single piece of rubbish within a quarter-of-a-mile radius of Melanie Golding's flat including the marshland has been assembled and labelled. There are over two hundred fag packets. Can you believe it? Over two hundred fag packets, six hundred sweet wrappers, nearly two hundred drink cans and thirty-eight contraceptives. Litter! Nobody thinks what it does to the process of investigation. No wonder we can't fucking solve anything. It's a joke. Do you remember those old films with lines of blue bobbies walking across marsh land and one of them suddenly goes, "Hey Governor, look at this," and picks up a dog end with the killer's fingerprints on it. God knows what they would have done with thirty-eight condoms. How can you police a modern society?'

Eddie Cole reached for a cigarette, lit it and blew a plume of smoke considerately in the direction of the door. After several exploratory dabs on the bedside table he located a glass of whisky which he attempted, partially successfully, to drink without raising his head from the pillow. Replacing the glass he again contemplated the ceiling. From Anita Flynn there came a slight but perceptible groan. Silence followed until Eddie Cole said, 'Eight footballs. There were eight footballs, all punctured of course. How do you play football on marshland? Three old sofas, two television sets, eight shoes (only one pair), all manner of underwear and a dinner jacket. Can you imagine that? A dinner jacket! Modern society is a mess. Oh, and a glass eye! Can you believe that? A left side glass eye. Brendan O'Hara was beside himself. Aylen's got a glass eye but it turns out to be the *wrong* eye. And do you know what?

The lady in the next door house said that hardly anybody went on to the marshes. She'd only ever seen one bloke four weeks before. In ten years! One bloke! Can you imagine what he must be like? Glass eye, dinner jacket, sixteen bottles of whisky, thirty-eight condoms. I'd like to meet him. I really would. I'd like to meet him.'

Eddie Cole stubbed his cigarette into the ashtray, split some more whisky into his mouth and on to the pillow and half turned to gaze at the raven hair which represented the back of Mrs Anita Flynn. 'No wonder we can't solve anything. The next time some journalist comes to me and says, "What are your main problems with policing serious crimes, Superintendent, drugs, gangsters, organised crime, the Triads, the Mafia, joy-riding, unemployment?" You know what I'll say? I'll say "litter." ' Eddie Cole looked at the ceiling and thought for a moment and then added, 'No, I'll say "litter and having a boss who is a complete wanker".'

Having found no response from his lover, Eddie Cole successively contemplated the state of his work, the state of his life and the state of his libido. The investigation was a mess. The ban on publicity was crippling. The search of Hackney Marshes had been passed off as an attempt to discover drugs, but already Melanie Golding's disappearance had been reported from three different sources, her tutor and two of her friends. What was wanted, thought Eddie Cole, was mass media attention. Pictures of Melanie, Nailor, Bedser, the secrecy was stifling. Would publicity put her at risk? Eddie Cole shrugged. She was almost certainly dead in any event. Nailor himself was bad enough, but Nailor in the grip of nineteenth-century nihilism . . .

Despite himself Eddie Cole suddenly became depressed. 'I'm fifty-five,' he said quietly into the darkness. Anita Flynn stirred beside him. 'Fifty-six.' 'All right,' said Eddie Cole, 'fifty-six.' To himself, he thought, 'Going nowhere. Can't solve anything. Lost in a sea of junk. A life surrounded by used condoms and deflated footballs. Got no hair; can't run; can only just screw; smoke too much; drink too much; swear all the time.' For the first time he thought, 'Why do I swear all the time? It's not even violent. It's just ordinary. I used to love English literature; got an A Level; read all the time. Now I use a vernacular with one adjective and a number of variants and derivations.'

Unusually doused with self-pity, Eddie Cole unhooked a hand and touched the black hair beside him. 'Twenty-two years,' he said softly, reflecting on his affair with Anita Flynn, 'twenty-two years,' and then softly into the night he said,

'And I was desolate and sick of an old passion . . .
I have been faithful to thee, Cynara! in my fashion.'

'Liar,' said Anita Flynn, stirring beside him.

Turning towards her, Eddie Cole slipped a hand across her stomach and uttered an old joke, 'Mrs Flynn, I think I'm going to need some help with my investigations.'

Turning to him, Anita Flynn replied, 'Superintendent, I want to give you all the help that I can.'

At precisely this point the mobile telephone rang. Anita Flynn listened briefly to the receiver before passing it to her lover. 'Brendan O'Hara. Says it's urgent.'

In the darkness Eddie Cole listened to the quiet voice of Sergeant O'Hara; Irish vowels rising slightly with repressed excitement. 'I am sorry to bother you, governor, but you need to know this immediately. It's Roddy Nailor.'

'We've got him?'

'Not exactly. We have a solicitor on the telephone. Says that Nailor has come to him as a client. Knows that we are looking for him. Wants to know why. Wants to know what will happen if he gives himself up. Wants to talk to us about terms and conditions . . . Are you there, guv?'

'Yes, yes, I'm thinking. Fuck it. Who is the solicitor? Is it that little Scotsman that farts?'

'No, guv, that's the strange thing. It's a guy called James Cameron from Dowsons.'

'Dowsons? Dowsons? Who are Dowsons?'

'I have just looked them up. They are a big firm in the City. Mainly commercial, some high-flying divorce, some commercial fraud. Not much crime that I can see. Nobody knows them at all. Oh yes, they have a department working for the Government. Procurement, export guarantees, that sort of thing.'

Eddie Cole stared at the ceiling. 'What the fuck is Roddy Nailor doing with an outfit like that?'

'Can't help you, guv. I suppose he must have plenty of money.'

'Of course he's got plenty of money, but he doesn't spend his own bloody money. He'll get Legal Aid. He's just out of the nick, for Christ's sake. He'd get Legal Aid before Lazarus.'

In the brief silence Brendan O'Hara said, 'What do you want me to do, guv?'

'Is he waiting for a reply?'

'He wants me to phone back within half an hour.'

'Phone him, tell him to come and see me.'

'Tomorrow morning?'

'No, no, tell him to come now. I'll be there in twenty minutes.'

'It's one o'clock in the morning, guv.'

'Tell him to come now. If he won't, phone me back. Otherwise I will be there.'

Anita Flynn watched Eddie Cole as he dressed. 'Special Branch,' she said, 'Special Branch, Customs and Excise, Security Services.'

Eddie Cole stared at her. 'What about them?'

'Dowsons. The solicitors. Work for them on difficult cases. Never heard of this chap Cameron but that's probably it.'

'How the hell do you know this?'

Raising both eyebrows, Anita Flynn stated the obvious. 'We do have other clients, you know.'

In his taxi Eddie Cole reflected on his work, semantic resolutions abandoned. What the fuck was going on? It was bizarre, monumental. Judge's beautiful daughter. Kidnapping. Grotesquely disfigured war heroes. Nailor. Junk Nazi philosophy. And now the bogeys. Special Branch? Security Services? Customs and Excise? What did it all mean? 'Me,' thought Eddie Cole bitterly. 'Why is it always fucking me?'

# Chapter 10

Brendan O'Hara met Eddie Cole in his office. 'He's here already. Been here for five minutes. Came straight from his offices in the City.'

'At one o'clock?'

'So he says. I've put him in my office. You can see him through the frosted door.'

'No, no, I don't give a damn what he looks like. Sit down and talk to me. Does Watson know about this?'

'Not yet.'

'Good. Try to phone him and put the phone down before he answers. Now we have a problem. Just one problem. Just a small problem. Just a tiny bit of a problem. We haven't got any evidence which is worth a row of beans. We *know* that it's Aylen because of the writing. We know he learned the writing at Bournemouth, and we know Roddy Nailor was at Bournemouth. We know that Roddy Nailor was banged up by Melanie Golding's dad, but apart from that the only link we have is a kidnap note couched in the same philosophical gibberish that Nailor's been stuffed with and the fact that Aylen is a bit fucking suggestible.'

'It's not enough.'

'Not enough, it's nowhere near enough.'

'If he comes in and gives himself up . . . to be interviewed?'

'He'll say nothing. Of course he'll say nothing. He's got a first class brief out there. So we tell him what he wants to know. We tell him that we know he's got this beautiful woman. And then we let him go? *If* she's still alive she will be dead within hours. Aylen too probably.'

Brendan O'Hara spoke quietly. 'We can't let him go.'

'And we can't get him in.'

Many years later, Brendan O'Hara would identify this as the moment when he first felt the force radiating from his boss. Much later he said, 'It was like becoming aware of a pulse. You could almost hear it. He was staring at me. I could see that his teeth were clenched. He suddenly appeared *possessed*.'

Eddie Cole said, 'If he comes in here, I'm not letting him go.'

'What about the evidence?'

'Something . . . of his is there at the flat.'

'Of Nailor's?'

'Yes, Nailor's. With his dabs on it.'

'Guv, it's all been dusted. It's all been tested. There's nothing on any of that stuff which is worth a row of beans.'

Later, much later, Brendan O'Hara would say, 'I watched him. I was frightened. He was pacing behind his desk. He kept muttering, "Something, there must be something." Then he said, "The eye!"'

'That false eye?'

'That's it. He must have touched it.'

'Guv, Roddy Nailor does not have a false eye.'

'But Aylen does. Aylen's got a false eye. Nailor could have touched it, looked at it.'

Brendan O'Hara walked across the office, placed both hands upon his boss's desk and said, 'Guv, it's the wrong fucking eye.'

Eddie Cole looked at his best sergeant and then, suddenly, smiled. 'Let's get him in.'

'We'll have to let him go.'

'We're not going to let him go. Superman is not killing anyone today. For a moment Eddie Cole stared at his desk, then he said, 'Go and get this smart brief but hold him up for fifteen minutes. Talk to him about something interesting like categorical imperatives. Fifteen minutes, that's all I need.'

In the quarter of an hour that followed Eddie Cole made himself busy. First he retrieved from a drawer in his desk a thin file marked 'Roddy Nailor'. From this he extracted a newspaper, holding it carefully in the extreme corner between his thumb and index finger. Briefly he checked the written boxes above the headline advertising the day's features thought most likely to attract attention. In the second box he read the words *Roddy Nailor Exclusive. Gangster turns Philosopher, Page 4.*

Carefully Eddie Cole selected from another drawer a transparent plastic envelope used for the retention of exhibits. Dropping the newspaper into the envelope, he sealed it with a white label and, having consulted a book marked 'Melanie Golding, Operation Judge', he wrote on the exhibit label 'Ex/EC/629A'. He then made an entry in the book. In the left-hand margin beneath Number 629 he wrote, '629A', and, selecting a pen identical to that with which the remainder of the page was written, wrote the words, 'Newspaper found at Melanie Golding's flat EC'.

Superintendent Eddie Cole smiled at his work, placed the plastic envelope carefully in his briefcase and left his office. Having waited unsuccessfully for the lift, he laboured up two flights of stairs to a room on the door of which was the legend 'Melanie Golding, Operation Judge – Exhibits Room'. Unlocking the door, Eddie Cole moved into a room piled high with plain plastic folders containing every form of ephemera from footballs to dinner jackets. On a table in the centre of the room lay a book similar to that in which he had transcribed his first note. On the top of each page were headings that read: 'Exhibit Number/Page/ Removed by & Purpose/Date Returned/Initial'. Eddie Cole selected the correct page, on which was written in the left-hand margin, '627, 628, 629' and carefully inserted the figures '629A'. In the next column he wrote, 'Removed by EC for Forensic Examination. 28.10.1988.' Having done so, he removed the white plastic folder containing the newspaper from his briefcase and, after a brief search along the shelves, found Exhibit 629, a manilla exercise book with Melanie Golding's name written untidily on the front. Next to it on the shelf he inserted '629A' and then immediately retrieved it, ensuring as he did so that the disturbance in the files could be noticed. Leaving the office he climbed three flights of stairs, and entered a further empty office marked 'Forensic' and beneath it 'Fingerprint Department'. In this room were several banks of computers and a desk, immediately before the door, on which was a triangular card bearing two enlarged fingerprints and the words 'Nothing can be done yesterday.'

Eddie Cole placed Exhibit 629A upon the desk and, selecting a message pad, wrote 'John – Please test today, immediately. Very urgent – EC.'

The policeman left the room, returned to his own office, sat behind his desk and assembled his features into the prehensile scowl which destroyed the hardest of them all. Within minutes came a knock on his door and Brendan O'Hara entered with a man whom he introduced as James Cameron. Eddie Cole assessed him in a matter of seconds as one to whom lying, manipulation and deceit were as natural as daily mastication. This, thought Eddie Cole, is going to be fucking difficult.

Save in their ages the two men could not have been more distinctly different. Eddie Cole, repellent of feature and slovenly of habit, observed before him a man whose meticulous dress, pale blue shirt, club tie and soft grey flannel suit matched perfectly the even features and the gold-rimmed glasses behind which blue eyes stared with apparent total indifference. The men touched hands. Eddie Cole said, 'Have you had some coffee?' and when the other nodded said, 'Do you want some more? It's bloody awful.'

'No thank you,' said James Cameron quietly. (Birmingham accent, thought Eddie Cole, odd.)

'You say that you represent Roddy Nailor?'

'I *do* represent Roddy Nailor.'

'Of course. Would you mind if I asked you for some proof of that?'

'Yes.'

'I see, well, how can we help?'

'My client informs me that he is on the Most Wanted list.'

How the fuck does he know, thought Eddie Cole. Aloud he said, 'I would be interested to know where he gets that information.'

'I am not at liberty to divulge that.'

'I see. We are not getting on very fast, are we? Do you want this recorded?'

'Why? Am I a suspect?'

'Of course not. I thought it might be wise for both of us.'

'I have a good memory, Superintendent, and I am sure we will both make notes immediately afterwards.'

'Very well, let us assume that Mr Nailor is right that he is wanted by us. Will he turn himself in?'

'That, I think, depends on the answers to a number of questions.'

'I suspect you are going to ask them.'

'Of course. First, and most obvious, why is he being sought?'

'I am afraid I cannot divulge that.'

'I see. We are still not getting on very fast, are we?'

'I can tell you that it is in connection with a serious crime.'

'Is there a warrant?'

'No.'

'Do you have evidence against him? Sufficient to arrest him?'

Eddie Cole looked evenly at James Cameron and said, 'I can tell you that we do not have sufficient evidence to arrest him. We wish to attempt, as we say, to "eliminate him from our enquiries".'

James Cameron's elegant face twisted with disbelief. 'You do realise, Superintendent, that I will record that, and should there ever be court proceedings, and it turned out that there *was* evidence of which you have not informed me, that it would be very bad, very bad indeed. It would almost certainly make the evidence unusable.'

'I am a superintendent, not a uniformed PC. What I tell you, as of this moment, is the truth.'

'There will be no arrest?'

'I have said once, and I will repeat it. We do not presently have sufficient evidence upon which to arrest your client. We want to ask him some questions.'

'Will it be clearly understood that any interview would *not* be carried out in accordance with the Police and Criminal Evidence Act and would not be used in any future proceedings?'

'I accept that.'

'Where do you want to see him?'

'Here, of course.'

'When?'

'As soon as Mr Nailor can make himself available.'

Smiling at the irony, James Cameron said, 'That will be two o'clock tomorrow afternoon.'

'Fine. Will you attend?'

'Of course.'

'Why does your client want to come in on a voluntary basis?'

'He has been in prison for ten years. He is going straight and wishes to be left in peace.'

'How very comforting. I will see you at two o'clock.'

As James Cameron was leaving the office, Eddie Cole said, 'Just one thing. Why did Roddy Nailor come to you? A bit out of his class, isn't it?'

'I am afraid,' said James Cameron, 'I cannot divulge that.'

# Chapter 11

At twelve o'clock the following day Eddie Cole received a report from his friend, Sergeant John Noble in the Fingerprint Department, together with the returned newspaper, Exhibit 629A, now heavily stained with the red dye that signifies the work of that department. Reading the report swiftly, Eddie Cole smiled with relief. He then took Exhibit 629A and replaced it in the Exhibit room. In the Exhibits Book he wrote, 'Returned from Forensic, 12.31 p.m.'

At two o'clock Eddie Cole sat in his office beside Sergeant Brendan O'Hara. In the corridor within hearing range were two young members of the CID, one of whom was armed. At 2.05 the door opened and a uniformed police officer said, 'I have a Mr Cameron and a Mr Nailor for you, guv.'

Eddie Cole said, 'Bring them in.'

Unless one carefully studied his eyes, Roddy Nailor did not resemble his reputation. Ten years in prison had left him lined and thin. Save for the eyes, nothing in the pale face revealed the monstrous cruelty and dementia which seethed within. The eyes were shocking: grey, immobile and cold as fish.

Eddie Cole rose from behind his desk. 'Mr Nailor, what a long time.'

'Yes, indeed, Mr Cole. Yes, indeed.'

'Been doing some learning, I gather.'

'Wouldn't interest you, Mr Cole, wouldn't interest you. Why you looking for me then, guv?'

Eddie Cole let the silence grow until it became a statement of menace. Then he said, 'What have you done with Melanie Golding?'

James Cameron said, 'Who is Melanie Golding?' At the same time Roddy Nailor said, 'Never heard of her.'

'Oh yes you have, Mr Nailor, oh yes you have,' said Eddie Cole, 'and I think you have as well, Mr Cameron, but to give you the benefit of the doubt I will tell you this: Melanie Golding is the only daughter of Elias Golding, the High Court judge. You have heard of him, haven't you, Mr Nailor?' Eddie Cole paused, looked into the eyes of James Cameron and thought, 'He knows, he knows it all.' He continued, 'On the twenty-second of October, Melanie Golding was kidnapped from her flat near Hackney Marshes. She has been missing ever since. She was kidnapped by a man known as Thomas Aylen, an ex-Marine Commando. You know him, Mr Nailor, don't you? *Don't you?*'

'Never heard of him.'

'Oh yes you have. He was learning to write at your college in Bournemouth, Mr Nailor, where you learned all that stuff about Nietzsche.'

'Lot of people there, Mr Cole, lot of people there. You forget names. Can you give me a face?'

Eddie Cole turned over a photograph that lay before him on the desk and pushed it quietly to the other side.

'Oh my God,' said James Cameron.

'You wouldn't forget *him*, Mr Nailor, now, would you?'

'Yeah, yeah, I recognise him. Who wouldn't? Makes you feel ill just looking at him.'

James Cameron said, 'How did he get like that?'

'He was blown up by a bomb, in Ireland. He was a hero.'

'What's this got to do with me?' said Roddy Nailor.

'He came under your rotten influence. You persuaded him to kidnap this girl.'

'Bollocks.'

'Oh yes you did.'

'Look, I've never heard of this woman, know nothing about her, who she is, where she comes from, where she lives. It's all fuck all to me.'

'You don't know where she lives?'

'Not a fucking clue.'

'Never been there or sent her anything?'

'Look, Mr Cole, I haven't been near Hackney for twenty years. No, I have never sent her anything.'

Eddie Cole took a deep breath and rose on his side of the desk. 'Will you repeat that for the record?'

'We agreed . . .' said James Cameron, before Roddy Nailor said, 'Of course I will.' Eddie Cole gestured to Brendan O'Hara who switched on the small grey regulation tape recorder which lay on the desk.

James Cameron said, 'I said nothing on the record, nothing. I must insist . . .'

'I only want the denial,' said Eddie Cole, 'no more questions, is that all right?'

'Fuck it,' said Roddy Nailor, 'you can have that.'

Eddie Cole spoke quickly, the rubric of statute, 'I am Superintendent

Cole. It is 2.41 on the twenty-eighth of October 1988. I am carrying out an interview together with Detective Sergeant Brendan O'Hara of Mr Roddy Nailor in the presence of his solicitor, Mr James Cameron. Will you confirm, gentlemen, by saying your names? You are not under arrest, but you are answering questions under suspicion of a crime, namely, the abduction of Melanie Golding. You are not obliged to say anything, but anything you do say may be taken down and used in evidence against you.'

Later Brendan O'Hara was to say, 'As we spoke our names into the tape recorder I suddenly had a feeling that something dreadful was about to happen. The next thing that Eddie did was to ask the question.'

'Have you any knowledge of Melanie Golding?'

'No.'

'Have you ever spoken to her, written to her or been to her flat at Hackney?'

'Never, never, never, I told you I've never heard of her, never had nothing to do with the bloody woman.'

'Have you ever communicated with her in any way, sent her anything, either yourself or through anyone else?'

'Never, never, never, I know nothing about the bloody woman.'

'Thank you,' said Eddie Cole, 'that is all, is there anything anyone wishes to add?'

In the silence Eddie Cole lent forward and checked the tape. He then stood above the other three and said, 'Roddy Nailor, I am now formally arresting you for the kidnapping on the twenty-first of October of Melanie Golding. You are not obliged to say anything, but anything which you say will be taken down and may be used in evidence against you.'

Roddy Nailor was on his feet shouting. 'You bastard, you fucking bastard.'

James Cameron, also on his feet, put a hand on his client's arm. 'You told me,' he said evenly, 'that there was no evidence to arrest him. You gave me that assurance yesterday and I want that recorded.'

'Certainly,' said Eddie Cole, and turned to Brendan O'Hara. 'Write that down, and we will all sign it.' Turning to James Cameron, Eddie Cole smiled a smile devoid of anything except contempt. 'When I said that to you yesterday we did not have the evidence that we have now.'

'I demand to know,' said James Cameron, 'what this evidence is and how it was discovered.'

'It is a newspaper found at Melanie Golding's flat. It contains an article written by your client. The article contains references to the same philosophical gibberish contained in the ransom note.'

'So what,' said Roddy Nailor. 'That proves fuck all.'

'It has your fingerprints on it. We discovered that this morning.'

Later Brendan O'Hara was to say, 'I didn't know what to do. I just didn't know what to do. I looked at him and said, "Guv," and that was all. Eddie just looked at me. I couldn't do anything.'

Roddy Nailor was backing towards the door, 'You swine! You bastard! You've fucking done it again. You bastard.'

As he reached the end of the room Eddie Cole said, loudly, 'Now.' The door opened immediately and Roddy Nailor turned into the arms of Detective Sergeant Brian Watling, whose regular attendance at the Central Gymnasium and pre-occupation with his own muscular body was demonstrated by the speed with which Roddy Nailor found himself pressed to the carpet of Eddie Cole's office, listening to the voice of his own solicitor above his head.

'I wish to protest very strongly. This was manifestly a trap and I was used to spring it.'

'You may protest to whom you like,' said Eddie Cole. 'Your client would now do himself a great favour if he told us the whereabouts of Melanie Golding.'

'Fuck you,' said Roddy Nailor to the carpet. 'Fuck you, fuck you.'

# Chapter 12

Unlike many ugly men Eddie Cole had no doubts about his appearance. When he looked into mirrors he perceived the reality without the comforting intervention of illusion. No attempt was made to compose the features, narrow the eyes or advance a favoured profile. Eddie Cole knew the truth and saw it. For this reason he generally avoided reflective surfaces. Unusual it was, therefore, twenty-four hours after the arrest of Roddy Nailor, to find Eddie Cole staring at his own reflection in the mirror of the fifth-floor washroom of Scotland Yard. The reason was simple and rare. Eddie Cole had come to talk to himself. More accurately, he had come for comfort. This happened on occasions, normally when Anita Flynn was unavailable or the subject matter (as now) was so serious as to prevent indiscretion. On those occasions the fifth-floor washroom was Eddie Cole's confessional. The man who stared from the silver rectangle was his friend, his counsellor, his confidant and his confessor.

'What the fuck is going on,' said Eddie Cole to his image, having carefully checked the cubicles and taken up position with his pendulous girth overhanging an enamel wash basin. 'What the hell is going on?'

'I'll tell you,' said the image. 'I'll tell you exactly what's going on. This is corrupt. Someone's got their snout in a trough. Someone's got his bread well into the fucking gravy.'

'Who?' said Eddie Cole. 'Who? What the fuck is going on? Is George Watson in on this?'

The face in the mirror twisted with contempt and disbelief. ''Course not, he's far too fucking stupid to be corrupt.'

'But is there some other game?' said Eddie Cole. 'What's he playing at?'

The subject matter of this monologue was a meeting from which Eddie Cole had just emerged in a state of considerable irritation. The meeting, which had lasted barely ten minutes, had taken place with Chief Superintendent George Watson. It had begun badly.

'Yes, ah yes, come in, Eddie, sit down if you like. It's about this Judge investigation. I got your note about Mr Nailsford . . .'

69

'Nailor,' said Eddie Cole.

'. . . Ah yes, Nailor. I got your note about this newspaper and the fingerprints. Why is it called Operation Judge by the way?'

'Because the girl, the kidnapped girl, is the daughter of a High Court judge,' said Eddie Cole.

'Oh, yes, yes. Well, it's a difficult one. Has Nailor said anything?'

'Yes, he said, "Fuck you, fuck you, fuck you."'

'Ah; who did he say that to?'

'Well, he had his face in the carpet at the time, but I think he was referring to me.'

'Yes, well you see, that may be the point. You know him of old, don't you?'

'I banged him up for fifteen years.'

'Ah yes, attacked an Indian, hadn't he?'

'Chinaman.'

'Ah yes, yes, yes, nailed his feet to the floor.'

'Well done,' thought Eddie Cole. 'Well done. Encyclopaedic.'

'I believe he said that he'd been fitted up at the time?'

'He said I'd forged his dabs on the hammer.'

'So there's not much love lost between you, then?'

'We're very close,' said Eddie Cole, regretting it immediately.

'Good Lord,' said Fast Track, 'how very odd.'

'No, sir,' said Eddie Cole, 'we are not very close. We are not friends. I think that Roddy Nailor would like to have me disembowelled.'

'Oh, I see, a joke. Yes, I see. Well look, Eddie, in these circumstances do you think it is a good idea if you go on with this case? There's fingerprints involved here too, I gather. Could get nasty. You know, cross-examination. Old vendetta. Vindictive. Taking revenge; that kind of thing.'

'I'm sorry, sir, why should *I* want revenge on him? He got the fifteen years, not me.'

'No, no, I can see that. It's just that a jury might not quite understand.'

'Juries,' thought Eddie Cole, 'do not consist of Fast Track Superintendents.'

'And then there's all this Nietzsche stuff, Superman and herd instincts and all that sort of stuff, a bit complex.'

'We don't need to go into all that. We've got his fingerprints.'

'Yes, but it might become relevant, and we might need someone who knows a bit about it. Some kind of academic.'

'Then I'll get one.'

'Yes, but, you see, it all gets a bit complex. Anyway, I understand it's going to be taken out of our hands.'

Eddie Cole stared at him. 'Who by?'

'Special Branch, I got a call from the Commander this morning.'

Eddie Cole was on his feet. 'Special Branch! This isn't Special Branch, this is police. Who needs Special Branch?'

George Watson shifted unhappily. 'Yes, well, but the whole thing, as I said, is a bit complex.'

'What do the Special Branch know about Hegel? The nearest they come to nineteenth-century moral philosophy is counting their fucking toes after target practice.'

'Eddie, please, I don't want that language used in here. It's not appropriate.'

With very considerable difficulty Eddie Cole said, 'Sorry.'

'That's all right, Eddie, I can see you're upset. But it's not all bad news. They want you to work with them. Are you all right? You've suddenly gone very red in the face. Would you like a glass of water?'

Eddie Cole spoke through his teeth. 'Who exactly is going to lead this team?'

'Jack Wagner. He's a Chief Superintendent now. I say, are you really feeling all right? You've gone awfully red now.'

'I cannot work with Wagner. I investigated him for corruption. I recommended prosecution. The Director let him off.'

'Yes, Eddie, I had heard about that, but it's many years ago isn't it? Bygones and bygones you know. In any case I don't think we have a choice so let's all make the best of it.'

Later, secure in his washroom confessional, Eddie Cole hissed at his image. 'Wanker! Wanker, Wanker Wagner. Of all the bent, fluffed-up septic pricks that I should get, I get Wanker.' And then, 'Why? Why? Work it out. There's something wrong. Something reeks. Think about it. Roddy Nailor. Roddy Nailor goes to that poncy firm of solicitors. Dowsons. They work for the Security Services, *and* Special Branch. Now we've got Special Branch on *this*. This is police work. *My* work.'

Eddie Cole steadied himself on the white porcelain hand-basin and smiled grimly at Eddie Cole.

'Well,' said the image, 'we shall see.'

Eddie Cole patted his own bald head and turned and made for the door. George Watson had said that Chief Superintendent Wagner had been told to give his assignment total priority and was on his way. By now the Wanker would have arrived.

# Chapter 13

Eddie Cole entered the operations room established exclusively for Operation Judge. It was crowded with men and three women. Varieties of garments could not disguise a uniformity of style. Uniformity of style could not disguise the clammy atmosphere of mutual hostility. The Special Branch had arrived.

Anger blackened the thoughts of Eddie Cole.

'My room,' he thought. 'My job, my fucking room. And now I've got Wanker.'

Jack Wagner came towards him, smiling with the condescension of appointed office. 'Eddie, long time.'

'Hello, Jack, you coming back to earth?'

'Not yet, Eddie, not yet. I'm just here to roll away the stone.'

'Good, good, manual work suits you, Jack. Plays to your strength. Know what I mean?'

Conversation in the operations room had subsided. Nineteen pairs of eyes, all partisan, watched their respective masters from whom mutual antipathy radiated like a pulse.

'Let's have a word in your office,' said Jack Wagner, smiling and turning toward the door.

As the two men left the room, Brendan O'Hara entered.

'Look after this, Brendan,' said Eddie Cole. 'Keep them apart. No biting or gouging.'

In Eddie Cole's office both men stood on the same side of Eddie Cole's desk.

'We are going to have to work together, Eddie,' said Jack Wagner.

'I wonder, Jack,' said Eddie Cole, 'why you always make me feel post-coital. You know, deflated, limp, slightly sick.'

'You are an ugly bastard, Eddie. In almost everything you do and say.'

'Funny, isn't it, and here's me always thinking you were so lovely. Lots of hair, blue eyes, rimless glasses, nice white teeth, shiny suit, shirt cuffs nearly clean too.'

With enormous satisfaction Eddie Cole saw Jack Wagner glance irresistibly downward towards his hands before tightening his lips.

'Nice cufflinks,' continued Eddie Cole. 'Are they real, those sovereigns or just, as they say, corrupt metal?'

'Fuck off, Eddie,' said Jack Wagner.

'You see, Jack, it's not just that I know you're a dishonest little shit. Dear God, Jack, I've worked with hundreds of dishonest little shits. Some of my best friends are dishonest little shits. True, in your case you're a humourless little bastard, but what of that? You were probably very unhappy when you were a baby. Perhaps they dropped you in the clinic. What worries me, Jack, about this, *really really* worries me, is why you? Why you, Jack? Of all the people they could have given me on this job, why does it have to be you? They must know, Jack. It's not that long ago now, is it?'

'Ten years, Eddie, nearly ten years.'

'Ten years, well, well, well, and you've hardly changed. You just look so *young*, so *wealthy*.'

'I didn't take that money, Eddie. I told you then, and I'm telling you now.'

'Oh yes you did, Jack. You took the money and you kept it. You and your little team. You know that bit of *Othello*, Jack: "Who steals my purse steals trash, 'twas mine, 'tis his, 'tis mine again." Except in your case it stopped with you, didn't it, Jack? 'Twas mine, 'tis his and then 'twas Jack Wagner's. There's something so seedy, Jack, about nicking what's been nicked already. Not giving back the swag. How much was it, Jack? Two hundred, two hundred and fifty thousand? Bank notes. Securicor van, wasn't it?'

'They got back all the money we found. They recovered it all.'

'But they didn't, Jack, did they? Because you had it.'

'You were the only one who believed it.'

'No, Jack, the others didn't *want* to believe it. You were their God, Jack, Olympian. The best thief-taker in London. There was nothing you couldn't do, Jack. Even I thought you were wonderful. And when they asked *me* to investigate *you*, do you know what I did, Jack? I nearly refused. Yes I did. I nearly refused. It seemed like man investigating God. Do you know why they chose me, Jack? You don't. I'll tell you why. They chose me because they thought I was a rough old copper. Loyal, tough. If anyone could be relied upon to close ranks it was me. But I didn't, did I? And do you know why? Because I'm soft? Because I'm fucking wet? No. I'll tell you why, Jack. It's because I believe we can do *anything*. We can bang them up, string them up, fuck them up, we can even fit them up, but the one thing we can't do, Jack, the one thing we can't do, is *take their fucking money*. Do you know why Gods stay Gods,

Jack? Not our silly old God, real Gods, *angry* Gods. Do you know why they're worshipped? They rain down pestilence and plague, suffering and misery, agony and pain. They carefully arrange for fire and brimstone, hurricanes and tempests, floods and droughts, earthquakes and volcanic eruptions, everything that fucks up and destroys what their miserable little worshippers, their acolytes, work their miserable little balls off to achieve every single day. They fuck it up and screw it up. Harvests fail, wars are lost, wives and children are raped and butchered, cities are raised, hanging, drawing, quartering, buggering, butchering, stretching, burning, gouging, blinding; all allowed by the angry Gods. And what do they do? Their followers, their worshippers, their acolytes, what do they do? They rebuild the Temple, they rebuild the altars, they rebuild the plinths, the alcoves and the Pantheons, and they *sacrifice*, they *sacrifice*. What they've got left after all the bloody mayhem. The precious residue of their lives. The pathetic ephemera of survival. They leave it on the altar. They make offerings to their Gods. And do you know why, Jack? Do you know why they still worship them? Do you know why they tremble then fall down? Do you know why? There are two reasons, Jack, only two. The first reason, Jack, these Gods, these angry Gods, are *feared and feared and feared*, and, secondly, Jack, these Gods, these angry Gods, are *not on the take*. They have not got their sticky Olympian fingers in the fucking till. They do not rip off and graft. They do not take sweeteners or earners or kick-backs or bunces or bungs or keep their bit of the swag. It's *still on the altar*, Jack. What the poor little bastards leave there on Sunday night is still there on Monday morning, Jack. The angry Gods don't want it, Jack. They don't want it because they are *Gods*, Jack, and it is enough to be *feared*. And what do you think would happen, Jack, if they took it? What do you think would happen on Monday morning if all that crap on the altar had disappeared? Taken up to heaven. What do you suppose would happen, Jack? I'll tell you what would happen. It's just so easy. You know what would happen? The bastards would start *complaining*. That's what they'd do, Jack, they'd start whinging. The next time their rotten hovels or skyscrapers disappeared in an earthquake, the next time their miserable boats or oil tankers turned over in a gale, the next time the hurricane flattens them or the sun burns them, or the war is lost, the next time that happens they will say, "It's not fucking fair. We gave you all those flowers and faggots and cakes and wine and virgins and tethered goats and sacks of rice, and," Jack, "bags and bags and bags of used fivers. We gave you all that, and *you took them*. And now we've got this fucking earthquake, bomb, blizzard, a war. It's not fucking cricket," And before you know where you are, Jack, before you know where you are, they're not Gods any more. They're just like us. On the take, on the make, on the fiddle, lining their nest, having a bit on the side. We know, we know; "everybody does it." But Gods don't do it because if they do they're *just like everybody else.* That's why they got the wrong guy to investigate you and your team, Jack. And you know why I can't bear your shiny fucking suit and your fake sovereigns anywhere near me, Jack? It's because when you do what you do you stop me being a God.'

In the pause that followed Jack Wagner said, 'I didn't think anybody could talk for that long.' Then he added, 'You're a pretty ugly God, Eddie.'

'I look ugly. Inside it's like the roof of the Sistine fucking Chapel.'

'God again. Did it ever occur to you, Eddie, that you might be becoming a bit paranoid? Failure perhaps. Gets to people after a while.'

Eddie Cole stiffened. 'I don't fail.'

'Well, Eddie, you haven't done very well on this case so far, now have you?'

Suddenly defensive, Eddie Cole said, 'It's very difficult, sensitive, I can't use publicity, but I have got Nailor.'

'Without proof.'

'There is proof . . .'

'Oh, come on Eddie,' Jack Wagner was suddenly angry. 'That fucking newspaper, so what? Any decent brief will rip it apart. Why did it go to Forensic so late? Why did you find it? Don't tell me you fitted him up because I don't want to know, but that's what they'll say and it looks *dreadful.*'

'It's enough to make a case. He'll have to give evidence.'

'Bollocks he will. Roddy Nailor's never been near a witness box in his life. And if he does, what if he does? What does he say? "This is vindictive. Of course it's Eddie Cole. He banged me up last time. Yes, I went to the Bournemouth Poly, and yes I was there at the same time as a man who appears to have kidnapped this girl. That's *why* he has picked on me. I know the girl is the daughter of the judge who sentenced me. That is a terrible coincidence, but so what? That is all it is. No one can prove that I influenced Aylen, set him on, controlled him, bent him to my will. I am not God. I am a gangster. Eddie Cole wants me banged up again. *That's* the coincidence".' Jack Wagner's hand went into the air to stop Eddie Cole's interruption. 'The newspaper. Ah yes, the newspaper. Very interesting. You know what he will say? "This is my article. This is *my* newspaper. Of course I had a number of copies. This newspaper I sent to Eddie Cole. I wanted to show him that I was making good. That I was not just a common or garden gangster, that I could write and *learn*, and I gave him, yes I gave him, the evidence he needed to plant." That's what he'll say, Eddie, even if he gets anywhere near the witness box. And you tell me, Eddie, you tell me now, why did that newspaper go to Forensic so late?'

'I did not consider it necessary to print it before. It suddenly came to me when I knew that Nailor was coming in. I hadn't realised its significance.'

'Oh *come on*, Eddie. This is an article written in a newspaper by the prime suspect, Target One. Have you gone stark staring mad?'

Eddie Cole's face turned to stone. 'I missed it. I made a mistake. Not everything was fingerprinted.'

'What, the footballs? Eight footballs not fingerprinted. Well they wouldn't be, would they? They're *footballs*. The sweet papers aren't fingerprinted, nor are the condoms. Of course they're not, but virtually everything in the flat has been through Forensic, and even the bloody glass eye found on the Marshes has been fingerprinted.'

'Aylen's got a glass eye.'

'Eddie, it's the *wrong fucking eye.*' There was a pause before Wagner continued. 'Eddie, we haven't got enough fucking evidence.'

'When we catch Aylen . . .'

'*If* we catch Aylen, and if we catch him alive.' Jack Wagner's sentence ended suddenly.

Noticing, Eddie Cole said quickly, 'Why shouldn't we catch him alive?'

'We may never get him at all.'

'Yes, yes, I understand that, but why might he not be alive?'

'I don't know. I don't know. It's always possible . . . men like that . . . do themselves in.' Eddie Cole watched him. 'Lame,' he thought. 'Very fucking lame. He knows something.' Aloud, Eddie Cole said, 'You know where she is, don't you?'

Jack Wagner crossed to the grimy window of Eddie Cole's office and inspected the brick wall visible twenty feet away. 'Maybe,' he said.

'What do you mean "maybe"?'

'I mean fucking *maybe*. We are beginning to get information.'

'Where from?'

'I can't tell you.'

'What do you mean? I am running this show.'

'No, Eddie, *I* am running this show and this is *my* snout. There have been deals.'

Eddie Cole looked at the back of Chief Superintendent Jack Wagner and then, with alarming speed, crossed the room and stood by his side.

He shook as he said, 'It's Nailor, isn't it? You're getting information from Nailor? You've done a deal with Nailor. That's why he's got those poncey solicitors, Dowsons, what's the game, Jack? What the fuck is going on? This man is not a snout, he's a killer. You don't do deals with men like Roddy Nailor, Jack. Now tell me. Where is she?'

Jack Wagner took his time in facing Eddie Cole, and when he did he looked straight into his eyes and said, 'You don't frighten me, Eddie. You're an ugly bastard, and you think you're God, but you don't frighten me, Eddie, and you don't tell me how to do my job. We think we will know in half an hour where this girl is, who she is with, whether she is alive and well and whether we can get her out, and then, Super-intendent, then I will let you know. Now, *I* am going to the operations room and *I* am going to talk to *our* squad. You will come with me and you will stand behind me and you will fucking *smile*. Your ugly face will radiate joy and contentment, and then, Superintendent, you will do what you are fucking well told. On this operation, Superintendent, there will only be one God, and you shall have no other God but me.'

# Chapter 14

Eddie Cole lay next to his mistress, confidante and most valuable snout, Mrs Anita Flynn. For the first time, when sober, Eddie Cole's fading libido had failed him completely.

'Don't worry,' said Anita Flynn, 'it happens to everybody.'

'I'm not worried about my dick,' said Eddie Cole irritably, attempting to stub out his second cigarette. 'Can't you get some new bedside tables? This is bloody dangerous.'

'All you've got to do is sit up.'

'I don't come here to sit up, I come to lie down.'

'Well that's all you've been doing so far,' said Anita Flynn. She looked at her lover and said, 'God you're an ugly bastard.'

'Jack Wagner called me that today.'

'Jack Wagner? What are you doing talking to him?'

'I didn't know you knew him.'

'Darling, I know *everybody*. Didn't you investigate him, after that Moffatt trial where they said part of the money had gone missing after arrest?'

Eddie Cole looked at her with admiration. 'God,' he said, 'Anita, you've got a mind like an elephant.'

'You know,' said Anita Flynn, 'you ought to write love poetry. You've got all the images. Now tell me. What's Jack Wagner doing in this?'

'He's been put in charge of this operation.'

'But he's Special Branch.'

'Of course he is, we've got the bastards crawling all over the office. I am worried about this, Anita; no, I really am worried about this.'

In the gloom Eddie Cole lit another cigarette and Anita Flynn gazed at him. 'I've never heard you say that before.'

'What?'

'That you're worried. Pissed off, yes, fucked up, yes, angry, yes, drunk, yes, but "worried"? You don't know how to worry. When did you learn this? Have you been on Day Release?'

'It's not a joke. There is something really wrong here. You know you said Dowsons were outside solicitors who acted for the Special Branch and their members?'

'Yes, it's true. Not many people know that but it's true.'

'So Roddy Nailor is going to the Special Branch's pet solicitors. And now we get the Special Branch running our case and Roddy Nailor, who I have arrested and charged with the offence, has become their snout. I'm sure of it. He hasn't *confessed*. There is no statement. They can't let him go without my agreement, so how could they do a deal? But I know Roddy Nailor is telling them where the girl is. They've been doing something this afternoon. I know. All the bastards left the office at three o'clock and there's a big meeting called for three a.m., yes, three a.m., this morning. Nobody's telling me fucking anything. What is it, Anita? What's going wrong? What's the relationship between Nailor and the Special Branch?'

In the gloom Anita Flynn said, 'I don't think it's Special Branch.'

Eddie Cole started dropping the ash from his new cigarette.

'What do you mean "not Special Branch"?'

'The relationship is with the Security Services, their masters.'

'Christ, with MI5, 6?'

'Maybe not the Service itself, someone in it, people in it or who was in it, powerful people by now I expect.'

'What do you mean, "by now"?'

'This goes back a long way if I'm right. I think it may be the Mackston business.'

'The Mackston business? Who the hell is Mackston?'

'Dear, dear, Eddie, you really should read a newspaper sometimes. Charles Mackston was Foreign Secretary in the Wilson Government in the 1970s.'

'Oh *that* Mackston, yes, I know that, but what's it got to do with this?'

'Be quiet for a minute. Sit up. Put out that cigarette, and I will tell you. That's better. Now, Charles Mackston was a Foreign Secretary in the last Wilson administration. Everyone knew that he had friends who did lots of business in Eastern Europe, mainly with the East Germans, and, I think, with the Poles, the Hungarians and also the Russians. Wilson knew some of them as well. Knighted some of them. Anyway, the Tory Opposition thought that Mackston could be a spy. They either thought he could be a spy or they thought it was a good idea that he looked like a spy. But rumours circulate. Then one day, in 1974 or 1975, I can't remember which, Charles Mackston's house is burgled. Lots of secret papers go missing and have never been recovered. Now Charles Mackston and Harold Wilson always thought that the burglary was done by the Security Services, shall we say "encouraged" by certain powerful elements in the Conservative Opposition. You may remember Wilson made no secret of it. The Security Services denied it and it was of course pointed out that the burglary was a pretty expert job. Since our Security Services, then and now, make a total mess of everything they do, their denial had some degree of credibility.'

'I remember this, vaguely,' said Eddie Cole. 'But what's it got to do with Nailor?'

'Nailor did it.'

'Did what?'

'The burglary, of course.'

'I don't understand. Why should Roddy Nailor work for the Security Services? Why should the Security Services employ Roddy Nailor?'

'Money. Also, it was said, there was a security link. Mossad I think. The Israeli Security Service. I forget the details, but it is something like this. When they were getting powerful in the early seventies the Nailors got illusions of grandeur and decided to go multinational. They had some operation in Israel, God knows what; drugs, arms. It brought them into contact with Mossad, painfully at first apparently. But Mossad soon realised that there were advantages to knowing some eminent British thugs. In return for money, and being left alone in the Middle East they could perform all kinds of unpleasant tasks that Mossad agents would otherwise have to do themselves. Harassing Palestinians in London among them. Mossad was always said to be very close to the British Security Services, and so there was a link. This is rumour. But, for whatever reason, there is little doubt that Roddy Nailor and his boys did the Mackston burglary. What they found, of course, was a lot of Foreign Office junk demonstrating the patriotic nature of the Wilson Government. Not what they were sent to get, but, nonetheless, they got it. That's the link. I suspect that Roddy Nailor is calling in his debts. He tried his bit of revenge. You screwed him up. Now he's getting some help in high places.'

'Why didn't he do it before, when I banged him up? Why didn't he do it then?'

'Darling,' said Anita Flynn wearily, 'darling, you banged him up in 1978. In 1978 there was a Labour government. Try telling a Labour government that you burgled their Foreign Secretary. Get it, do you? Trying hard?'

'How the hell do you know all this? How the hell do you know all this?' said Eddie Cole, sitting up smartly and stubbing his cigarette carefully into the ashtray.

'We get all types here,' said Anita Flynn, 'we get lawyers, doctors, civil servants, spies, judges, and a few politicians, Tories mainly. We don't only get ugly sozzled drooping coppers you know. Now *do not* light another cigarette.'

# Chapter 15

Eddie Cole settled into the back of his taxi and looked at his watch. 2.30 a.m. Plenty of time. The premises of Mrs Anita Flynn occupied the top three floors of a Victorian office building in Drury Lane. Twenty minutes to Scotland Yard, at the most. He wanted to see Brendan O'Hara before the briefing began at 3 a.m. Eddie Cole reached into the front pocket of his briefcase and pulled out a mobile phone, the battery of which, on inspection, was quite flat. 'Fuck,' said Eddie Cole.

'Sorry?' said the taxi driver.

'Fuck,' said Eddie Cole.

'Right on,' said the taxi driver.

Leaning forward Eddie Cole secured the glass partition with a murmur of apology and sat back in order to cogitate. He still didn't quite believe it. Suppose it was right? Suppose Nailor had some kind of political pull? What kind of deal could they do? Whatever Jack Wagner had said, there was *a case* against Nailor. It did not just rely on the newspaper. The newspaper simply pulled it together. Here was a motive and here was direct association with Aylen. Aylen's part was provable beyond doubt by the identification of the ransom note and, once the kidnap was ended and Aylen was arrested, *he* would probably put Nailor in the frame. There was always the possibility he would plead guilty and turn Queen's Evidence. Even if he did not give Queen's Evidence, suppose he fought the case, did not plead guilty, any confession made by him implicating Nailor would still go before the jury. Certainly, the jury would be told that Aylen's confession was not evidence against Nailor, but so what? No one believed the jury would take the slightest notice of that, unless of course, thought Eddie Cole, Aylen doesn't survive.

Quite suddenly there came to Eddie Cole a feeling he had thought long extinct. A lurching sickness somewhere above his pendulous gut. The unmistakable rush of acid, the by-product of adrenalin. Aloud he said, 'That's it, that's the deal, Aylen's not going to survive. If he survives he implicates Nailor and Nailor's case is near hopeless. Fuck. Fuck,' said Eddie Cole. 'There's going to be an execution.'

Staring at the back of the driver's neck he suddenly stiffened again.

Aloud he said, 'It's not just Aylen, it's Bedser too, and any others. Jesus.'

Sweat formed on the bald head of Superintendent Eddie Cole. He felt cold, old, he murmured, 'Jesus'. What could he do? Tell George Watson? One might as well go to Whipsnade and tell a penguin. Go to the Commissioner? Stop the operation? *It was the Commissioner who had ordered this. The Special Branch were the Commissioner's men.* 'Dear God,' thought Eddie Cole, 'I am *not* going to witness murder done.' Then, suddenly again, he thought, 'Nailor. He's done it. Superman. He is controlling it all. Murder by proxy, kidnapping by proxy. Total control.'

Eddie Cole closed his eyes and turned his head towards the roof of the cab. Five minutes and he would be there. Stall the operation. Stop it in its tracks. Get hold of Jack Wagner. Tell him that he knew what was happening. Even if he couldn't prove it, it would certainly stop it. Again Eddie Cole reached for his mobile phone. Dead. Fuck, fuck, fuck, fuck. Five minutes. Enough time to call it off. Do it properly. Mount the operation with his own people. Easy.

Relieved, easier, he watched the Embankment pass before the window of the taxi. Two minutes later he was stationary outside the steps of Scotland Yard. Thrusting a card into the taxi driver's hand he said, 'Charge it.'

'Can't, guv, it's not my firm. Don't do it.'

'Fuck, fuck, fuck,' said Eddie Cole, delving into his pocket for money.

'Right on,' said the taxi driver.

'Keep it,' said Eddie Cole, before turning and jumping the steps. Past the desk, Eddie Cole flashed his warrant card to the station sergeant who, without a word, operated the automatic lock that gave access to the interior of London's biggest police station. Up the stairs, two at a time. Breathless on the second floor, Eddie Cole appeared in the operations room at 2.55 precisely. Empty. Empty, that is, except for Sergeant Brendan O'Hara gazing unhappily at an enlarged photograph of a neat, squat, suburban house pinned on the notice board beside two rough room plans representing its interior.

'Brendan,' said Eddie Cole, 'where the fuck is everybody?'

'Gone, guv. They brought the briefing forward to 1.30. I couldn't get you on your mobile. Not working. Your wife said you were here. They're going in at four o'clock. Battering rams, Special Branch are all armed. Our boys are going for the ride.'

'Jesus,' said Eddie Cole. 'Brendan, where the fuck is that?' He pointed to the notice board.

'It's in St Albans. Apparently that's where they're holding her.

There's four of them: Bedser, Aylen and a pair of heavyweights from Cardiff, brothers called Jones. I've never heard of them.'

'Brendan, where's your car?'

'Haven't got it, guv. Came by cab.'

'Brendan, we have got to get a bloody car.'

Eddie Cole had the internal telephone in his hand. A thick finger punched out the internal traffic number. Busy. 'Fuck, fuck, fuck.' He dialled again. And again. And again. 'Fuck, fuck, fuck.' Finally he said, 'Let's go, for fuck's sake.'

Eddie Cole running through Scotland Yard. Brendan O'Hara, easily keeping pace, says, 'What's the matter, guv, we'll get there.'

Eddie Cole stopping, staring at Sergeant Brendan O'Hara. 'Brendan, they're going to kill them.'

'Who, the S.B. . . .?'

'*The S.B. are going to kill them. All of them. Maybe even the girl.*'

Brendan O'Hara, looking carefully at his boss. Sniffing for alcohol. 'Why, guv, why?'

'It's Nailor, they've done a deal. It's Superman. Don't you see? It all *fits*. Nailor, he's *controlling* this. Don't you see?'

'Guv,' says Sergeant Brendan O'Hara, 'I think you ought to calm down.'

'I am perfectly fucking calm,' says Eddie Cole through what remain of his teeth. 'This is not a joke, Brendan. Jack Wagner practically told me. He nearly told me and I missed it. Aylen's not coming out of this alive, nor is Bedser. Nor is anybody else there who can identify Nailor. I have *got* to stop it.'

Brendan O'Hara stares unhappily at his superior, who is also, he suddenly realises, his friend. 'Guv, you must go to Watson.'

'Watson? I might as well talk to a lampshade. There is no point in talking to fucking Watson. *We* have got to stop it.'

Eddie Cole entering the traffic room. 3.05. The uniformed sergeant smiles politely. 'I need a fucking car, now.'

'Haven't got any, guv. All out.'

Eddie Cole's face within two inches of the sergeant's nose, no longer smiling.

'Listen my friend, there is going to be a murder. Four probably. Get me a fucking car. *Now.*'

The sergeant does not retreat. 'There's a Metro. Got a flat. In the yard. The keys on the desk.'

Eddie Cole and Brendan O'Hara jacking up a white Metro. Eddie Cole and Brendan O'Hara heaving at wheel braces, locating flanges, cursing. Eddie Cole says, 'Fuck, fuck, fuck, fuck, fuck.'

Brendan O'Hara says, 'Guv, could you keep quiet for a minute.'

Eddie Cole says, 'I'm not speaking.'

3.20. Eddie Cole is watching the speedometer as Brendan O'Hara, trained police driver, accelerates to eighty miles an hour on the Finchley Road.

'Can't this fucking thing go any fucking faster, Brendan?'

'Guv, I can feel the floorboards on both sides of my foot.'

'Jesus,' says Eddie Cole.

3.40. Eighty miles an hour through Mill Hill, past Apex Corner. 3.45, crossing the M25. Signpost. St Albans – 8.

'We're going to make it,' says Eddie Cole, who is reading the Operations Map torn from the blackboard before departure. 'Don't go into St Albans. Turn left here, *here*, fuck, fuck, fuck, fuck. You missed the fucking thing.'

'At this speed I need more time,' says Sergeant Brendan O'Hara, 'we would have been on our fucking roof.'

3.48, at the next roundabout. 3.50, back at the turning. 3.55, 'left here,' says Eddie Cole, 'now right, then left again.'

3.58, road block. Eddie Cole running forward, Brendan O'Hara beside him.

'It's all right, it's all right, it's me, boys. Where's the fucking house?'

'Down there, guv. About a hundred yards on the right. Number 35. Guv, where have you been?'

Eddie Cole beginning to run down the street. Seeing silent figures, black assault suits, monstrously pregnant with protective vests, moving together across the street, crouched, intent. Eddie Cole hears the battering ram. One single massive shunt. Seconds later the firing starts. Eddie Cole, turning past the privet hedge, meets his first obstruction. 'Can't go in, guv, armed squad only.'

'Fuck you,' says Eddie Cole, as his shoulder hits the flak jacket and the man goes down.

Firing, still firing. Eddie Cole through the door falls on a body immediately inside the hall. The body is wearing assault clothing. The flak jacket is no good. The blood is gushing from the right eye. Past the first room. Two more bodies on the floor, one naked, the other in jeans and a leather jacket. More firing. Eddie Cole up the stairs. At the head of the stairs 'Bonkers' Bedser faces him. In his right hand a gun. There is then a shot. Bedser's eyes stare towards the ceiling. Slowly he falls towards Eddie Cole. Passing him, crashing to the small landing, remains wedged against the balustrade. Eddie Cole turning left across the landing past a figure in assault clothing and into the rear bedroom. Eddie Cole turns to the man who saved his life, 'Where are they?'

'Try the cellar, guv.'

Eddie Cole, breathless, down the stairs. In the hall a narrow door reveals an inner light. Down the steps into a cellar, a playroom perhaps. A bed. On it a girl tied. Is she naked? Later, much later, Eddie Cole would say in all truth he could not remember. At the end of the bed Jack Wagner stands above a man lying on the floor. From this figure one hand, gloved but empty, thrust forward in submission. Eddie Cole hears the girl cry, 'No, no.' Eddie Cole throwing himself forward. Jack Wagner, caught off balance. Arms suddenly spread wide. The single crack of a pistol shot and Melanie Golding's voice becomes silent. Blood flowing from the side of her head as she falls back from the side of the bed to the floor. Her bound hand remains aloft in a grotesque parody of liberation.

Jack Wagner's head smashes against the open drawer of a chest and his gun falls to the floor. Eddie Cole, seizing the weapon, turns to see Brendan O'Hara push past a blue figure in the doorway. Both men stare at each other before Sergeant O'Hara says, 'Christ, guv, what the fuck have you done?'

# Chapter 16

The offices of Special Branch occupy one floor of New Scotland Yard. There are twenty-six rooms, of which numbers 9, 11 and 13 are equipped for conferences. In the smallest of these, three days after the dawn raid on St Albans, a meeting took place between Chief Superintendent Jack Wagner of the Special Branch and Superintendent Eddie Cole. Both had a deputy. Next to Eddie Cole sat Brendan O'Hara and in an identical position beside Jack Wagner sat Stuart Patterson whose perfectly aimed bullet had terminated the violent life of Harry 'Bonkers' Bedser.

By common consent no notes were taken.

'Is this being recorded?' asked Eddie Cole.

Jack Wagner shrugged. 'Does it matter?'

'Not much. I don't want you to feel shy, that's all.'

'I'll try not to. Well, Eddie, you certainly fucked that up.'

'Oh I see,' said Eddie Cole, '*I fucked it up*. Here was me thinking it was your operation. Here was me thinking that the Special Branch had taken control. Here was me thinking that you moved the briefing forward so that I *wouldn't be there*. I must be barking mad. Now at least we know what happens when you employ the Special Branch. Four men dead including one of ours and a kidnapped judge's daughter in a coma, with a bullet in her brain, unlikely to survive the week. Wonderful police work. You should have been on the Somme.'

Jack Wagner's eyes narrowed into the smallest of slits. 'The girl has a bullet in her brain because you knocked me over. If you had not come in like a roaring bull the girl would be alive and well.'

'And Thomas Aylen would be dead.'

'So what?'

'You know, Jack, I will put up with a lot of things in routine policing. A bit of graft, a bit of buncing, energetic questioning, even the odd creative confession but I will not have deliberate execution on my patch. Call me soft-hearted. Call me old-fashioned. But I remember my time at the Hendon Police School. Lesson one, day one, do not execute your suspects in the interests of the State.'

'I would be very careful, Eddie, if I were you.'

'Careful! My dear Chief Superintendent Wagner, not a word will pass my lips. This was a *brilliant operation*. Masterminded by one of the greatest coppers of his generation. But I want you to know what I know, Jack, about this whole nasty business. Do you know why? Because *I* want to be safe, Jack, and I want to see Roddy fucking Nailor back in Parkhurst where he belongs.'

Chief Superintendent Jack Wagner smiled a long smile and then said, 'I wanted to tell you before we did it. We are going to let him go.'

Eddie Cole's voice became as soft as silk. 'You are going to let him go?'

'There is no evidence against him Eddie, not now. You see, Thomas Aylen has made a confession.'

'Where?'

'Here. We interviewed him last night. He's coughed the whole lot. You want to see it? You want to see a copy? Here it is.' With splayed fingers Jack Wagner's hand descended on a document before him, reversed it and with the same movement propelled it across the desk.

'That's it. It's all there, the whole thing. You want to read? Go ahead.'

Eddie Cole did not move. 'You can't have taken a confession. The boy's ill. You know he's ill.'

'Oh really? Now how do I know that? He seems perfectly all right to me. Doesn't look too nice but even you wouldn't be improved if half your face was blown away, now would you? But he's a clever boy. Went to Cambridge. Read philosophy. Did you know that, Superintendent? Nice coincidence, isn't it? So we took a chance. Asked him if he really wanted a solicitor and do you know? He said he didn't and so out it all came. We had to prompt him now and again but it's all there. All recorded. The whole beastly thing.'

Eddie Cole, motionless, still did not touch the papers before him. 'You will never get this in evidence in a trial. You knew he was ill. He's got Monkey's Syndrome or whatever it's called. He's totally suggestible. He'll do whatever you tell him. Say whatever you tell him. *Sign* whatever you tell him. Even Alan Barlow will tell you. He's got half a fucking brain. You can't take confessions from suspects with half a brain with no solicitor. The trial judge will chuck it straight back in your lap.'

Jack Wagner, relaxed, happy, continued, 'Oh yes, Alan Barlow, your friend the great police psychiatrist. Well, we spoke to him. Yes, we did, surprise you does it? Well, we did, got him on the phone last night. Do you know, I think he may have had a few. I told him we had got the girl. I told him she was in a coma. I told him that the seed of Aylen's loins were deep inside her cervix. Don't get up Eddie. You didn't know that either? Well it's true. The DNA isn't through but the early tests, the old tests, you remember them, indicate that it can only be Aylen. So he had her, my friend, your war hero with half a brain has apparently got nothing wrong with his cock. That's what I told Alan Barlow. And I said to him, "Alan," I said, "we *need* to interview this guy. We need to find out if there is anything else wrong with the girl. We need to do this quickly, Alan old boy, and he doesn't want a solicitor." And do you know what he said? He said, "Say you have spoken to me and I've told you it is all right." You surprised Eddie? You know your precious shrink better than anyone else. You were on the Lurcher trial, weren't you? Good old Ivan Lurcher. Took his instructions from a glass dog on the mantelpiece. Set light to his women. Barking, barking mad. Now you took a confession from him, didn't you, Eddie. Do you remember what Alan Barlow said about him when they suggested he was half way to Ongar? "Bollocks", that's what he said, "bollocks". Well this is just the same. I'm covered, Eddie. Completely covered. Aylen's coughed. Do you want to read it now?'

Still Eddie Cole did not move. 'You will never get this past a judge. Whatever Alan Barlow says, this guy is not Ivan Lurcher. He is not an evil bastard, he is sick. His brain has gone. He is one of the fucking herd. He's just like us. He does what he's fucking well told. And you told him what to say, didn't you?'

'I think you had better read, Eddie, it's all in the transcript. Do you want me to give you a precis? Save you reading it all? You do, right, well I'll tell you. First he tells us how brilliant he was, then he tells us about Ireland. How he has felt bitter ever since. Bitter about the Establishment. Bitter that nobody recognises this. So he went to Bournemouth Poly. He was going to become a clerk. This Superman, this genius, this Sports Personality of the Year. He was going to become a disfigured, grotesque clerk. And at Bournemouth Poly he met "Bonkers" Bedser, the psycho-pathic pederast. Nice pair, mad and bitter and bent. And so they hatched a plan. They were going to kidnap the daughter of a High Court judge. Why? For two reasons. For money and because they wanted to *show that they could*. That they had power. He wasn't a disabled, grotesque fucking clerk. And, what's more, he had the money. He had the money. He had the bonuses and the accelerated pension et cetera et cetera that the grateful Services gives you when you have been blown apart. So when they got out they recruited two friends of Bonkers and they kidnapped the girl and they took her to St Albans. And do you know who rented the house in St Albans? Do you know whose name the house is in? Don't even bother to look. Thomas Aylen. All fits together, Eddie. All fits together. And when they got her into the house he had her. I shouldn't bother to read it if I were you Eddie. Not pretty reading even for an old hard bastard like you. Bonkers got the guns and so they settled down to wait. And then we arrived and everything would have been absolutely fine if *you* hadn't arrived, Superintendent, and fucked it all up.'

Eddie Cole, still motionless, said, 'What about Nailor? What does he say about Nailor?'

'Nailor! Roddy Nailor? I think he mentions him once. He says that Bonkers Bedser said the girl to kidnap was the daughter of Judge Golding. He was the bloke who banged up good old Roddy Nailor and besides that he was a fucking Jew. Bonkers Bedser does not like Jews. He's just a teensy weensy bit anti-Semitic. Maybe that saved the girl from his attentions as well. Who knows? That's what Aylen says about Roddy Nailor. That and nothing else. Now do you see why we are going to let him go?'

Eddie Cole rose from his seat, picked up the statement, folded it neatly and placed it in his inside pocket. 'Very interesting,' he said, 'very interesting indeed. Now let me tell you what happened. You have fitted this boy up. He has Menkies' Syndrome which means that he will do anything you want and anything that you say. You know that and Alan Barlow knows that. Whatever Alan may say to you on the phone when he is pissed, he will not say anything like it in court. You know full well you will never get that statement in evidence. And what is more, Chief Superintendent Wagner, you don't want or need to get that statement before a court. You know this poor bastard can't give evidence because if he does he will say what anyone tells him to say and that means he is a sitting duck in cross-examination, even to the pillocks who are employed by the Crown Prosecution Service. He is caught in the girl's room. You *say* he had a gun (and *no one* can say otherwise) and his sperm is found inside her. You don't need anything else. This boy is a sitting duck. Why you need this statement is so that you can let Roddy Nailor go. Once you have let him go Aylen is finished. They probably won't even let him plead not guilty. "Unfit to plead", they will say, and off he will go to Broadmoor or worse for the rest of his life. Well done Superintendent Wagner. Well done the Special Branch. Well done, if I am being recorded, to the security forces. This nasty, regrettable, sordid, disgusting, fatal business is now wrapped up. That's it, isn't it, Jack?'

Jack Wagner shook his head and said 'Dream on Eddie, dream on. Nice try.'

Eddie Cole leaning forward slowly on the desk. 'Haven't you forgotten about the newspaper?'

Jack Wagner made a gesture of annoyed impatience. 'Oh really Eddie, really. The *newspaper*. Don't you understand you dim fucker, I am doing you an enormous favour. You talk about fitting up? You'd fit up Mother Teresa if you had a fucking chance. Oh I am not suggesting,' said Jack Wagner with resignation, 'that you'd do it for money Eddie. You do it because they are guilty. Or worse still, because you believe that they are guilty. Worse still, because you think you are God. What is truth, Eddie? You tell me. Truth is what you make it, isn't it? That newspaper evidence will be ripped apart in court. It is about as seaworthy as a drunken Irish priest. It's got plant written all over it. The number, the late discovery, the late fingerprinting. And you have done it *before*. It will all come out. Ten years ago Roddy Nailor was banged up because his prints were found on a hammer. They said you had planted it then. Eddie, you will end up in the dock, charged with perjury, perverting the course of justice and just about everything else they can get on a charge sheet. They may even review Roddy Nailor's conviction. He'll get a pardon and a million in the bank. Fuck the newspaper Eddie, forget it. Now let's draw stumps. Let's go and have a beer like we used to a long, long time ago.'

Eddie Cole leaned further forward. 'Jack,' even quieter now, 'Jack you know full well that you can't let him go unless I agree. If I let the press know about this evidence and the fact that you have let Roddy Nailor go, then the shit will hit the blades as never before. And, Jack, I might even start asking questions in public about the Special Branch. Why are you here Jack? This is police work. You remember all those rumours about Roddy Nailor burglarising the Foreign Secretary? Do you, Jack? There, you didn't know I knew? But I do and I can prove it. Don't ask me how, Jack, because you might just say that I fitted you up. But if Roddy Nailor walks away from this your life as a centurion of the people may be very fucking short.'

Much later Brendan O'Hara was to say, 'I thought no one would ever speak again, until Jack Wagner said, "You are a fool, Eddie Cole, you are a fool and you have always been one. Don't do this."'

Eddie Cole smiled his ugly smile, nodded to Brendan O'Hara and both men left the room.

Jack Wagner turned to his junior officer. 'This is going to be a major, unprecedented, ghastly fucking unstoppable disaster. Who for? That's what I would like to know.'

Beyond the door Eddie Cole turned to Brendan O'Hara. 'Brendan, I want that girl guarded twenty-four hours a day by one of ours, no, two of ours. You as much as possible. While she is in a coma she is safe. If she knows anything, anything about Nailor, then she is in danger. If she wakes up I want you to see her. Do you understand? Only you. Everything she says I want it recorded. I want it recorded under a "threat of death" caution. Do you understand, Brendan?'

Brendan O'Hara looked closely at his chief. 'Guv, this is getting very nasty. Shouldn't you go to someone at the top, the Director, the Commissioner, the Home Secretary?'

'Now Brendan,' said Eddie Cole kindly, 'for a Jesuit Mick you do have the most wonderful lovely touching faith in the integrity of the British fucking constitution.'

# Chapter 17

By agreement with the Director of Public Prosecutions, the Home Secretary and the Commissioner of Metropolitan Police, a press release was faxed to the editors of all the national papers simultaneously at 9 a.m. on the morning of 2 November 1988, by which time the surrounding roads in St Albans had been cordoned off. The carnage at number 35 had been photographed from a thousand angles, plotted, dissected, measured and sketched. Melanie Golding had been taken by ambulance to a sanatorium at Watford and subsequently to the Ardingley Military Hospital. The bodies had been removed. The press, of course, had been at the cordon within twenty minutes of the shooting. By six o'clock television cameras and film crews were in place and the decanted, sleep-eyed inhabitants of St Albans were in violent demand to provide any fact or speculation to compensate for the firm and obdurate silence maintained by the assembled police. Some residents became exasperated.

'What exactly did you hear?' demanded an enthusiastic BBC reporter of an elderly man in a tartan dressing gown.

'An enormous crash, about twenty shots, the sound of broken glass and a great deal of shouting and screaming.'

'Had you heard anything like that before?'

'Of course, in St Albans; this is a well-known war zone.'

When it was finally issued the official press release was terse and factual.

On 22 October 1988 Melanie Golding, the daughter of a High Court judge, was abducted from her home in Hackney. Following an intensive police investigation it was discovered that she was held against her will in an address in St Albans, Hertfordshire. At 4 a.m. on 2 November police officers from the Serious Crime Squad and the Special Branch, under the Command of Chief Superintendent Jack Wagner, entered the premises in order to effect Miss Golding's release. They encountered armed resistance and gun fire was exchanged. One police officer, Detective

Sergeant Ian Davidson, was tragically killed as were three men inside the building, all found to be armed. During the gun fire Melanie Golding was herself injured and is presently in hospital in a critical condition. Name and location of the hospital is withheld. One man found within the premises is assisting the police with their enquiries. He is identified as Thomas Aylen. Identity otherwise withheld. Terrorism of any kind is not, repeat not, suspected.

In his office at the top of the *Evening News* building, the chief editor, Charlie McGrath, read and re-read the fax. Standing before him was Alex Bentley, his chief crime reporter and one of Fleet Street's finest, who, Charlie McGrath noticed with some relief, was only slightly drunk.

'Jesus,' said Charlie McGrath, 'Jesus wept, what a cock-up. This is brilliant. Who's this Thomas Aylen? Aylen? Aylen? I know the name? Why do I know it?'

Before him Alex Bentley shrugged expansively, releasing a distinct and unpleasant odour from beneath his apparently regimental blazer.

Charlie McGrath picked up the phone. 'Cutting room please. Well go on, try. Yes, it is urgent. Sit down, Alex, for God's sake. Yes? Right? Thomas Aylen, what do we have on Thomas Aylen? Yes, A, Y, L, E, N. No, do it now please. This is urgent.' Charlie McGrath drummed his fingers on the front of the *Daily Mail* and stared unhappily at his crime reporter. 'God you look bloody awful. Why don't you join a gym or something? Have a heart attack.'

'Olympic glory wouldn't suit me,' said Alex Bentley happily. 'Couldn't stand the envy of my friends.'

Charlie McGrath was suddenly attentive. 'What? Yes, yes! That's it. Right, get every cutting you've got up here at once.' Replacing the phone he spoke carefully to his chief reporter of crime. 'Now listen to me Alex. This is going to be the biggest story that you have ever covered. This guy, the kidnapper, is a former Marine Commando and a war hero from Northern Ireland. I remember it all now. He was blown up with a booby-trap. He's lost half his face and a lot of other bits. He is a grotesque. This is wonderful. The judge's daughter, so they say, is an absolute cracker. This is wonderful. Beauty and the Beast. Now I want this to be our story. Do you understand? Our story. We will beat everyone tonight and I want to stay ahead of this. See *everyone*. Her friends, her family, his friends, his family, his old school teachers, her old school teachers. Everyone. Jesus, this is wonderful.'

# Part II

---

## TRIAL

# Chapter 1

Mary Shelley arrived at the Clerks' room at 35 King's Bench Walk, precisely thirty-five minutes late and carrying an enormous box within which were twelve ring binders full of closely-typed paper. The overall weight, perhaps fifty pounds, she bore without difficulty towards the desk of the senior clerk, on to which she allowed it to fall with satisfied aplomb.

'The Aylen/Naylor brief,' she announced impressively. 'Sorry I'm a bit late. Is she ready?'

'Miss Wilson is always ready for you, Miss Shelley. Would you like a cup of coffee?'

'No thank you Stephen, the client's father is coming at eleven o'clock and there are things we must discuss.'

'I will take you straight in. Nicholas will bring the papers.'

'Don't worry,' said Mary Shelley. 'I'll take them in. We don't want the little chap to do himself an injury.

Mary Shelley scooped up her box and majestically followed the senior clerk from the room under the admiring glances of the remaining staff. Mary Shelley was an Amazon. Six foot three in her socks, she rose to a majestic six foot six on the high heels she insisted on wearing on every occasion save when stamping the Welsh hillsides, which she did twice a month at the head of her large and complaining family. Despite her great height and bulk she was perfectly formed and a prodigious athlete. She was a renowned sybarite, an International Amnesty observer, a dedicated feminist and, by all accounts, an enthusiastic, expert and alarmingly noisy lover. Otherwise she was untidy, headstrong, and drank too much. She was a governor of several schools and a trustee of several charities dedicated to the welfare of children and animals. A tireless worker for the Labour Party, she was allowed to canvass only in strong Tory areas where she stalked majestically, spreading fear and alarm before her. She was much loved by her many friends, including the illustrious and diminutive QC Jane Wilson, with whom she had been at school and shared a dormitory and a short lesbian experience, and whom she had now briefed to appear for Thomas Aylen in what had been described and broadcast as the Trial of the Century. She followed Jane Wilson's senior clerk up the Chambers staircase towards the conference room bearing half a hundredweight of papers as most women would carry a handbag.

'We must get pissed again together sometime soon, Stephen. You can go on telling me about Essex. Lovely place, full of clients.'

'It would be a great pleasure, Miss Shelley,' said Stephen, meaning it, and pausing to open the panelled door. 'In here, Miss.'

Beyond the conference desk Jane Wilson rose to greet her old friend. 'Hello Frankenstein. You know Gilbert Smith.'

'Yes I do. You can call me Frankenstein.'

Gilbert Smith, small, square, earnest and about to embark on the biggest challenge of his short legal career, smiled nervously and took hold of the enormous hand which was thrust towards him.

'I brought two set of papers here, one for each for you. There is not much in it which you haven't already read in my summary and in the newspapers.' She sat heavily on a mock Chesterfield sofa and looked straight at her Queen's Counsel. 'We've got problems, haven't we?'

'Just a few. About a thousand, to be precise. How is the girl? Still in a coma?'

'Yes. The bullet is lodged next to the brain. They are waiting for the swelling to go down before they operate. That may never happen.'

'What about our man? Have you seen him?'

'Several times. Last time, yesterday. Extraordinary. You prepare yourself but it is still a terrible shock. Two centuries ago they would have forced him to put a bag over his head.'

'Can you take instructions? There is no statement in the papers.'

'Oh yes, you can take instructions but they are not *his* instructions. They're *your* instructions. He will say anything you want him to say. He is quite slow, thinks very hard, obviously does his best. I will give you an example. I recorded the first part of our conversation.' Mary Shelley opened her briefcase and extracted a typewritten document upon which were written lines of dialogue. 'This is it.'

'Question (me): "Did you kidnap Melanie Golding?"

'Aylen: "No, no, no, did not kidnap her."

'Me: "What did you do with her?"

'Aylen: "Tried to help her. No good. Not strong enough. Only one hand." (He has only got one hand, you see, the other one was blown off in the explosion.)

'Me: "Did you do her any harm?"

'Aylen: "No, no, no harm at all. Love her." (Quite extraordinary, that

98

reply. No idea what it means. His vocabulary is limited by the speech defect and sometimes bizarre.)

'Me: "How did you get involved? Did anyone suggest this to you?"

'Aylen: "Nailor, Roddy Nailor. Bedser. Two others. Don't know their names."

'Me: "Did you try to stop the police when they came in the house?"

'Aylen: "No, no. Tried to help. Was knocked to the ground. Going to be shot."' Mary Shelley looked up from her documents. 'He has difficulty speaking but the meaning is quite clear and intelligible. Sometimes he uses strange words like "love", slightly childish.'

Jane Wilson was frowning on her side of the desk. 'That sounds all right. The instructions are clear enough.'

Mary Shelley raised her wide eyebrows. 'So far, so good but now listen to this.

'Me: "But that's not right, Thomas, is it? Can't be right. It's not what you told the police."

'Aylen: silence.

'Me: "What you told the police was that you did this on your own with Bedser. That it was your idea with him. Because you felt bitter about your treatment after Ireland. That's right, isn't it?"

'Aylen: silence.

'Me: "That's right, isn't it."

'Aylen: inaudible.

'Me: "I'm sorry Thomas, I didn't hear that."

'Aylen: "Yes."

'Me: "Yes what?"

'Aylen: "My idea with Bedser."

'Me: "Your idea with Bedser to carry out the kidnap. That's right, isn't it?"

'Aylen: "Yes, that's right."

'Me: "And Nailor had nothing to do with it, did he?"

'Aylen: silence.

'Me: "Did he?"

'Aylen: "No, no."' Mary Shelley pushed the document on one side. 'It goes on like that. After that I took him back the other way. Told him he hadn't done it. Told him he was right that he had tried to protect her. Then he agreed with that. I'm no psychiatrist, but I think I can see what is happening. He has a natural inclination to tell the truth. His memory is virtually intact and thus, over a period of time, he reverts to his true personality and his perception of events is accurate although his speech is impaired. Immediately his recollection is questioned he begins to doubt. Only very little pressure causes him to abandon the account that he has given. Very little more and he will agree with precisely any version of events which is placed before him. In other words he is totally malleable. He has no judgement, cannot resist argument and will accept any state of affairs, any hypothesis, notwithstanding the implications and consequences, not least to himself.'

'The archetypal sheep, member of the herd,' said Jane Wilson.

'Precisely, in the circumstances of this case, the supreme irony.'

'Let us forget the interesting metaphors. Have we received anything from our psychiatrist?'

'I have a preliminary report. It is John Heathcliffe at the Maudsley. I have spoken to him on the phone and he is confident that his view will not change. Aylen has Menkies' Syndrome. It arises from severe damage, traumatic or clinical, to the right frontal lobe of the brain. It removes the critical faculty. It is the part of the brain which apparently governs argument, rationality, the capacity to *disagree*. The subject of Menkies' Syndrome becomes ultimately suggestible. It is a recognised syndrome. Rare but clinically undoubted. Anyway there is no doubt he's got it. In those circumstances the first question we need to ask, I need to ask *you*, is whether we can legitimately accept instructions?'

'You say that his initial accounts are consistent?'

'Precisely. I have seen him three times. On each occasion he begins with a consistent though incoherent account as you have heard. He denies being part of the kidnapping and maintains, to the contrary, that he attempted to stop it. I have deliberately not attempted to obtain great detail. At this stage I am interested only that we have enough to enter a plea. Guilty or not guilty.'

Jane Wilson considered her friend carefully. 'I think we have. We know he has this condition and we know that his initial account is consistent, and consistent with innocence. In those circumstances I think we can accept instructions. The next, and the most difficult issue, is whether he is fit to plead. Gilbert has done some work on this. What's the answer, Gilbert?'

'Normally the legal tests are quite simple, but in this case it becomes very complex. Essentially there are three questions: can the defendant comprehend the nature of the proceedings? Is he capable of participation in the trial and providing instructions and, lastly, does he, if necessary, understand the meaning of the oath? As I perceive it, our man understands that he is charged with serious criminal offences, indeed as serious as it is possible to get. His initial instructions are, as Mary says,

consistent. He is capable of entering a Not Guilty plea. Can he understand the trial? The answer to that appears to be "probably". The
interesting question arises in connection with his own evidence. This is
a case in which he *must* give evidence. Even if we succeed in excluding
the confession (which we both think we probably will), the evidence
against him in the absence of an explanation is overwhelming. He is
caught at the scene, in the cellar. According to the lead copper he is in
possession of a gun and there is every indication that his sperm is found
in the victim. He wrote the ransom letter. Of the remaining potential
witnesses, three are dead and one is in a coma. Roddy Nailor is hardly
likely to be of great assistance. The only witness we have is Aylen
himself. He may give a coherent account at first but in cross-examination
he is a sitting duck. By the time John Wilkin has finished cross-
examining on behalf of Nailor, he will have admitted any crime that's
put to him. In other words he cannot give evidence. If he cannot give
evidence then he will be convicted.'

With some impatience Jane Wilson said, 'What is your view?'

'In my view we have no choice but to run Unfit to Plead. It is a matter
for the jury to decide in a separate trial before the main action. The way
we run it is to maintain that he cannot properly comprehend the oath.
Where the critical, rational and logical processes have been destroyed,
how can a man understand truth? He may swear to tell the truth but what
is the point of that if he cannot *do* so?'

'Interesting,' said Mary Shelley. 'Surely it will be said that it is
possible to comprehend the nature of the oath even if one is incapable of
keeping it? What is Truth?'

'Precisely. That is the problem.'

'What about the prosecution?' Mary Shelley turned to her leading
counsel.

'I have spoken very briefly to Edward Boyd, pompous ass that he is. I
get the distinct impression that they would not oppose the issue of
fitness. Nailor's team will, of course, be overjoyed. With us out of the
trial the only real evidence against him is this interesting newspaper
with his dabs on it. As a piece of evidence it is about as strong as the paper
itself. It absolutely reeks. When that's gone Nailor walks and that's it,
end of the Trial of the Century.'

'There is just one thing,' said Mary Shelley. 'If we succeed and the
jury find him Unfit to Plead, what happens to him?'

'He goes to Broadmoor, for life.'

'For *life?*'

'Effectively, yes. There is no way out. If he did ever become fit to plead then there would be a further trial but this condition is, apparently, incurable.'

The telephone on the desk before Jane Wilson rang once. 'Yes,' she said, 'right.' Placing her hand over the receiver she said, 'It's his father, Colonel Aylen. I think we have agreed, haven't we? Unfit to Plead? Can we have him up now?'

# Chapter 2

At precisely the time at which the fate of Thomas Aylen was discussed at 35 King's Bench Walk, the team representing Roddy Nailor plotted their strategies in the Chambers of John Wilkin overlooking the lawns and gardens of Gray's Inn. Immediately before this consultation John Wilkin had undertaken an energetic discussion with his clerk, Samuel.

'Legal Aid?'

'Yes, sir.'

'But Samuel, this is Dowsons, Dowsons, Samuel, they wouldn't notice a Legal Aid brief if it came in with the fleet.'

'I'm sorry sir, that's what it is.'

'Samuel, did you know this when you accepted the bloody thing?'

'No, sir. I rather assumed, sir, like you, as it was Dowsons, that it was real money.'

'Samuel, I've got nine children. Nine. My school fees cost a hundred thousand a year. I've got three wives, three; one up and running, two cashiered, none of them showing the slightest sign of doing an honest day's work. I have a house in Tuscany. I entertain the Prime Minister. My mortgage is almost as big as my school fees. Legal Aid? Samuel, I might as well go and drown myself in a barrel of sack.'

Samuel observed the figure of his Head of Chambers and principal source of income and reflected quietly on the size of barrel which would be necessary for such an immersion. 'That would be a bit rash, sir.'

'Samuel, I have *dependants*. It's not me, Samuel. I can live on anything, roots, a handful of rusks. Have you any idea of how much they pay you on Legal Aid?'

'Shouldn't be too bad, sir. It's the Trial of the Century after all.'

'Samuel, the Legal Aid Office couldn't care less if this was the trial of St Thomas à Becket. I am going to have to return it.'

'I think that would be very unwise, sir. It is Dowsons. They did specially want you, sir.'

'Specially wanted me, did they?'

'Yes, sir. They came to you first. They said it was a sensitive case.'

'Why did he go to Dowsons? This gangster. Why Dowsons?'

'I really don't know, sir.'

John Wilkin stared unhappily at the leather top of his desk and mentally calculated the value of the silver ink stand. 'How long is this case going to last, Samuel?'

'Depends entirely on the other bloke, I gather, sir. If he fights the case it is good for a month or so. If he doesn't it should be pretty quick. I gather there is not much evidence against our chap.'

'There is no bloody evidence at all. Just a newspaper with some fingerprints on it. A bloody obvious plant by Buster Cole. Oh well, I suppose it could be worse. When is this chap James Cameron coming to see me?'

'He's here now sir. Been here for ten minutes or so.'

'All right, let's have him in. Get Preston as well, will you.'

Samuel left the room and five minutes later Preston Lodge, John Wilkin's junior, arrived at his leader's room. At the age of twenty-eight Preston Lodge was regarded as one of the most successful and ruthless juniors at the Bar. He had a mind like a knife and a tongue (as a judge once memorably observed) like a Russian knout. His ability to distil and analyse the most complex of cases was legendary.

'I gather this is Legal Aid?' he said as he entered the room.

'Sod off Preston. Do your duty like everybody else. Oh, hello, James.'

In the doorway behind Preston Lodge, James Cameron of Dowsons appeared, together with Samuel Jacob.

'Thank you Samuel, get someone to bring us some tea, will you? Nice to see you, James. You know Preston, don't you. He is just complaining about this case being on Legal Aid. I don't mind of course. Delighted to do my bit for the underprivileged. Malnourished gangster and all that. Why are you doing it anyway?'

James Cameron settled his legs beneath the table, removed his gold-rimmed glasses and began to polish them with a handkerchief from his upper jacket pocket. 'Doing a favour for some important clients. I think you ought to know Nailor's got some pull in high places. Don't know what it is. Haven't asked. Don't want to. Best if you didn't ask me. 'Fraid we are all stuck with the Legal Aid. Whoever is running this show can't be seen to be paying for it. Dare say we will get our reward in Heaven, wherever that is on the Southern Region. Anyway, we have just got to do our best to get this dangerous maniac released. Doesn't look as though it will be too difficult.'

'I agree,' said John Wilkins. 'What do you think, Preston?'

Preston Lodge's face narrowed with concentration. 'I'm not sure that

I do. On the face of it the only real evidence linking Nailor to the girl is the newspaper found in her flat together, of course, with the lie that he told about it. Our guy says it is a plant and there is a lot to suggest that he's right. The only evidence of finding it is Buster Cole. The exhibit number has got an 'A' suffix which means it was inserted, or may have been inserted, after the event, and it's not fingerprinted until the actual day when Nailor delivers himself voluntarily to the police station after Cole had been informed. If it was just that we would be walking on air. It doesn't need the best cross-examiner at the English Bar to rip that apart. Or the worst for that matter. The problem, as I see it, is the ransom note and the undoubted connection between Nailor and Aylen at the jolly old Bournemouth Poly. The note contains this half-baked, philosophical gibberish which is exactly what Nailor was studying.'

James Cameron interrupted. 'Aylen did philosophy too.'

'Yes, I know that, but Aylen did philosophy at Cambridge and got a Double First. The stuff in this note is sub-11 plus, whatever that is.'

John Wilkin interrupted with more vigour. 'Oh come on, Preston, really. The jury will never understand that. Hegel, Kierkegaard, Nietzsche, it's all gibberish to them. What is the Crown going to do? Give them a course on nineteenth-century philosophy? This is garbage and this isn't? And besides that, this guy Aylen has got Monkey Nuts Syndrome or something. He's sick. Who knows what Monkey Nuts Syndrome does to advanced Hegelian metaphor? Of course he could have written it.'

'Yes, yes, all right. But that's another thing. It's Menkies' Syndrome by the way. And not too much ridicule, because this chap is a war hero, whatever else he has done. Menkies' Syndrome means, as I understand the papers, that he is highly suggestible. Highly susceptible to influence and manipulation. It's his only defence (if it is one). He goes into the witness box and says it's all down to Nailor. We took advantage of him. Put him under pressure, guided him. It's a form of duress.'

'This is a defence?'

'Who cares if it's a defence? When the jury hear about what he did in Northern Ireland they will want to acquit him. When they hear what Nailor did to that Chinaman ten years ago they will want to convict us. It's not easy.'

James Cameron looked worried. 'But if Aylen gives evidence John will destroy him. We've already established that.'

'Exactly, but don't you see? If John destroys him in the conventional sense, makes him change his evidence completely, we are simply demonstrating precisely what Aylen's case is setting out to prove. Aylen is the follower, the herd, the mindless bovine chump, and our guy is the diabolic machine. That's the problem.'

'Christ,' said James Cameron unhappily. 'This is a bit bloody difficult.'

John Wilkin looked from his instructing solicitor to his junior and smiled. 'I think,' he said evenly, 'that this problem may be more apparent than real.'

Both men regarded him closely.

'I have been speaking to Edward Boyd. I had dinner with him last night. Jane Wilson has been talking to him. She is Aylen's leading counsel. She's been making noises about Fitness to Plead.'

'Ah,' said Preston Lodge.

'You will have to forgive me,' said James Cameron. 'What exactly does that mean?'

'Aylen is found Unfit to Plead. In other words he can't stand his trial. A separate jury sorts that out. If that works then we are tried on our own. Then, without putting too fine a point on it, we put all the blame on Aylen. All we have to get round is the planted newspaper. Not difficult in my view. We walk and Eddie Cole ends up in the dock for perverting the course of justice. All very right and proper. Justice is done, et cetera et cetera.'

'What about the Menkies' Syndrome?'

'I have given that some thought. In our trial, without Aylen in the dock, the Crown can't run it. They cannot do that for the simple reason that we cannot examine Aylen, either in the witness box or with our own psychiatrist. We have no power to subject a co-defendant to medical analysis and so would be hopelessly prejudiced. No Menkies' Syndrome, no war hero, just a disillusioned, disfigured soldier working out his monstrous grudge, together with Bonkers Bedser the psychopathic pederast from Manchester. So let us sleep easy in our beds. I don't think we have much of a contest, Legal Aid or not.'

All three men smiled the contented smiles of the professionally fulfilled as tea arrived in blue porcelain cups.

# Chapter 3

When Colonel William Aylen entered her room in Chambers, Jane Wilson's first reaction was surprise. Having never met a colonel from the Brigade of Guards, she had anticipated something much bigger. Something, indeed, approximating to the size of Mary Shelley who sat beside her. A small, wiry man preceded Stephen through the door and took each hand in turn, smiling politely, almost diffident.

'No, thank you,' he said, refusing tea. 'I have just had some at the station. I was early, you see.'

Jane Wilson began. 'Colonel Aylen, we are very grateful to you for coming to see us. We all thought it essential to speak with Thomas's parents in this case.'

The colonel nodded and was silent.

'I understand from Mary that you have had all the case papers and read them.'

The colonel nodded briefly. 'I have not seen any psychiatric or medical reports.'

Mary Shelley said, 'They are being prepared at this moment. Our own psychiatrist and the prosecution psychiatrist have both seen Thomas in the last week.'

Jane Wilson continued, 'They are, of course, very important in the context of this case, but we do have the benefit of the medical reports from Ardingley where your son was treated following the accident.'

The colonel's eyebrows lifted perceptibly.

'I am sorry,' said Jane Wilson, 'I am not entirely sure how to describe it.'

'Attempted murder, I should think.'

'Of course; in any event, after the attempt to murder your son he was treated at Ardingley Military Hospital and we do have the reports, which I think you have seen.'

The colonel nodded.

'The first thing which we must consider is the plea which is to be entered to the separate counts on the indictment.'

Colonel Aylen noticeably stiffened but said nothing.

'As you know, your son has been charged with murder, kidnapping and rape . . . '

'How is the girl?'

'As far as we know she is still in a coma. The bullet is still lodged in her brain and it is thought unsafe to remove it. Apparently she has moments of consciousness and there is some hope that she will recover in some way. However, the trial is due to start in six weeks so she may clearly be discounted as a witness.'

'Can we not obtain a deferment, an adjournment or whatever it is called?'

Jane Wilson shook her head. 'Not in this case. The Crown and our co-defendant Nailor are anxious to proceed as soon as possible. The level of publicity has already put the whole trial in jeopardy. Besides, there is no clear prognosis. It may be months or years before she recovers. If she recovers at all. And then we have no knowledge of what she will say.'

The colonel looked straight at Jane Wilson. 'I do.'

Uncomfortably Mary Shelley intervened. 'We may, of course, *assume* what she will say but we do not *know*. In any event it is quite inevitable that the trial will proceed without her. The first question we must ask ourselves, whatever the condition of Melanie Golding, is the nature of the plea which must be entered *if* a plea is to be entered at all.'

The colonel leaned forward, his back straight. 'If at all?'

'Precisely,' said Jane Wilson. 'If at all. It is possible at the beginning, before the trial has even commenced, to raise the issue of Fitness to Plead. This becomes a separate issue to be tried by a separate jury. The law is not entirely straightforward, but, in broad terms, we need to show that Thomas is unfit to stand trial because of his mental condition. Either that he does not understand the nature of the plea, guilty or not guilty, or that he is incapable of conducting the trial, giving proper instructions or giving evidence upon oath. It is the last two matters upon which we need to concentrate.'

'You think he will not tell the truth?'

'No, that is not the point. In these circumstances the truth is not relevant,' said Mary Shelley, regretting it immediately.

'Not *relevant?*'

'What Mary means,' said Jane Wilson, 'is that the central issue is the mental *ability* to give coherent instructions and to give evidence on oath. Whether those instructions are true or untrue is not a consideration.'

'So,' said the colonel evenly. 'Providing there is an ability to give lying instructions and lie on oath then Fitness to Plead does not arise?'

'Precisely,' said Jane Wilson, not entirely happily. 'Many defendants give instructions which are untrue and many, unhappily, lie on oath. It does not mean that they are not fit to stand their trial.'

'Go on,' said the colonel.

'Whether we raise the issue is a matter for us. It *can* be raised by the court or even the prosecution but it would be very rare for either to do so if the defence objected. In this case, effectively, the choice lies with us, I think. Whether we make such an application depends entirely on a number of issues.' Jane Wilson held up her hand and counted on her fingers. 'First, are we likely to succeed? In other words, is there is a good case for saying that Thomas is unfit? Second, what is the strength of the prosecution's case and the likelihood of an acquittal? Plainly if the case is very weak then it may be in a defendant's interest to contest it if he possibly can. Third, what are the possibilities of a future recovery? I hope all this is clear. Ultimately the decision is one to be taken by your son if he is able to provide us with coherent instructions (which rather begs the question). In this particular case, given Thomas's rare mental condition, we wanted some assistance from yourself.'

'How can I help you?'

'Your son suffers from a rare mental condition known as Menkies' Syndrome.'

'I know.'

'It affects the rational and logical functions of the brain. The ability to resist orders and persuasion. The ability to argue and reason.'

'Does it affect the ability to perceive the truth?'

Startled, Jane Wilson said, 'I don't know. I don't think so. It merely means that you are easily deflected from it and swiftly perceive that to be true which is, in fact, untrue.'

'That is a condition unhappily common in many human beings. Perhaps even those who attempted to murder my son.'

'Perhaps.'

'Are you suggesting they are not Fit to Plead?'

'No, no, of course not.'

'And,' said the colonel, turning to Mary Shelley, 'are we likely to succeed in this . . . attempt to show that he is Unfit to Plead?'

'We think that we are. The prosecution is unlikely to contest it. The jury is bound to be sympathetic given your son's record.'

'*Sympathetic?*'

'Perhaps that is the wrong word. More likely to accept our arguments.'

'I see. And if they do *accept our arguments* and find that my son is Unfit to Plead (whatever that has to do with the truth) then what will become of him?'

After a brief and awkward silence Jane Wilson said, 'He will go to Broadmoor.'

'To a prison for the insane?'

'It is a hospital.'

'It is *called* a hospital. For how long will he remain in Broadmoor?'

'Until he is fit to stand his trial.'

'Menkies' Syndrome is incurable.' In the ensuing silence Colonel Aylen moved his steady and intense gaze to each of the three lawyers before him. He settled upon Gilbert Smith. 'Do I understand correctly? If we raise this issue we say, in effect, my son is incapable either of discerning the truth, the difference between right and wrong, or of maintaining the truth. He is therefore not even able to maintain that he is not guilty. If we *succeed* in this course he will be sentenced to Broadmoor *Hospital* for the remainder of his life.'

Gilbert Smith inhaled sharply. 'That is not how I would have put it, but in effect it is right.'

The Colonel's gaze returned to Jane Wilson. She said, 'I know what you are saying, Colonel Aylen, but we must look at the alternatives. The case against your son is very strong. One, he wrote the ransom letter; two, he is discovered in the sealed room where Melanie Golding is held prisoner, tied to a bed; three, according to the Chief Superintendent who led the charge, he was in possession of a firearm; four, I am sorry to mention this but it is unavoidable, there is the plainest forensic evidence that sexual intercourse had occurred between them. As yet we have not taken complete and coherent instruction from your son and *deliberately so*. If we reach the conclusion that it is best for him and best for you that we raise the issue of Unfitness to Plead, then we should take that decision now before attempting to obtain instructions in full and take it on the basis that the unequivocal medical evidence suggests that any instructions we receive will be unreliable. I do not have an ethical problem with that if it is the best and wisest course.'

'Have you asked him whether he is innocent or guilty?'

'Yes. He tells us he is not. But he gives way under the smallest pressure.'

When he next spoke the Colonel shifted his gaze and looked at the lawns of the Temple, across which the long shadows of the late summer reached towards the rows of plane trees and the dark river beyond. 'Miss Wilson. Let me tell you something about my son. We all hope for good children. I do not mean pious or wet or dull or studious or indulgent. I mean good children; brave, honest, funny, independent, thoughtful, considerate and with as much wisdom as their condition allows. When we have them we tend, do we not, to overlook their faults. We do so in the hope that they will be what we want them to be. I have two other children. To both of them I extend that indulgence. To one, remarkably so. Thomas was rare. He had many advantages. He was a beautiful boy and a beautiful man. He had a fine brain, swift, intuitive, retentive. He was a fine philosopher. He deserved his Double First. Ironically he was obsessed with proof. To distil the essence of truth. He was an ontologist. Above his desk at college and at home he had a quotation (from Voltaire I think), "*Plaider le faux pour savoir le vrai.*" You know it? "Allege that which is false to discover that which is true." What a supreme irony. He was a fine sportsman, had great energy and wild enthusiasms. He *belonged*. He tried to save most things. Children from dying, the rainforests, people from sickness, cruelty and poverty. He was no saint. Indeed he was an atheist. He drank, smoked and fell madly in love with a number of women, several of whom loved him. He was funny and rich and passionate and wise. Despite our background – Home Counties Army – he was an unrepentant socialist, and ran the University Labour Club, to the amusement of his friends.

'We were all surprised when he joined the Marines. Until he told me why. He said he wanted to *keep the peace.* Naïve perhaps, old-fashioned, but typical. He signed on for five years. He was in his fifth year and his second tour of duty in Ireland. He had fallen in love with an Irish Catholic girl. Not supposed to be allowed but she appeared to come from the right family. When he had leave they went to the Lakes of Killarney and stayed in small hotels. He wanted to marry her. One day she gave him some information. She said there would be a terrorist attack on the Strenath Road. Small arms were to be taken to the area in a civilian car which was to be left on a road in Armagh for the arms to be collected. He was given the information to use, which he did. The car was a booby-trap. He was lucky to live. Two didn't. It happened because he believed that she had told him the truth. That is the story of my son, Miss Wilson. The last part is not common knowledge, indeed it is a state secret. The girl has disappeared and, in any event, the only evidence against her would be a broken disabled boy with Menkies' Syndrome.

'You asked me for what assistance I can give. I suspect that you are really asking me to make a decision on my son's behalf. The choice, of course, is his. Let me say that if it were mine I would never, *never*, allow my son to do anything other than fight this case to the bitter end. You know he has been duped and beguiled by men with an extraordinary capacity for evil. He is no more capable of rape or murder or kidnap than he is of returning to read philosophy at Cambridge. Now if he were well he would fight this case with all his strength. To my imperfect judgement the fact that he is ill simply makes the task more difficult for him, for us and for you. I am not a fool. I know that criminal trials are not about the truth. I know they are about proof, burdens and standards of proof and the niceties and complexities of evidence. But, at the end, this is his only chance to avoid a life which will be a living nightmare. He must take it and we must take it. Finally, do not think that I do not understand the difficulties that you face. Ultimately if he gives evidence he will be a hopeless, helpless sitting target, but then, perhaps, that may be his best position. I have seen soldiers miss such things absolutely.' The colonel transferred his gaze to Jane Wilson and smiled.

She smiled back and said, 'Thank you, Colonel Aylen. I think you have told us all that we want to know. We will go into battle as best we can.'

One hour later, after the colonel had left, Jane Wilson phoned Sir Edward Boyd in his Chambers. After their conversation Sir Edward called in his junior, Miss Antonia Black.

'Well, my darling, we are in business. Aylen's pleading not guilty to everything. Jane Wilson's made about fifty demands for evidence. Her war-paint is on. We have a battle on our hands. I had better phone John Wilkin.'

John Wilkin, still in Chambers, was enjoying a glass of chilled Chablis with Preston Lodge when the telephone rang. He listened intently, his face in an elegant grimace. He held the stem of his glass between his thumb and forefinger, moving the liquor slowly against the light of his desk lamp. At length he said, 'Thank you, Edward. No, no, you are just the messenger. Thank you very much.'

Replacing the receiver, he stared at Preston Lodge. 'That's it. Aylen's fighting. We've got a battle on. Four to six weeks in the Old Bailey. On Legal Aid. Oh my dear God! On Legal Aid? My family! My wives!'

# Chapter 4

'Go away,' said Emily Thompson. 'Go away or I shall call the police.'
'Now there's no need to be nasty,' said Alex Bentley, 'I only want
a bit of information and help.'

Emily Thompson was standing at the doorway of her house; the
Headmistress's House. 'Melanie Golding left this school nearly eight years
ago in unhappy circumstances. I do not wish to be reminded of them. Nor
should I be bothered and pestered by people like yourself simply because
she has become involved in some kind of criminal activity.'

'It's a question of public duty.'

'Nonsense, absolute nonsense. Now take your foot from the door and
go away or I will call the police.'

'I don't care if you call the police. They won't do anything to me. I'm
within my rights. I'm from the national press.'

'You're drunk,' said Emily Thompson, wrinkling her nose with
distaste. 'And you've had some kind of accident down the front of your
blazer.'

'I am not drunk,' said Alex Bentley nobly. 'And I have not had an
accident down the front of my blazer. That was one of my colleagues.'

'I do not care who has had an accident down the front of your blazer.
You smell revolting. You are not coming in here and if you, or any of
your *colleagues*, attempt to approach any of the girls,' Emily Thompson
shuddered, 'then I shall call the police immediately. Now go away!'

Alex Bentley surveyed his antagonist with interest. He found it easier
if he slightly closed one eye and drew the other into focus. Unfortunately
he knew that this had a regrettable effect on his appearance. It also
caused him to sway slightly. He considered making threats based on the
Power of the Press but decided, instead, on charm. 'Now look, don't let's
be bloody unreasonable about this. I don't want much. This is a human
interest story. All that I want is a few minutes' interview with you, a
couple of members of the staff who remember her. You know the sort of
thing, mother figures and perhaps some old school photographs, you
know the kind of thing. Sports photographs. Girls in gymslips, you know
the kind of thing . . .'

It had become quite clear to Alex Bentley, even through his single eye, that this approach was not having the desired effect on Emily Thompson. Indeed the reverse might be the case. For almost the first time in his thirty years as a crime journalist Alex Bentley felt a spasm of physical fear. 'All right, all right, no photographs, but just an interview. All right? Just an interview with a couple of her teachers. You know, the mother figures, those she looked up to, hero-worshipped. You know the kind of thing. Goes on in all girls' schools.'

Emily Thompson looked down at Alex Bentley's foot, the toe of which was placed immediately inside the door jamb. The door was old-fashioned, of heavy oak construction. Emily Thompson reflected that if she opened it to its full extremity and then slammed it as hard as she could it might, in fact, sever the end of the toe. She was even calculating grimly that the soiled suede material would form little protection when suddenly her eyes narrowed and she thrust out her forearm. 'What's that? On the gymnasium roof?'

'Ah, yes,' said Alex Bentley uncomfortably. 'It's Benson.'

'Benson! What is Benson?'

'He's our photographer. Well, he's freelance, actually. Nice chap. He is trying to get some nice photographs of the girls. You know, back-ground pictures.'

Emily Thompson made a noise in the back of her throat which would have caused prehistoric men to fall silent in their caves. Then she hissed, 'Background pictures. I see.' Pushing past Alex Bentley she covered the small quadrangle before her and reached the side of the gymnasium, a single-storey building on which Benson could be seen crouching, barely fifteen feet above her. 'Mr Benson, Mr Benson, get off that roof this instant. Do you hear me? This instant!'

It was at this point Benson made the first of two mistakes. Raising himself to his knees he looked down to the figure of the headmistress, arms akimbo below him. After a moment's thought he thrust into the air his right arm, at the extremity of which was the unmistakable gesture that the English bowmen directed heroically towards the French Knights at the Battle of Crecy.

Emily Thompson stared upwards. 'Right,' she said. 'Right.' Turning on her heel she marched back to her front door. 'Get out of the way,' she said to Alex Bentley, before disappearing into her house. Seconds later she reappeared, carrying what Alex Bentley was subsequently to describe to the police as a 'projectile'. 'It was a hockey ball,' Miss Thompson then observed, shortly. 'Medium weight, twelve and a half ounces.' Swiftly she returned to her place below the gymnasium roof and delivered what was subsequently to be described in the police report as 'a sporting second chance'.

'Mr Benson, Mr Benson, leave that roof immediately. Do you hear me, Mr Benson? Immediately.'

Prosaically, Benson's second gesture was identical to his first. Then, possibly to add a little colour to his defiance, he raised his camera to his eye and directed the lens towards Miss Thompson herself. This unfortunate act rendered him temporarily unsighted and thus unprepared.

Alex Bentley, as previously recorded, was suffering from the classic focusing problems of the advanced alcoholic. Through one eye he observed Emily Thompson drawing back her right arm, her wrist crooked, and leaning backwards to the extent that her left foot left the ground.

'Right,' she said.

In her youth Emily Thompson had captained England at both hockey and lacrosse, had opened the bowling for the women's national cricket team and had narrowly failed to qualify for the Olympic discus. With his deficiencies of vision Alex Bentley perceived only a blur followed by the violent shattering of glass, a short scream and silence. Thereafter he instinctively flattened himself against the wall as Emily Thompson returned across the quadrangle and through her door which she slammed behind her. Seconds later the door reopened.

'If you don't bugger off the same will happen to you,' she said evenly before the door closed for the last time.

As it transpired, fortune favoured the brave. The skylight through which Benson fell was situated immediately above a pile of rubber mattresses intended to soften descent from the high beam. No girls were in the vicinity and the first that class 4A observed of the *Evening News* photographer was his descent accompanied by a cloud of glass from the gymnasium roof. Hitting the rubber mattresses he bounced once and was still. It further transpired that his only injury was a broken forearm which had crushed the telescopic lens of his Nikon.

The police arrived in the person of PC Oldfield from Devizes Station. Like many West Country police officers, Mr Oldfield was a strong devotee of monastic education for girls and was proud of the reputation that St Augusta's provided for the area. Having formed a swift and accurate view of the primary facts, he proceeded to summary justice. 'We don't like pederastic people round here,' he observed to Alex Bentley. 'Particularly them that carry cameras.'

'I'm not a pederastic person,' said Alex Bentley. 'I'm a crime reporter.'

PC Oldfield sniffed at the non sequitur. 'And what's he when he's at home then?' indicating Benson, doubled over nursing his broken wrist. 'I suppose he's a trained steeplejack is he, doing a bit of practice on the gym roof. Now before you say any more I'm going to give you gentlemen a choice. You can come down to the police station with me while I carry out a thorough check into your pederastic activities. This normally takes about twenty-four hours and word gets round the local farmers pretty quick. However hard I try, it is difficult to stop them guessing when you will be let out. They don't like pederastic activities in Devizes. Either that or I can let you off with a caution. That means you sign a statement admitting to your pederastic tendencies and swearing as a condition of your caution that you never come here again. Now you decide.'

However deep his commitment to the relentless search for justice, Alex Bentley was well versed in the codes of his profession. 'All right, all right, I understand.' Then, indicating the figure of Benson now moaning quietly over his broken arm, 'he'll sign the caution. He was the one on the roof.'

'Oh no. You both sign or you both come down the nick.'

Thus it was that within half an hour Alex Bentley and the unhappy Benson were free men standing at the entrance to St Augusta's by their Toyota car.

'What about his arm?' said Alex Bentley in a rare moment of compassion. 'Where can we get it treated?'

'If I were you,' said PC Oldfield, 'I would wait until I get back to London. Doctors round here don't like pederastic people either. If you get one of them to treat that arm he might not be able to use it for anything. Might even *lose it altogether*. Now you get along back to the *Evening News* and write a nice story.'

# Chapter 5

'Publicity's gone a bit flat,' said Sir Edward Boyd to Antonia Black. 'Nothing in the *Evening News*. Trial's four weeks away. Maybe they're losing interest.'

The two prosecuting counsel were seated in their room at the Old Bailey. That morning the trial judge had conducted the first pre-trial review, the purpose of which was to identify preliminary points to be argued before the trial and to set an agenda for the trial itself. Such hearings are deeply unpopular with practitioners at the criminal Bar. To understand precisely why, it is necessary to understand the attributes of the criminal barrister. These are few but essential. The first, which they share with journalists, is an affected indifference to the pain, suffering, loss, poverty and mind-wrenching violence daily inflicted in the course of criminal activity and the mindless, hopeless, destructive forms of punishment employed in retribution. The carapace of cynicism is more important to the criminal barrister than his wig and gown. The other essential attribute, again shared with journalists and also with members of the acting profession, is the ability to master a large number of interrelated facts on a deliberately superficial level. Trials, like all theatrical performances, have a finite life. Aside from curiosity, culture or anecdote, long-term factual recollection has no value beyond the end of the proceedings. Indeed, assuming the brain to have finite capacity (in the case of many criminal barristers it is very finite indeed), then the swift obliteration of memory is not only likely but essential. The mind must become a *tabula rasa* upon which can be written the next drama of murder, rapine, theft, robbery, fraud or deceit. Once this interesting mental process is understood then the aversion to the pre-trial review is obvious. If this court hearing pre-dates the trial by, say, two months, then unless the case is one of unusual size and complexity it will be necessary to prepare for it twice, since in the intervening weeks other trials will have wiped out recollection with the efficiency of an incoming tide.

To this explanatory note should be added the simple fact that no criminal barrister would begrudge doing the work twice. The complaint comes, of course, from the fact that he is paid only once. There is a further, psychological, aversion. The pre-trial review is not part of the battle. It is a phony war, a meaningless skirmish. Decisions may be retracted. Provisos are endlessly attached. Reviews are conducted secure in the knowledge that in the heat and mayhem of battle the niceties of previous treaty may be flung to the winds.

Thus it was with noticeable reluctance that the prosecution and defence assembled in the court of Mr Justice Phillips, a reluctance most poignantly articulated by Mr John Wilkin, QC, the unwilling recipient of Legal Aid.

'Do you know how much I get paid for this?' he demanded of Preston Lodge. 'Two hundred and fifty quid, that's what I get paid for this. Two hundred and fifty quid. My God, my wives, my children.'

At the far side of the court other serious matters were under discussion between Sir Edward Boyd and Jane Wilson, concerning the exchange of psychiatric reports.

'Jane,' said Sir Edward in a tone of resignation, 'I am supposed to have had your psychiatric report ten days ago.'

'I know, Edward, I know. I have only just received it. I will let you have it as soon as I can.'

'It is *important* in this case.'

'Do you think I don't know? I cannot perform miracles or drive psychiatrists. If you want an order get one for me to produce it.'

'*Jane*, of course I don't want an order. Just let me have it within seven days.'

'Fine.'

Further conversation between lawyers was interrupted by the arrival on the Bench of Mr Justice Phillips. A decent man and convivial company, Bob Phillips had one impeccable qualification to be the presiding judge in the criminal Trial of the Century, namely that he knew virtually nothing about crime or criminal law. His practice at the Bar had been conducted entirely in the Chancery Division, where he had made a considerable fortune rearranging the family trusts of the rich. He had rarely appeared in court and never, in twenty-eight years at the Bar, confronted a jury. To this day Britain remains one of the few legal systems in the world (the others, like India, are clones of the British system) where a legal pedigree consisting entirely of the consideration and construction of wills, codicils, deeds and bonds is regarded as a suitable, indeed essential prerequisite for conducting trials involving, for instance, bestiality, sodomy, rape and robbery.

Mr Justice Phillips' ignorance of criminal law and practice and, more importantly, his inexperience in the myriad forms of conventions and deals which govern, informally, the criminal process made him nervous. This nervousness reflected itself in a judicial hauteur which belied the man beneath. It also led him to rely heavily on the pronouncements of prosecuting counsel, particularly if they enjoyed the eminence and reputation of Sir Edward Boyd, First Treasury Counsel, England's most famous prosecutor and a man for whom the word gravitas might have been freshly minted.

On this, the first hearing of the Trial of the Century, Mr Justice Phillips began at a brisk pace. 'Sir Edward,' he said, nodding and smiling briefly at the voluminous advocate who had risen to his feet. 'Let us dispense with the introductions. I know everybody here.' With that he directed a *sourire passant* along the rows of counsel's benches. 'A number of preliminary matters, if you would. First, I see that we are attended by a large number of the Gentlemen of the Press. The judge inclined his head towards the press benches, which were uncomfortably overfilled, wondering, as he did so, why one of the reporters in the front row, wearing a dirty blazer, appeared to be looking at him with one eye. 'Do we require any orders to be made about publicity at this stage?'

'I think not. As this is, in part, a rape trial, the name of the victim would in normal circumstances be withheld from the press. However, as your Lordship knows, this matter achieved such extensive, indeed unstoppable publicity at the time of the arrests that any such order would be quite useless. The lady in question is not a witness, and indeed, is incapable of being so.'

'Thank you,' said the judge, making a clearly defined tick on the papers before him. 'Next, Sir Edward, will there be changes to the existing indictment?'

'No, my Lord, the counts will remain the same. Aylen is charged with murder, kidnap and rape; Nailor with kidnap alone.'

'The murder charge relates to the death of Sergeant Davidson who was killed when the house was stormed?'

'That is so. Davidson, of course, was not shot by Aylen. He was shot by another member of the group who was himself shot and killed. Aylen was in the cellar, also armed. The Crown say that this is a clear case of joint enterprise. The responsibility of one is the responsibility of all."

Mr Justice Phillips sifted the papers before him. 'Tell me, Sir Edward, in these circumstances why is Nailor not charged with the murder as well?'

'We have given considerable thought to this. It is obviously borderline. The existence of the newspaper with his fingerprints upon it, together with his denial of any contact with Miss Golding, provides clear evidence of participation and presence at the flat. The extent of that participation, however, is unclear, particularly in relation to the use of firearms. After very careful consideration we have reached the view that we could not invite the jury to be sure that he knew of the weapons. He may well be fortunate but that is the Crown's decision.'

'Very well, Sir Edward, it is, of course a matter for you. I simply wished the position to be clear. Now, may I also enquire whether there will be issues as to the admissibility of evidence?'

'I think that *that* is a matter for my learned friends. I gather that there are such issues in both cases.'

John Wilkin rose smartly to his feet and draped himself upon a lectern, on the outer extremity of which a large brass plaque bearing his own name reflected his immaculate wing collar and pink and rounded chin. 'We have one issue which concerns statements made by my client at the time of his arrest at the police station. The issue is simple. We say that they were obtained by means of a trick and should be excluded as unfair under the provisions of Section 78 of the Criminal Justice Act. We are all agreed that this issue should be decided in the course of the trial.'

The judge frowned and turned the page of his notebook. 'Let me understand the significance of this. As I understand it, the prosecution relies heavily on a newspaper said to have been found at the victim's home. In this interview, to which you object, your client Mr Nailor denies any contact with Melanie Golding. He also denies any contact with Aylen. The significance of his statement to the police is that it excludes any innocent explanation for the presence of the newspaper. That is right, is it not?'

'Precisely,' said John Wilkin.

'So,' continued the judge, 'if I rule that the interview is inadmissable, the case against Nailor is much weaker. All that the jury will have is the mere presence of the newspaper with your client's fingerprints. Is that right?'

'That is the point precisely, my Lord.'

'Thank you, Mr Wilkin. For the present I will rule that this evidence should not be put before the jury. I will consider its admissibility when Superintendent Cole gives evidence. Now, Miss Wilson, do you have any such issues to raise?'

'My Lord, we do. Following his arrest, as your Lordship will have seen, Thomas Aylen made a full confession to the police. The admissibility of that confession is in issue. As with my learned friend, we rely upon Section 78 and also upon a number of specific breaches of the Codes of Conduct including a failure to ensure the presence of a solicitor or other legal representative. The defendant is a person under a disability.'

Mr Justice Phillips' eyebrows rose imperceptibly. 'Is it suggested that Mr Wagner knew of these disabilities?'

'My Lord, it will be.'

'Very well. If this matter is to be tried in the absence of the jury when will it be done?'

'We are again agreed, subject to your Lordship's directions, that this matter should be tried before your Lordship in a "trial within a trial" at the appropriate time of the evidence. That will be when Mr Wagner gives evidence himself.'

'Very well. Finally, Sir Edward, are there any other matters of law which I can deal with now or at the beginning of the trial or which I should consider in the time that I have available?'

'My Lord, I think not, save possibly for the question of Fitness to Plead.'

At the end of counsel's row Jane Wilson's head jerked upwards in surprise.

'Ah, yes, Fitness to Plead,' repeated the judge. 'On whose part exactly?'

'The first defendant, Thomas Aylen.'

'Ah, yes. What do you say, Miss Wilson?'

Glaring briefly at her opponent, Jane Wilson rose to her feet. 'My Lord, we have no application to make. I repeat, *no application to make* relating to Fitness to Plead. There will be no preliminary issue.'

'You say that your client is under a disability in relation to the alleged confession. Is this not a disability which affects his fitness to stand trial?'

Jane Wilson's lips set in a tight line. 'My Lord, we have considered this matter with very great care. We have had the benefit of psychiatric assistance and, I repeat, we are not raising the issue of Fitness to Plead.'

Sir Edward Boyd rose again to his feet. 'My Lord, I only raised the matter since technically at the end of the day it remains a matter for your Lordship to decide. If your Lordship took the view that Aylen was unfit to plead, or *might be*, then it would be a matter for your Lordship to raise. As yet *I* have not had the benefit of seeing my learned friend's psychiatric reports which, of course, she must serve on the prosecution if they are to be used. I do *not* ask your Lordship for any order in respect of this matter but the Crown must reserve its position, particularly if we are to *assist* your Lordship in any way on this issue.'

'Ah, I see. Well, Sir Edward, I am very grateful to you as always. I am not, as you know, totally familiar with these procedures and it is useful to know where my full responsibility lies.' The judge turned to Jane Wilson. 'Miss Wilson, is this right? Do I understand that no psychiatric report has yet been served upon the Crown?'

Speaking as clearly as possible through clenched teeth, Jane Wilson replied, 'My Lord, that is right. I have told my learned friend that I will provide him with a copy within seven days.'

'That leaves very little time before the trial, Miss Wilson. I must say I am surprised, *very surprised*, that Sir Edward has not seen such a report to date. Sir Edward, do you require any form of order?'

'No, my Lord. If my learned friend tells me I will have it, I will have it.'

'Just so, Sir Edward, very reasonable and proper. Finally, Sir Edward, how long is this trial scheduled to last?'

'It is difficult to judge, my Lord. Perhaps as long as four weeks.'

Beside him on counsel's bench, John Wilkin flinched and muttered, 'My God. My wives, my families.'

'I'm sorry, Mr Wilkin, did you say something to me?'

'No, my Lord, no. I was just saying that I hoped it would be rather shorter.'

'I am sure we all hope that, Mr Wilkin, but justice must run its course in its own way. I will mark the case down for six weeks. Are you all right, Mr Wilkin? I thought you didn't look well but perhaps it was just the expression on your face. Very well, gentlemen, Miss Wilson, we will see each other again on the fifth of June.'

As the court cleared Jane Wilson manoeuvred herself to the side of Sir Edward Boyd. 'What are you playing at, Edward?' she said in a voice which contained several layers of permafrost. 'What's all this about Fitness to Plead? I *told you* it was not an option.'

'Well, you never know, do you,' said Sir Edward smoothly. 'Things may change and I haven't seen your report.'

'Don't talk rot Edward. You know I told you you would have it in seven days. And you didn't have to tell the judge. We had an agreement.'

'Temper, temper, old thing. Our agreement was that we did not have an order, and anyway, now you will have to give it to me, won't you?' Sir Edward smiled sweetly.

In order to arrest his forward motion Jane Wilson took three steps ahead and turned to face him. 'I want to know what game you are playing, Edward. Something's up. Why do you want my guy out of the picture? It doesn't make sense. He's the only chance you have got of getting Nailor. If he gives evidence he'll put Nailor right in it. You *know* that, don't you?'

'My dear Jane,' said Sir Edward, in a voice reminiscent of molten lava, and aware of the rage his expression invoked. 'My *dear* Jane, I am running this little show and I will do it my way. If my way involves getting rid of your little mad man off to Broadmoor, then that is a matter for me. There may be other reasons, but, to draw for a moment on your own chosen vernacular, I suggest that you mind your own business.'

# Chapter 6

Eddie Cole lay in bed with his mistress, the incomparable Anita Flynn.

'You've stopped smoking,' she said in a tone somewhere between wonder and admiration. 'You haven't had a single bloody fag. You been going to aerobics or something?'

'I'm trying to give it up in bed. It's dangerous and bad for the libido.'

'Well it certainly seems to be working. That wasn't bad.'

'Thanks a lot. Confidence building. I must get a string vest.'

Anita Flynn smiled at her favourite policeman in the darkness of her room. 'You do that. But seriously, something is wrong. I can feel it.'

In the darkness Eddie Cole nodded his head. 'There is something happening I do not understand. I was in court last week. Aylen's got this Monkey's Syndrome. He could go Unfit to Plead. Not surprisingly, his brief's not having it. It's as good as an admission of guilt and you end up in Broadmoor with the nutters for life. He's got a good brief, a woman, but good.'

'Hooray,' said Anita Flynn.

'Anyway, she tells the judge she's going to try and get rid of the confession that Jack Wagner bullied out of him on the basis of psychiatric evidence. Then the prosecution – *us* – in the person of Sir Edward "Boomer" Boyd raises the issue of Fitness. Why? We all know Nailor put him up to it. Aylen's only chance of walking out is to say so. Our case against Nailor becomes one hundred per cent stronger when Aylen gives evidence. That way we get them both. Nailor for setting him up, Aylen for being a gutless dupe on account of having half a brain. Justice is done. Nailor gets life for kidnapping. Aylen gets life which the poor sick bastard spends in torment at Nutters' Hall. Justice done all round and that's an end to it.'

'I told you,' said Anita Flynn. 'Nailor's pulling the strings. You said yourself Jack Wagner and his mob went to St Albans to kill that boy. Maybe the girl too. Nailor's calling the shots. It all goes back to his employment by the Security Forces and burglarising the Labour government. I have told you this. There is not much point in running this place, collecting all this priceless knowledge, passing it on to the Terror of the London Underworld, if you can't remember it.'

'I know, I know,' said Eddie Cole, 'but he didn't kill Aylen. I saw to that. He didn't even wing him. The others went down. Bedser and the other gorillas. But the boy's still there. They got a confession out of him without naming Nailor but I've got the newspaper. They can't let Nailor go so they are both in it. The only explanation for trying to stop the trial against Aylen is that Boomer Boyd is also taking his instructions from Nailor, or Security Services, or the Special Branch and that means the DPP. I don't believe it. I just don't believe it goes that far up.'

'Innocent abroad,' said Anita Flynn. 'Wandering unsupervised.'

'No I'm *not*. I do know this game. Coppers are bent. Some solicitors are bent. Some counsel are bent, but on a deal like this it just doesn't happen. This is the Director, for God's sake. The *Attorney General*. Government. Something else is going wrong. I don't know what it is but it looks as though they are trying to lose Nailor. It won't do me any good. By that time they would have torn my balls off in the witness box. John Wilkin is going to try to boil me in oil. Every time he looks at me in court I see saliva running down his chin. I don't care. I've done my job. But if they let that demented bastard Nailor go, Superman with a shotgun, God the gangleader, then someone else is going to get killed. Perhaps a lot of people.' Eddie Cole picked up his whisky and poured some into the corner of his mouth. 'We need some more evidence.'

'How's the girl?'

'Still in a coma. They can't get the bullet out. I've got Brendan O'Hara there twenty-four hours a day. Two of our men with him. I won't let anyone near her. Particularly Jack Wagner. But she's gone, dead. Brendan says sometimes she murmurs. A couple of times she has opened her eyes. She tries to say something but then it all goes blank. She's a beautiful girl. I think Brendan's getting quite soft on her. Anyway, maybe she'll wake up. Maybe Jack Wagner will go straight. Maybe George 'Fast Track' Watson will go into a monastery. Maybe seven dwarfs will arrive and wake her from a long sleep. I think we are fucked.'

'Now that's a good idea,' said Anita Flynn.

# Chapter 7

Jane Wilson had not been entirely candid with Sir Edward Boyd about the psychiatric report which had been obtained on behalf of Thomas Aylen. Certainly the report had been delivered late and certainly at the time of the pre-trial review the report had been in her possession only a matter of days. However, the real reason for her reticence was a nagging unhappiness with its contents and, particularly, its conclusion. Thus, on the same day on which Eddie Cole spoke with such affection to Anita Flynn, Jane Wilson, Mary Shelley and Gilbert Smith were in urgent consultation with Dr John Heathcliffe, one of England's most eminent psychiatrists and pedants.

'Let's get this straight,' said Jane Wilson, 'he's got Menkies' Syndrome, right?'

'Undoubtedly.'

'This affects the right frontal lobe of the brain?'

'The *front* of the right frontal lobe.'

'Very well, the front of the right frontal lobe. The effect is to reduce resistance to intellectual pressure. The victim changes his personality, right?'

'Not exactly.'

'Well, what exactly is it?'

'The victim's personality remains unaltered. What he or she was so he or she will remain. The grasp of reality is unaltered. This is not a psychosis. It does not induce schizophrenia. The victim does not believe that he is Napoleon or she is Josephine. Nor can he or she be induced to such a belief. What is affected is the capacity to make value judgements or, more accurately, the capacity to *maintain* value judgements in the face of persuasion or pressure. To give you an analogy, the brain has a springboard mechanism. The springboard is the process by which we question information or, most important, commands or inducements. It is this capacity which is damaged. This results in an inability or relative inability to withstand persuasion or reject commands. Because of this there is a danger that the "victim" under extreme pressure or persuasion will act in a way which is entirely "out of character", insofar as that term has any meaning.'

'Does this mean that the victim has no perception of right or wrong, good or evil?'

'Not exactly. As a behavioural psychiatrist I prefer to regard such matters in terms of empathy with others, guilt and a perception of consequences. All of these things will remain basically unaltered. The victim is not suffering from a personality disorder. He is not a psychopath, to use the well-known dustbin category. He has a "normal" perception of guilt and empathy and has the normal thresholds of gratification.'

'I don't understand that.'

'He is not unusually self-obsessed. Forgetting the present circumstances the Good Soldier is the best analogy. The Good Soldier is trained to obey orders. That is not a moral precept, it is an essential precondition of the job. The extent to which the condition does or should overcome the moral or rational instincts is, of course, a celebrated subject for debate. A person with Menkies' Syndrome cannot resist an order and is seriously disabled in the face of persuasive argument. The extent to which this is varies. The effect or influence is no more permanent than it would be with any of us. Similarly, of course, they are liable to the conflicting argument. Put shortly, they will obey the command which is last given.'

'Like a child?'

'Similar.'

'Good,' said Mary Shelley.

After the psychiatrist had left with Gilbert Smith, Jane Wilson removed a bottle of wine from her cupboard together with two glasses.

'Isn't it a bit early?' said Mary Shelley.

'Good God, no, I need to think.'

After pouring two large glasses Mary Shelley looked at her friend. 'Cheers,' she said. 'You're not happy, are you?'

'No. We have a serious problem. We must call the psychiatric evidence to avoid the confession. If we don't avoid the confession we may just as well all go home. If we do call the evidence Boyd and Wilkin will both argue that we are Unfit to Plead. Off we go to Broadmoor and Nailor walks.'

'Is there a way round it?'

'God knows. Cheers.'

# Chapter 8

At 10.30 a.m. on 5 June 1989 the jury panel of eighteen men and twelve women, from whom the apostolic twelve would be chosen, was ushered into the back of Court One of the Old Bailey, where they sat silent as though in the presence of the great. Thirty pairs of eyes shifted across the vast room absorbing an atmosphere created deliberately to summon up the first handmaiden of Justice, namely Fear.

At the furthest extremity of the court, fully one hundred feet distant, a wall of panelling rises to the height of a small house. At its apex are set three giant chairs, and above the centre of these a gigantic sword is suspended before the royal crest. No Venetian doge could have asked for a finer setting. Occupying the near middle of this darkened amphitheatre, the raised dock thrusts the prisoner into an elevated cage, walled on three sides by glass and on the fourth, directly confronting the judge, by iron rails providing the reality and metaphor of incarceration. In the well of the court figures in black gowns perform tasks incomprehensible. Beside them sit the ranks of the Bar. Three in silk robes, three in stuff, and behind them yet more barristers without immediate employment, some to learn and some to watch. Above their heads the waiting jury hears the shifting feet and muffled voices of the public gallery, full to its capacity of two hundred seats arranged in ordered rows in the foremost of which sit the curious and committed, several of whom have queued on the streets of Holborn throughout the cold summer night. Despite the ambient temperature, however, the court room is warm and, during the course of the following days will become increasingly, near-intolerably hot, heat proceeding from the assembled multitude and the great lights of brass and iron suspended from the plaster moulded roof full forty feet above the dock. In this space the defendants now appear, scarcely noticed from the cells beneath. This then is Court One of the Old Bailey, the most famous and feared Palace of Justice of them all.

As though moved by some common consent, at half past ten the great courtroom fell quiet. Whispers exchanged in the public gallery and on counsels' benches gradually subsided into a universal reverence from which the human condition will never be divorced.

Fully four minutes passed. One nervous laugh was stifled before the oak door behind the judge's platform swung open and four men with swords and black garters solemnly enacted a ritual dance, ludicrous in any other circumstance. Following his courtiers, Mr Justice Phillips, splendid in the red and ermine of a full judge, moved to the right hand of the three seats, bowed to his court and, whilst still in the process of taking his seat, began the process of justice.

'Sir Edward, I think that the defendants have already been arraigned and have both pleaded Not Guilty to all counts.'

'Yes, indeed, my Lord.'

'Thank you,' said Mr Justice Phillips. 'Sir Edward, is there any reason why we should not swear the jury?'

'My Lord, there is a matter of law to be considered before I open the Crown's case. It may be convenient to swear the jury now in order to release them and the remaining members of the panel until a suitable time.'

'Very well. Let the jury be sworn.'

Jane Wilson watched intently as twelve members of the jury were selected from the panel. Finally seven women and five men sat facing her across the well of the court. Three obvious professionals, she thought; two of them women. One man, young, sharp, something in the City. The remainder solid-looking enough, save for one of the younger women, twenty perhaps, from whose left ear dangled a long silver chain, looping across the side of her face before attaching itself with what appeared to be a safety-pin to the side of her nose. Her shoulders were bare and both were heavily covered in tattoos. As Jane Wilson watched she saw her scowl at Sir Edward Boyd.

'Attitude problem,' thought Jane Wilson, and smiled.

On entering the jury box several of the jury glanced at the dock. Jane Wilson observed two of them narrow their eyes with involuntary grimaces.

'Sympathy and horror,' she thought. 'King Kong, Frankenstein's monster.' With that thought she leaned forward to her friend Mary Shelley, occupying a large area of the solicitor's table, and said, 'Not a bad lot, could be worse.'

The jury having been selected, Mr Justice Phillips dismissed them. 'Ladies and gentlemen, as you may have heard, there is a matter of law for me to consider in your absence. There is no secret about this. Matters of law concern me alone, just as matters of fact are for you alone. Thus, from time to time, it will be necessary for you to leave the court and indeed it has happened already. I ask you please to return sharp at two p.m. when Sir Edward Boyd may open the case for the prosecution.'

As the jury left the court Sir Edward Boyd turned to John Wilkin and said, 'It looks as though this *may* be shorter than we thought.'

'Oh I hope so,' said John Wilkin fervently.

'Sir Edward,' began the judge, 'I imagine that the only matter we need to deal with at the outset is Mr Aylen's Fitness to Plead.'

'My Lord, just so.'

'Am I right, Miss Wilson, that there is no application from the defence to have this issue tried? You do not want to have to try to persuade the jury that your client is Unfit to Plead?'

'My Lord,' said Jane Wilson, rising to her feet, 'that is precisely so.'

'However, that it is not quite the end of it. As I understand it, *I* have a duty here. If I come to the conclusion that the defendant may not be Fit to Plead, then I can initiate an enquiry with a jury. Is that right, Sir Edward?'

'Exactly so, my Lord.'

'And without wishing to enter this arena, Sir Edward, would you invite me to consider this matter on the basis of the psychiatric reports from both the Crown and the defence with which I have *now* been provided? They are from two very eminent psychiatrists, both known to me, Mr Barlow for the Crown and Mr Heathcliffe for the defence. Is that right?'

'Exactly so, my Lord.'

'Well, I have done. I have read the psychiatric reports carefully and it seems to me that save in one or two important respects, they are in agreement. The *present* view that I have formed is this. The defendant is Fit to Plead. Everyone is in agreement that *at the moment* he understands the charge. He is capable of understanding his plea of guilty or not guilty and giving Miss Wilson instructions. If he were not able to give her instructions then I am sure she would tell me. In other words his will is free until someone tampers with it. No one is going to tamper with it in this court, at least until he gives evidence, *if* he gives evidence. On that I am going to retain an open mind. If it occurs to me at any stage during the course of the trial that Aylen may have *become* Unfit to Plead then I will stop the trial. A new jury will be impanelled in order to consider that matter at that stage. Let us hope it does not happen. If it does a great deal of time and money will be wasted but justice will have been done. This is an unusual state of affairs. I have never heard of Menkies' Syndrome. It occurs to me, however, as a vulgar layman, that if it means that the will is free until it is tampered with by others then, as a matter of fact, the syndrome may be a lot more widespread than anyone thought. Now does anyone disagree with this approach? I will say straight away that I will take a good deal of persuading.'

On counsel's benches no one moved.

'Good,' said Mr Justice Phillips. 'Let us meet again at five past two when Sir Edward will begin to open this case.'

After the court had risen two meetings took place. John Wilkin conducted one of his rare conferences with his client, Roddy Nailor, in the forbidding cells below the Old Bailey. As a general rule John Wilkin had a serious aversion to discussion with *any* clients. In the case of Roddy Nailor this rule had become an axiom. However, when his client demanded to see him (which was now the case) there was little he could do to avoid it.

'What's all this mean?' said Roddy Nailor, his pale eyes narrowed and his fingers drumming the desk. 'What's going on? How does it look for us?'

John Wilkin leaned forward towards his client, 'Mr Nailor . . .'

'I've said, call me Roddy.'

'Yes. Mr Nailor, you may rest assured that the whole business has just improved enormously. If the psychiatrists are right, this chap Aylen will automatically crack up under examination. Once he comes under pressure from me or Sir Edward Boyd, if I'm right, he'll change his tune and admit anything. If he does, one of two things happens. Either any allegations against you are effectively withdrawn or the judge, at that stage, will decide that he is Unfit to Plead and the whole of this trial comes to an end. That issue, the issue of Fitness to Plead, is then tried by a separate jury. The jury finds he is unfit *because the judge will tell them to*, Aylen goes off to Broadmoor and the Crown find that they don't want to proceed against you on the basis of one newspaper. By then I hope we will have destroyed that piece of evidence. The judge has given Jane Wilson a serious problem and has done us a lot of good, so, Mr Nailor, you may sleep easy in your bed.'

'I want to get out of this fucking place. I have been banged up for ten years and I don't want to stay here much longer.'

'Mr Nailor,' said John Wilkin, smiling politely, 'let me assure you that your early, and I mean, *early* release is my primary and urgent consideration.'

The second meeting was between Eddie Cole, Jack Wagner and George Watson.

Eddie Cole began. Looking hard at Jack Wagner, he said, 'We have got to keep Boyd away from this Fitness to Plead stuff.'

George Watson intervened. 'Why exactly do you say that, Eddie?'

Eddie Cole turned to his superior officer and spoke with exaggerated care. 'Because if Aylen disappears out of this trial we lose all the evidence against him, which is in reality the best evidence against Nailor; the mental condition, duress, everything. It provides the essential link to the main man.'

'Oh come on, Eddie.' Jack Wagner adopted a smile calculated to taunt. 'We have still got your newspaper, or are we getting a bit less keen on that as we get closer to giving evidence?'

Before he could reply, Eddie Cole's mobile phone rang. When answered, the voice of Brendan O'Hara was heard speaking with quiet urgency. 'Guv, I'm sorry. I know you're busy but I need to talk to you urgently.'

'Phone me in two minutes, Brendan. This meeting is just finishing.'

Shortly after the two chief superintendents left him Eddie Cole was again listening to his sergeant.

'Guv,' said the Irishman in reply to the immediate protest, 'I'm sorry. I know, I know, you have just started, but it's important guv. She's waking up. No, I can't get much. She comes and goes. Sometimes she won't speak about it at all. Then she's having treatment. It's very difficult. But I'm worried, guv, there's something really wrong here. And I *mean* wrong. She hasn't told me much but I can feel it.'

Eddie Cole stared at the defaced notice on the wall of the police room. 'Truth,' he thought, 'may be about to emerge.'

'Listen, Brendan, just stay with her, all right? How many of the lads have you got there? Right, I'll send two more. Stay with her. Take a statement. Remember they don't give her much hope of surviving this. So when you get the statement make sure she understands that she is in imminent danger of death. Get it recorded. Have you got that?'

'Yes, guv,' said Brendan O'Hara. 'Yes, guv, I've got all that.'

'And for God's sake, Brendan, don't let the bogeys anywhere near her. Do you understand? Not anywhere near her. The first sign of Wagner's merry men let me know, *immediately*. Do you understand? And, Brendan, if you get any orders or directions from anyone except me – and I don't give a fuck who it is – that's the Commissioner, George Watson, anybody, then *don't* do anything. Misunderstand it. Do you understand? Say you didn't hear it properly. Say you never got your brain around it. You're a bloody Mick, they'll believe that.'

'Thank you guv. I'll do my best.'

'Good lad Brendan,' said Eddie Cole, 'good lad'.

'What was all that about then?' said Jack Wagner to Eddie Cole as they stood in the passageway outside Court One waiting for the doors to open.

'Nothing, different case. Robbery at Golders Green. Furniture van full of kitchen units.'

'Kitchen units? Kitchen units?'

'Yeah, you know. Cupboards, drawers, that sort of thing.'

Jack Wagner looked closely at his fellow police officer and then said, quite suddenly, 'What's the news on Melanie Golding?'

'Dunno. Still in a coma according to Brendan O'Hara. He's up at the hospital with a couple of my boys. They're *armed*. They have got instructions to shoot *anyone* who tries to get in there. In the head.'

'I think I might pop up there and see her,' said Jack Wagner. 'May go tomorrow.'

'Wouldn't do that if I were you Jack. You wouldn't like it in Ardingley. They play bridge and things and talk about Japanese Noh theatre. They also have real regimental buttons on their blazers. And we really don't want anybody else getting shot now, do we?'

'Are you threatening me Eddie?'

'Threaten you, Jack? *Me?* Good God no. I just don't want you to become a social misfit. It can be so embarrassing.'

# Chapter 9

Sergeant Brendan O'Hara spoke slowly for the benefit of the portable tape recorder which lay on the hospital pillow beside Melanie Golding's bandaged head. 'Please repeat after me: "I, Melanie Golding, wish to make a statement. I make it of my own free will knowing that it may be tendered in evidence and that I shall be liable to prosecution if it contains anything which I know to be false or do not believe to be true."'

After the recital, he said, 'Do you understand that?'

'Oh yes,' said Melanie Golding, 'I understand that very well. I may be sick but I am not stupid.'

'Good,' said Brendan O'Hara from his bedside chair, 'Now this: "When making this statement I realise that my life is in danger and that I may not survive until such time as it is given in evidence. I appreciate that, under the rules of evidence, this statement may be received by a court as evidence in the event of my death. In so far as it may be relevant it is my express wish that this should occur in any trial relating to the events described in this statement." Do you understand that?'

'Oh yes,' said Melanie Golding again, 'I understand that very well. Should I start now?'

'Whenever you're ready.'

'Right,' said Melanie Golding. 'On Friday the twenty-second of October of last year I attended my lectures at the London University School of Politics and Philosophy. I left in the afternoon at about five p.m., having decided to cut my last lecture on Schopenhauer to return home to write an essay.

'On my way back I stopped at the small supermarket at the corner of Marsh Lane run by Mr Ranjit. I always shop there. He is expensive but he works late hours and supports five children in Bangladesh. By the time I left the shop it was quite dark. As I walked along Marsh Lane I sensed that I was being watched. I cannot describe why but I simply knew that somebody was watching me. I was not frightened as I could see several other people walking towards me from the end of the lane. As I passed them I could see clearly that they were young men, approximately eighteen to twenty years old. One white and two West Indian.

Shortly afterwards I turned into the front gate of 14 Marsh Lane, which is a house converted into flats and in which I have the first floor. I opened the front door and definitely closed it behind me. I did not turn on the light in the hall but looked back through the stained glass window which forms the upper part of the door. My view of the street was, of course, blurred but I distinctly saw a figure move across the front of the house and disappear towards the end of the lane where an alleyway connects the road to the open marshland. This extends along the back of Marsh Lane at the end of the gardens. The balcony of my bedroom overlooks this area. I turned on the light, climbed the stairs, unlocked and opened the door of my flat and closed and locked it behind me.'

'Do you always lock it?' said Sergeant O'Hara.

'Never normally. I hate locked doors. I went into the kitchen and unpacked the groceries. I had the normal things, milk, some tea, some bread. I also had the makings of a stew, as my godparents, the Stokers, were coming to lunch on the Sunday. I was still a little uneasy after my experience in the street and I imagined that I heard a noise coming from my bedroom. It was very faint and stopped immediately. I thought then that it was my imagination (and indeed I still do). I made myself some tea and some toast, went into my living room, turned on the television and watched the news. Afterwards (it would have been seven p.m. or thereabouts) I made myself another cup of tea and went into the bedroom in order to change into my tracksuit which I wear in the evenings if I am working. As soon as I entered the bedroom I noticed that the balcony doors were open. This was not unusual. I sleep with the doors open and frequently forget to close them in the morning when I leave. I like open doors and I like fresh air. I changed out of my clothes, my jeans, shirt and sweater, and went into the bathroom to shower. The shower is part of the bath itself and protected by a shower curtain which can be drawn the length of the tub. Whilst in the shower, of course, I could hear nothing in the flat. After several minutes, I turned off the water, left the shower, put on my tracksuit and went back into the bedroom to start work at my desk. I was writing an essay on Kierkegaard.

'How do you spell that?'

'K-i-e-r-k-e-g-a-a-r-d.'

'Who is he?'

'He was a nineteenth-century Danish philosopher. He was a wonderful man, free-thinker, the last of the ontologists. Do you know how he proved the existence of God?'

'Tell me,' said Sergeant O'Hara.

'He wrote, "If there is no God, to whom should I make my complaint?" Isn't that brilliant?'

'I don't know,' said the police officer. 'I am a Jesuit.'

Melanie Golding looked up from the pillow, smiled and continued. 'It was quite warm and I left the balcony doors open. I sat down at my desk, with my back to the doors and turned on my computer. I had already made the notes and I intended to work from them for a couple of hours before going to bed. The machine makes a quite audible high-pitched hum. I find it irritating so I turned on my radio and tuned to the independent classical station where they were playing extracts from Brahms' Symphonies. I kept the radio soft as the balcony doors were open. This was not really necessary as my downstairs neighbour, Mr Stoppard, is quite deaf and the people upstairs were away. I worked for about an hour, then I made myself a cup of coffee and poured myself a glass of wine. I returned to my desk and had been working for about another twenty minutes, sufficient time to finish the wine, when I became absolutely certain that someone, or something was in the room behind me.'

'Did you hear them?'

'No, at first I heard nothing at all, but I had an overwhelming sense of *presence*. I sat very still and concentrated on the keys of my computer.'

'Were you frightened?'

'No, not at all. I know it is extraordinary but I felt, suddenly, amazingly *calm*. I also felt completely detached. It was as though I was watching myself from a position above my head. Visually everything became startling clear. I can remember noticing that one of the letters on the keyboard (the "k" I think) was beginning to fade, and I can remember thinking, absurdly, that I should repair it with ink or graphite. Then I saw his reflection.'

'There is a mirror?'

'No, but I have on my desk a brass lamp. It is, in fact, a converted shell-case. Jim Stoker gave it to me for a birthday. The surface is highly polished and lacquered. The reflection is, of course, on a curved surface and distorted, but movement is immediately apparent.'

'You saw something move?'

'Quite clearly. I saw one figure which moved slightly towards me. I continued to sit very still and then something came to me which I will never forget.' Melanie Golding's voice, previously firm and conversational, faltered and stopped. Alarmed, Sergeant Brendan O'Hara watched tears begin to form in her eyes, and instinctively he reached for the girl's hand which lay on the reversed sheet of the hospital bed.

Melanie Golding smiled. 'It's all right, I can finish this but then I would like a break.'

'Of course. Can you tell me what you noticed that was so strong?'

'It was the smell,' said Melanie Golding. 'So strong, so overpowering. I think, please, I would like to stop there. I need some sleep.'

# Chapter 10

At 2.15 Court One of the Old Bailey was fully assembled and Mr Justice Phillips took his seat. Over three hundred people listened in cathedral silence as the judge arranged his papers, opened a new notebook with a faint snap and turned to counsel's benches. 'Yes, Sir Edward.'

So began the Trial of the Century, presided over by a judge who knew little or nothing about crime. It placed upon trial a mentally and physically disabled hero who had confessed to a crime which he did not commit and a deranged psychopathic killer who had not confessed to the same crime which he most certainly did commit. Against the first, a born Olympian deprived by bloody accident of the power to defend himself, the evidence of fact and circumstance provided an overwhelming and crushing weight. Against the second, a born villain, the evidence extended barely beyond a page of newsprint conjured from deliberate deception and falsehood to achieve a greater truth. Against the first, the State, which he had served and for which he had sacrificed his body and his mind, pursued conviction, condemnation and shame. Against the second, agents of the same State worked in dark concert to procure his liberty and compound their debts. And all the while the Delphic oracle of Truth lay in her coma, watched day and night by an Irish copper who might once have been a priest.

Thus above the proceedings in Court One the forces of Truth and Justice, Power and State, Goodness and Evil, Conscience, Punishment and Pain were locked like jealous Homeric Gods. And of this the jury of five men and seven women upon whose simple verdicts rested the hopes of gods and men remained in total and complete ignorance.

Like a giant cormorant Sir Edward Boyd rose above his lectern, re-assembled the row of gold pens which glittered against the green baize, selected one and, with exquisite care, effected a small, unnecessary, alteration on a page in a ring binder beside him. As he did so the silence in Court One of the Old Bailey, already profound, became grey with intensity. Slowly the bloodhound eyes rose to meet those of the jury and he began.

'Ladies and gentleman of the jury, in this case I appear to prosecute, together with my learned junior Miss Antonia Black. In a moment I will introduce those who represent the defendants and outline the facts, but first a word about the nature of this case and the notoriety it has achieved. This is a case of kidnapping, rape and murder. In the dock are two men,' he paused and raised a left hand, causing twelve pairs of eyes uncontrollably to swivel towards the object of his observation, 'very different in character and appearance. The first defendant alone is charged with all these offences. The second defendant is charged only with that of kidnapping. However, you may feel when the facts are known to you that he bears a heavy responsibility for the tragic deaths that occurred. You all read the newspapers and will be aware that the facts behind this trial have been widely reported. Indeed, some of the press have been preoccupied with little else. As a result of this you must be aware that the allegations in this trial concern the kidnapping, in October last year, of Melanie Golding, the daughter of Mr Justice Golding, a judge of the High Court. That kidnapping, say the prosecution, was carried out by the first defendant, acting on the instructions of the second defendant. The defendants, as I say, are very different men. The first, you may think, is a poor creature, disabled and, some may say, hideously deformed. But, for all that (and, in part, because of that), he is a man of impeccable background and character. The second defendant, say the prosecution, is a gangster. A man steeped in crime and villainy. In normal circumstances, ladies and gentlemen, such matters would be concealed from you. Your deliberations would take place in ignorance of the criminal background and propensities of those in your charge. In this trial that background forms an essential part of the case. It was, indeed, the principal spring and motivation which lies behind these terrible crimes.

'The first defendant's name is Thomas Aylen. He sits on the extreme left of the dock as you observe it and is represented by my learned friend Miss Jane Wilson QC and her junior, Mr Gilbert Smith. Let me say straight away that the appearance of the first defendant is, to say the least, unfortunate.' (Within the jury box several eyes shifted uncomfortably to the dock, hesitated, blinked and returned to those of Sir Edward Boyd.) 'That appearance is not only a grave misfortune but was caused, let me tell you at once, during the course of dedicated and loyal service to this country in Northern Ireland. Nearly three years ago whilst serving in the Marines he took it upon himself to examine a car parked on a road in the County of Armagh on a route which would, shortly thereafter, have been travelled by a local bus, full of people. The car was booby-trapped and the injuries which he sustained were quite ghastly, resulting in what is self-evident today. Why do I mention this terrible circumstance? It has relevance for three reasons. First it is a matter which you can, of course, if you wish, place to his credit.' (Within the jury box several heads nodded in agreement.) 'But the second matter of relevance is emphatically to his discredit. It is idle to suggest that he does not know of the grotesque, indeed horrific, nature of his appearance. He it was, the Crown will say and prove, who carried out the actual abduction of Melanie Golding in the dark of the night in October last year. Imagine, if you will, how much worse that ordeal must have been made (at least initially) by the knowledge that she was in the power not only of an abductor but of one whose aspect brings to mind the famous grotesques of literature. The third matter of relevance concerns his meeting with the second defendant. For it was during the course of his rehabilitation at a college in Bournemouth that he met his co-accused, a very different man.

'Let me now turn to the second defendant, Roddy Nailor, who is represented by my learned friend Mr John Wilkin and his junior, Preston Lodge. As I have already said, I will deal in some detail with his criminal past. As I have also said (which I now emphasise again), that past is relevant only because it establishes clearly the motive and indeed the mainspring behind the crime with which we are now concerned. The abducted girl was, as you know, the daughter of a distinguished High Court judge. That judge, Mr Justice Golding, presided over Roddy Nailor's last trial, over ten years ago, in this very court building. He was sentenced to fifteen years' imprisonment. As you will already have realised, the crime for which he was sentenced was serious indeed. He, no doubt together with others, had kidnapped a Chinese man by the name of Lin Won-Ki and inflicted upon him grave injuries which culminated in both his feet being nailed to the floor of a warehouse in London.'

Sir Edward Boyd paused and was pleased to notice expressions of shock and disgust from three of the jury. Two others, he observed, glanced quickly at the dock, the compulsive, fascinated search for the definitive appearance of evil. Sir Edward Boyd's great head remained unmoved. The pause was intentional but restrained and the Olympian gravitas rigidly maintained.

Five words followed before the interruption. 'It is for that crime ...'

The shout echoed immediately into the vaults of the court. Roddy Nailor, on his feet, one arm thrust out pointing at the side of Sir Edward Boyd's yellowing wig. Roddy Nailor's face contorted with the uncontrolled venom of the deranged. 'It's a fucking lie! A fucking lie! I was stitched up by that fucking bastard.'

Roddy Nailor's arm described a flat arc, his finger stabbing the air in the precise direction of Superintendent Eddie Cole sitting, impassive, on the benches reserved for the police. One dock officer, already on his feet, moved towards Nailor and took his arm, which was to be his last recollection for some hours as Nailor's forehead crashed into his own, rendering him instantly senseless on the floor of the dock. Brief fighting ensued, moving backwards in the dock and through the door which gave on to the stairs to the cells. In the court the sounds of mayhem receded gradually into a collective stillness. In the public gallery murmuring fell away as the eyes of Mr Justice Phillips swivelled across it. Several jurors appeared shaken. One began to cry. Sir Edward Boyd, motionless, continued to hold the jury. John Wilkin QC, representing Roddy Nailor, rose slowly to his feet, anticipating command. Mr Justice Phillips spoke softly into the void.

'Mr Wilkin, I will rise for fifteen minutes. At the conclusion of that time I would like you to tell me whether your client proposes to spend the rest of this trial in the dock or in a cell. At the moment, and in the interests of justice, he still retains a choice. That choice will not survive a further volcanic eruption.'

After the judge and jury had left, the court filled with chatter and the nervous laughter of tension relieved.

Sir Edward Boyd spoke to his friend John Wilkin. 'Clever chap your client, thoughtful.'

John Wilkin smiled without humour. 'Cerebral, deeply cerebral.'

# Chapter 11

When the court resumed Sir Edward Boyd continued his opening to the jury; seamless narrative punctuated only by solicitous enquiry designed to establish between himself and his listeners the Delphic relationship that would ensure, throughout the trial, his implicit and calm authority. Sir Edward Boyd was in control. He did not merely sound reasonable, he radiated rationality. Above all the mantle of Fairness lay upon him like his silk gown which glowed gently in the dull light of the afternoon court. From him fell repeated exhortations on the dangers of premature judgement – 'Ladies and gentlemen of the jury, beware of this evidence and weigh it carefully. Remember that when it is tested by the skill of my learned friends in cross-examination. Events proceed quickly. Mistakes can easily be made, even by the most honest observer.' When he made these observations he would smile at the jury, a smile so wise and yet so sad that it invited, and invariably received, silent nods of approval and considered mutual trust. So *fair*, so *even-handed*, so . . . *wise*. It is possible, years later, that some of this jury might come to suspect, or even to realise, that those passages of the evidence which were most solemn, most *fair*, were of virtually no consequence to the prosecution case. And then there was compassion. In unveiling allegations of fearful depravity and violence no anger emerged from Sir Edward Boyd. Rather a sadness, a weary heartfelt acknowledgement of the painful wickedness of the world. And sometimes an air of incredulous, bewildered perplexity. 'Ladies and gentlemen, this act, this terrible act, through lust, revenge, depravity or sickness of mind? Who knows? Who knows?'

Later, much later, some of the jurors would reflect on the effect of those sad, rhetorical enquiries. 'Well,' they thought, looking across the court, '*he* may not know, this decent, kind, honourable, *fair*, lugubrious, charming, knowledgeable, (really quite handsome) Queen's Counsel, *he* may not know but *we* know. Lust and depravity, that's what it is.'

And so, with meticulous care and meticulous accuracy, Sir Edward Boyd from reason created prejudice, from even-handedness created the partisan. From his very fairness he created the desire for retribution. Melanie Golding could rely on *them*. Melanie Golding would be avenged.

Sir Edward had covered the discovery of the kidnap. Within their bundles the jury were directed to the photographs of Melanie Golding's flat. They were directed to the upturned chair, the student's notes in disarray. Also the posters and the pictures pinned upon the wall. 'How much of this disarray, this . . . *mess* was caused in the abduction, and how much simply the normal scattered ephemera of a busy, disorganised and, by all accounts, brilliant student life, is of course impossible to assess in the absence of Melanie Golding herself.' Polite smiles from the jury. He is so *fair*, so eloquent and *fair*. Sir Edward continued, 'You will hear, ladies and gentlemen, from Mr Justice Elias Golding, a High Court judge, indeed *the* High Court judge who sentenced Mr Nailor so many years ago thus providing, say the Crown, the motive for this terrible crime. But remember, ladies and gentlemen, in *fairness* to the defendants, he is a father like any of us, and if he appears to be distraught, distressed, it is bound to awaken feelings in all of us, but do not . . .' Sir Edward's voice became grave, '. . . do not allow those feelings of sympathy, empathy, to introduce prejudice against these men.' Sir Edward smiled, the jury nodded and the damage was done.

Sir Edward continued. He dealt with the searches, with the exhibits, most of scant relevance, discovered at the scene. 'All, save one.' He paused and concentration deepened. 'Found at the scene was something else. Something of crucial importance in this trial and critical to the case against Roddy Nailor. It is in itself a surprising exhibit. It is *this*.' So saying, Sir Edward Boyd reached behind him, confident that his junior, Miss Antonia Black, would place unbidden between his fingers Exhibit 629A, which he then held aloft between thumb and forefinger. 'A newspaper, as you can see; a copy of the *Evening News* dated the twenty-seventh February 1988, but it has a special significance, or rather, to be accurate, two matters of special significance. First, it contains within it an article by the second defendant, Roddy Nailor. That article has been copied for you and is at page 368 of your jury bundle. Do *not* look at it now, please,' said Sir Edward, as hands reached compulsively for the ring binders set out on the jury desk, 'it is enough that I tell you that the article concerns the nineteenth-century philosophers Friedrich Nietzsche and Georg Hegel. Some of you may be conversant with these philosophers. But I suspect that some of you will not [polite smiles]. It may be that the content and burden of their philosophies will have some relevance in the trial; however, for the moment the significance is simply the authorship of this article. Ladies and gentlemen, you will ask yourselves, immediately, what has a man who, we are told, is a gangster, steeped in villainy and violence, to do with articles on nineteenth-century mid-

European moral philosophy? The answer is simple. Shortly before his release Mr Nailor had the good fortune to be accepted on what I believe is called a Day Release Course at a college in Bournemouth. Indeed he was to be awarded qualifications. It was at that college, ladies and gentlemen, that he met Thomas Aylen, his co-accused. Mr Aylen was there for a quite different purpose, namely rehabilitation. A course to re-learn the skills violently torn from him in the explosion to which I have referred.'

The jury were silent, watching. They were working it out. Sir Edward helped them. 'And so, members of the jury, what a coincidence is here. Here is the man, Aylen, who we can prove beyond any doubt (and almost certainly beyond any argument from my learned friends) was the actual abductor of Melanie Golding. The man, indeed, as you will hear, who is *found to be* her kidnapper at the dreadful ending of this criminal venture. What a coincidence that Roddy Nailor should be at the same institution at the same time as that man, the man who abducts the daughter of the judge who sentenced Roddy Nailor to fifteen years' imprisonment in 1978. What a coincidence is this? Ladies and gentlemen,' Sir Edward's voice dropped an octave, 'you will remember please, *in fairness* to the defendants, that if coincidences did not exist the word coincidence would not exist either. There are cruel tricks of fate which cause the finger of suspicion unjustly to point to those who are innocent. You will bear this in mind at all times in *fairness* to them.' Several of the jury cast glances of overt hostility towards the dock. They had the point. 'But the coincidence is not all.' Slowly, Sir Edward opened the transparent plastic folder and extracted a copy of the *Evening News*. As he did so he pointed to blotches of what appeared to be red ink covering the front page. 'These, members of the jury, are the unmistakable traces of the fingerprint expert's work. And whose are these fingerprints? They are the fingerprints of Roddy Nailor. Of even more significance is this. Pinned to the top of the newspaper is a handwritten note on a scrap of paper. It simply has upon it two words, "Page 4". It is upon page four that the article is written. Ladies and gentlemen, the writing on this short document is of crucial importance to the case. You will hear evidence from an expert that this writing is almost certainly that of Roddy Nailor himself. Now look, if you would, at the newspaper itself which I hold up before you. Plainly it has been folded into four. The creases are still apparent, and, indeed, at one edge the creases have become tears. Please understand that what I say to you now is an hypothesis. It is only a theory. But it may well be that this newspaper was folded thus in order to be placed into a convenient envelope known as quarto size.' Reaching behind him, Sir Edward produced magically just such an envelope, to which he compared the newspaper before the jury's eyes. 'This, of course, is only an envelope. It does not otherwise figure in the case. It is correct to say that no such envelope was found at Melanie Golding's flat. But is it not likely that this envelope would have been destroyed? If it was not sent by post then it arrived at her flat by some other means. Perhaps carried by Aylen who was her abductor. But, by whatever method, a newspaper which once belonged to Roddy Nailor, which has upon it his undoubted fingerprints, which carries a document with his handwriting, has been found at the flat of Melanie Golding. Why? The Crown say that there can only be one reason. This newspaper was sent, or carried, with the intention that it should convey some form of threat. Some form of sinister frightening message. A message which could no doubt be summarised thus: "Roddy Nailor, the gangster whom your father sentenced, is now free or about to be free." Alternatively it is possible to suggest that the very content of the article itself contains a threat. This may be far-fetched but it is a possibility which cannot and should not be overlooked. The article deals largely with the philosopher Friedrich Nietzsche. In due course the Crown will call an expert on the writings of this gentleman, but it is enough for me to say at this stage that Mr Nietzsche put forward the idea that there existed, within mankind, a race of Supermen. Men not subject to the normal rules, the normal restrictions on behaviour, normal ethics, and normal considerations of other men. They exist above mankind as a species. Because of this status they may do as they please. This is the message contained within the article written by Roddy Nailor, and may be, I say only *may be*, intended as some form of warning. Bear in mind, please, that the prosecution say only that this *may be*. It must be rare indeed that a prosecution points to a motive embedded within the body of nineteenth-century philosophy. In these courts we are lawyers, not philosophers. We deal in fact, not fantasy [smiles all round], and in *fairness* to these defendants you must examine the possibilities of that motive with every great care. However, it is right that you bear it in mind.

'Now, members of the jury, I will come to the terrible events which followed. The events which led to the final bloody apprehension of the first defendant and the tragic deaths which occurred.' Sir Edward paused, glanced at the court clock and effected a look of surprise. 'My Lord, I see the time has reached four fifteen . . .'

'Very well, Sir Edward,' said Mr Justice Phillips, 'that would be a convenient moment to rise.' The judge turned to the jury. Ladies and gentlemen, this ends what has been for you the first day of the trial. Do bear in mind that what you have heard so far is not evidence, it is simply the opening of the prosecution. In fairness to the defendants, do not reach any conclusions until such time as you have heard the evidence and, preferably, all of the evidence.' The jury nodded as their minds closed. 'Do not talk about this case to anybody outside your own number because they may attempt to influence you, having not heard the evidence. If you discuss it amongst yourselves, keep an open mind.'

Mr Justice Phillips rose and a packed courtroom rose with him. He disappeared from view and entered the judge's corridor behind the courts. After a short distance he encountered his fellow judge, Mr Justice Curtis, also leaving his court, and the two men fell into step towards their respective rooms.

'Well, how's it going?'

'Edward Boyd's doing his usual job. The milk of human kindness is dripping from his fangs.'

# Chapter 12

James Cameron was unusually excited. 'We've got him!' he said to John Wilkin and Preston Lodge. 'We've got him absolutely cold.'

'Go on,' said John Wilkin. 'It isn't by any chance going to make this trial shorter, is it?'

'It may well do. I have heard from the Governor at Grafton Hall Open Prison. They have managed to find the records of prisoners' letters and postage which relate to last February. It was just a hunch. I never knew they kept them and neither did Nailor. But they do. The prisoners don't know it, but they do.'

Preston Lodge leant forward and tapped the desk. 'The newspaper.'

'Exactly. The newspaper.'

'Somebody help me?' said John Wilkin.

'Eddie Cole says he found the newspaper in Melanie Golding's flat. And that it's got Nailor's fingerprints on it, and it *does*. Nailor's explanation, which we haven't told anybody yet, is that he sent a copy of his newspaper to Eddie Cole by way of an unpleasant joke, together with a short note. Nailor says Cole planted that newspaper. Which is why it has got Nailor's dabs on it. So far we have only got Nailor's word for it. But now we've got *this*.' James Cameron took a number of documents from a folder before him, extracted a facsimile copy and passed it to John Wilkin.

'It's the fifth entry down. That's the log of prisoners' letters. Normally they only log the envelope and the address, together with the description such as "personal letter". In this case it was clearly a copy of the newspaper because he needed a special envelope. So what is recorded is "Superintendent E. Cole, Serious Crime Squad. Copy *Evening News*".'

John Wilkin read the entry with exaggerated care. When he looked up his soft, pink face was a smile of content. 'This is wonderful, absolutely wonderful. Do we have a statement to prove it?'

'Being made by the Assistant Prison Governor even as we speak.'

'Cole is finished. Cole is finished: this is the end.'

'Nemesis by newspaper.'

Preston Lodge spoke. 'Sorry to interrupt the general joy. But how do we use it? As I see it we can either show this to the Crown and hope to bring the whole trial grinding to a halt now or we can wait until Cole gives evidence in two, three days' time, then break him in cross-examination. We have a choice.'

John Wilkin looked closely at his junior. 'You are the criminal expert, Preston, what do you think?'

'I favour cross-examination. If we give it to the Crown then they will investigate it. We won't be part of the process. They will want an adjournment. Other coppers will have to be drafted in to do it, another force probably. They may try to cobble together a case without a news-paper on the basis that Cole hasn't yet given evidence and is anyway not the senior officer in the case. Doubtful but possible. Anyway, messy. I say let Cole give evidence, prove the finding of the paper and then destroy him. The effect will be devastating. They could not possibly go on after perjury on that scale. In any event it passes into the hands of the judge who would never let it continue. So we wait for three days, get in perfect order, statements ready, then we crush him.'

John Wilkin turned to his instructing solicitor. 'What do you think, James?'

'I agree with Preston.'

'Good, I agree too. Wait three days, then goodbye Buster Cole, goodbye case. Preston, let us have a glass of Chablis if you would be so kind as to fetch and pour.'

As Preston Lodge assembled the glasses and began to fill them, John Wilkin relaxed into the leather of his chair, and smiled his cherubic smile and closed his eyes. 'Free,' he said softly, 'free at last.'

James Cameron looked up in surprise, 'I didn't think you cared for our client much.'

'Oh Cameron dear, not Nailor – not the client. Me, my wives, my children.'

# Chapter 13

Melanie Golding and Sergeant Brendan O'Hara were talking about Nietzsche. More accurately, Melanie Golding was talking about Nietzsche, and Sergeant Brendan O'Hara was listening. He had arrived early and found her propped on her pillows and staring across the hospital lawns. She looked at him carefully.

'Sergeant O'Hara, indeed. We were talking.'

'Yes, we were talking yesterday. I was taking a statement from you. You were kidnapped, abducted. We were talking about Thomas Aylen. You became very upset and we had to stop. If you remember they gave you an injection.'

Melanie Golding smiled. 'Mr O'Hara . . .'

'Brendan.'

'Brendan, I remember so little. Do you understand? It is like living in fog. Sometimes, suddenly, it lifts and I can see completely clearly. Yes it *is* like that. It is visual. There is a sudden clarity of images and sensation. You see, I *know* I cannot remember. It is strange, weird. If I know I cannot remember, *why* can't I remember? If I know something is not there, if I know there is something missing, then it must be there, mustn't it? *Cogito ergo sum.*'

'Descartes,' said Brendan O'Hara.

Melanie Golding looked up from her pillow. 'Yes, Brendan, yes. I did not know you were a philosopher.'

'I am a Catholic,' said Brendan O'Hara, 'a Jesuit.'

Melanie Golding eyes widened. 'Ah, the sworn enemy.'

'Enemy of what?'

'Secular reason, rationality.'

Brendan O'Hara smiled. 'We are not all so blind.'

Melanie Golding suddenly became intense. 'You see, it is relevant, isn't it? I cannot remember. I know something terrible happened to me. Something else too. I don't only feel fear. There is something else, something powerful. I can't identify it. But I know it's there. What is important, Brendan, is this, isn't it; when I remember, then what I remember must be the truth. The words, the images, have not been distorted, disfigured by recent memories. There is nothing I *want* to be true or do *not want* to be true. It is there, inside me, like a lost book, a lost documentary record, accurate, contemporaneous, unassailable.'

'Would it help if I read you what you have already told me?'

'No, for exactly that reason.'

'Or,' said Sergeant Brendan O'Hara softly, 'if I told you the results of the medical tests that have been carried out?'

On the pillow Melanie Golding shook her head violently. 'No, no. Don't you see, if I am told part of the story, or even part of the results, then my imagination will work. And when memory comes there will be a blurring, a distortion, between the real and the imagined.'

'Does it help to talk at all?'

'I think so, and I like you being here ... Brendan. I feel safe. I have no pain.'

An idea came to Brendan O'Hara. 'When you read your philosophy, did you study Nietzsche?'

'Friedrich Nietzsche? Oh yes. A monster.'

'Why? What did he do that was so terrible?'

'He created a philosophy in which there is a moral vacuum. He postulates the existence of human beings who are beyond convention, beyond law, beyond social inhibition, beyond what he would describe as the cluttered instincts of the herd. These human beings, these Supermen, are devoid of self-doubt, self-analysis, beyond even self-belief (which presupposes a positive effort of belief).'

'Such people exist,' said Brendan O'Hara, 'we call them psychopaths.'

'Yes and no,' said Melanie Golding. 'It is true that your psychopaths are so defined because it appears to us that they had no conscience, no guilt. But they *lie*, do they not, Brendan?'

'Oh yes,' said Sergeant Brendan O'Hara, 'they lie all right.'

'Why?'

'What, when they are caught? To avoid being convicted.'

'Convicted and what?'

'Sentenced.'

'Yes, and why do they seek to avoid sentence?'

Brendan O'Hara looked at the grey eyes, staring at him from the pillow, and thought, 'My God, this is a beautiful woman.' Aloud he said, 'Fear?'

'Precisely,' said Melanie Golding. 'Fearful Gods are no Gods at all.'

'Who said that?'

'I did,' said Melanie Golding. 'To be charitable to Nietzsche, his Supermen are philosophical concepts. It is possible to interpret his writings psychologically. A recognition of the moral deficit in us all. The longing in us all to be Olympian. To possess the ultimate power of not caring about anything. No fear, no punishment. Indifference to conscience, indifference to pain. Indifference to emotional investment or emotional blackmail. Indifference to self.'

'Indifference to enjoyment?'

'Ah, "is Nietzsche's Superman hedonistic? – discuss." The answer is, I think, "if he wants to be." But that begs the interesting question of *want* without *desire*. Can one desire without caring whether the desire will be fulfilled? If one desires and cares that it is fulfilled then that, in itself, presupposes *disappointment*. Can God be disappointed? Can a Superman acknowledge the "pangs of unrequited love"? How can one *want* whilst being indifferent to the object of wanting? You tell me, Brendan. You are the Jesuit.'

Brendan O'Hara smiled. 'I am also just a copper.'

Melanie Golding's grey eyes set on the face of the policeman above her. It was an Irish face. Dark, wide-eyed. A large mouth, curled hair. Romany perhaps. A tinker's great-grandson. Melanie Golding said, 'I think you're more than just a copper, Brendan.'

Brendan O'Hara felt himself flush. 'I don't think so,' he said, leaving his chair and walking to the window. Before him the grounds of the Military Hospital stretched to the institutional fencing, beyond which the road to London could be seen between the trees. In the flower beds set within the lawns men were planting mature shrubs. 'Azaleas,' said Brendan O'Hara softly.

Behind him he heard a sudden intake of breath. Turning quickly he said, 'What is it?'

'It's coming, Brendan, I can see it. I can remember.'

# Chapter 14

The court sat late. It was 11 a.m. before the jury filed into the jury box to hear Mr Justice Phillips say, 'Ladies and gentlemen, I am sorry that we are late in starting. There were, I understand, some legal difficulties to be resolved between counsel in the case. We are now ready to proceed. Yes, Sir Edward?'

Sir Edward Boyd, already standing behind his lectern, nodded to the judge and re-asserted his control. He allowed a moment's silence before saying, 'Good morning, members of the jury.'

The jury in the Trial of the Century was estimated by the press to have an average age of thirty-five. Faced by Sir Edward Boyd, most were reduced irresistibly to their early classrooms. For a moment they sat cross-legged in short trousers and blue skirts on the shining parquet floor of the school hall as they said, dutifully, 'Good morning.'

Sir Edward continued his narrative. 'After the kidnap, ladies and gentlemen, there was, of course, widespread police activity. You will not have heard of it because there was an embargo on the news. Nonetheless, after nearly three weeks the police were no nearer to solving this terrible mystery. After three weeks, you will hear, officers of the Special Branch became involved. This, as you may know, is an elite part of our police machinery.'

Sitting behind Sir Edward Boyd, Eddie Cole's ugly face became an unstoppable and hideous grimace.

'Shortly afterwards the police had their first stroke of luck. An anonymous informant provided information which proved to be all too dreadfully correct. As a result of that information, on the second of November last year armed officers of the Special Branch, together with police officers who had been investigating the case, surrounded a house, a quite normal suburban house, in the town of St Albans. May I ask you please to look in your bundle of photographs at photograph number sixteen.'

Six bundles of photographs were duly located and, upon turning to number 16, the jury looked down at an unremarkable detached residence set behind a privet hedge and a lattice gate. The bourgeois embodiment of conservative middle England.

'It is,' continued Sir Edward, 'an unlikely setting for the drama which followed. In order to understand the events which occurred, let me take you now to a plan of the house. Within your jury bundles would you turn please to page twenty-six.'

In the pause which followed as ring binders were assembled, Sir Edward turned to his junior, Miss Antonia Black. 'Is this going fast enough?'

'It's fine, stick at it.'

'Again, an entirely unremarkable house. At the top you see a plan of the upstairs bedrooms, four in all, the largest at the back. Below that you see a plan of the ground floor, two rooms and a kitchen. Between the rooms is a doorway. That gives on to steps which lead to the cellar. This had at some stage been used as a playroom. In October 1988 it was employed for a more sinister purpose.

'As a result of the information which they had received the officers in the case knew that the house contained five people. Melanie Golding, Thomas Aylen, and three other men who the Crown say were involved in the crime, all now dead.' Sir Edward paused and watched as the jury assimilated the first intimations of carnage.

'Also as a result of the information that they received, the officers thought they knew the whereabouts of all five people within the house. You will hear, ladies and gentlemen, from the officer in charge of this operation, Chief Superintendent Jack Wagner, what the police believed when they stormed these premises. If you turn to page twenty-seven you will see the same plan with initials to indicate the position of the occupants of this house *as the police believed*. In the back bedroom, the largest, you see the initials MG and TA. It was in this room, so the police believed, that Melanie Golding was being held, her immediate captor being the defendant Thomas Aylen. In the middle bedroom you see the initials HB. It was here that they believed Harry Bedser was sleeping, and in the front room the initials AJ and TJ, being Alan Jones and Terry Jones, who, say the prosecution, were armed and dangerous accomplices who had taken part in the abduction and subsequent imprisonment of Melanie Golding. That is what the police *believed* and thus it was that the decision was taken to storm the premises at four a.m. precisely. The timing is obvious, is it not, members of the jury. At that time of the year those engaged in the operation would have had the benefit of very early light and total surprise. Those inside the house were most likely to be unsuspecting and asleep. At four a.m. precisely six hand-picked officers from the Special Branch stormed the front door of the premises using a mechanical battering ram which, you may be surprised to learn, can remove the entire door frame in a matter of a split second. Simultaneously, three officers entered the rear of the premises using the same means. At the front and rear a further ten police officers, some from Special Branch and some from the Criminal Investigation Division, waited as reinforcements. You may imagine the scene, members of the jury, the terrible noise as the doors were shattered, the sudden rush of men, all armed, storming the stairs in order to attain the landing and the upper bedrooms where, they believed, the kidnappers and Melanie Golding were located. I emphasise *they believed*. In fact, as you will learn, that belief was a tragic error and the result was carnage. Within the space of minutes four people were dead and one was terribly injured.'

Sir Edward Boyd paused. The jury watched in silent awe, anticipating the meticulous dissection of mayhem and violence.

'In all *fairness* to the defendants, ladies and gentlemen, and, in particular, to the second defendant, remember that events such as these happen with enormous speed. Sometimes things may not appear as they seem. But we have the benefit of collective recollection, do we not? Five police officers, all members of the Special Branch, and also we will be assisted by evidence from two police officers from the CID, Detective Sergeant Brendan O'Hara and Superintendent Eddie Cole. These last two, you will hear, arrived somewhat later, and it is, perhaps, because of that late arrival that the most terrible misadventure occurred. For ease of reference I will refer to the first group of Special Branch officers as "the assault party". Mr O'Hara and Mr Cole I will refer to by name. When the officers give evidence, of course their names will be given to you, but, for the present, it is easier to treat them as a group. This group was led by Chief Superintendent Jack Wagner, who will be the final officer to give evidence. All the assault party were armed with handguns and wore protective clothing or, as it is sometimes referred to, flak jackets. At four a.m. precisely, as I have told you, the automatic battering ram was applied to the door of the house. The hydraulic mechanism operated perfectly, and with one blow the entire door effectively disappeared. The officers, you will remember, believed that all the members of the gang were in the upstairs rooms. Unhappily this turned out not to be the case. The two Jones brothers were asleep in the downstairs living room immediately to the right of the door and marked "A" on your plan. As the assault party moved across the hall shots came from this room and one of the police officers, Sergeant Davidson, was tragically struck on the right side of his face by a bullet which cost him his life. Two of the assault party returned fire and both brothers were killed. Post-mortem examination subsequently revealed that both men died from bullet wounds to the head. Undeterred, the assault party continued up the stairs – can you follow this on your plan, ladies and gentlemen – led by Chief Superintendent Wagner. Intent first on freeing the victim, they turned towards the rear bedroom where, they had been informed, Melanie Golding was being kept. The room was empty. In the meanwhile other officers had discovered a cellar door. From behind this male and female voices could be heard. Chief Superintendent Wagner was called down and gave the order that he should go first into the cellar alone. In this room he found Melanie Golding, lying on a bed and manacled to the pipework that ran behind it. In the same room, guarding her, was Thomas Aylen. The tragedy of this man's life has already been recorded by me. Good, decent and brave he once undoubtedly was. However, the depths to which he has sunk and the evil by which he is now possessed was demonstrated immediately. He was armed with this handgun.'

With precise assurance, Sir Edward reached behind him and was handed a transparent plastic wrapper.

'This,' he said, holding the package aloft, 'is a Smith and Wesson thirty-five. A deadly weapon of great power. So confronted, Jack Wagner, whose firearm was not to the ready, charged Aylen and knocked him to the ground before a shot could be fired. Aylen's firearm, you will hear, was subsequently found on the floor under the bed. Chief Superintendent Wagner stood above him ensuring that he could pose no further threat either to the police officers or to Melanie Golding herself. It was at this point that a terrible misadventure occurred. Super-intendent Cole, who had arrived late upon the scene, first climbed the stairs and was confronted by the man Bedser who had been hiding in the front bedroom. Undoubtedly he would have shot Mr Cole had he not been shot dead himself by an armed officer who had remained in the front bedroom. Having observed the death of Bedser, and without realising that the principal danger was effectively past, Superintendent Cole launched himself down into the cellar. There, unhappily, he cannoned into the back of Jack Wagner who, thrown momentarily off balance, fell across the floor. At that very moment, his own firearm discharged. By the most dreadful of all coincidences the bullet struck Melanie Golding at the side of her head, fracturing the skull and causing extensive haemorrhage which has, in turn, placed pressure on her brain and rendered her comatose to this day. By that bullet this tragic young woman has, perhaps, been robbed of her life or at least the enjoyment of it. Also, of far less significance, this trial has been robbed of the testimony of a victim who could have spoken in detail of the criminal acts which were perpetrated during the course of her abduction and subsequent imprisonment. One thing, however, is clear.' Sir Edward's voice fell an octave. The jury stiffened, instinctively braced for the awful. 'Upon subsequent medical examination it was revealed beyond doubt, that Melanie Golding had been the subject of sexual assault. Male spermatozoa were found within her body. Now, members of the jury, as you may well know, it is possible to identify with exactitude the person from whom those juices have flowed. In this case there is not the slightest doubt that the perpetrator of this rape upon a defenceless woman was the defendant Thomas Aylen.'

Two of the jury stared straight at Sir Edward. Three looked down towards the floor and one, a woman of perhaps fifty, carefully dabbed her eyes. Seven of the jury turned irresistibly to the grotesque face in the dock.

(Afterwards, in the Robing Room, Antonia Black was to say, 'Verdict assured. You should have *seen* the expression on their faces.')

'Well, members of the jury,' said Sir Edward, closing one ring binder which he replaced in a rack before selecting a second, larger file, 'that is the outline of this terrible case. Remember, as I have said, in *fairness* to the defendants, that these allegations must be proved beyond doubt, but, in reality, ladies and gentlemen, can there be a shred of doubt in this case? Let me tell you a little about the law.

'Kidnapping is the unlawful abduction of a human being against his or her will. That is simple. In this case there can be no doubt, can there, that a kidnapping occurred. The only conceivable issue lies in the identity of those who carried out the act. In the case of the second defendant, Aylen, there can be no doubt that it was he. He was arrested in the very room where this unfortunate girl had been kept. In the case of the defendant Nailor the matter is a little more complex but nonetheless clear. In order to commit any crime it is not necessary actually to be the person who wields the gun or the knife, or even the cheque book. It is enough that you have organised, counselled or procured a person to do so. That is the allegation against Nailor. His is the brain behind these offences. He the mastermind. The Crown, however, does not allege that he was a participant to rape. For it would be necessary for him to have foreseen the likelihood of such an act in addition to the abduction. There is no evidence upon which the Crown could rely for you safely to convict on that count.

'Next I come to murder. As I have told you, one police officer, Sergeant Davidson, was tragically killed during the course of this assault. He was not shot by Aylen. However, you may be clear that Aylen was a part of the same group. That the group were all armed. That they were determined to resist, together if necessary, the assault of the police and the release of their captive. If that is the case they were acting together; we lawyers say "in concert". If that be right, and you are sure that that is the case, then all are guilty. Aylen, as you know, is the sole survivor of that group. No murder charge is pursued against the second defendant. Perhaps you may think that is unfair. But there is no evidence that the second defendant was aware of the use of firearms by the actual abductors, or that they would show a joint determination to use them. In those circumstances, perhaps mercifully you may think [nods from the jury], no charge of murder is pursued against him.

'Finally, rape; rape is any unlawful penetration of the female vagina by the male penis. In this case there is no doubt that such sexual intercourse occurred since the residue of Aylen's semen was found within her body. Was it without her consent? You may think, ladies and gentlemen, that there is little better evidence of duress than the plain visible evidence that a woman has been tied, mercilessly, semi-naked and humiliated, to a bed.' Eleven jurors nodded and one unaccountably but definitely shook her head. It was no matter. It meant the same thing.

'And so, members of the jury, I come at last to the evidence. The first witness will be Mr Justice Elias Golding, a judge of the High Court and father of the victim of these crimes.'

# Chapter 15

'Do you want to start from the beginning?' said Brendan O'Hara as he pressed the record button.

'No,' said Melanie Golding. 'I remember it clearly, I remember what I've told you. I was in the flat. He was standing behind me.'

'Yes, yes,' said Brendan O'Hara. 'That is where we were. Can you remember what happened?'

'Yes, yes I can, quite clearly.'

'Do you want me to ask questions or will you just tell me?'

'It's all right, I can tell you. I could sense that he was behind me. I have a lamp, a table lamp, it is brass and made from an old shell-case. It was a present from my godparents, the Stokers. The surface is shiny and round but reflective and it is possible to see distorted images. In it I could clearly see a man, although I could not discern his size or shape. At first I thought he was black because the face appeared to be dark. But then I realised that the features were blurred. The eyes appeared white and I knew it was some form of mask.'

'How did you feel? I'm sorry, I'm sorry, go on.'

'No, please ask what you need to. It was curious, even then I felt no *fear*, none. Indeed it was the reverse. I felt a kind of warmth. It is difficult to describe. It was physical but also, in a way, heartening, *invigorating*. It was as one wakes up in a cold room in a hot country and opens the shutters. You are suddenly submerged in sunlight and warmth. It was the same. But above all there was *no fear*.'

'Did you feel that you knew him?'

'No, indeed I was quite certain that I did not know him in the sense of acquaintance, but the feeling, the sensation, was in some way familiar.'

'What did you do?'

'I sat up, quite straight. I felt myself squaring my shoulders, and then I spoke to him. I can tell you the exact words that I used. I said, "I do not think that you have come to hurt me."'

'What did he say?'

'Nothing, there was silence, so I said, *and I had no idea why*, I said, "I think it is you who have been hurt."'

'How remarkable.'

'Yes, isn't it? Knowing what I know now it was extraordinary. But I did say it.'

'Do you want to record it?'

'Yes, yes, of course, it's the truth.'

'It is just,' said Sergeant O'Hara, with some hesitation, 'that if you ever gave evidence, in court, people might find it difficult to believe.'

Melanie Golding's grey eyes widened with amusement. 'Sergeant O'Hara,' she said, 'people always believe in me. They know I am the truth.'

'But,' said Brendan O'Hara uncomfortably, 'this statement may have to be used on its . . .'

'If I die? That is what you mean, isn't it, Brendan? If I die, here, then you will have to try to use the statement without me. I know a little law. A statement made in contemplation of death. I know all that. But don't worry, Sergeant, if I tell the truth it will ring out from the page.'

'Go on,' said Sergeant Brendan O'Hara, 'tell me the truth. What happened then?'

'After I'd said that, about his being hurt, I saw the reflection begin to move towards me. I think I realised immediately that there was something wrong with his walk. There was a dragging sound. Now, of course, I know what it was, but even then I perceived some form of disability, of pain. It was as though one had seen, indistinctly, a wounded bird flapping in undergrowth, the same feeling of helpless sympathy. The reflection soon became too big for the surface of the lamp and all I could see was a blur of colour and movement. When he stopped I knew he was very close behind me. I could hear him breathe and then the smell. I mentioned the smell before, didn't I?'

Sergeant Brendan O'Hara nodded. 'Yes, you did.'

'It was extraordinary. I think perhaps it was the smell which stopped any fear. It was as though it were my smell. They say we all have our own scent but, except at its most extreme, we cannot smell it ourselves. But I felt as though this was *mine*. I had never smelt it before but it had an extraordinary familiarity. Not sweet, not bitter, not pungent, just human. I sat quite still and then said, "Tell me what you want."'

'Did he reply?'

'Yes, but not to the question. The next thing I saw was a hand come across my shoulder and reach towards the wall in front of my desk.'

'Was it gloved?'

'No, no, it was not *that* hand – I know now of course – no, this was his good hand.'

'His left hand?'

'Yes, Sergeant, do not prompt me. I will not make mistakes. It was his left hand, and I can remember thinking when I saw it, despite everything, despite my . . . predicament, I remember thinking how beautiful it was.'

'Beautiful?'

'Yes. Do not sound so shocked. I am telling you the *truth*, and it *was* beautiful. Strong, wide, large-boned.'

'Did he touch you?'

'No, no, not at all. He pointed beyond my desk to a Greek quotation I have upon the wall, and then he spoke. He spoke in Greek and he pronounced it perfectly. In order to do so, of course, it would be necessary to read and understand the script.'

'What did it say?' said Sergeant Brendan O'Hara.

'In Greek,' said Melanie Golding, 'it means, "Ignore the unwritten rules."'

'Did he say anything else?'

'Yes, yes. He said that. He said, "Ignore the unwritten rules."'

'It's a funny motto,' said Brendan O'Hara.

'It's my motto,' said Melanie Golding, 'I believe it, don't you?'

'Not really,' said Brendan O'Hara, 'but go on.'

'He then said, "Demosthenes".'

'The name of the author?'

'Well, he *thought* it was the author. Actually it's not but it doesn't matter. I can remembering thinking, bizarre isn't it, but I can, I thought "Rapists and murderers do not mention Demosthenes even in error." Strange, isn't it?'

'It is,' said Sergeant Brendan O'Hara. 'Yes, yes, it is.'

Melanie Golding's head turned on the pillow. Her eyes fixed on the window overlooking the hospital ground and there was silence.

'Go on, go on, please.'

'Don't rush me, Brendan. I am getting tired. It's beginning to go. I am losing the images.'

'Please, please,' said Sergeant Brendan O'Hara, now standing above her bed, 'please, Melanie, try.'

'I knew, I knew that I must turn round, and so I stood up and heard him take a pace backwards. Then I turned and looked straight at his face, only it was not his face because, as I knew, he was wearing a mask, it was a balaclava, and so I saw only his eyes. I realised immediately that there was, in reality, one eye. One, a poor attempted replica of the other, was obviously glass. The other looked into mine.'

'Can you describe it? What did you see?'

'Pain. I saw pain and something else, which I got to know later so well. It was surprise. The expression, you know, that you see on the face of a child, a baby, staring at things as though for the first time, waiting for instruction, waiting for identification. I don't know how long we stood like that, but it may have been minutes before I spoke.'

'What did you say?'

Melanie Golding gave a soft laugh. 'You will not believe this, Sergeant O'Hara, but I said, "Aren't you going to take your hat off?"'

'I don't believe you,' said Sergeant O'Hara.

'Yes, you do,' said Melanie Golding, 'for it is the truth. But the next bit is worse, if you are looking for something easy for your jury; the next bit I hardly believe myself. As he just stood there I reached out and took hold of the balaclava and lifted it from his head.'

Melanie Golding turned her head and looked at the window.

'What did you see?'

Melanie Golding said nothing. Brendan O'Hara leant forward with alarm as he watched her eyes slowly begin to close. Gently he lowered his head towards the pillow and said, 'Tell me, Melanie, you must tell me. I know it was a shock, grotesque.'

'No, no,' said Melanie Golding, her voice receding, 'it was wonderful.'

# Chapter 16

Elias Golding entered the witness box, called by Sir Edward Boyd himself. A stately forensic dance then ensued to the soft melody of mutual regard. Yes, he was a High Court judge, yes, he had had a long and distinguished career at the Bar – 'like yourself, Sir Edward, if I may say so.' Yes, he was Melanie Golding's father. He had brought her up in substantial part by himself after his wife departed.

'I do not wish to intrude, Sir Elias, but what was your relationship with your daughter? It may have some relevance.'

In the ensuing short pause, sympathy filled the court like a vessel.

'I . . . think we were quite close. Our politics did not entirely coincide but I believe that is almost normal.'

Watching the jury, Jane Wilson was pleased to observe that not all of them smiled. The girl with the earring scowled at the ceiling. 'I like her,' thought Jane Wilson, 'one of us.'

The duet continued. Yes, he had received the note while dining at the Garrick. Yes, that was his regular location on Friday evenings. Anyone observing him for a couple of weeks would know this to be the case. No, he did not open the document until the following morning. No, he did not realise the significance of the letter or that it related to his daughter.

'Forgive me, Sir Elias, but are you aware that the doorman himself has made a statement to the effect that he had told you the letter concerned your daughter?'

'I am aware of that statement. I cannot comment, of course, on its accuracy. All I can say is that it did not get through to me. I'm afraid I was in the middle of a rather engrossing conversation. Had I realised it concerned Melanie I would, of course, have read it. I assumed it was some kind of bill from the club.'

Mary Shelley leaned forward to speak into the ear of her leading counsel. 'He's lying, isn't he?'

Speaking from the side of her mouth, Jane Wilson replied, 'Of course he is, but it doesn't help us to point it out. The jury have the point.'

Mr Justice Golding's evidence finished on a somewhat subdued tone.

'When you discovered the contents of the letter the following morning, I think you phoned Melanie's flat and got permanent engaged tones?'

'I did.'

'And then placed the whole matter in the hands of the police?'

'First I went to see my neighbour, Lord Justice Stoker; you have a statement from him, I think. Then we went to Scotland Yard together.'

'Finally, Sir Elias, just this. It is admitted, but I ask you nonetheless. Was it you, ten years ago, who sentenced Roddy Nailor to fifteen years' imprisonment for grievous bodily harm?'

'It was.'

By agreement John Wilkin examined first and was brief. 'I have only one question. When you sentenced Nailor did he utter any threat or message, to yourself or anyone, or do anything other than, if I may use the expression, "go down quietly"?'

'He made no threat or menace. No trouble of any kind.'

'Thank you, Sir Elias.'

In the short pause that followed, Mr Justice Phillips looked down at counsel's bench. 'Do you have any cross-examination, Miss Wilson?'

'My Lord, I do. I am sorry, I was talking to my junior. Sir Elias, may I take you, I hope without causing any distress, to a photograph of your daughter's bedroom, taken on the Sunday following her disappearance. Do you have it? Now, you can see that the bed is in a state of disarray. Perhaps nothing unusual about this. In the foreground we see a number of cosmetic items scattered on the floor. Can you help us as to whether this would be normal?'

'I'm afraid I can't, no.'

'If you look carefully beside the bed, you will see an item lying beside the bedside table. Can you discern what it is?'

'It looks like an alarm clock.'

'Precisely, Sir Elias, I can tell you that it *is* an alarm clock. What we can see is the back of the alarm clock. The face is against the carpet and, I can tell you, it has been broken as though it has been crushed into the carpet itself. The time on the clock is eight minutes past nine.'

'I see.'

'Are you able to tell us if the alarm clock was normally in good, undamaged condition?'

'I cannot. I can only assume that it was.'

Sitting the second row of counsel's benches, Preston Lodge watched with interest. He knew Jane Wilson to be a fine, calculating advocate.

'Why,' he thought, 'has she asked such a crass question? There must be a reason.'

Jane Wilson, continuing, appeared to change the subject. 'You tell us that the kidnap note was delivered at eight forty-five. Thereafter, as I understand it, your evidence is that no telephone call was made to the flat by you until the following morning. Is that right?'

'Yes, that is right. Of course, with the benefit of hindsight . . .'

'I am not criticising, Sir Elias, I am simply attempting to ascertain these important times. In the morning the telephone was permanently engaged.'

'It was.'

'Precisely. We now know that the telephone wires had been cut at the point at which they entered the house, which caused the phone to appear busy or engaged.'

'I see.'

'What would you say if I suggested to you that the note was delivered very much later?'

'It was definitely not.'

'Definitely?'

'Because I remember precisely what time it was we sat down to dine. Eight thirty. When the note arrived I had not finished my first course, which had been placed upon the table when we sat down.'

'Sir Elias, is it not possible you are influenced by hindsight?'

Elias Golding looked at his inquisitor and narrowed his eyes. 'What are you suggesting? Oh, I see, I see where we are going. If the note was delivered at eight forty-five and the struggle took place at eight minutes past nine, I would have been told of the kidnap *before it had taken place*, that's it, isn't it? I could have stopped it.'

The jury, suddenly interested, stared fixedly at the witness box, and from some of them hostility emerged.

Jane Wilson continued, 'It is not for me to put speculation to you, Sir Elias, I simply elicit facts. However, since you raised the hypothesis, is it correct?'

'That seems very unlikely. Why should I receive a kidnap note before the kidnap takes place, in time to stop it?'

Mr Justice Phillips intervened. 'Sir Elias, please, I must ask you not to put questions to counsel. We are dealing with hypothesis which is, in any event, not a proper subject for cross-examination.' So saying the judge turned a stern gaze towards Jane Wilson.

Jane Wilson smiled her sweetest smile. 'Your Lordship is *absolutely* right. These are all matters of comment and argument rather than cross-examination. However,' she added smartly, turning once again to the jury and before the judge could intervene, 'since you do ask me a question, Sir Elias, I will respond. It is patently folly to provide you with a letter before the crime was committed. So either the participants are very foolish or else the timing of the abduction was for some reason delayed. Either by circumstance, or because *somebody did not do what they were supposed to do?*'

The judge's voice cracked with irritation. '*Miss Wilson*, you know perfectly well that is not a question, it is a comment.'

'I do apologise; one sometimes gives way to temptation.'

'Resist it, Miss Wilson, *resist it.*'

'That was absolutely brilliant,' said Mary Shelley between mouthfuls of a bacon sandwich.

'Thank you, Frankenstein,' said Jane Wilson. 'We didn't establish much but the guns have started firing.'

The two women were seated on either side of Jane Wilson's desk. Also present, eating lunch out of paper bags, were Gilbert Smith and his new pupil Anthea Gray.

'Did you enjoy yourself, Anthea? Any problems?'

Jane Wilson believed in using barrister's pupils. 'Ask for their opinion,' she would frequently say. 'If you listen to them they will tell you what the jury are thinking.'

'I enjoyed it very much,' replied Anthea Gray. 'The judge seemed to get rather angry with us. I thought it was quite unfair.'

Jane Wilson smiled. 'Good. Let's hope the jury think so. Actually it was perfectly fair. I was breaking the rules and we all knew it. You are not supposed to use cross-examination for making comments. However, if you judge it right you can often persuade your witness to comment to you. Elias Golding couldn't restrain himself from telling me that my timings were unlikely. This enables me to comment back.'

'It's better than that,' said Gilbert Smith. 'The whole idea has now been placed into the jury's mind that somebody (obviously our man) was not doing what was expected of him. Now they can work it out for themselves.'

'And what people work out for themselves,' said Mary Shelley, 'they are much more likely to believe.'

'What have we got this afternoon?'

'Scenes of Crime Officer,' said Gilbert Smith, 'more interesting stuff in store.'

# Chapter 17

Detective Sergeant Alan Parsons was the best Scenes of Crime Officer in England. His reputation was vast and his talents were legion. Unlike most of his colleagues who had arrived at the job when they were too old, too tired, too exhausted or too drunk for operational policing, Alan Parsons had seized his vocation with the ardent enthusiasm of youth. He had volunteered.

By the time he arrived at Melanie Golding's flat his career as a SOCO had lasted for twenty-five years. Twenty-five years he had spent arriving at every hour of the day or night at the frozen scenes of human carnage. No one touched the scene of crime before he arrived. If they did his fury was terrible. What he required was the scene of crime suspended and distilled at the very moment when the hand of the perpetrator moved on. Sometimes he would enter a room or a bank or a vehicle knowing as he did so that what he observed was *precisely* what the criminal had left. On other occasions subsequent events had obscured this clear view. Sometimes he found the charred remains of a scene deliberately destroyed by fire. Sometimes there were the signs of brief recovery. A victim left for dead altering with the last painful spasms of life the perfect tableau of crime.

Within this world involving the minute examination of the aftermath of death and loss, despair and pain, Alan Parsons was a quiet genius. Unlike most of his colleagues who confined themselves to the basic business of record and examination, photographing, sketching, video-taping, fingerprinting and collection of weapons or clothing, blood and hair, Alan Parsons strode forward into dissection and analysis. Experience and intuition had fuelled a burning desire accurately to reclaim the past. From apparent ephemera he sought and found causation. Famously, on arrival at any scene, all other participants, police, public, medical personnel, were summarily expelled. In the room or bank or cellar or field Alan Parsons would stand alone, his eyes shifting across the background scenery of evil deeds. Sometimes he moved, squatted, lay down, his eyes fixed upon objects of apparent total irrelevance. The foot which left the imprint on the door, the body which dislodged the chair, the hand which placed the cup on the table, or thrust the knife into the throat, did so again and again in the mind of Alan Parsons, and then again until there emerged a sequence, a causation, and the imaginings clarified into the violent actions of the past. Thus through his skills he enjoyed an Olympian perspective. He could *see* the crime. Sometimes he could see the criminal himself (or, rarely, herself). The size, the dexterity, the age, the anger, the motive, all of these achieved renewed life in the mind of Alan Parsons. Before long his reputation had been turned to scholarship. He lectured regularly to police forces in every part of the world, even displaying to the uncomprehending Chinese the minute details of the British suburban bedroom, pointing carefully to the position of the candlewick bedspread from which could be deduced the proximate acts of human depravity.

For those who used and valued his talents Alan Parsons performed two distinct services. Firstly, in accordance with the rigid parameters of his job, he recorded and assembled the forensic material of investigation. This ultimately became his final report, used, if necessary, for the process of law and the conduct of cases. For those whom he knew and trusted he provided a second report. This document was invariably treated as confidential. It crossed the border between expertise and speculation and as such its only use was to assist detection. As a witness Alan Parsons confined himself to the hard factual material of scientific examination devoid of inspired perception.

On the morning of 7 June 1989 at 10.30 a.m. he stepped quietly into the witness box in Court One at the Old Bailey, laid his files on the ledge before him and took the oath. For the next hour, examined in chief by Miss Antonia Black, he provided the detailed and deadly results of his investigations. The state of Melanie Golding's flat could be seen in the bundle of photographs. There were twenty-six in all, showing in various degrees of detail the living room, bedroom, hall and bathroom. Attention was drawn, without comment, to one overturned chair and a quantity of academic notes scattered on the floor by the desk. In the bedroom the bed itself was in a state of disarray, otherwise nothing appeared untoward save for an alarm clock crushed face downwards into the carpet. This was photographed from three angles in considerable detail. The clock had been stopped at 9.08.

'Was there any sign of a forced entry?' asked Antonia Black.

'No. But the doors which give on to the balcony from the bedroom were both open.'

'Open in the sense of unlocked or standing open?'

'Standing open.'

'Did you discover anything else in connection with the balcony?'

'Yes, a ladder was lying on the ground below.'

'Could this ladder have provided access to the balcony?'

'Undoubtedly so, yes. There is a separate photograph of the ladder after I had placed it upright, from which it can be seen that the top extremity is within two feet of the balcony ledge.'

'Was there a thorough fingerprint examination of the scene?'

'Indeed. Fingerprints were lifted from many areas of the rooms, the hallway, the bathroom and also the balcony and the ladder.'

'Were any fingerprints lifted from any documents found in the room?'

'Not at that stage, no.'

'I will come to that later. The fingerprints which were taken from the rooms and from the ladder, were these subsequently the subject of examination against police files?'

'They were.'

'Can you summarise your findings?'

Alan Parsons sifted through his files and extracted a number of documents bearing enlarged photographic images. 'Throughout the flat and on the balcony there were a large number of fingerprints of common origin. These related to prints from the fingers, thumbs and also the palms. These were subsequently found, on analysis, to correspond with fingerprints taken from Melanie Golding herself.'

The judge intervened. 'These fingerprints from Melanie Golding were presumably taken after she had been rescued.'

'They were.'

'They were taken whilst she was unconscious?'

'They were. We had no choice. They were taken with the consent of her father.'

'I was not criticising, Detective Sergeant. I merely wished to ascertain the fact. Please continue, Miss Black.'

'Were there any other fingerprints or palm prints found?'

'A number, yes. Subsequently some of these were identified as belonging to friends or relatives of Melanie Golding whom we were able to contact as a result of information obtained from her father.'

'Were any other fingerprints found which relate to anyone connected with this case?'

'They were. A number of fingerprints and palm prints were lifted from different parts of the flat and also from the balcony and the ladder which could subsequently be identified as belonging to Thomas Aylen, the defendant. We did not, of course, have samples of his fingerprints until after his arrest.'

From counsel's bench Jane Wilson rose to intervene. 'My Lord, in order to assist your Lordship and ladies and gentlemen of the jury, I can say now that there is no issue here. The defendant's fingerprints which were found in all these locations are admitted to be those of my client.'

'There is no issue that your client was present in this flat?'

'I can do better than that, my Lord, I can tell your Lordship that there will be no issue that my client was in the flat at the time when Melanie Golding left it.'

'I see. Well, thank you. There you are, members of the jury, I am sure you will have noticed that Miss Wilson, as always, chose her words with considerable care. Are there any other matters to be dealt with by this witness, Miss Black?'

'Yes, my Lord, just one. Did you find any traces or signs of blood during your investigations?'

'Yes. There was a small quantity of blood which was found on the skirting board in the corner of the room directly opposite the desk. A scraping was taken at this time and was sent to the laboratory for analysis.'

'I think that you can tell us at this stage, Mr Parsons, what was the result of this test?'

'The blood corresponded on analysis with that of Thomas Aylen.'

'Thank you,' said Antonia Black, smiling down at her leading counsel, 'unless I am instructed otherwise that is all that we require, Mr Parsons.'

Jane Wilson began, 'Mr Parsons, may I tell you, if you do not already know, that during the course of the police operation to free Melanie Golding four men were shot and killed. One of them, unhappily, was a police officer. The other three were armed, dangerous and apparently part of the gang who were guarding this unfortunate lady. Were you aware of that?'

'I have become aware.'

'Of the three men who were part of the gang, two were brothers, the Jones brothers, and one was a gentleman called Bedser. All three had a substantial number of previous convictions and all three had convictions for serious violence. Were you aware of that?'

'I was aware of that.'

'In those circumstances, Mr Parsons, it would be inevitable, would it not, that all three would have their fingerprints on file in the police computer?'

'That is correct.'

'Am I right in saying that none of the fingerprints found at Melanie

Golding's house, despite the obvious involvement of these three, that none of those fingerprints belonged to these three men?'

'That is correct. If any of the unidentified fingerprints had been theirs, then the computer would have revealed it.'

'It is possible of course that they were there but, unlike Aylen, took the elementary precaution of wearing gloves?'

'Of course.'

'Thank you. Now may I come to the state of the room and ask you to look at the general photograph at the beginning of the album which shows as much of the living room as the lens can cover. The remainder of the room is to be found in photograph two. Now first of all, this is a large room is it not, measuring some fifteen feet by twenty?'

'Approximately, that is right.'

'At first sight the room appears to be untidy but there is no obvious sign of violence. Do you agree?'

'I think that is a matter of opinion, but if you ask for my opinion I would agree.'

'You have identified three areas which contain some evidence of a struggle. First the desk where papers have been left on the floor in disarray. Do you have reason to suppose, looking at the room as a whole, that this did not simply represent untidiness?'

Sir Edward Boyd rose majestically to his feet. 'My Lord, I don't want to interrupt my learned friend, but this really is a matter of opinion and conjecture. It is essentially a matter for the jury what they make of the state of the room.'

Mr Justice Phillips looked down at Jane Wilson. 'What do you say to that, Miss Wilson?'

'We do not agree. Mr Parsons is highly trained and experienced in these matters. He is an expert and is therefore entitled to give his opinion.'

'With that I am afraid we do not agree,' said Sir Edward Boyd; 'Mr Parsons is an expert in the discovery and recovery of evidence, not its interpretation. That is a matter entirely for the jury.'

Mr Justice Phillips raised a hand to stop further argument. 'It is a very narrow line. For the moment I propose to allow Miss Wilson to cross-examine in this vein but I will be watchful. If that line is crossed then I will stop you, Miss Wilson. Please continue.'

'I had just asked you, Mr Parsons, before I was interrupted, why you say this is not mere untidiness?'

'I had the opportunity to consider the other documents surrounding the desk. Whereas it appears clear from the general condition of the flat that Miss Golding was generally untidy, her student notes and other documents pertaining to her studies were kept in immaculate form. The notes which were scattered on the floor all relate to one subject and would otherwise have been chronological. They were not. In this respect they differed from every other file or bundle of notes within the room. I think that this resulted from the desk being violently jolted.'

'Violently?'

'Yes, I think so; the documents were some little way from the desk and you can see there is a bare patch on the surface which would or may have accommodated a pile of paper.'

'Thank you. May I now come to two other areas of the room? In the exteme far corner of the room, approximately twenty feet from the desk, a chair was found on its side. Is that right?'

'Yes, that is right, it is one of the dining chairs from the table. Before you ask for my opinion as to the reason, I will tell you that in my view this chair was not directly knocked to the ground. The table, itself a heavy object, received a violent shock which, in turn, caused this chair to fall on to its back. I base that conclusion on the condition of the carpet. In it there were four clear indentations which corresponded with the feet of the table. In each case these were approximately six inches from the actual position of the table legs. I conclude that the table was moved and moved *once* (there are no other such indentations). The force dislodged the chair which had been drawn against the table and then fell from view behind the table itself. Anyone attempting to tidy the flat after such a struggle may well have failed to notice this article of furniture beneath the table itself.'

'Thank you very much, Mr Parsons. I now come to the third area of the room which is, again, in one of the corners. In this area you found a quantity of blood on the skirting board, subsequently analysed to be that of Thomas Aylen. A photograph was taken of this blood, which you will find at photograph nine.'

In the jury box twelve pairs of eyes gazed downwards at an enlarged photograph of human gore.

'It appears from the photograph that this blood is smeared against the skirting board, is that right?'

'That would appear to be the case.'

'It is distinct from a pattern of dropping blood which would leave literally droplets and trails?'

'That is entirely correct. It is my view that a wounded part of the body was pressed against the skirting board.'

'I can tell you, Mr Parsons, if you do not already know, that at the time of his arrest a matter of days later the only open wounds found on Thomas Aylen were to the head and face. Did you know that?'

'I did not know that. I believed he had injuries to his arm and also, I think, his leg.'

'That is in part correct, Mr Parsons. He had an unhealed recent fracture of the left ulna, the bone below the elbow and a fracture of the left ankle. Neither of these, however, produced open wounds. Now, Mr Parsons, assuming this to be the case and assuming that there are not other recently healed wounds, it would appear, would it not, that his forehead or face had been in contact with the skirting board?'

'Really, *oh really*,' said Sir Edward Boyd, rising to his feet with even greater difficulty, 'I don't want to appear fractious but the witness is being asked to draw inferences from the evidence which are plainly matters for the jury.'

'I think you are right, Sir Edward,' said the judge with an air of resignation, 'but I am going to let Miss Wilson continue. It seems to me that the conclusion which she asks the witness to draw is so obvious and inescapable that no harm will be done by airing it in court at this stage. I agree that she is effectively making a comment which could be made later but you did have the benefit of a very long opening speech, Sir Edward, and I am going to allow her a little indulgence.' So saying Mr Justice Phillips turned and smiled benignly at the jury who obediently smiled back.

'Now tell us the obvious conclusion, Mr Parsons.'

'The conclusion is, as you say, obvious. Assuming there were no other recently healed wounds and assuming that the blood was left on the skirting board at the time when the fingerprints were left and assuming that to be on the day when I examined the premises, then either Mr Aylen's forehead came into contact with the skirting board or else someone or something deliberately transferred the blood by deliberately smearing the blood firstly from the forehead and then on to the board. Very unlikely in all the circumstances.'

'Thank you, Mr Parsons,' continued Jane Wilson. 'I have only one other matter of concern. In the bedroom, beside the bed, the alarm clock was found face down, broken and its hands fixed at eight minutes past nine. In your view, was force applied to this instrument in order for this to occur?'

'There is no doubt of that. The buttons and dials at the rear of the clock had all been bent and distorted. The glass face is broken. The hands themselves are not bent or distorted from the driving mechanism. The alarm is clockwork and partially wound so I think it is possible to say that this clock was stamped upon next to the bed at precisely this time.'

'This would indicate the possibility, at least, of a struggle, perhaps the same struggle, taking place throughout not only at least three corners of the living room but also into the bedroom itself?'

'That is indeed the case.'

'Total area covered by the struggle fifty square metres?'

'I am sure you have calculated it correctly.'

'Despite his disabilities, Thomas Aylen remains a powerful man?'

'I imagine so.'

'Melanie Golding is a woman of twenty-five?'

'So I am told.'

Seeing Edward Boyd rising beside her, Jane Wilson hurried the question, 'If Aylen was the *attacker*, is it likely that, given their respective strengths, a struggle would have covered so wide an area *and* involved Aylen's damaged face being pressed against the skirting board?'

The judge spoke, his eyes raised towards the ceiling of the court, 'Do not say anything, Sir Edward, you are right. That question is for the jury and not the witness, *as Miss Wilson well knows.*'

As Jane Wilson resumed her seat, John Wilkin rose, placed both hands upon his lectern and asked his first question. 'I have no issue with you, Mr Parsons, over your findings but there is one matter which I want to deal with which is of importance to my client. It concerns a newspaper, exhibit 629A. I wonder if you could see the original. While it is being handed to you I will invite the jury to look in their bundles at exhibit number 368 which is a copy of the front page of this document. Now, Mr Parsons, that you have it in your possession I would like you to consider it. You will see that at the top of the front page there is what I am reliably informed is known in the world of journalism as "a flag". It is, in effect, a small advertisement for something which appears within the newspaper itself. This "flag" refers to an article by my client, Roddy Nailor, who is described as a famous criminal. Is that right?'

'So it would appear.'

'The newspaper itself, you have the original, bears upon it the unmistakably pink markings of fingerprint analysis, does it not?'

'It does.'

'Now tell me, Mr Parsons, you are the Scenes of Crime Officer, the "SOCO". Have you seen this document before?'

'I have not actually seen it until today.'

'You have been aware of its existence?'

'Yes, I have. I have been told about this document.'

'You did not send it to be analysed?'

'As I have said, I did not send any documents for fingerprint analysis. I had no reason to suppose that there were any of relevance. There were, after all, many hundreds of documents. This was a student's flat.'

'I appreciate that, Mr Parsons. And no criticism is intended. However, had you been aware of a *newspaper* and a newspaper in a prominent position, a newspaper in a prominent position which contained an article by a notorious *criminal*, then would you not have considered that to be relevant?'

'I think I would have done. I never saw that newspaper at the flat.'

In the court a deep silence had descended. Such a phenomenon is well known to those who live and work within the criminal justice system. It is the collective instinct of the herd sensing danger.

'You did not see the newspaper in the flat?'

'That is what I said.'

'Forgive me for the repetition. Now I would like you to look at photograph number eight in our first bundle. Do you have it? Good. And you, members of the jury? Excellent. Now this photograph, Mr Parsons, this photograph shows the top of the desk, does it not?'

'Yes, indeed it does, from a little distance.'

'Yes, indeed. But the top of the desk is clearly visible. Now tell me, Mr Parsons, do we see any sign of *any* newspaper on that desk?'

'I can see no such document.'

'Precisely. Now we are a little distance from the desk. Would you care to borrow my magnifying glass in order to inspect the photograph more closely?'

'There is no need for me to do so, Mr Wilkin. I have already examined this photograph in the manner you suggest, when I learned of the existence of this newspaper.'

'You have already examined it. Oh I see, very interesting. So you will agree with me that there is no sign on the photograph at all of any such newspaper?'

'There is none.'

John Wilkin allowed the silence to linger and deepen while he looked with apparent worried concern between the witness and the jury. Then he said, 'Forgive me for digressing, Mr Parsons, you I think have been a Scenes of Crime officer for many years?'

'Twenty-five.'

'Indeed and you and I, Mr Parsons, in that time have known each other very well, have we not, on both sides of the fence, as it were?'

'Oh God,' thought Jane Wilson, 'he's laying it on with a trowel.'

'We have, Mr Wilkin.'

'And I think it would be right to say, would it not, that in your craft, the analysis of the scenes of crime, you have probably the most distinguished record of any officer in this country?'

'That it is not for me to answer and, in any event, it is not a very big craft.'

John Wilkin smiled at the witness and then the jury in order to acknowledge the becoming modesty. 'Of course, but I am right, am I not, that you have lectured in your craft in many countries of the world?'

'I have been fortunate enough to be asked to do so.'

John Wilkin sprang the trap. 'So, to recapitulate, we have here a newspaper which, on its very face, bears information which you acknowledge to be highly relevant to the investigation. As you know it allegedly comes from the desk. At the time it was photographed this desk had been inspected by one of the most experienced and distinguished officers in your craft, namely you, Mr Parsons. The newspaper *cannot have been there*, can it?'

Faced with the question, Alan Parsons in a single moment rehearsed in his mind the conversation which had taken place between himself and his friend and long-term colleague Superintendent Eddie Cole, head of the Serious Crime Squad. The conversation had taken place two weeks before the start of the trial.

'Where, Eddie,' he had said quietly, 'did this newspaper come from?'

'It came from the girl's desk.'

'Eddie, I have been in this game for twenty-five years. I went over that room with my eyes wide open. This is a newspaper with Roddy Nailor's face and name all over the front of it. *A newspaper*. Even if it hadn't had his mug on it I would have wanted to know the date and the edition in case it showed when the girl had gone missing. Eddie, my friend, I would *never* have missed this trick. I've seen the photographs and the video. You can't see this paper anywhere. You cannot do this, Eddie. They will fry you alive this time.'

'I knew Roddy Nailor had that girl. I know what he can do, Alan. He is probably not the most evil man on the planet but he's in the top ten. He's Olympic class, Alan. If I'd let him go he would have killed her. When I'm in charge in the world, Alan, people like Roddy Nailor don't do that. Now I'm telling you, Alan, that this newspaper was on that desk. It may have been buried under other things. It may not have been immediately apparent but that newspaper was on that desk.'

'Eddie, look at the photographs, there is no sign of it. Not even a bulge.'

'Alan, my old friend, that newspaper was on that desk.'

'You know what they'll do, don't you, you know what they'll do. They'll have me in the witness box. They'll go through the whole business. The nature of the paper. The photographs. The video. Then they will haul out all my CV. The most famous scenes of crime analyst in the world. A modern Sherlock Holmes. And they'll say "That newspaper couldn't have been there, could it?" And I'm either going to say "It couldn't have been there", which is the *truth*, or else I'm going to have to say "I don't know, maybe it was there and maybe it was not", in which case not only am I breaking the rules and the habit of a lifetime but also in this the Trial of the Century my entire reputation of a quarter of a century will be on a funeral pyre.'

All of this went through the mind of Alan Parsons in the silence of Court One and in the blinking of an eye. Fortunately John Wilkin was not averse to repetition. 'You're obviously considering the matter carefully, Mr Parsons. Let me put it to you again. That newspaper *could not* have been there, could it?'

In the witness box Alan Parsons smiled a thin smile, looked straight at the jury and said, 'I don't know. Perhaps it was there, perhaps it was not. If it was I missed it.'

Sir Edward Boyd, troubled, rose again. 'Since everyone has apparently asked for your opinion and got it, Mr Parsons, I do not want to be left out. I want to return to the question of the newspaper. My learned friend Mr Wilkin has suggested to you that, given your experience, the state of the desk and the nature of the newspaper, you could not have missed it. You said in answer to him that it was possible. Is that indeed the case?'

Alan Parsons paused, tightened his grip on the edge of the dock, allowed himself one penetrating stare into the eyes of Superintendent Eddie Cole who sat impassive on the police benches below him and said, 'It is perfectly possible. I am fallible like anyone else. It is perfectly possible that the newspaper was there.'

Sir Edward Boyd shrugged and turned to the judge. 'My Lord, that may well be enough for today. I can tell your Lordship and the jury that for the next two days I will be calling police officers and neighbours to deal with the assault on the premises. Most of it will not be in dispute.'

'Very well, Sir Edward, ten thirty tomorrow members of the jury. I hope that you will agree that it has been an interesting day. Science can be fascinating.'

# Chapter 18

'I am worried,' said Eddie Cole in the darkness.

'Not again,' said Anita Flynn.

'I am giving evidence tomorrow. I am entitled to be worried.'

'It's never bothered you before.'

'It's not the evidence, it's the consequences. In truth we have only got the newspaper. The newspaper relies entirely on me. If I fuck it up Nailor walks. If Nailor walks he could do anything. He's barking mad and totally dangerous.'

'Well on behalf of the Great British Public, Hostesses, Call-girls and Prostitutes Division, I urge you not to fuck it up.'

'I'll do my best,' said Eddie Cole into the blackness. 'I will do my best.'

'I am worried,' said John Wilkin.

'Really?' said Preston Lodge, pausing in the act of pouring a second glass of claret for his leader. 'Not about doing Eddie Cole tomorrow?'

'No, now we have the prison record he is pretty much dead meat. No, I'm worried about *our* client and, for that matter, about our solicitor.'

'Anything in particular or just a general aversion to psychopaths and toffs?'

'I can't understand why they are so bloody smug. It's as though they *know* that they are going to win. I know the evidence is not strong but unless I break Cole on the wheel tomorrow there is probably just a case for him to answer. In that case he goes into the witness box and God knows what a mess he'll make of that, and then he'll be in the dock when Aylen gives evidence and points the finger at him. I cross-examine him. He completely changes his account but everyone knows he's got Menkies' Syndrome, so it doesn't matter. This case is not easy. Why are they so bloody confident?'

'Total belief in their counsel maybe.'

'Maybe,' said John Wilkin, 'maybe.'

'I'm worried, Frankenstein,' said Jane Wilson as they left the main entrance of Wormwood Scrubs.

'What's the problem?' said Mary Shelley, helplessly scanning the road for a taxi.

'Our client is not telling us something. It's about the girl. There is something missing from this account.'

'Perhaps he's trying. He is, after all, very ill, mentally.'

'No, he knows what he's telling us and what he's not. There's something which he won't say.'

'I'm worried,' said Brendan O'Hara to the senior nurse who had entered Melanie Golding's room. 'She has been completely motionless for two days since the operation. Can you tell us anything? Is there a prognosis?'

'The prognosis,' replied the nurse, reading the notes she had removed from a rack at the foot of the bed, 'is that she is a very tough girl and lucky to be alive. They have removed the bullet from her skull. It has caused considerable damage to the outer layer of the brain and she has a severe subdural haemorrhage, a blood clot. Whether that disperses or whether it continues to grow and place intolerable pressure upon the brain is simply a matter of conjecture. If the bullet had not been removed she would have died in any event. I don't think that answers your question, Mr O'Hara, does it?'

'How long will she remain unconscious before she becomes better or worse?'

'I am afraid it is quite impossible to say. Minutes, hours, days, maybe weeks, maybe longer. When she wakes she may be normal or not. Everything is monitored, her heart, her pulse, her breathing, the sensory waves from the brain which are carried on that wire which you see behind the bandages. They are all on my screen next door, Sergeant O'Hara. There is really no need for you to remain.'

'I have orders to remain and besides that, I want to.'

The senior sister raised one eyebrow, revealing a perfectly green orb.

'Irish,' thought Brendan O'Hara, 'just like me.' Aloud he said, 'Where are you from?'

'A *very* long time ago, Sergeant O'Hara, my people came from County Cork. Just like you.' Ignoring his surprise, she replaced the notes, straightened the bedcovers and left the room. At the doorway she said, 'This is a very beautiful girl, Sergeant O'Hara. I hope they all burn in hell.'

Alone Brendan O'Hara, careful not to touch the bed itself, leaned over the sleeping face. 'Inside there,' he thought, 'is the Truth.' Aloud he said, 'Come on darling, come on.'

Against her pillow Melanie Golding, turbaned in bandages and invaded by tubes, slept the sleep of the dead.

# Chapter 19

Sir Edward Boyd dealt with the essential preliminaries before asking, 'Mr Cole, you were originally in charge of this police operation, were you not?'

'I was.'

'I think I can lead you over this early ground about which there has been no dispute . . .'

'Careful,' muttered John Wilkin next to him.

'I always am,' replied Sir Edward cheerfully at full volume, causing three of the jurors to smile.

'I think your first contact was with Mr Justice Elias Golding who brought you the letter which we have all seen?'

'That is the case.'

'Did there come a time, Superintendent, when you, together with a number of other officers and Mr Golding himself, went to Melanie Golding's flat in Hackney, and there did you obtain entry by means of a key in Mr Golding's possession?'

'We did.'

'The Scenes of Crime Officer, Mr Alan Parsons, was he also present at the scene?'

'Yes, he was, I had made arrangements for him to be there first. I wanted the most experienced man that we could possibly get.'

'When you arrived was the scene similar to that which we could see in photographs one to nine?'

John Wilkin, burly and outraged, was on his feet. 'Really my learned friend must be careful. He *must not lead* on the state of the room. He knows there is a serious issue.'

Sir Edward Boyd held up a hand in mock supplication. 'My learned friend is *absolutely* right. Of course I know there is a serious issue. That is why I chose to use the word "similar". As I understand the case there is no issue as to the general state of affairs and . . .'

'Gentlemen,' said Mr Justice Phillips, 'please do not squabble. Sir Edward is quite right. The word "similar" was carefully chosen and cannot cause offence, but do be careful, Sir Edward, we want to protect

Mr Wilkin's health. He's gone quite red.' Mr Justice Phillips acknowledged the gratifying titters from the jury before nodding to Sir Edward Boyd that he should continue.

'Did you find the room in a *broadly similar* state to that which we find in the relevant photographs?'

'It looks very similar. The photographs were not taken by me, they were taken by one of the SOCO team.'

'SOCO?'

'The Scenes of Crime team. They took the photographs and the fingerprints and the other samples.'

'Is that the first operation that is carried out?'

'That is correct. Alan Parsons always insists that nothing is moved prior to his arrival unless there is an emergency. Here there was none. Besides he was indeed the first to arrive.'

'After the SOCO team had carried out their tasks what then occurred?'

'We carefully inspected the flat. It was quite obvious that the girl, Melanie Golding, might have been abducted and so we took possession of large numbers of items for analysis and, if necessary, subsequent fingerprinting. Some of these items were selected by the Scenes of Crime Office, and others by myself.'

'How were they so collected?'

'They were placed in large plastic bags. One different bag for every category of document or item. Thus items found on the table, the dining table, were placed in a separate bag. Items from the mantelpiece likewise. Also from the floor of the living room.'

'And the desk?'

'Items from the desk were placed into a separate bag, I think, from recollection, bag number six. There may have been two or three bags, each numbered six. These were subsequently taken to the police station, examined and identified by number.'

'How were they so identified?'

'All the items from bag six contained the prefix six, thus items were exhibit sixty-one, sixty-two et cetera.'

'And when they reached sixty-nine?'

'Then they became six-ten, six-eleven, six-twelve, six-thirteen et cetera. This is a relatively new system. It is done in order immediately to identify the areas where items are found.'

'When the bags are returned to the police station who is responsible for their labelling and storage?'

'That would be any member of the squad who was available to carry it out. It is not a popular task.'

'Is it something that you would do as the officer in charge of the case?'

'Very rarely.'

'Did you do so in this particular case in respect of any items?'

A now familiar silence fell upon Court One and gathered intensity. Even to those newly arrived in the public gallery, impossibly attempting to gauge the nature and progress and importance of the trial below them, it was apparent that a moment of truth had arrived.

In the silence Eddie Cole answered. 'I was involved in only one item. That is numbered 629A. It is a newspaper.'

On counsel's benches pens scratched furiously to ensure a verbatim record of potential destruction.

'Perhaps you would tell us, Superintendent, how that came about.'

'Certainly. It is my invariable practice, in a case as important as this, carefully to check the exhibit bags before they are stored. I do so in order to ensure that exhibits have not inadvertently been left in the bags. It happens on occasions and it happened here. At the bottom of bag six I found this newspaper. It is necessary to reach into the bags since they are made of black polythene.'

'So items are not visible from the outside.'

'Precisely.'

'In those circumstances, Superintendent, would the exhibit label be in your writing?'

'It would.'

Turning to the judge, Sir Edward addressed the court. 'My Lord, as you know, Superintendent Cole was involved in the later arrests. They do not directly affect the exhibits and on one matter we require your Lordship's guidance as a matter of law. It has been agreed between myself and my learned friends that we should take Mr Cole's evidence in two parts and that he should be recalled to deal with subsequent matters. I would therefore invite my learned friends to cross-examine at this stage on that evidence which he has given. Mr Wilkin is most affected and he will cross-examine first.'

'A sensible course. Yes, Mr Wilkin.'

John Wilkin rose and assembled himself behind his lectern. He was a big man of stern, unyielding presence and, on occasions, a savage wit, and his reputation as a formidable cross-examiner had provided much of his substantial fortune.

'Superintendent Cole, may I ask you first please to look at photograph number eight in our bundle. Do you have it? Good. That photograph shows the desk, does it not, before any of its contents or documents upon it were removed?'

'It does, yes.'

'Tell me, Superintendent Cole, can you point out the newspaper on that desk?'

In the witness box Eddie Cole did not lower his eyes. 'No sir, I cannot. I cannot see it there.'

'Superintendent Cole, you did not look at the photograph.'

'I did not need to, sir. I have already examined it very carefully for precisely this point. I was aware, of course, that it might be suggested that the newspaper had not come from that source.'

Even whilst making notes furiously on counsel's bench Preston Lodge could not resist a smile of admiration. 'God,' he thought, 'this man is *good*. A lesser man would have looked at the photograph. If he had been examining it *before* the trial then the impression to the jury must be that he thought that it *should* be there. Clever, very clever.'

The effect was not lost on John Wilkin who then, attempting to regain lost ground, made an uncharacteristic error. 'When you looked, Superintendent, did you *really expect to see it?*'

'Oh no,' thought Preston Lodge, 'oh no, slow ball outside his leg stump. That's going over the boundary.'

'Of course I expected to see it, sir. I would not have looked otherwise. I have actually employed a microscope and obtained enlarged copies of these photographs which are available if you wish to see them. They tell nothing else. It is not possible to see the newspaper on the top of the desk.'

'Clever,' thought Preston Lodge, 'depressingly clever. Thirty-love to Cole.'

Effortlessly caught in the trap, John Wilkin had no choice but to bluster. 'I was not informed that there were enlarged photographs, Superintendent. We have not seen them.'

'I am very sorry about that, sir. Since they reveal nothing in addition to the smaller photographs I thought it unnecessary to bring them to anyone's attention. Also, sir,' added Eddie Cole with a small smile, 'I had rather assumed that the defence solicitors would do what I have done. Indeed I think I see some enlarged photographs on the desk before you Mr Wilkin.'

'Forty-love,' thought Preston Lodge sadly.

'I am going to suggest to you, Superintendent, that the reason why we cannot see it on the desk is because *it was never there.*'

'As I say, sir, I did not see it there because I did not collect the contents of the desk. However, I think that your assertion is most unlikely, sir, impossible in reality.'

'Why do you say that, Superintendent?'

Below John Wilkin's lectern Preston Lodge perceptibly winced. The open question. He can say what he likes.

'Because all the bags were sealed at the flat and were opened only in the exhibits room. The newspaper was found by me in the bag. I have also carried out enquiries among my team. They do not specifically remember the newspaper because they simply swept the contents of the desk and the documents on top of it into plastic bags. I would expect no less.'

'My God,' thought Preston Lodge. 'Game to Cole. I bet he has actually asked them. When they give evidence, if *we* ask them that's just what they'll say. "Superintendent Cole asked me that sir, I couldn't say." This man is an evil genius. He is a God.'

John Wilkin, aware of the state of play, was glaring across his lectern. 'Superintendent Cole, this is, is it not, the most important piece of paper in the case against Mr Nailor?'

'That's a matter of comment, isn't it, Mr Wilkin?' interjected the judge, making a bad situation worse.

In the witness box Eddie Cole, affecting not to notice the judicial intervention, had already answered. 'I am well aware of that, sir, and I would agree. That is why I have been so *worried* about its provenance and taken these precautions.'

'Ah,' thought Preston Lodge. 'He's overdone it.'

John Wilkin, sensing the same, visibly brightened. 'Yes, well I expect you were worried, Superintendent, and I expect you had good reason to be so. But let us move on. Now this document, which you agree is the most important document in the case, just happens to be found, abandoned, in the bottom of a black plastic bag, in the exhibits room, by you. When you found it were you alone?'

'Can't remember, sir, to be frank.'

'Searching for a piece of incriminating evidence?'

'No, sir, searching for inspiration.'

'God,' thought Preston Lodge, 'the jury are laughing.'

'Tell me, Superintendent; this document is labelled 629A. Why, if the system is as you tell us, was it not labelled 630?'

'I wanted to make it quite clear, sir, that this document had been found by me and was in a different category to the other documents.'

'It was not in the hope that its arrival would go unnoticed in the middle of the exhibits bundle?'

'Certainly not, sir. Quite the reverse. The purpose was to draw attention to this document as different rather than attempt to make it appear the same. Even then I was aware that questions might be asked, since it was obviously an important document, and I wanted to make it quite clear from the start what had happened.'

'Clever,' thought Preston Lodge, 'clever but *flawed*.'

John Wilkin moved in. 'So, even at that stage you considered this document to be important because, of course, it forged a link with Nailor.'

'That is right, obviously.'

'Obviously! So it was. Why should Melanie Golding have an old copy of the *Evening News*, nine months old, on her desk relating to Nailor?'

'Precisely, sir.'

John Wilkin charged. 'And so, Superintendent, realising just how important this newspaper was, you immediately sent it to the Forensic and fingerprinting department in order to have it examined?'

'No, sir, I did not.'

Dense silence had descended again from the ceiling of the court to the well below. Many eyes watched Superintendent Eddie Cole.

'Why, Superintendent, did you not do so?'

'Because I am fallible. My first reaction, to be blunt, was that Melanie Golding had purchased this newspaper months previously when she observed the connection with her own father. I assumed that it had remained there through inadvertence. It was only subsequently that I formed the clear view that Nailor was a suspect. This view had no direct relationship with the newspaper, save for the fact that I was aware that Nailor had taken a course in philosophy and it had been pointed out to me that the ransom note contained references to somebody called "Nasty".'

'Nietzsche,' said John Wilkin involuntarily and cursed himself.

'As you say, sir. I had not myself heard of him. It was only after I began to suspect Nailor that I suddenly realised the potential signifi-cance of the newspaper. I then delivered it to be fingerprinted with all urgency.'

'This man,' thought Preston Lodge, 'is an Olympian. Thank God we have the ammunition to break him.'

'It was only,' continued John Wilkin grimly, 'after Mr Cameron, Mr Nailor's solicitor, had come to see you and before Mr Nailor gave himself up, that you thought to have this vital work done?'

'I am afraid that is right, sir. It was at that point that I saw the light. I am very pleased that I did.'

'Please,' interjected Mr Justice Phillips warmly, 'do not comment on the evidence, Superintendent. Just answer the question. You know the rules.'

'Of course, my Lord, I'm sorry.'

'Very well,' said John Wilkin, in apparent resignation. 'What I must suggest to you, Superintendent, is grave. I wish to suggest that you, and it can only have been you, were responsible for planting this newspaper in the exhibits room and pretending that it was found in Melanie Golding's flat. Do you understand?'

'Oh, I understand, sir. The allegation is completely false.'

'You don't appear to be surprised that I am making it, Superintendent?'

'No sir, I am not in the least surprised, I know your client of old. He has made this false allegation before.'

'Ouch,' thought Preston Lodge, 'now we really must hit him.'

As though at his junior's command John Wilkin adopted an air of apparent defeat and said, 'Tell me, Superintendent, had you seen this newspaper before?'

There was a perceptible pause before Eddie Cole said, 'No, sir.'

'Are you sure about that?'

'Yes, sir.'

'Got him,' thought Preston Lodge, watching as his leader turned a page of his file and looked down at the prison record of letters sent.

John Wilkin's voice assumed a hard edge. 'Superintendent Cole, on the twenty-seventh of February 1988 Roddy Nailor sent you this newspaper under cover of a prison envelope, did he not? Before you answer that question, Superintendent, I want to tell you that the prison records show precisely that. You had this newspaper nine months before Melanie Golding was abducted, did you not?'

Many pairs of eyes turned on Superintendent Eddie Cole who stared impassively at his interrogator. Then he said, 'Certainly, Mr Wilkin, I received a *copy* of this newspaper from your client together with a letter. But it was not that copy.'

'My God,' thought Preston Lodge. 'He saw it coming, he saw it coming. We've blown it.'

In the silence which had descended John Wilkin attempted to rebuild his case. 'Now I suppose you are going to tell us, Superintendent, that the newspaper which was sent to *you*, which is apparently a different newspaper from this, has gone missing or been lost.'

'Oh no,' thought Preston Lodge, 'oh no.'

'No, sir,' said Eddie Cole brightly, 'I've still got that. It's here in my briefcase. You can have it if you like, sir. I expect it may have your client's fingerprints on it as well. If they weren't brushed off in the post.'

To break the pregnant pause which held the court John Wilkin was forced to deliver the weakest ball of all. 'You're lying, Superintendent. You're lying,' he repeated as he sat down heavily on counsel's bench.

'No, I'm not, sir,' said Eddie Cole, 'here it is.' The thud, thud of the locks on Eddie Cole's briefcase sounded across the court like blows from an old leather glove. A second later triumphantly he held aloft a copy of the London *Evening News* proudly advertising their publication of the philosophical ramblings of a crazed mind.

Sir Edward Boyd arose. 'I have no re-examination my Lord, save to ask formally that *this* copy of the Evening News be exhibited,' he said, smiling politely towards Mr Justice Phillips who was examining the newspaper intently. 'Does your Lordship have any questions?'

Surprisingly and for the first time Mr Justice Phillips nodded his head. 'Yes, yes, Sir Edward, I do, but I want to check my notebook first. I see it is five to one; that may be a suitable moment to adjourn. Sir Edward, I am afraid that the court cannot sit this afternoon for administrative reasons. We will meet again tomorrow morning when there are some questions I wish to put to Mr Cole.'

The robing rooms of the Old Bailey and the dining rooms where counsel meet have a shabby eccentric charm. Piles of old forgotten paper containing the statements of countless forgotten witnesses to human wickedness are stacked untidily on every available ledge. On them rest wig boxes, old gowns, collars and sometimes long-discarded ties and pairs of trousers, causing mild amusement and speculation. The dining room serves canteen food on long tables adjacent to noticeboards bearing advertisements and exhortations, many of considerable antiquity. Generally these are friendly places. The ruthless competition of stage or media or parliament is largely absent from this well-knit group in the front line of a legal system still fiercely attached to ritual trial by combat. Anecdotes of trial disasters are mainly kind, a tacit recognition of the ease with which Error attends the heat of competition. To this gentle rule, however, there are exceptions. Unhappily for John Wilkin his cross-examination of Eddie Cole was a prime example. John Wilkin was regarded with the cordial distrust and faint dislike accorded to most civil practitioners straying into the criminal arena. Regarded as 'too clever by half', they suffered from the defensive prejudice that their vast brains preclude their being good advocates in court. Thus when one of the ilk of John Wilkin took a pasting from an old copper the news spread like fire and the reaction was merciless. As soon as John Wilkin brought his plate to the long table it began.

'Had a good morning then, John?' came from an elderly criminal hack who had failed to take silk on nine previous occasions, accompanied by barely concealed snorts. 'These old London coppers, a piece of cake you know. Not up to you civil buggers used to cross-examining bankers, actuaries and the Rolling Stones.'

John Wilkin was not a bad man. He could take a joke. Quietly he laid his knife and fork across his unfinished food, rose from the table, smiled and said, 'Why don't you lot just fuck off.'

# Chapter 20

'Where did you get it?' said Anita Flynn in the darkness.

'Get what?' said Eddie Cole, removing the whisky glass from his lips.

'The second copy of the *Evening News* in court. You said it was the one that Nailor had sent you. Where did that come from?'

'Like I said, Nailor sent it to me.'

'Rubbish,' said Anita Flynn, 'bloody rubbish. Please remember, Superintendent Cole, I have known you *very* well for a *very, very* long time. I am, among other things, your best snout which means you can tell me anything. Now, just as a matter of interest, where did *that* newspaper come from?'

'Well, do you know?' said Eddie Cole, staring at the glowing end of his cigarette, 'it's just possible that I bought it at the time it was published. I can't quite remember now but I might have done out of curiosity to read that bloody article. Now maybe that's what's happened.'

'What I do not understand, Superintendent, is this. If you bought that copy of the newspaper at the time it was published from a newsagent then it would not have Roddy Nailor's fingerprints on it, now would it?'

'I suppose that must be right.'

'But in court you said, according to the report, that it was the one that Nailor sent you *and that it probably had his fingerprints all over it*. What happens if they take it and test it? What happens if they find no fingerprints on it? Doesn't that make rather a nasty mess?'

'Mrs Flynn, let me tell you something about the forensic process. At the moment Roddy Nailor's little team don't *know* whether his dabs are on it or not. It has not been tested. What they *do* know is that I have said that they may be on it. They will think that it is unlikely, *very* unlikely that I would say such a thing if his dabs were *not* on the newspaper. So they have got a terrible choice to make. If they get that newspaper tested and find that his fingerprints *are* on it then they have completely destroyed their own allegation of plant. For that reason they don't dare do it. They are much better off simply asserting that I am lying. Now do you understand? Where's the ashtray?'

'On the floor. Anyway, what happens if your own lot, the prosecution team, decide to have it tested? What happens then?'

'Mrs Flynn,' said Superintendent Eddie Cole, 'this is what I wanted to find out and I have. No one has asked for this newspaper to be tested. As for my own side the only explanation for their stunning silence is that they are playing the same game as Nailor's lot. They don't want to wreck Nailor's defence or *risk* wrecking Nailor's defence and so the whole thing remains suspended. Only I know whether his fingerprints are, in fact, on the newspaper. Even Roddy Nailor isn't sure because, under all the psychopathic bluster and crap, all the rampant ego and Superman psychology, he thinks I can walk on water. And besides that, Mrs Flynn, it may just be that if anyone dares have this newspaper fingerprinted that they *will* find Roddy Nailor's fingerprints on it.'

In the darkness Anita Flynn could make out the bare profile of her lover's face. Inexplicably, for a moment, she felt afraid.

'If you bought that newspaper from a newsagent it couldn't have his prints on it, could it?'

Eddie Cole's profile disappeared as his face turned towards his mistress. He spoke softly in the pillow. 'On exhibit 629A we found Nailor's fingerprints on the front page. He must have left them there when he folded the newspaper prior to sending it to me. No other part of the newspaper was fingerprinted. But it is at least *likely*, is it not, that he would have read his own ghastly little article. If so, then his fingerprints are *likely* to be on that page as well, are they not? Now it might just be possible, might it not, to remove the pages from one copy of the *Evening News* and put them into the other? So it just might be that the newspaper which I produced today will reveal Roddy Nailor's fingerprints, but not on the *front*. It is just possible that his fingerprints will be found on the inside pages where the article is printed. Do you take the point, Mrs Flynn? Fingerprints on both papers in different places.'

Suddenly serious, Anita Flynn said, 'You are a dangerous bastard, Superintendent Cole. Have you no respect for the truth?'

'Roddy Nailor kidnapped that girl and would have killed her. You know that, Anita, and so do I. In this business *I* am the Truth and the Way and the Light.'

# Chapter 21

Mr Justice Phillips knew little about the criminal law but he had a fine legal brain and his practice at the Chancery Bar had allowed him to earn a great deal of money. A prudent man, he had invested much of this money in a large share portfolio wisely spread through gilts, government bonds and equities. For this reason he took a regular interest in the stock market and habitually purchased the *Evening News*, not to admire its tabloid journalism but to check upon the progress of his personal fortune as revealed in the prices of his stock. It was this habit which had caused him to make a significant and worrying discovery during the course of the trial. This had, in turn, resulted in his unusual decision to direct a number of his own questions to Superintendent Eddie Cole. This decision he had announced immediately before the rising of the court, partly because the end of the court day had been reached early and partly because he wanted further time to reflect upon his discovery.

What had happened was this. When exhibit 629A had first been produced in court, the original had been shown to the jury and finally, in accordance with normal procedure, to himself sitting on the bench. At first he had simply glanced at the newspaper, knowing, as he did so, that the important parts, namely the front page and the page bearing the Nailor article, had already been photocopied and were contained within his bundle of documents. The original newspaper had then remained, through inadvertence, upon the judge's bench. The court usher had been distracted at the moment when she would normally have removed it and placed it on the exhibits table. Subsequently, during Alan Parsons' evidence, the mind of Mr Justice Phillips had wandered. This was during a lengthy period in the evidence when Alan Parsons was simply producing the exhibits found at Melanie Golding's flat which had little relevance to the trial, and which were, in any event, clearly set out in his witness statement already in the judge's possession. During this period the judge allowed himself to be deflected, and as a matter of habit and idle curiosity had opened the *Evening News* at the page containing the share prices which had prevailed in February 1988. The judge had noted the prices of his own stocks and had reflected, with some quiet satisfaction, that the intervening eighteen months had seen a reasonable, if not spectacular, rise in his personal fortunes. Shortly thereafter the newspaper had been retrieved from his bench and been replaced (as it should have been) among the other exhibits. In due course Super-intendent Eddie Cole had given evidence and had been cross-examined with conspicuous lack of success by John Wilkin. At the climax of this forensic conflict Eddie Cole had produced (with some drama) the copy of the same newspaper which, he claimed, had been sent to him by Roddy Nailor. This newspaper had, itself, been made an exhibit.

In due course, by the same process, the newspaper had arrived upon Mr Justice Phillips' desk. This was shortly before the final exchange in court. Whilst these exchanges took place the judge, now weary of a lost cause in its dying phases, had flicked through the pages of the newspaper and had allowed his eye to run down the column of figures of share prices once again. It was then that he noticed something which caused him, at first, nothing but a mild spasm of interest. The share prices were different. From this the judge swiftly concluded that the two newspapers were, in fact, different editions. Since the *Evening News* ran to four such separate editions during the course of the day this was, in itself, not unusual. The only mildly surprising point was that Roddy Nailor should have purchased, or more accurately, had purchased for him, two newspapers at different times of the day. It was simply this small matter on which Mr Justice Phillips wished to reflect before putting his own questions to Superintendent Eddie Cole. Thus, on rising from the bench, he asked the usher to provide for him both the newspapers in his room. It was here that he made the most significant discovery. The two news-papers were, to all outward appearances, identical. On the front and back pages the headlines and copy were, indeed, the same save in one respect. Next to the newspaper's title on one copy appeared the words 'closing prices', indicating that this was the last edition of the day. Turning to the share prices the judge observed that these were indeed at the levels which he had at first observed. He then turned his attention to the second newspaper and, as much from curiosity as otherwise, turned to the business section to observe the day's events from the comfortable benefit of hindsight. What he saw caused him to start in his chair. Above the page containing the tiny figures representing the progressive health of companies there appeared the words, 'Widespread losses in late selling. Closing prices down.' What the judge had discovered was that the newspaper which was, undoubtedly, on its face, the early edition purported to contain the closing prices, whereas (as he rapidly ascertained) the latest edition of the newspaper contained news (on the business page) of the earlier day's trading. At first the judge reflected on the possibility of error within the printing process of the *Evening News*. This he swiftly discounted. A dreadful possibility then began to dawn upon him.

Rapidly he flicked through the pages of the newspaper and ascertained a terrible truth. The *Evening News* followed a conventional tabloid format. Thus double pages were folded around each other to produce the ultimate convenient size. Most sheets therefore contained four pages of newsprint, two closer to the front and the other two closer to the back. Thus the counterpart to pages one and two were the final pages thirty-three and thirty-four. When Mr Justice Phillips extracted the page which contained the Stock Exchange results he discovered that the corresponding page towards the front of the newspaper contained the article written by Roddy Nailor.

Mr Justice Phillips knew little about the criminal law but in logical deduction he had no match. Grimly he remembered the words of Superintendent Cole spoken from the witness box, 'I expect you'll find your client's fingerprints on that as well.' Thus was revealed to Mr Justice Phillips the secret which was to be imparted by Mr Eddie Cole to his mistress a matter of hours later. As Eddie Cole lay in that darkened room discussing the wider parameters of truth, he did so in blissful ignorance of the revelation that had already occurred at the highest level.

Having made his discovery Mr Justice Phillips sat and contemplated action. Finally he called his court clerk into his room. Upon the desk lay the two newspapers in their plastic containers bearing the exhibit numbers.

'I want you,' said the judge carefully, 'to take personal possession of these exhibits. They are to be retained in the highest possible security and no one, but no one, is to touch or tamper with them. Do you understand?'

'Perfectly,' said the clerk, his eyes wide with enquiry. 'I will make sure they are put into the principal court safe.'

'Who has access to this safe?'

The clerk's eyes widened still further with surprise. 'Only myself and the deputy chief clerk. She is away on holiday. For present purposes, only myself.'

'Very well,' said Mr Justice Phillips, 'please ensure that they are taken there immediately and that they are not unlocked or released until my arrival in the morning, when they should be brought straight to me.'

After the court official had left, bearing the fruits of Nemesis carefully before him, Mr Justice Phillips looked at his watch and cursed quietly. He was invited to a boring dinner at the Athenaeum at which he had undertaken to speak. Tonight, of all nights, he could have avoided this. Wearily he began to remove the red cloth of office and, having done so, retrieved his dinner jacket from the court cupboard and after barely twenty minutes was sitting in his official car on the way to his assignation. His thoughts remained full of his discovery and its consequences. The trial would have to be stopped. Investigations would be put in train. The evidence (in reality the *only* evidence) against Roddy Nailor was now in ruins. He would have to be released.

In the rear of his car Mr Justice Phillips murmured to himself, 'Why do they do it? Oh *why, why, why* do they do it? Superintendents, Chief Superintendents, gods of all they survey, of impeccable reputation and social standing, possessed of power unsurpassed. Why, *oh why, why, why* do they do it?'

While Mr Justice Phillips was making his discovery, Preston Lodge, in the cells of the Old Bailey, was having trouble with his client, Roddy Nailor.

'Well he fucked that up all right, didn't he? I thought he was supposed to be the best brief in the fucking universe. The jury were laughing, fucking laughing, and all at the bit about the Chinaman trial. He got it in first. "I know your client of old, sir." He *used* it. We didn't hit him with it. He hit us. Christ, it was a fucking disaster.'

Preston Lodge looked away from his client at James Cameron, who, in turn, looked at the floor. Conflicting emotions played within Preston Lodge. On the one hand was a personal dislike for an odious client. On the other hand he personally agreed. John Wilkin had fucked it up. Eddie Cole had seen them coming. Not only seen them coming but lain in wait, in ambush.

'I don't think it's that bad . . .' he began weakly.

'No, no, it's not "that bad", it's not "that bad" at all. It's fucking *terrible*, that's what it is. *Terrible*. Now the jury know I've got form. Know I've shouted plant in the past and this Elephant Man I sit next to all day is going to say it's all down to me. Where is fucking Wilkin anyway?'

Preston Lodge looked unhappily across the table at his client. 'I am afraid he had to go to a meeting in his Chambers and . . .'

'Bollocks he did. He knows he fucked it up and he doesn't want me to tell him. Well you tell him from me, you tell him I'm not fucking happy. You tell him that if I don't get out of this there is going to be fucking trouble. A lot of very big heads are going to do a lot of rolling.'

James Cameron intervened. 'Roddy, just take it easy. I was watching them. Some of the jury simply didn't believe Cole. Some of them may have done, but that's enough. Just remember there is more to this trial than one witness.'

Roddy Nailor looked at his solicitor through hooded eyes. 'I think we ought to do something. Something serious now.'

'Will somebody tell me what's going on?' said Preston Lodge. 'What's something serious?'

'Listen,' said James Cameron, turning suddenly towards Roddy Nailor, 'just relax all right? We all have our bad days and our good days but *everything is all right*. Do you understand? Everything will be all right.'

'Well I hope so,' said Roddy Nailor slowly, 'I just fucking hope so. It's that Eddie Cole. He gives me the shits. One day I'm going to have him. I'm going to wire him up to a plug and turn him black.'


'Nice chap, our client, isn't he?' said James Cameron as he walked with Preston Lodge along the silent corridor of the Old Bailey, now nearly deserted.

Preston Lodge stopped by the doors of the lift. 'James, is something happening we don't know about? Is something going on?'

James Cameron looked squarely at his junior counsel. 'Don't ask,' he said, 'just don't ask. Now I'm going back to the City to sort out some stockbrokers and I'm not going to think about Roddy Nailor until tomorrow.'

# Chapter 22

At half-past ten that evening Mr Justice Bob Phillips sat in the library
of the Athenaeum. Dinner over and speech made he had retired to
this majestic room in order to be alone and think. Gently revolving the
brandy in his glass he stared into the coal fire and thought of Eddie
Cole.

What would happen to him? Attempting to pervert the course of
justice. He would fight the case of course. He, Bob Phillips, would be a
witness. He had discovered the damning evidence of plant. Once that
was known other facts achieved a deadly significance. The finding of the
newspaper. The late decision to fingerprint. The photographs of the
desk. They all built up an overwhelming case. What did superintendents
get for attempting to pervert the course of justice? Seven years? Eight?
And what happened to them? Prison was a terrible place for fallen
coppers. The higher they were the harder and more miserable was their
fall. Years of beatings, 'accidents' in the washroom, until the relief of an
open prison brought the torture to an end. Why did they do it? Why did
they do it?

Mr Justice Phillips drained his glass and prepared to leave when a
voice spoke unexpectedly behind his shoulder.

'Good speech. Enjoyed it very much. Can I get you another one of
those?'

The man who now stood between Bob Phillips and the fire was only
slightly familiar. Slim, athletic, fifty-something, sixty perhaps. Silver hair
neatly cut and a suspicious tan.

'You may not remember me but we were, in fact, at Christ Church
together. I was two years ahead of you reading French. Adams, Richard
Adams.'

'Of course, you've got a half Blue, tennis.'

'Squash actually. Same sort of thing. Let me get you another one of
those.'

'No really.'

'I'm only having one myself and then I'm going home. Need the last
train.'

'Thank you. But it will only be one I'm afraid. I'm in court in the morning and have a difficult day in store.'

While Richard Adams got the drinks, Bob Phillips tested his recollection. In relation to Richard Adams there was something on the edge of his memory. A shadow. Something vaguely dislikeable. When he returned Bob Phillips accepted his brandy. 'Thank you, very kind. Tell me, were you in politics?'

Richard Adams settled himself in the next chair, crossed his legs and arranged the creases of his trousers. 'Good memory. I dabbled a bit. Conservative Association actually. Not much came of it. I thought about trying for Parliament but went into the Civil Service instead. Foreign office first, then Home Office. Under Secretary, nothing special.'

'Are you still there?'

'Sort of. I've done some interesting stuff. Security services mainly. That sort of thing. Cheers.'

Bob Phillips looked at his companion closely. 'Are you a member here?'

'No, but I have visiting rights and I came to hear you. Nice to have a chat. How's the Trial of the Century?'

Bob Phillips turned and glanced around the empty room, a gesture which he immediately regretted. 'Why did I do that?' he thought. 'Why do I feel *threatened*?' Aloud he said, 'It's going slowly. The papers are full of it. There are some over there.'

Richard Adams smiled at the obvious deflection. 'The best of it is not in the papers, I gather.'

'What do you mean?' said the judge sharply, placing his brandy firmly on the table between them. 'What do you mean?'

'Oh, I gather there is a background. Nailor and Cole go back a long way. And there is this poor bugger with Menkies' Syndrome, complicates things. All very difficult.'

'You seem to know a lot about this?'

'Quite a lot really. I gather Cole has done well in the witness box. I've been told that things look rather bad for Nailor after today.'

Watching him Mr Justice Phillips said nothing. Adams continued, 'I am also told that there is some question about Aylen. It is Aylen, isn't it? Some question about Aylen being Unfit to Plead. I understand that that decision had been deferred?'

'If you are asking me,' said the judge with deliberation, 'if you are asking me, then that is correct. It is a difficult decision. He is plainly ill but no one wants to confine him to a life in Broadmoor without trial.'

'Absolutely. Still, as *I* understand the matter, *if* Aylen was found Unfit to Plead then the trial would have to stop, would it not? And then the prosecution would have to decide whether they would proceed against Nailor on a new trial. *Without Aylen*. Am I right?'

'You are right.'

'And I suppose without Aylen in the dock ready to put the finger on Nailor the prosecution might just decide that there was no point in going on, despite Superintendent Cole's clever performance to date. It might even be, of course, that after a few years in Broadmoor the authorities might decide to move him quietly to a nice sanatorium. Somewhere his parents could visit him regularly. That way quite a lot of justice would be done.'

When Richard Adams' voice stopped the library in the Athenaeum became very quiet. The fire, on its last embers, gave no noise and the distant voices from the dining room had now disappeared with their owners into the London night.

The judge's voice was cold with warning. 'What are you saying to me and on whose behalf are you saying it?'

Both questions remained unanswered.

'Roddy Nailor has an interesting past. He has a number of attributes which don't involve hammers or nails, electrodes, or electric saws. Sometimes men like Nailor can provide outstanding service to their country. Unknown, unheralded and unsung. It would be a great pity, even a great *injustice* if these services were completely unrewarded.'

'I am quite sure,' said Mr Justice Phillips, 'that those who represent Roddy Nailor will place all these good qualities before the court in due course.'

'Ah, well there's the problem, you see. There are some things so wonderful that they cannot be allowed to shine. In those circumstances we can only be grateful that the great powers of law and justice *may* be exercised with regard to a Greater Good. I am sure you will agree.'

'Not entirely.'

'I think that it is helpful to understand that these powers of influence are so important, so central, so *vital* to the interests of the Greater Good that they are also *rare*. Only in the most exceptional circumstance is such influence brought to bear.'

'And if this "influence" does not succeed? If the object of this "influence" is not persuaded? What can be done then?'

Richard Adams performed a shrug, close to irritation, and drained the remainder of his brandy.

'I don't think,' he said, arranging himself for departure, 'I don't think that this influence has ever failed on the *very rare occasions* when it has been used. Who knows the powers of the mighty. No doubt they are terrible but mercifully unused. In any event,' he said rising, 'how very nice to see you again and to listen to your excellent speech. I live on Clapham Common. My name is in the book. If you would like to talk to me I would be delighted to have another little chat. Please don't get up. I see you have not finished your brandy.' Without waiting for a reply Richard Adams turned on his heel, the silence of the library being momentarily disturbed by the quiet shutting of the mahogany door. Alone, Mr Justice Phillips lifted his glass and was alarmed to note that his hand was shaking.

Later, alone in his study, Bob Phillips sat and surveyed the dreadful landscape of doubt. Outrage and irony welded together. Here was the ultimate abuse of power. The bully, the gangster and the killer protected by the machinery of government itself. But what government? How high did this go? How powerful? On arriving home Bob Phillips had phoned an old friend, now a Permanent Secretary in the Cabinet Office. Richard Adams was real all right. 'Powerful chap,' his friend had told him. 'Slightly shadowy. Makes deals in very high places. Avoid at all costs.'

Then came irony. In the court safe at the Old Bailey, and known only to Mr Justice Phillips himself, lay the incontrovertible proof of the perversion of evidence. Proof which would free Roddy Nailor in any event and, in all probability, would effect his pardon for past crimes and render him grossly enriched at the State's expense. Mr Justice Phillips stared at the top of his desk. Why had he not mentioned this to Adams? 'Don't worry,' he could have said, 'Nailor is out in any event. Tomorrow morning the case against him will be broken. He will be free, free to place his evil talents at the disposal of the State and, by reason of the power that he possessed, above the law and laws of ordinary men.'

Now what should he do? He could go to the highest authority. The prime minister if necessary. He could recount in all its detail the conversation in the Athenaeum. To what effect? Without its own atmosphere, its own innuendo, the conversation was little enough. A concerned enquiry of an informed acquaintance. As to the information about Nailor it could be dismissed as a misinterpretation. He heard the voice of Richard Adams, 'Completely misunderstood. Totally misinterpreted. I simply said that men like Nailor are *often used by* Government agencies. As a matter of fact I said it was very undesirable,' et cetera, et cetera.

It was not until the early morning that Mr Justice Phillips fell into a trouble sleep. Two hours later, at seven a.m., his alarm awakened him and his apprehensions.

At nine o'clock precisely Bob Phillips set out for the old Bailey. He did so with the step of a man in whom all dilemmas have been resolved. Mr Justice Phillips knew his duty and was going to do it.

# Chapter 23

When he arrived at his room in the Old Bailey Bob Phillips summoned his court clerk, who arrived after five minutes carrying the two exhibits.

'No one has touched them except me,' he said immediately, 'I put them in a discrete part of the safe and they were unmoved this morning.'

'Thank you,' said the judge, 'please leave them on my desk and, if you could, organise me some coffee.'

When the clerk returned about twenty minutes later he observed that the two newspapers lay apparently untouched in position where he had left them.

'Edward Boyd is trying to organise his witnesses,' he said; 'he asked me to enquire whether you still had questions for Superintendent Cole?'

'Oh yes,' said the judge firmly, 'oh yes. Tell Edward Boyd it will take ten minutes or so. You can take those in and put them back on the exhibits table.'

In Court One of the Old Bailey it had not gone unnoticed that the judge had retained the two exhibits, causing various speculations on counsel's benches.

'I wonder,' said John Wilkin to Preston Lodge, 'what he has seen in those newspapers? He seemed very interested yesterday. I think you should have a really good look at them, Preston. Do it this morning. Get them from the exhibits officer after Cole has given his evidence.'

At half past ten precisely Mr Justice Phillips resumed his seat and the courtroom, still packed to overflowing, fell silent.

'I'll call Superintendent Cole again,' said Edward Boyd, and Eddie Cole, already positioned below the witness box, climbed the short row of steps and smiled politely towards the judge whose face remained cold as stone.

'Superintendent Cole, I wanted to ask you some more questions about these two exhibits, 629A and the newspaper which you produced yesterday which, I think is now exhibit 121. I wonder if you would have them both before you in the witness box. Thank you. The jury can follow this on the photocopies with which they have now been provided.

Now Mr Cole, at first sight these two newspapers appear to be identical copies of the *Evening News* for the twenty-seventh of February 1988, do they not?'

'They do. They do,' Eddie Cole looked down at the two front pages and then frowned. 'No, they are not absolutely identical.'

'Precisely,' said the judge, 'there is one significant difference, is there not? They are different editions of the evening paper for the same day. Everything on the front page is identical, including the headline and sub-headings and the important "flag" relating to Mr Nailor's article. However, on exhibit 121, your newspaper which you produced yesterday, there also appears the words "late edition" and "closing prices". Do we all see that, members of the jury?'

In the jury box eleven heads nodded obediently and the girl with the safety pin scowled.

'Superintendent Cole, I want to ask you if you had noticed this before today.'

'No, this is the first time I have seen this difference.' Eddie Cole was a professional. Thirty-two years in the Metropolitan Police, living close to the edge of most forms of danger, enabled him to face disaster with apparent sangfroid. This was no exception. He looked evenly at the judge and smiled a polite smile of mild surprise. Beneath the surface things were rather different.

'Oh fuck!' thought Eddie Cole to himself. 'Oh fuck, fuck, fuck, fuck! Goodbye Superintendent Cole, hello hard labour.'

The deep primitive silence, already described, had now fallen upon the court. This stillness which precedes the sudden kills.

'It would appear, therefore,' continued the judge, 'if you are right about the delivery of these newspapers, that Mr Nailor sent two copies of this newspaper to two different persons, yourself and Melanie Golding, but chose to send two different editions.'

'That would appear to be the case. But I can see a possible explanation for that.' Eddie Cole was running but he was not down. 'It may well be that he was provided with different editions by different people.'

The judge looked hard at his witness. 'That, Superintendent, is simply speculation.'

'Indeed it is. I can do nothing else.'

Mr Justice Phillips' eyes had narrowed for a moment and met those of Superintendent Cole involuntarily. Both nodded imperceptibly in the mutual acknowledgement of a shared truth. A smile spread across the judge's face. 'Yes, Superintendent Cole, for what it is worth that was my speculation as well.'

Turning briskly to Sir Edward Boyd, he said, 'Thank you, Sir Edward, that's all I want to ask. Does anyone have anything arising from that?'

On counsel's benches there was a universal shaking of heads, until John Wilkin rose as though motivated by afterthought. 'There is just one matter my Lord. I think before your Lordship brought it to our attention none of us had appreciated that these newspapers were indeed different editions. For my part I would like to have them thoroughly examined, which can be done after the court rises this evening by my learned junior, Mr Lodge, if the exhibits can be made available to him, under supervision of course. If we discover anything of interest, may I assume that Mr Cole can be recalled to deal with such a point?'

'Of course, Mr Wilkin, of course that will be done. I think that Mr Cole will give evidence again in any event when we deal with the police operation and the arrest in St Albans. You will have a further opportunity to cross-examine him then, or, indeed, at any earlier time which may be convenient. I rather doubt if Mr Cole is going to travel very far. Am I right, Superintendent?'

'Australia, if possible,' thought Eddie Cole, and said, 'No, my Lord, I will be here every day at the court's convenience.'

'Well, there we are,' said Mr Justice Phillips pleasantly. 'Perhaps the usher could give those two exhibits to Mr Lodge who will, of course, undertake to return them in precisely the same condition as he found them. Now, Sir Edward, I gather that we now come to that part of the evidence that deals with the police operation and the arrest at St Albans. Distressing though this may be, I rather doubt that very much of this evidence will be an issue. We shall see.'

For the remainder of the morning Sir Edward Boyd called evidence from police officers, members of the Special Branch and other forces who had taken part in the catastrophic rescue of Melanie Golding at St Albans. As anticipated by the judge, very little of the evidence was the subject of dispute. The first police officer, a sergeant from the Special Branch called Neil Atkins, told of the assault on the house and the use of the battering ram. He spoke of the armed resistance which was encountered immediately after the first charge, from a downstairs room from which such resistance had been wholly unexpected. He had been beside Detective Sergeant Davidson when he was shot and had himself returned fire which had been responsible for the death of one of the Jones brothers. He had remained in the downstairs part of the house in order to check and clear the remaining rooms which were, in the event, empty. He had swiftly learnt that Melanie Golding was not, as expected, in the upper rooms from which he had heard firing. He had assisted Chief Superintendent Wagner, who was leading the operation, to open the one remaining door which, it transpired, led to the small cellar. He himself had not entered the cellar behind Chief Superintendent Wagner. He had intended to do but, at that moment, had been distracted by the arrival of Eddie Cole. Not immediately recognising the superior officer (who was not a member of the Special Branch) he had attempted to stop him from entering the premises in accordance with his general instructions. He had been brushed aside and had watched as Superintendent Cole first mounted the stairs a short way and then, having observed the shooting of Bedser, immediately returned and disappeared into the cellar. From the cellar Atkins had heard one shot and confused shouting. He learned later, of course, that this shot had critically wounded Melanie Golding. That was the end of his evidence. Thereafter he had assisted in the clearance operation and the subsequent debriefing.

Jane Wilson cross-examined. 'I have only this to ask you, Mr Atkins. You, I think, assisted Mr Wagner in opening the cellar door?'

'That is correct.'

'It would appear therefore, would it not, that the cellar door was locked?'

'Yes, it was securely locked.'

'And am I right that the door was locked from the *outside*?'

'That is correct. It was locked from our side. The key was in the lock which is why it took our attention in the first place. There was also a bolt.'

'And the bolt, am I right in suggesting that this was also in place? That is to say, the door was bolted as well as locked?'

'That is correct.'

'So it is a statement of the obvious, is it not, that both people within the cellar were, in effect, prisoners?'

Sir Edward Boyd was on his feet. 'I do wish my learned friend would choose her words with more care. If she means that both people within the cellar were apparently unable to obtain egress without some assistance from the outside, then she is undoubtedly right. The term "prisoner" is prejudicial in the case of Aylen. It is a statement of the obvious that he may well have been a guard rather than a victim. That is, of course, the Crown's case.'

'I am quite sure,' said Mr Justice Phillips, smiling at the jury, 'that the ladies and gentlemen had these matters well on board and will not be deflected by any looseness of language.'

In the jury box eleven heads nodded and one face scowled.

'Do you have any further questions, Miss Wilson?'

'None at all, my Lord,' said Jane Wilson, thinking, 'Why is he being so affable? Something has happened to him.'

John Wilkin took his turn. 'So, Mr Atkins, to summarise, there were, in addition to Melanie Golding, four men in the house, Bedser, Aylen and the Jones brothers?'

'That is correct.'

'Tell me, Mr Atkins, as a police officer, do you have any previous experience of any of these men?'

'Only the Jones brothers, from some years back.'

'Where was that?'

'I had a spell of duty in Cardiff during, I think, the Jubilee celebrations. I was part of an operation which led to their eventual arrest. Both, if I recollect, received long prison sentences for extortion.'

'That was in Cardiff, am I correct?'

'That is right.'

'Can you confirm, Mr Atkins, from your knowledge that Cardiff was (if I may use the vernacular) their "patch"? They were not known London criminals?'

'That is correct.'

From the Bench Mr Justice Phillips intervened. 'They do get about a bit you know, Mr Wilkin.'

'Just so, my Lord, just so. I have no further questions.'

During the rest of the morning a succession of police officers gave their similar accounts of the mayhem of the early morning. At the conclusion of the evidence, in the small and ill-equipped library provided for the services of counsel at the Old Bailey, Preston Lodge was carefully examining exhibits 629A and 121, the newspapers upon which the entire future of the Trial of the Century and Superintendent Eddie Cole hung in the balance.

# Chapter 24

Post-coital Eddie Cole lit a cigarette and propped himself up against the pillows.

'Something's wrong,' said Anita Flynn, 'I can feel it.'

'Not wrong, more like catastrophic. I hope you enjoyed it. That may very well be our last.'

'I wouldn't say that, I thought you were getting better.'

'It's not me, it's where I'm going. They don't let you out for extra-marital sex and the way they treat coppers in there they will probably chop it off anyway.'

'What are you talking about?' said Anita Flynn. 'Where are you going?'

'Who knows? The Scrubs, the 'Ville, Brixton, Sing-Sing, Alcatraz, Robben Island?'

Anita Flynn's raven head loomed out of the darkness. 'What have you done? You are not joking, are you?'

'Not joking, not joking at all. It's the newspapers. I fucked it up. The joke is I didn't even have to do it. It was just a bit extra. The final demonstration of truth. All unnecessary.'

'What *are* you talking about?'

'I told you. I changed the pages which contained Nailor's article. I reckoned that Nailor would have been unable to resist looking at his own handiwork and so his dabs would have been on the inside page as well as the front. By putting it in the second newspaper then there was a strong probability that his dabs would be in both of them. *If* they had dared to test the second paper for fingerprints then they would have found precisely that. Bingo! End of Nailor's case. Off he goes to Parkhurst. But what I didn't realise was that the newspapers were *different editions*. My *Evening News* was the late edition which has the closing prices on the Stock Exchange. The earlier edition has different prices. I wasn't able to get the originals back but I have looked at the photocopies we took. The back page which corresponds to the Nailor article carried those closing prices. So the *earlier* edition, 629A, has got the *closing* prices. The judge has been looking at the papers. He's obviously missed it. But this morning he drew attention to the fact that they *are* different. Nailor's people have asked to see the two newspapers so they can be thoroughly checked. There is no way that they will miss it. Back I go into the witness box and get fried on a grid iron.'

'What will happen?'

'Oh, the trial will be stopped. This is in reality the only evidence against Nailor. The Crown offers no evidence against him. He gets acquitted. Then there is an enquiry. The Chinaman case will be reviewed. As I provided the main evidence in that case and *that* evidence was fingerprints on a fucking hammer, that will be deemed to be unsafe. Full pardon. Compensation for ten years in the slammer, say two million and probably a knighthood and the Queen's medal. Sir Roddy Nailor fucks off to the south of France on his yacht. The press goes berserk about miscarriages of justices. Then comes the trial of good old Eddie Cole. *Ex*-Superintendent Eddie Cole. *Two* miscarriages of justice. One narrowly avoided. Ten years down the steps with my good old bollocks hanging on the first bath house that I visit. With Nailor gone Aylen doesn't stand a prayer. How can you say you were acting under duress applied by Saint Roddy fucking Nailor, the well-known victim and class hero? Everyone will close ranks. He'll go Unfit to Plead. Off to Broadmoor with the *real* maniac bastards and his bollocks will end up on the wall just like mine. Lovely. Well done E. Cole. That's what you get for trying to play God.'

'Can't you get hold of the newspapers? Put the pages back where they came from?'

'No chance. Thanks but no chance. When the defence asked to look at them the judge, as a sensible precaution, and to protect everybody of course, ordered that the individual pages should be marked by the court usher. The whole thing is set in stone. I watched them being marked immediately the judge handed them back this morning. Unless Preston Lodge has completely lost his marbles (and they're just about the biggest marbles at the criminal Bar) then by now they will have the whole thing stitched up and, after the caning I gave him in court yesterday, John Wilkin will be dribbling into his steak au poivre.'

'Can't you bring out all the stuff about Nailor? The Security Forces. The burglary of the Foreign Secretary. The whole involvement of the Special Branch?'

'It's not going to help, is it? I thought of that. I haven't got a grain of evidence and I can't exactly *make any* now, can I? That really would be asking for the rack and transportation. And what's worse, it provides motive. If I say that I believed that Nailor is guilty of all of this and burglarising the Government twenty years ago, they will think I am completely barking and shove me in Broadmoor with poor old Aylen. *And* they will set up a paranoid obsession with Nailor which provides the motive for fitting him up. No, I've turned it inside out and upside down. There is nothing I can do, Anita my darling, except get my old boy working as often as possible while I've still got him.'

In the darkness Eddie Cole started with surprise as the hand of Anita Flynn touched the side of his face, stroking between his chin and the bald ridge of his forehead.

'That's nice,' he said.

'You know something, Superintendent Cole. You're not a bad bastard. You're a *bastard*. It's odd isn't it? I've known you for twenty years. I can't think of a single rule that you haven't broken. You're above it all. You don't care. You take the most terrible risks, but never, never, never once in all that time have I known you do anything that was *wrong*. What am I saying? Everything you do is wrong but it's not *wrong*.'

'Mrs Flynn, Mrs Flynn, I do believe you're crying.'

'Don't be such a bloody idiot. It's just that cigarette smoke getting in my eyes. Now put it out and drink that whisky and I'll go and get another bottle and you can drink as much as you like and I will do some wonderful things to you Superintendent Cole so when they chop it off in Wormwood Scrubs they will wonder what the hell you have been doing to it.'

At that point the telephone rang.

'It's for you,' said Anita Flynn, 'it's Brendan.'

'Brendan, what the fuck is it? It's a quarter past bloody twelve.'

'I know, guv, I know. I can't control when she wakes up. She doesn't know what time of day it is, she's hardly been conscious for the last nine months.'

'All right, Brendan, all right. I'm sorry. What have we got, Brendan? Has she given you any more?'

'Not exactly, guv. All I've got so far is Aylen definitely in the flat. They've had a short conversation and she'd seen his face. Yes I know, guv, I know. I've told you this and she hasn't actually given me any more. I can't even manage to get her to sign that. But since they took the bullet out she's different. Her expression is different. She doesn't thrash about. She's much more calm. Twice she's woken up and looked at me and tried to speak. Her eyes are totally clear and twice she has said she can remember. She knows who I am and she says "Brendan I can remember it all." But she can't stay with it. Very quickly she just goes back. But I think we are close. I really think we are close. Can you do anything to stop this trial?'

'What do the doctors say?'

'Well that's the problem. They won't say anything that's different. Could be weeks, could be months, could be years. They don't see what I see. They haven't sat with her day and night like I have. They don't know that she's *different*.'

'Brendan, my old bugger, my old Mick,' said Eddie Cole, 'I'm afraid it's not enough. They won't adjourn this trial. Nailor's been in the nick for ten years. Unless the boys in white coats tell us she's going to be all right in a specified time then we are pissing in the wind. And also, Brendan, my old mucker, we have much bigger problems than this. No, I can't tell you on the telephone and probably never will. I am afraid this ship is inches from the rocks and the captain just jumped it. Now don't *you* worry. It's got nothing to do with you and you will be all right. You go and sit by your lady and contemplate your navel or whatever you Jesuits do. If you want to pray you can pray for her and pray for my poor old dick.'

'Guv, you sound terrible. What can I do?'

'Absolutely nothing, Brendan. Absolutely nothing, unless you can walk on water or raise the dead or feed the fucking world. Now go back to your lady and look after her.'

In the darkness Eddie Cole heard the cupboard door swing and the slight, swift grinding of a bottle uncapped. Holding his glass towards the figure beside the bed he said, 'Don't turn it on.'

'Would I do something like that,' said Anita Flynn, 'with an ugly bastard like you. Now let's get started.'

# Chapter 25

Eddie Cole arrived at the Old Bailey after five hours' sporadic coitus and a bottle and a half of whisky. He was, so he subsequently maintained, in a perfect condition to be arrested. Unhappily, on entering the police room set aside for the trial of Nailor and Aylen, he discovered George 'Fast Track' Watson in deep conversation with Jack Wagner. George Watson was making one of his rare visits to the court in order to 'keep up to date'.

'Good morning, Eddie,' he said without rising. 'I say, you don't look at all well.'

Jack Wagner wrinkled his nose. 'Doesn't smell well either. Been hit by a runaway still?'

'I think you ought to sit down, Superintendent Cole.'

'I had a bad night. My uncle died suddenly. Terminal cunnilingus.'

'Good Lord,' said George Watson, 'I'm so sorry. Had he been ill long?'

'About ten minutes. Got him quite suddenly. My mother took it very badly.'

'I thought your mother was dead?' said Jack Wagner.

'Only briefly,' said Eddie Cole, 'she's fine now and living in Margate. Can we get on?'

'George has come down to see how we are getting on. I've told him it's all going very well. I *even told* him how you stitched up John Wilkin. Generous bugger, aren't I?'

George Watson interrupted, 'I have been to see Edward Boyd. He tells me that the prosecution case may finish within a matter of days.'

'It may be a lot quicker than that,' said Eddie Cole. 'Maybe today.'

'Good Lord,' said George Watson, 'how extraordinary.'

Jack Wagner's eyes had narrowed. 'Do you know something I don't?'

'Now where,' said Eddie Cole, 'would you like me to begin on that one?'

'Never mind,' said Jack Wagner, 'we need to go. They want us in court at half-past ten sharp. Some barney about the newspapers I gather. Our precious exhibit 629A.'

'Surprise me,' said Eddie Cole.

At 10.30, Mr Justice Phillips took his seat and the courtroom, which remained full to capacity, settled in anticipation of the day's drama.

John Wilkin was on his feet, which the judge acknowledged with a raised eyebrow of faint surprise.

'My Lord, before the case continues there is a matter of some seriousness which I must bring to your Lordship's attention.'

'Yes, Mr Wilkin, what can I do for you.'

'My Lord, it concerns the two copies of the *Evening News* to which your Lordship drew attention yesterday. Your Lordship will remember pointing out that they were, in fact, different editions.'

'Indeed I did, Mr Wilkin. Indeed I did.'

'Your Lordship will also remember that I informed your Lordship that we intended to carry out a thorough check of the two newspapers in the light of your Lordship's observations.'

'I do indeed, Mr Wilkin. Has it been done?'

'My Lord, that is the point. I am afraid it has not. We have encountered a difficulty with which I would ask your Lordship's assistance. As you know the exhibits are held by the exhibits officer in the exhibits room which has been specifically designated to this case. The room itself comes under the control of the court's staff. It is apparently a rule that this exhibits room is locked at four thirty. It has been quite impossible for Mr Lodge to examine the newspapers in any detail. The exhibits room, likewise, is not *opened* until ten fifteen in the morning which also provides no reasonable time for this work to be carried out. It would, of course, be possible for Mr Lodge to conduct his inspection whilst the court was sitting. However, we are rapidly approaching evidence which will be of considerable importance to my client and I would wish Mr Lodge to be in court.'

'What would you like me to do, Mr Wilkin? You know that I have no control over the court's administration whatsoever.'

'I wonder if I might ask your Lordship to rise early today, say at three o'clock, in order to give Mr Lodge and his pupil and my instructing solicitor a good hour in which to carry out this work. I anticipate that it will be sufficient. There are only thirty-four pages in the newspapers.'

The judge turned to prosecuting counsel. 'Sir Edward, does the Crown have any observations on that?'

'None at all, my Lord. Indeed it may very well be convenient. I can inform your Lordship of the future conduct of the trial. We have proceeded at a faster pace than we anticipated. This morning I propose to call two or three neighbours of the premises in St Albans who may be of assistance to the court. Thereafter I have been told that I can read formally the medical evidence relating to Melanie Golding, so that will be comparatively short. I then come to the arrest of Mr Nailor by Superintendent Cole which, of course, .took place *before* Melanie Golding was released. Your Lordship will be aware that this evidence is the subject of a legal challenge. My learned friend will seek to exclude it from the trial. At that point, therefore, we may dispense with the services of the jury while that matter is considered by your Lordship. We may arrive at that point before the lunch adjournment and may well finish that part of the trial today by three p.m. That will enable my learned friend and Mr Lodge to consider the newspapers and, if necessary, I will recall Superintendent Cole tomorrow morning.'

The agenda having been set, the Trial of the Century continued. As it did so Eddie Cole abruptly left the police benches in the well of the court and made a painful journey to the lavatories reserved for prosecuting officers, where he was violently sick. Immediately afterwards he telephoned Anita Flynn.

'How nice to hear you,' she said, 'where are you then, Alcatraz?'

'There are times when I think you have got a pretty funny sense of humour.'

'I have an abiding faith in the forces of light and justice. What happened?'

'They haven't looked at the bloody things yet. They couldn't get them out of the court's administration. I've just been sick.'

'I'm not surprised. You drank nearly two bottles of whisky and misbehaved badly. I think I'm beginning to believe your publicity. No mortal man could do that. So, another day's freedom. What are you going to do?'

'I have got to give fucking evidence again this afternoon. This trial is going like a missile. They have agreed a lot of the evidence. I'm on this afternoon dealing with Nailor's arrest. Can't concentrate. Feel ghastly. There is something wrong with my vision. I have to close one eye in order to focus. Eddie Cole giving evidence is not going to be a pretty sight.'

'What are you doing tonight?'

'Packing my toothbrush, reading my Baedeker on British Gaols. Nothing much.'

'You had better come here. I had arranged to entertain some *very* important people from the Middle East but I've taken quite a fancy to old coppers who are about to be castrated. I'll tell the sheikhs that the girls have got headaches.'

Leaving the police room Eddie Cole turned left and collided with Alex Bentley. Both men peered at each other suspiciously through one eye.

'Hello Eddie,' said Alex Bentley.

'What do you want?' said Eddie Cole.

'I want some inside track. I'd like to know what's really going on. What's happened to the girl? What's all this stuff about these newspapers? Is there going to be a story?'

'The story is that everything is going beautifully and that the forces of light and justice and joy are bound to prevail. What have you done to your blazer? If I were you I'd send it to some industrial cleaners. Now I must fly, I've got to give some evidence.'

As Eddie Cole walked past him Alex Bentley said, 'How's Anita Flynn? Still doing the business?'

Eddie Cole stopped dead in his tracks, turned and delivered his next sentences with his nose less than one inch from Alex Bentley's open eye. As he did so an extraordinary mixture of vapours were released into the corridors of the Central Criminal Court. 'Do you know how they killed Edward the Second in Berkeley Castle? You don't, do you? Now I am going to tell you because you're an ignorant, drunken pillock. They rammed a red hot poker straight into his anus. They did it so that there would be no marks on the body and also because he was homosexual and they had a pretty funny sense of humour. Now I want to tell you, Alex that if you even so much as breathe that woman's name here or anywhere else, aloud or in writing, then what will happen to you will make Edward the Second's stay at Berkeley Castle look like a package deal at fucking Tenerife. And don't think I'm being funny. In my job I meet some very odd people who owe me some very odd favours.'

As Eddie Cole walked back to Court One, he said to himself, 'Now why oh why? Why oh why did I do that?'

In Court One of the Old Bailey the trial of Nailor and Aylen was moving towards Nemesis at a steady pace. Three residents of St Albans gave evidence of their observations of the days preceding the police operation which released and crippled Melanie Golding. The house in question had been vacant for some time. Some weeks before the police operation they had all become aware of activity. A number of men appeared to have taken up residence. The house was furnished and the only deliveries were of food and drink. The men had kept to themselves and given no trouble before the night of the shooting. To all three witnesses Jane Wilson had carefully pointed out her client, observing each of them to narrow their eyes and glance downwards in sympathy and disgust.

'May I take it that you did not observe Mr Aylen in the vicinity of the house at any time?'

'No, I did not.'

'And, for reasons which must be obvious to everybody, had you seen him it is unlikely that you would have forgotten, do you agree?'

'I agree.'

Following upon their evidence, five medical reports were read as agreed documents. The first four related to those killed on the morning of November 2. The police officer Ian Davidson, 'Bonkers' Bedser and the Jones brothers had all died of internal injuries caused by bullet wounds. Ian Davidson had been shot three times, once in the eye.

Finally Antonia Black read the agreed medical report on the condition of Melanie Golding. On admission to hospital she was deeply unconscious. Examination revealed the presence of a bullet lodged beneath the dura and adjacent to the brain on the left side of her skull. Subdural haemorrhaging had occurred over a wide area, causing pressure upon the brain itself. The decision had been taken to leave the bullet in situ, carefully monitoring the quality of blood and taking appropriate medical steps against the spread of lead poisoning. Further disturbance within the subdural cavity (it was decided) would run the risk of further uncontrolled haemorrhage. The only other injuries were to her wrists which bore abrasions consistent with being bound or handcuffed. Internal examination revealed that sexual intercourse had occurred recently and a quantity of male semen was removed from the cervix. Subsequent DNA analysis had revealed beyond doubt that this emanated from Thomas Aylen.

During the reading of this report Jane Wilson observed the jury and reflected, as she had often done, on the power of human imagination. The cold, academic analysis advanced in the clinical vernacular created an impact far greater than that conveyed by the crude description of violence or pain. As the jury worked to understand the significance of the established facts, images like sharper splinters were embedded in the brain. Melanie Golding incarcerated, bound and raped, helpless in the power of the grotesque. Some stared at the desk before them. One of them cried and several allowed themselves to watch the dock for minutes at a time in silent fascination.

For the first time Jane Wilson felt the dull weight of inevitable misfortune. 'We can't do this,' she thought. 'Maybe Broadmoor is best. Maybe we should let him go.'

Finally, before the recall of Superintendent Eddie Cole, evidence was produced as to the physical condition of Thomas Aylen. By common consent the nature and consequences of his mental condition was deferred to the expert psychiatrists assembled on both sides. The consultant neurosurgeon from Ardingley Military Hospital referred merely to 'severe damage to the frontal lobes of the brain' before passing to the physical defects and disabilities. The bomb had apparently exploded as Thomas Aylen had passed the car, which resulted in the full impact being delivered to his right-hand side. The bottom half of his right arm had simply been destroyed in the blast, no amputation being necessary other than the creation of a stump below the elbow. Vast soft-tissue injury had been caused to the right buttock and leg. The right testicle had been destroyed. From these injuries there had been partial recovery. He was able to walk without sticks or crutches but only by dragging the right leg behind him in order to use it as a prop for further momentum. A prosthesis had been attached to the right arm which he had learnt over several months to operate by flexing the remaining muscles and ligaments. The electrical impulses so deployed gave him some dexterity with a metal claw grip at the end of a jointed aluminium shaft. For obvious cosmetic reasons these two 'fingers' were encased in a black glove. The witness then turned to the facial injuries. These were very extensive but, remarkably, affected only the right-hand side. Thus in left profile Thomas Aylen was virtually unchanged. On the right the blast had effectively burnt away all the flesh and crushed the facial bones from the forehead to the jawbone. The eye socket was totally depressed. Many operations had been carried out by a team of cosmetic surgeons, grafting large areas of skin and bone from the left leg and arm. No skill or craft, however, could recover any sense of normality. The right side of the face remained a fallen slab, the mouth on that side resembling little more than a blackened hole without control or motion. This obviously proved a severe impediment to speech. Further clinical details of deformity followed. The jury became inattentive. They had before them the visual testimony.

Jane Wilson cross-examined. 'These injuries were all caused by one enormous blast?'

'Yes they were.'

'So great was the blast that two other men in the immediate vicinity were killed instantly?'

'I believe that is the case.'

'From the hospital records is it possible to tell whether Aylen was conscious or unconscious when he arrived at the first hospital in Armagh?'

'It appears from the record that he was conscious. I must say I find this extraordinary but perfectly possible.'

'If he was conscious it is likely, is it not, that he would have suffered terrible pain?'

'Quite unendurable.'

'I see from the hospital records, "patient in grave discomfort but co-operates". Would you like to translate that for us?'

'Yes. This is a classic understatement employed in clinical notes. In reality, in lay terms, it means that the patient was in terrible pain.'

'And "co-operative", would I be correct in assuming that his means that the pain was being borne with considerable fortitude?'

'That would be the case. It is an indication that despite his suffering Thomas Aylen was able literally to co-operate with his medical staff.'

Sir Edward Boyd was on his feet, 'My Lord, I really don't want to interrupt my learned friend but I wonder where this is going? No one has questioned Thomas Aylen's bravery and credentials. Indeed we were at considerable pains to endorse these during the course of our opening and have done so at every opportunity.'

'Good,' thought Jane Wilson, looking at the jury, 'they don't like him interfering with this. They think it is unfair.'

Mr Justice Phillips, observing a similar reaction, gave it voice. 'Yes, well, Sir Edward, you are probably technically right. But it is entirely understandable that the jury should wish to know the character of the man in their charge at first hand. Whether, in the long run, it assists Mr Aylen's cause is, of course, a matter entirely for them. I shall let Miss Wilson continue.'

'I had, in any event, nearly finished. I have only this. According to the hospital notes, for how long did his treatment continue?'

'Approximately one year.'

'Thereafter he was transferred to the rehabilitation unit and was taught, amongst other things, to write with his left hand?'

'That is right. It was to assist him to follow some kind of clerical occupation.'

Jane Wilson nodded and resumed her seat.

John Wilkin rose. 'The picture that we get is of a young man of considerable bravery and fortitude?'

'That is right.'

'A man perfectly suited for the calling of a soldier or Marine?'

Beside him on the bench Jane Wilson was beginning to stir in opposition. Her eyes met those of the judge before the witness answered.

'That is not really a matter for me. It may be thought to be obvious that such qualities were quintessentially military.'

'Just so. Forgive me for seeking the obvious again, but they are not qualities necessarily associated with clerical employment?'

'I am a consultant neurosurgeon and not an expert in the psychology of employment. But if you wish me to answer, that observation appears reasonable.'

'Someone with these undoubted qualities might well find the prospect of clerical work deeply frustrating, might they not?'

Jane Wilson was on her feet. Unnecessarily, as it transpired.

'Really, Mr Wilkin,' said the judge with an impressive frown, 'you know perfectly well that that is not just simply comment, it is comment to a witness with no conceivable qualifications to make any observations upon it.'

John Wilkin smiled a broad smile of transparent and disingenuous charm. 'My Lord, I am so sorry. We *all* stray from time to time and I am no exception. I do hope your Lordship will forgive me.'

'Once, Mr Wilkin, once. Thereafter the milk of human kindness will run very thin indeed. Do you have any further questions?'

'No.'

'Sir Edward. Do you have any re-examination?'

'No, my Lord.'

'I see. Well, that is very convenient. We will take the luncheon adjournment and after lunch I think we shall have the pleasure of seeing Superintendent Cole again, will we not? Mr Wilkin, I see that you are on your feet again. What can I do for you?'

'My Lord, as soon as Mr Cole returns to the witness box a matter of law and admissibility will arise for your Lordship's consideration.'

'And it will not concern the jury, Mr Wilkin, am I right? Yes? I thought so. Well, ladies and gentlemen of the jury, there you are. You may have the afternoon off. I will see everyone else at two o'clock.'

As the judge rose in order to be escorted from his Bench, John Wilkin turned to Jane Wilson and murmured, 'He's learning very fast, isn't he? The jury absolutely love him. I think they will do *exactly* what he tells them. I do wonder what that will be?'

As the court cleared, Eddie Cole stood watching the small knot of barristers discussing the strategies and tactics of the coming battles. Despite the inner turmoil caused by whisky and the direst apprehensions he smiled an ugly smile. They were, he reflected, like ancient geographers attempting to understand and plot the maps and topography of a future world. They little knew that lying before them on the exhibits table were two newspapers containing ancient news, the inspection of which would utterly destroy the entire landscape upon which their calculations were based.

# Chapter 26

At 2.15 Superintendent Eddie Cole re-entered the witness box. The volcanic effects of whisky and lack of sleep had now subsided into a dull, pervading pain. Normal vision had been restored but black 'floaters' hovered before his eyes like angry and silent mosquitoes. The court and public gallery remained crowded. The empty seats in the jury box provided a gaping contrast to the surrounding crush. In the absence of the jury the atmosphere of the court changed, as though, in a theatre, the front row of the stalls had decamped. The critics upon whom success or failure ultimately hung had gone about their business.

Sir Edward rose to his feet. 'My Lord, we are agreed on counsel's benches that I should deal very briefly with the evidence in chief. Your Lordship has a copy of Mr Cole's statement and this part of his evidence is at page 496 of your Lordship's bundle. It concerns the arrest of Mr Nailor. With your Lordship's leave I will simply ask Mr Cole briefly to rehearse his evidence before cross-examination.'

Mr Justice Phillips nodded his approval and Superintendent Eddie Cole began.

On 27 October 1988 Mr James Cameron, a solicitor from Dowsons, had come to Scotland Yard, anticipating, rightly, that his client Roddy Nailor was sought by the police. No information had been given to Mr Cameron relating to the investigation, but he was told that Nailor was required *only* for questioning. He was told that there was insufficient evidence to warrant his arrest or charge. On the following day he attended with Nailor and a short interview took place. By prior agreement this interview was not recorded in accordance with the Police and Criminal Evidence Act. This was done deliberately to render the interview informal and inadmissible in any future court proceedings. Certain events, however, had occurred after James Cameron's previous visit and before his return with Roddy Nailor. The most important of these was the discovery of the fingerprints on the newspaper which was found in Melanie Golding's flat. The purpose of the informal interview was to ascertain whether there could be an innocent explanation for the presence of this newspaper. When it appeared that Nailor would deny any association with Melanie Golding or, indeed with Thomas Aylen who was known at that time to be the kidnapper, the status of the evidence changed. At that critical stage Nailor was asked whether he objected to the proceedings taking place on a formal basis and being interviewed under caution. He expressly consented to this step and a short interview was recorded in accordance with the Code of Practice. Nailor continued to deny any association with Melanie Golding and, in those circumstances, he was arrested and charged. The earlier 'informal' discussion was immediately recorded in writing with the assistance of Sergeant Brendan O'Hara who had been present throughout.

Following this account Edward Boyd resumed his seat and John Wilkin rose to cross-examine. 'Superintendent Cole, may I begin by saying that the account you have given of the conversations between yourself and James Cameron and Mr Nailor is, in substance, agreed. There is the odd difference of recollection but nothing with which I need trouble you at this stage.'

'Thank you.'

'What I wish to explore and ascertain is your own state of mind as the police officer in charge of his investigation. At the time when James Cameron came to see you, his client, Roddy Nailor, was on a police wanted list. Is that correct?'

'That is correct. He was on the Most Wanted list.'

'Just so, but no warrant had been issued for his arrest. Is that also correct?'

'That is correct. There was no warrant. We wished firstly to ascertain the whereabouts of Mr Nailor and secondly to interview him. At the time when James Cameron came to see me we did not have sufficient evidence to arrest him.'

'In the time that elapsed between that visit and this subsequent interview with Mr Nailor it was ascertained that Mr Nailor's fingerprints were on the newspaper.'

'That is correct, as I have said.'

'Bear with me, Superintendent. So you were aware at that stage that this new evidence was available to you?'

'Obviously yes.'

'Yet when he arrived there was no arrest. Why was that?'

In the short silence which ensued Eddie Cole saw it coming. 'God,' he thought, 'the fucking rules. I should have prepared this better.' Suddenly he felt very tired. It was all a waste of time anyway. As soon as the newspapers were inspected the trial would come to a grinding halt.

Why bother with the charade? At that moment Eddie Cole gave up. 'I don't know.'

'I beg your pardon?' said John Wilkin, sensing, for the first time, real blood, 'I *beg your pardon?*'

'I said I don't know.'

'Superintendent Cole, how long have you been in the police force?'

'Thirty-three years.'

'And for nearly ten years you were Head, were you not, *Head* of the Serious Crime Squad, dealing with the most serious offences and most serious criminals in the country?'

'I was and I am.'

'Now let us look at this with some care. You know full well, do you not, in accordance with the rules, that when there is sufficient evidence to arrest a suspect he should be arrested and cautioned. That is right, is it not?'

'Of course.'

'The whole reason why this first arrangement had been made, the *informal chat*, was because there was insufficient evidence to arrest. Since you did not change that arrangement you must have considered, when Mr Nailor arrived with his solicitor, that there *still* was not sufficient evidence for him to be arrested and cautioned. That must be right, mustn't it?'

'I suppose so.'

'You suppose so?' In five minutes John Wilkin had grown physically in size. 'You *suppose* so?'

'One moment,' said Mr Justice Phillips, 'one moment please, Mr Wilkin.' With obvious deliberation the judge turned to face the witness box. Despite the indifference and weariness that had fallen upon him Eddie Cole was surprised at the concern on the judge's face. 'You must know, with your experience, that "I suppose so" simply will not do. Mr Wilkin is right, is he not? If the newspaper, in itself, with the fingerprints provided sufficient evidence to arrest and caution, then that *must* have been done. I am right?'

'Yes, my Lord.'

'In considering whether to allow this evidence I must proceed on one of two alternatives. Either you considered that there was insufficient evidence and were justified in continuing on an informal basis or else you considered that there was sufficient evidence to arrest and charge. In that case the caution should have been given *at that stage*. Now please address the question. What is the answer?'

Faced with no conceivable choice Eddie Cole walked into the trap.

'It must be that we did not consider that there was sufficient evidence to arrest and caution.'

'Notwithstanding the existence of the fingerprints on the newspaper?' John Wilkin's voice cracked like a flail.

'Yes.'

'In those circumstances we may take it, may we not, Superintendent Cole, that you did not contemplate arrest at the time that Mr Nailor came to see you. That must be right, mustn't it?'

'That would depend on the answers that he gave to the questions,' said Eddie Cole, and perceived through the dullness that beset him the fatal flaw of the answer.

'But, Superintendent, the very nature of the questions was such that they *could not* have formed evidence against Nailor. The plain fact is, Superintendent, is it not, that you deliberately started this interview on an agreed informal basis, notwithstanding the fact that you knew full well that what was said *without caution* would subsequently be used immediately to support this arrest. That is the truth, is it not?'

'No, it is not.'

'I see.' John Wilkin had won and he knew it, and it radiated across the lectern in waves of menace. 'I see. Now tell me, Superintendent Cole, it is right, is it not, that immediately after you told Nailor that he was to be arrested you issued a command by using the word "now"! If necessary we can listen to it on the tape.'

'There is no need to listen to the tape. Yes I did.'

'And that was a pre-arranged signal?'

'Obviously.'

'A pre-arranged signal to carry out an arrest?'

'Yes.'

'An arrest which you did not contemplate would even take place?'

Silence descended upon the court. The afternoon was hot. In the shafts of light which fell from a candelabra, dust hung and danced like lace.

'I will repeat the question again, Superintendent, an arrest which you *did not think was going to take place.*'

'We were prepared for an arrest.'

'Meticulously prepared, Superintendent. The plain truth is that this was a trap set for Nailor with the assistance of his own solicitor?'

'Yes.'

On the bench Mr Justice Phillips lifted his head, laid down his pen and stared at the witness. 'I beg your pardon? Did you say that this was a trap?'

'It was not my word.'

'But you agreed with it?'

'In essence.'

Again, through the blur of alcohol, tiredness and defeat, Eddie Cole registered surprise at the expression on the judge's face. Frustration, annoyance certainly but, unaccountably, regret.

Slowly Mr Justice Phillips turned to counsel's benches. 'I need trouble you no further, Mr Wilkin. The evidence of this interview plainly must be excluded in accordance with all the rules and authorities.'

John Wilkin, a smile barely suppressed across his pink face, nodded with acknowledgement.

Turning to the witness box, Mr Justice Phillips continued, 'I cannot but observe, Superintendent Cole, that it is a very great pity that police officers as experienced and distinguished as yourself do not obey the rules of interrogation that have been so clearly laid down in Code of Practice. It comes, I know, from a feeling that you are above such things. With your rank and the gravity of the cases that you investigate there is a belief that the rules do not matter. But they do, Superintendent, they do. I do not believe that this was deliberate. I believe that, in your anxiety to achieve the freedom and wellbeing of Melanie Golding you went too far without thought or premeditation. Also, perversely, I commend your candour in this court. Obviously there was an element of trap, which no court can condone. You may leave the witness box. Now Mr Wilkin, I see that the time is just gone three. We agreed, I think, that we would rise early to enable Mr Lodge to inspect these interesting newspapers.'

'Your Lordship is absolutely right, but I must say I had completely forgotten.'

'Very well,' said Mr Justice Phillips. 'We will reconvene at ten thirty tomorrow, when I think we will hear evidence of the arrest of Aylen and his subsequent interrogation.'

Sir Edward Boyd nodded in agreement and the court adjourned.

'That was bloody good,' said Preston Lodge, assembling his files into order. 'That's made a lot of difference.'

John Wilkin beamed upon him. 'Revenge is sweet, revenge is sweet, but where does it leave us? Do we get out at the end of the Crown case? Have they got enough evidence left?'

'I don't know,' said Preston Lodge thoughtfully. 'They have still got the newspapers, the association with Aylen at Bournemouth and the philosophical stuff, but that's all. They cannot positively exclude innocent possession without this evidence. There is always the possibility that it got there via Aylen or some other means unspecified. In my view I think they may still have just got enough to keep the case running after half time. And that's when our problems really start. Are we going to put our hero in the witness box to be fried alive by Edward Boyd *and* Jane Wilson? She's bloody good, incidentally. And we have got to watch our back. Aylen may give evidence. If we *don't* then we are hopelessly exposed.'

'That will all depend, will it not,' observed John Wilkin, 'on whether or not the judge raises the issue of Fitness to Plead. If he does then this trial is all over. Aylen goes off to Broadmoor and, given what's happened today, the prosecution will never go on against us alone. Sufficient unto the day, Preston, my dear boy. Now go and read those interesting newspapers.'

At four-thirty on the same day the same subject was considered by Jane Wilson, Gilbert Smith and Mary Shelley. They sat at Jane Wilson's desk, an early bottle of Pinot Grigio between them.

'Have an olive,' said Mary Shelley pushing the bowl towards Gilbert Smith, 'take one and pass on.'

She chewed for a moment, extracted a stone from between her teeth and placed it on the saucer of her empty teacup. 'John Wilkin did well. Losing that evidence was bad for us. We have got to keep Nailor in this frame. Can we put the evidence back in against him?'

'I've been thinking about that,' said Jane Wilson. 'Gilbert's done some research on it. I don't think we can. We may be able to do so if Nailor gives evidence and suggests, in some way, that our chap had the newspaper and left it in the flat. But he is not going to do that even if he gives evidence. He will simply say that the newspaper was sent to Eddie Cole and is a plant.'

'Is there still a case against Nailor? If the judge lets him out at the end of the prosecution case it will be a disaster. Try running duress by someone who has just been acquitted. It's a big problem.'

'My own view,' said Jane Wilson, 'is that the Crown have still got *just* enough. What worried me is the attitude of Edward Boyd. He is showing a marked lack of enthusiasm to get Nailor down. I don't understand it. If John Wilkin makes a submission of no case to answer and Edward Boyd waves it through then we may as well go to Broadmoor and have done with it. Incidentally, do you think we need to look at these newspapers ourselves?'

'I don't think so,' said Jane Wilson. 'I can't see that there is much in it. Let's see if Preston Lodge discovers anything. It's their business and not ours.'

# Chapter 27

'How did it go?' asked Anita Flynn

'I got murdered. In cold blood. I just lost it. Whisky, shagging, imminent imprisonment. They all got to me. Then John Wilkin turned me on a spit.'

'What does it mean?'

'The case against Nailor is much weaker but none of it matters. By now they will have sussed out the change in the newspapers. I'm first in the witness box tomorrow. Whatever happens then will make today look like a game of volleyball. Still, at least it will all be over.'

'Oh I don't know,' said Anita Flynn. 'I like these long goodbyes.'

At ten thirty precisely, for the third time in as many days, Super-intendent Eddie Cole mounted the steps of the witness box in the Old Bailey. The jury, expectant, had reassembled.

From his elevated position Eddie Cole could see the working papers spread across the counsels' desks. Lying before John Wilkin the two copies of the *Evening News*, apparently identical, lay like the books of Old Testament prophets, pregnant with accusation.

Sir Edward Boyd had risen to his feet but was interrupted.

'I wonder,' began John Wilkin, 'if I could raise one matter with your Lordship concerning the two copies of the *Evening News*, exhibits 629A and 121?'

'Of course, Mr Wilkin. Is this a matter we can all share or do the jury need to go on their travels again?'

'No, my Lord. It is something from which I feel we can all benefit.' As he spoke John Wilkin carefully took a newspaper in each hand. 'Your Lordship will remember observing that the newspapers were different editions and would therefore have contained different material. As your Lordship knows, my learned junior, Mr Lodge, has had the opportunity to check the two editions in order to ascertain whether there is any significance in that point which may affect the trial. I can tell your Lordship now that the newspapers differ in only one important aspect, which concerns share prices on the Stock Exchange.'

In the witness box Eddie Cole closed his eyes, took one deep breath and waited for the blow to fall.

'I can tell your Lordship as a matter of interest that share prices fell quite dramatically during the latter part of the day. That fact is recorded in the latter edition. I am pleased to say that there is no indication that this economic movement was in any way connected with my client's views on nineteenth-century philosophy. Your Lordship may be confident that that is the only matter of any significance. I hope that is of assistance to your Lordship and members of the jury.'

When he opened his eyes Eddie Cole could observe the polite smiles which still lingered on the faces of the jury in acknowledgement of the weak joke. Edward Boyd rose to his feet and began the proceedings of the day.

'Mr Cole, I know you have been in the witness box before and you will realise that you are still on oath. I want now to deal with the events of the second of November which culminated in the dawn raid on the premises at St Albans. When you give your evidence it would be of assistance if you could have before you the photographs and plan of the house in question. Ladies and gentlemen of the jury, you now know where to find these documents.'

In the short pause that followed while documents were assembled and the court usher placed the exhibits on the top of the witness box, Eddie Cole irresistibly lifted his eyes to meet those of the trial judge. From his bench Mr Justice Phillips, for the briefest of moments, held his gaze before lifting his own head to look with brief but rapt attention at the Latin inscription at the foot of the royal crest above his head.

'Domine dirige nos,' thought Eddie Cole, ' "God guide us". Well well well. Well well *well*.'

The remainder of Eddie Cole's evidence passed without significant event. Yes, he had missed the police briefing. He was not aware that it had been brought forward in time. Through inadvertence the batteries on his mobile phone were dead. Arriving late he had driven with all speed to St Albans and had arrived at the very moment that the assault on the house began. Immediately on entering the house he had seen the bodies of Detective Sergeant Davidson and the Jones brothers. On mounting the stairs he had observed the shooting of Bedser. Realising that the upstairs bedrooms were empty, he had descended the stairs and had seen the open cellar door. The speed with which he had descended the cellar steps had caused him to lose his balance and collide with Chief Superintendent Jack Wagner. It transpired that this accident had tragic consequences, namely the discharge of Chief Superintendent Wagner's firearm which had caused the injuries to Melanie Golding. Medical assistance had been summoned immediately (it was in fact on hand in the street). He had remained at the scene until Melanie Golding was taken by the ambulance. Thomas Aylen was arrested by Chief Superintendent Wagner and departed with officers of the Special Branch.

'Two more questions please,' said Sir Edward Boyd, his voice assuming a solemn tone. 'The condition of Melanie Golding. She was, of course, badly injured. What else can you tell us about her?'

'The cellar had obviously been turned into some form of a cell. There was a bed and a mattress on the floor. She was on the bed which was adjacent to metal pipework which obviously served the central heating system. One hand was handcuffed to these pipes.'

'Handcuffed?'

'Yes, these were not police handcuffs but they were of a type readily available in numerous shops. They were not toys.'

'What else can you tell us about her condition?'

'She was partially clothed, wearing what appeared to be a man's shirt. Other than that she was naked. There were two blankets beside her on the bed.'

'Thank you Mr Cole. That is all that I have to ask.'

John Wilkin, by an inclination of his head, indicated that he had no questions in cross-examination and, beside him, Jane Wilson rose.

'I have very little for you, Mr Cole. We already know that the cellar door had, before your arrival, been bolted on the outside. When you reached the bottom of the cellar steps Thomas Aylen was on the floor, was he not?'

'Yes, he was.'

'As far as you can see was he offering any form of resistance?'

'None at all. He had one arm raised in the air.'

'In a gesture of defiance or supplication?'

Sir Edward Boyd rose to his feet. 'I'm sorry to interrupt my learned friend again. Can Mr Cole really interpret the mind of the defendant? He can surely only describe the gesture itself.'

Mr Justice Phillips assumed a tone of weary resignation. 'Sir Edward, I will allow Miss Wilson to continue. To employ the use of the modern vernacular, Miss Wilson is seeking a description of "body language". Is that not right, Miss Wilson?'

'Your Lordship expresses it better than I could hope.'

'I think not, Miss Wilson, but it will do. Let us have an answer to the question Superintendent, defiance or supplication?'

'Supplication, without doubt.'

'That is all, thank you, Superintendent.'

And so Eddie Cole left the witness box a free man, by courtesy of an incorruptible High Court judge who could rearrange newspapers. The court rose for the lunch adjournment and within ten minutes he was in telephone communication with Anita Flynn.

'Where are you,' she said, 'the Gulag?'

'I am in heaven.'

'How nice. Any good clients around? Arabs, Japanese, members of the Royal Family?'

# Chapter 28

Superintendent Eddie Cole was sitting opposite his old friend Alan Barlow in a pub in Greek Street.

'Two more, Norman,' said Eddie Cole, raising his whisky glass in the direction of the bar.

'Get off your bloody arse,' replied the proprietor. 'Where do you think you are, Raffles?'

Eddie Cole purchased the drinks, returned to the table and looked squarely into the liquid eyes of the psychiatrist. 'Cheers.'

'Cheers Eddie. What is this stuff?'

'Norman's best, don't ask.'

'It could do without the water. What can I do for you, Eddie? Is this a social event?'

Without moving his gaze, Eddie Cole drank half his glass and set it down before him. 'I have been reading your report in the Aylen case.'

'I hope you enjoyed it.'

'Not entirely. You say that Aylen has Menkies' Syndrome.'

'Correct. Whatever that means, he has got it.'

'You also say that he was fit to be interviewed and understood the nature of the confession he made to Wagner.'

'Absolutely right. Wagner phoned me. Asked whether it was safe to interview the man in view of his obvious disabilities. I told Wagner to go ahead. Can't remember a lot about the conversation but broadly that's it. It is all in Wagner's statement anyway.'

'Alan, old friend, this is what I do not understand. When we were trying to find the girl long before the arrest, you came in and told us about Aylen. You told us that Menkies' Syndrome came from the destruction of the right frontal lobe of the brain and it made you totally suggestible, a robot.'

'Not totally suggestible, not necessarily. Sometimes it hardly affects you at all. Not many people know much about it.'

'Alan, that is *not* what you told us. You told us this boy was in danger of falling completely under the control of someone like Nailor, particularly in view of the fact that Nailor had gone totally barking mad and believed he could fly with a cape. If that's right it couldn't possibly be safe to take a confession from him. If he is likely to be manipulated by Roddy Nailor then he would be putty in the hands of an old pro like Wagner. What's changed? What's the game?'

Alan Barlow drained the remainder of his whisky glass and frowned. 'God, that's bloody awful. Want another?'

'Not yet. I want to know. Something happened to change your mind. I want to know what it was.'

Alan Barlow looked straight at Eddie Cole, and drew him into sharp focus. 'When I gave you the first opinion I did not know that he had shagged her on a bed to which she was chained in the cellar of a house in St Albans.'

'What difference does that make to his mental condition?'

'In itself, nothing, but it does, at the very least, demonstrate a certain element of enthusiasm. It's not just an intellectual process. In order to do what he did you have got to get your pecker up. You may remember doing that, Superintendent. I, myself, have a dim recollection. It is just possible to shag to order. I gather that the Zulus do it. But as I say it does require a certain level of motivation.'

'Suppose it wasn't rape?'

'Superintendent, what are you saying? She was chained to the bed. In a *cellar* in *St Albans*. In a *locked* cellar. There are all kinds of funny practices in this world. Some people enjoy setting their partners alight, covered in petrol, as post-coital recreation, but there is nothing in Melanie Golding's case history, eccentric though some of it is, to suggest that she liked it in handcuffs in a cellar in St Albans with the modern equivalent of Quasimodo. So let's stay in the real world, shall we. Now do you want another one of those?'

'All right. Make it a large malt.'

When Alan Barlow returned to the table, Eddie Cole continued. 'I am being serious, Alan. I can't tell you why, but I am. There is no evidence yet worth a row of beans but suppose, just suppose, this was not rape. Does it make a difference?'

'The answer to that question is that it makes a difference to me but it has nothing to do with clinical analysis. If you were to ask me whether I would have allowed Jack Wagner to take that confession if there had been no rape then the answer is, as you know, certainly not. But then that's all hypothesis now, isn't it? I have said what I have said. It is in the report.'

'Alan, even if he had raped the girl, it can't make any difference to the effects of Menkies' Syndrome when under pressure in an interview.'

Alan Barlow shook his head. 'Superintendent, I am not making myself clear. Of course, it might not make a difference academically, intellectually, clinically or according to the fucking text books but *it makes a difference to me.* Ivan Lurcher was about a hamper short of a picnic. You knew that, I knew that. He was completely barking mad. Totally psychotic. But when illness causes murder, torture and rape don't ask me to give them a defence. Anyway Eddie, let's get away from the glorious theory. What is all this about? I thought you were prosecuting this trial. This is a confession. Don't you want the thing? What do you want? Acquittal? Have you been on a Civil Liberties Convention?'

'I want a conviction, Alan, but I want Nailor. As to the burnt boy, to be brutally frank, I couldn't give a toss. I hope he has a comfortable and protected life weaving baskets but I *want* Nailor. This is not an ordinary criminal. This is not even a very bad ordinary criminal. This is not even the worst ordinary criminal. This man is pure evil.'

Alan Barlow looked closely at the familiar shape before him. Quietly he said: 'You are shaking, Eddie. I can see it. I can *feel* it. Are you all right?'

'Of course I am not all right. I have been drinking Norman's fucking whisky. What you don't understand, Alan, are the mechanics of this trial. We can convict Aylen. I have so much evidence it is embarrassing. But if I convict Aylen with this confession I lose Nailor. Let me spell it out for you. Aylen's defence (his only defence) is that he was under duress from Nailor as a result of his mental state. If that defence succeeds, Nailor must go down, providing, of course, that he doesn't walk out, courtesy of the judge, after the prosecution case. If Aylen's defence fails it is still possible to convict Nailor but very unlikely. All the evidence I have is my copy of the *Evening News.* But most important is this. Aylen's confession makes no mention of Nailor whatsoever. If it goes into evidence it is Nailor's best birthday present since his first junior tool-kit. Another?'

'I think I know what you are going to say to me, Eddie, and if I am right I am going to need a large, a very large, straight malt, sufficient, if necessary, to induce immediate and permanent amnesia.'

When Eddie returned to the table, Alan Barlow inspected his new drink.

'I think,' he said, 'that it will probably not be possible to get more alcohol into that glass. I am surprised Norman didn't kiss you.'

'He tried, of course, but I rejected him. Now drink that and listen to me. That report, your report, has already gone into court. The judge has a copy. When you give evidence you will be cross-examined by Jane Wilson. You know her?'

'No.'

'Well, I can tell you she is pretty bloody good. She's got her own shrink.'

Alan Barlow interrupted. 'A lightweight, from the Maudsley.'

'All right, all right, I know you could have him fried on toast but Jane Wilson is no fool. She is going to suggest to you that your analysis is not wholly safe as you had not examined Aylen at the time.'

Interrupting again, Alan Barlow said: 'That's nonsense. His condition is clinical, already proven. I would have had to rely on the clinical history in any event. Examination would have told me nothing.'

'I know, Alan, will you please *listen*. She is going to suggest to you that Aylen should have been examined before he was interviewed. *Listen*, she will suggest that it *might* have made a difference to your view. All you have to say is "maybe". "Maybe" will be enough. If the judge thinks that it is even possible that Aylen should have been examined then he cannot let the confession in. "Maybe" is all you have to say.'

'Eddie, I have been doing this job for thirty years. I have been in the witness box more times than you have bought straight malt whisky. I have never said "maybe" to anyone.'

'Precisely. In those circumstances they are bound to believe you.'

'I can't do it. I have a reputation.'

'If you leave your evidence unchanged then you are effectively ensuring that Aylen's confession goes in evidence. If that happens we will almost certainly lose Nailor. If we lose Nailor it is only a matter of time before someone else is maimed or killed. He will think he can do anything. What about your reputation then?'

Both men held each other's eyes in a weary, silent dialogue of mutual history. Finally Alan Barlow lifted his glass and drank a quarter of a pint of whisky in one slow movement. As he placed the glass on the table his Welsh baritone was as steady as slate. 'Superintendent Cole, you are a bastard. But you are *my* bastard. I do not know what I am going to do but I am going to think. In particular, I am going to make full use of the frontal lobe of the right hemisphere of my brain. In case you have forgotten that is the one that provides our will to resist even the most persuasive shits in the business.'

# Chapter 29

In Jane Wilson's Chambers, Thomas Aylen's defence team was taking stock.

'Well,' said Jane Wilson, helping herself to a chocolate biscuit, 'here we are at the Rubicon. Only the great Jack Wagner to give evidence and then the confession. Is our shrink ready?'

'He will be in court at ten thirty tomorrow morning,' said Mary Shelley. 'I want him to see Jack Wagner give evidence, get an eyeful of the blazer and gold cufflinks. I want him to know the enemy.'

'Is he going to come up to proof?'

'I think so. As you know, he is an odd little bugger, but I went through it with him again yesterday. On the main points he is pretty clear. Aylen is ill. Menkies' Syndrome makes him suggestible, *possibly* totally suggestible, certainly he was in no fit state to undergo an interview. Wagner should have known that and, even if he did not know it, the confession is totally unsafe. I don't think he will go back on that.'

'What about the physical injuries?'

'At the time Aylen was interviewed these had been treated and there was no reason to suppose that, in themselves, they would have affected the fairness of the confession. He had recent fractures of the left ulna and lower leg but they were undisplaced. Painful certainly, but not sufficient to affect the mental process. Our psychiatrist wants to know when he will be giving evidence.'

Jane Wilson jotted times on to her blue notebook. 'Ten thirty Wagner gives evidence. We should reach the confession by eleven thirty. Then the jury goes out and we commence the trial within a trial. He will give evidence of the confession but that will not take long. The judge has all of the documents and presumably will have read them. I cross-examine Wagner eleven forty-five, probably until one o'clock. At two fifteen the Crown will call the other interviewing officer, I can't remember his name, Blodwyn or something, which will be largely formal at this stage. I think we will have our expert in the witness box at two thirty. The judge already has his report so I can take him quickly through his evidence. Then I hand over for cross-examination to

Edward Boyd. God knows how long he will be. He cross-examines like the groundsman at Lord's cricket ground. Mows the pitch one way, mows the pitch the other way, gets off and has a good look and then does it all again. He will certainly be the rest of the day, I would have thought. Then the following day we have Alan Barlow telling the judge that Aylen has a mind like a razor. That's the game plan. I would like our shrink to stay while Barlow gives evidence and I cross-examine. After that he can go. What's the matter with you, Gilbert? You look as though you are constipated. Have a biscuit.'

'No, thanks,' said Gilbert Smith, 'but I am worried. I know we have been here before but I am still not convinced. Shouldn't we let the confession go in before the jury without challenge?'

'Oh God,' said Mary Shelley, 'not again.'

'Look,' Gilbert Smith leant forward and spoke directly to his leader, 'even if we exclude the confession there is still a massive case against us. Aylen was undoubtedly in the flat. His fingerprints are all over it and he undoubtedly wrote the kidnap letter. That's how they got him in the first place. He is found in the cellar together with the victim and in possession of a gun. *I know* that we say the gun was planted but that's between him and Jack Wagner. Finally he has obviously had sex with the girl who is found manacled to the bed. The case against us is massive, even without the confession. The only defence is duress based on the Menkies' Syndrome. There is no better evidence of Menkies' Syndrome than the fact that he coughed the whole thing immediately, conveniently, on demand from Jack Wagner, the nice policeman in the fake club blazer. Why don't we let the jury hear it and then cross-examine Wagner for the first time in front of them and bring out the mental stuff? The jury is bound to be sympathetic given our client's background, and the Menkies' Syndrome is undeniable. Wagner, as we all know, is an odious self-seeking shit and the jury is bound to dislike the fact that he interviewed an injured war hero who was an intellectual sitting duck.'

'Gilbert,' said Jane Wilson with resignation, 'we have been through all of this before. Of course there may be some advantages but, at the end of the day, this is a confession. It sets it all out in loving detail. This may be the fiction of Jack Wagner but it doesn't sound like it and our man signed the bloody thing. Jack Wagner is an odious shit, granted, but some of the jury will like gold cufflinks and fake blazers. Some of that jury may even own them. Not the girl with the pierced nose, certainly, but it is unlikely that she will end up as the foreman of the jury doing a Twelve Angry Men. If that confession goes in then the jury will have it in writing for the whole of the rest of the trial. They will take it with them for pleasant reading when they retire. Those of them who want to convict will have the perfect text to read out to their brethren. I have *never* allowed a confession to go before a jury which I thought could be excluded.'

Gilbert Smith interrupted. 'I know, of course, that must be the normal rule, but this is not a normal case. This is just about as abnormal as it is possible to get. And the fact that he has Menkies' Syndrome is not in dispute.'

'That, Gilbert, is precisely the final point. Jack Wagner, cunning bastard that he is, phoned Barlow before he took the confession. Barlow had looked at all our man's case papers during the course of the investigation. Barlow said he was fit to be interviewed. I know he didn't examine him and probably should have done but the condition, although rare, is well-known and Jack Wagner can say, legitimately, that he phoned Britain's most eminent police psychiatrist who gave him the green light. We know that Britain's most eminent police psychiatrist was almost certainly pissed. That is a pretty good assumption unless Jack Wagner happened to hit a precious moment unknown to Barlow since his mother's milk, but we can't cross-examine on that basis. Furthermore,' continued Jane Wilson, holding up her hand against objection, 'Alan Barlow will then give evidence in front of the jury. Drunken charlatan he may be but he is a *professional* drunken charlatan. The Lurcher case proved that beyond any doubt. Juries love him, mainly because he tells them what they all want to believe about psychiatric illness. What do you think, Frankenstein?'

Mary Shelley shrugged her enormous shoulders. 'Gilbert's obviously got a point, but in the end I agree with you. But then, darling, I always have.'

'Right,' said Jane Wilson, 'that's it. Over the Rubicon and confusion to the forces of Wagner. Now one quick glass of wine before I start some serious preparation.'

# Chapter 30

The origin of the English legal system, insofar as it concerns the resolution of disputes between individuals or between individuals and the State, is trial by battle. The principle of justice upon which it was based was crude but simple. Where a dispute arose both sides employed champions who then fought in an arena until one or other lost as a result of incapacity or death. As a way of obtaining a just result, the system had a number of obvious imperfections. The first of these was the indisputable fact that whoever employed the biggest bully was likely to win. Since these champions all charged a fee, the normal laws of commerce dictated that the more ferocious champions commanded the highest figures. This resulted in the second obvious imperfection, namely that victory was likely to be secured by he who could afford the largest fee. It would have been surprising if the finest intellects of the Middle Ages had not grasped these simple implications and, indeed, they did. Justification lay, it was argued in the existence of God. If truth and justice were on your side, it was argued, God would intervene in the battle to ensure the just result. It is thought unlikely that this theology had the slightest effect on commercial realities. Litigants continued to employ the biggest thug that their resources would allow in order to provide an insurance against divine oversight.

These elementary principles of justice are still clearly visible in the British trial, revealing a touching and continuing faith in the adversarial process. Paid bullies have been replaced by barristers and divine intervention has been usurped by the English judge. The rules have been tightened up and death, incapacity or surrender has been replaced by the verdict. Otherwise many of the essential principles remain intact. As a result of this interesting and unique historical development, the English system (unlike many others) has nothing to do with truth. It relies entirely on *proof*, which is a quite different matter. This, in turn, accounts for the importance in English trials of the *voire dire* or 'trial within a trial'. The purpose of this process is to attempt to withhold from the jury evidence which is deemed to be unfit for their contemplation. Whether evidence falls within this category is a matter for the judge to decide, exercising the Olympian function with which history has endowed him. It was upon this exercise that Mr Justice Phillips had embarked to exclude Roddy Nailor's interview and he was now about to do so again in the case of Thomas Aylen. At the point of Thomas Aylen's confession the jury would be suspended whilst the judge deliberated on the principles of fair play. If the confession of Thomas Aylen was excluded the jury would reassemble in order to consider, in sublime ignorance, an imaginary world across a playing field rendered divinely flat. All of this relied upon the premise that the judge, Mr Justice Phillips, could apply the rules of battle with the unobstructed perspective of truth, which ignored the power of Superintendent Eddie Cole and a bottle of whisky in Greek Street.

At 10.30 on Thursday morning, Court One at the Old Bailey assembled for the final act of the prosecution case. The judge was about to arrive. Sir Edward Boyd, QC, draped across his lectern, rearranged his gold pens. Next to him John Wilkin, QC, concentrated heavily on a number of arithmetic calculations made on the back of his notebook which revealed, on close inspection, the daily disparity between his domestic expenses and potential payments under the system of Legal Aid. Next to him Jane Wilson surveyed the jury who themselves had fallen silent, anticipating the daily entrance of the high priest of justice. Jack Wagner stood waiting behind the steps which led to the elevated witness box, while Eddie Cole sat impassive in the well of the court, conscious of the steady malevolent glare radiating from the dock.

At that very moment Anita Flynn was welcoming several early visitors from the Middle East. In the depths of the Hampshire countryside Melanie Golding stirred, opened her eyes and saw for the first time with total clarity, the wide-eyed features of Sergeant Brendan O'Hara. These in turn became suddenly radiant with genuine, uncomplicated joy. Meanwhile, at 10.35, Mr Justice Phillips entered his court, settled himself below the sword of justice, nodded to the jury, arranged his notebook and indicated with a tilt of his head that the next and, possibly, final phase of battle should begin.

# Chapter 31

Chief Superintendent Jack Wagner mounted the steps into the witness box, held the Bible an uncompromising distance above his head and recited the oath. Radiating the poise of experience, he spoke directly at the jury, an unflinching position which he constantly maintained. In the well of the court, Eddie Cole stared fixedly at the wooden panelling of the dock and strove to remember the historical works of Sabatini, in which the tortures of Torquemada and the Spanish Inquisition are set out in graphic detail. Sir Edward Boyd began with his accustomed gravitas and for half an hour Queen's Counsel and Chief Superintendent performed a practised dialogue. Yes, indeed, he was Chief Superintendent Jack Wagner. For the last four years he had been one of three senior officers in the Special Branch. He had been asked, unusually, to take over control of the present case due to its obvious complexity and the sensitive identity of those involved. It was also clear that little progress was being made in the detection. He, Chief Superintendent Jack Wagner, had taken control from Superintendent Eddie Cole, who had nonetheless remained on the case. Superintendent Cole was an old acquaintance from the CID and they had, in the past, worked successfully on many important assignments.

Very shortly after his secondment to the case, he, Chief Superintendent Jack Wagner, had obtained information which enabled him to identify the house in which the kidnapped Melanie Golding was being held. This was the house, photographed from several angles, within the court bundle. A briefing had been held for officers who were to take part in the rescue attempt at Scotland Yard at 1.30 a.m. Unfortunately it had been impossible to contact Superintendent Cole who was elsewhere engaged on police business.

The information with which he, Chief Superintendent Jack Wagner, had been provided was, unhappily, only partially correct. The house was correctly identified but the position of those within the house was not accurately described. As a result of this, gun-fire was exchanged immediately upon entry. (He was the first through the door.) In that cross fire Sergeant Davidson, an officer in the Special Branch, was killed.

Having ascertained that Melanie Golding was not held (as was believed) in the upstairs rear bedroom, he (together with one other Special Branch officer) had descended into the cellar of the house, which he had discovered was locked and bolted from the outside. Behind him, he now understood, the man Bedser (apparently the mastermind of the kidnap team) had emerged from an upstairs bedroom where he had been hiding and was himself shot by another Special Branch officer acting in self-defence. Descending into the cellar (photographs of which he was able to identify) he was confronted by the defendant, Thomas Aylen, carrying a gun in his left hand. The victim, Melanie Golding, could be seen lying on a bed in the corner of the cellar room. So confronted, he, Chief Superintendent Jack Wagner, had charged Aylen, knocking him to the ground and causing the gun he had previously been holding to fall beneath the bed itself. He had then drawn his own weapon and ordered Aylen to remain lying on the floor under arrest. It was at this precise moment that a most unfortunate and tragic accident occurred, namely the arrival of Superintendent Cole. No doubt in an excess of enthusiasm, Superintendent Cole emerged at great speed from the cellar steps, colliding heavily with his, Chief Superintendent Wagner's, unprotected back. Knocked completely off balance, he had instinctively clasped his hands, one of which held his own revolver. The resulting shot struck Melanie Golding in the side of the head. He was aware that the bullet remained lodged below the skull, causing deep and probably permanent coma. Had he had any warning of the arrival of Super-intendent Cole? Unhappily he had not but, of course, this was the type of mistake which can easily be made in a highly volatile situation, inducing panic.

Arrangements were immediately made for Melanie Golding to be taken to the nearest hospital, together with Aylen. It was discovered that Aylen was suffering from undisplaced fractures of the left arm and right lower leg. Since they were undisplaced it was possible to treat them by conventional strapping and plaster. Pain-killers were also administered. Aylen was released into police custody after six hours with the full consent of the medical team at St Mary's Hospital.

At this point, Chief Superintendent Wagner paused and directed his attention towards the judge. Mr Justice Phillips addressed himself to prosecuting counsel. 'I think I am right, Sir Edward, that a matter now arises which concerns me alone and not the jury?'

'Precisely so, my Lord, it is a matter of law which concerns your Lordship alone.'

'Very well. Miss Wilson, I think this is your application is it not?

238

Perhaps you could give me an estimate? For how long will it be possible to release the jury?'

Jane Wilson rose behind her lectern. 'My Lord, it is a matter of some substance. It is now, I see, half past eleven. Today being Thursday, I would anticipate that the jury could now begin a long weekend with a view to recommencing the trial on Monday morning.'

Mr Justice Phillips turned to the jury. 'Well, there you are, members of the jury, you may enjoy a long weekend. We will not be so fortunate but I look forward to seeing you again on Monday morning.'

As the jury filed from court an usher approached Eddie Cole and tapped him on the shoulder. 'Superintendent Cole, I have a message for you. Would you please phone Sergeant Brendan O'Hara as a matter of great urgency.'

In the police room Eddie Cole found all the telephones in use with a queue already formed. Cursing, he obtained a quantity of coins and sought the nearest public phone, in the corridor outside Court Thirteen. Here he dialled the given number and, almost immediately, Sergeant Brendan O'Hara answered his mobile telephone.

'Guv, listen, this is important. She has come round. No, it is not like it has been before. She has *really* come round. Her eyes are completely clear. So is her speech. It is a complete miracle. She has even been allowed to sit up. She tells me she has total recall. She wants to make a statement. I haven't done anything yet, guv, before I spoke to you.'

In his public, half-open booth Eddie Cole shovelled more coins into the slot. 'Brendan, listen carefully, I want to make sure that I have got this right. She is completely conscious, right? Good. What about the doctors, do they say she can give a full statement? Good. Now, this is what to do. Give her the death caution again. You know, statement made in anticipation of death. Got it? Then give her the tape recorder. Do not ask her a single question. Do you understand. Not a *single* question. Let her tell the story. Let her do it in her own words and into the tape. I want this coming out crystal clear, whatever it is. I don't want any fucking brief knocking this out on the grounds of pressure. Has she said any-thing? Anything at all? Anything about Nailor? Nothing at all yet? Now do that exactly. You stay with her and one of our team. *Do not let anyone else know.* Do you understand? No one at all at this stage. Particularly not George Watson or Jack Wagner and don't let the bogeys anywhere near her. Do you hear, nowhere near her. Shoot the bastards first. That girl is in danger. No, I am not joking. She is in real danger now. What? The trial? We have Jack Wagner doing the dance of the sugar-plum fairy in the witness box. Yes, it was. Very unpleasant, but I took it well enough.'

Superintendent Eddie Cole replaced the receiver. Noticing that £2 remained unused, he struck the side of the box, which returned nothing. This small preoccupation delayed his turning towards the corridor. As a result he did not see Alex Bentley, crime reporter of the *Evening News*, who had, throughout the totality of the conversation, been standing immediately behind his back, one eye almost closed as he digested information through the filter of post-alcoholic pain. Whilst Eddie Cole attempted to regain his coins, Alex Bentley slipped sideways towards the court reports' room. Shortly thereafter he was speaking urgently to his boss. After listening for five minutes, the editor pronounced, 'We can't use it.'

'What do you mean "can't use it"? This is the scoop of the century. Girl wakes. The truth is told, et cetera et cetera. You can't do this to me.'

'Listen Alex, I can do this to you and I will. This is one half of a conversation. There is nowhere near enough detail, and this is a judge's daughter for God's sake. This is not some murdered tart. This is also the middle of a trial. If we get this wrong, it is contempt of court. That means a judicial pole straight up your arse and through what remains of your liver. Do you understand? We cannot use it.'

Alex Bentley replaced the receiver and attempted to focus on a photograph of Fleet Street hanging, crooked, on the wall. 'Fuck him,' he said softly. 'If he doesn't want it, I know a man who does.'

Alex Bentley returned to Court One as proceedings began in the absence of the jury. As he entered, he found Preston Lodge, junior for the Crown, about to leave on an errand.

'Half a tick,' said Alex Bentley, adopting a stage whisper and placing his mouth close to the side of the barrister's face, 'how long is Jack Wagner going to be in the witness box?'

'About another hour,' replied Preston Lodge, trying not to inhale.

'Good,' said Alex Bentley in the direction of the retreating wig, "cos when he gets out of the witness box I want to talk to him.'

# Chapter 32

In the absence of the jury the atmosphere of Court One changed perceptibly. Dramatic irony was no longer necessary. Disbelief, hitherto willingly suspended, gave way to reality. Circumlocution gave way to professional vernacular.

Sir Edward Boyd completed the examination of his witness. 'After Aylen's discharge from hospital was he taken to Scotland Yard and there interviewed?'

'He was.'

'A full transcript of that interview is available and we have all seen a copy. Will you formally produce the original? Thank you. There is no need in these circumstances for it to be read since his Lordship is well aware of the contents. Just tell me this: it appears that the interview was conducted by yourself and Sergeant Derby but no solicitor was present.'

'That is right.'

'Tell his Lordship why that was.'

'Aylen indicated quite clearly before the interview began that he did not want anyone present and, in particular, did not want the services of a solicitor. You will see in the early part of the transcript that I again asked him whether he wished anyone to be present in order to assist him and informed him of his rights. As you will see he continued to indicate that he did not wish to have any such assistance. In those circumstances I had no choice but to continue the interview. Every effort was made to ensure that it was fairly conducted and he was reminded from time to time of his rights.'

'The interview lasted, I think, for a little over an hour, and shortly thereafter Aylen was charged with offences of kidnap, rape and murder, the precise charges he now faces on the indictment?'

'That is absolutely correct.'

Sir Edward Boyd resumed his seat. Unexpectedly, next to him, John Wilkin rose behind his lectern.

Mr Justice Phillips raised his eyebrows. 'Do you have any cross-examination? This doesn't seem to affect you very much.'

'Thank you, my Lord, I have only one question. It is this. Chief Superintendent, I am right, am I not, that in the whole of your dealings with Aylen, from his arrest in the cellar to the time he was charged in Scotland Yard, he made not one single mention of Mr Nailor, in relation to the offences or otherwise?'

'I can read, Mr Wilkin,' the judge interjected; 'we do not have a jury in court.'

'Just so. I have no wish to annoy your Lordship but sometimes there are conversations which are not recorded in writing and I simply wish to ascertain, now and in the absence of the jury, that there were no such conversations relating to Mr Nailor.'

'There were none.'

'Thank you, Chief Superintendent.'

Jane Wilson came directly to the point of cross-examination. 'Chief Superintendent, I am going to suggest to you that this interview should never have occurred. You know that, do you not?'

'I had anticipated as much, Miss Wilson.'

'Before I come to the precise reasons I can take up the theme just explored by my learned friend. I want to suggest to you that there were indeed conversations with Aylen which were not recorded, either directly or on any subsequent document. Do you understand?'

'That suggestion is false.'

'After his arrest at St Albans, Aylen was taken to St Mary's Hospital in an ambulance, was he not?'

'He was.'

'You and another officer, Sergeant Derby, went with him in the ambulance, did you not?'

'We did.'

'The ambulance men and paramedics were seated in the front of the ambulance, were they not?'

'I do not entirely recollect. Possibly they were.'

'I suggest to you that they were. Their written statements confirm it. That being the case, you and Sergeant Derby were alone with Aylen in the body of the ambulance itself.'

'As I say, I cannot recollect but that would seem to be likely.'

'During the trip to this hospital, there was a conversation?'

'There was no conversation at all.'

'The journey time is, I think, approximately twenty-five minutes. Are you suggesting that there was total silence throughout?'

'I may have passed the odd comment to Sergeant Derby. Administration, that sort of thing, but there was no conversation, whatsoever, with

Aylen. He was, if I recollect, lying on the ambulance stretcher with his eyes closed.'

'Chief Superintendent, let me suggest what you said to him. You told him that he would be expected to confess. That he would be required to confess to kidnapping Melanie Golding as a result of the intense bitterness he felt following his injuries in Ireland and the subsequent lack of any recognition by the authorities. You told him that if he made such a confession it would be in his own best interest. You told him, furthermore, that he had carried out this act together with Bedser whom he had met at Bournemouth and the Jones brothers who had been recruited by Bedser. You told him that Bedser's motivation was money. You told him that he should confess to being in possession of a gun, provided by Bedser; that he was guarding the girl at the time of the raid on the house and that, shortly prior to that, he had subjected her to a sexual assault. You told him all of that in the ambulance and, furthermore, you told him that if he did not co-operate further harm would come to Melanie Golding herself. In other words you told him, in detail, what to say, in the interview which subsequently occurred. That is correct, is it not?'

In the witness box Chief Superintendent Jack Wagner looked calmly at his questioner, then half turned to face the judge. 'There is not one word of truth in those allegations.' Turning again to face Jane Wilson, he continued, 'Given the state of my knowledge at the time, such conversation would, in any event, have been totally impossible.'

'In what respect?'

'At the time I was in the ambulance, Melanie Golding had not been examined. She was, indeed, in an ambulance herself. I had no way of knowing that she had been subjected to any form of sexual abuse, let alone rape.'

'Precisely, Chief Superintendent, you had no way of knowing that sexual intercourse had occurred but you did know that there had been close intimate contact between them because the unidentified source of your information had told you that, had he not?'

'I had no such knowledge and no such information.'

'In order to test that reply, Chief Superintendent, perhaps you would be good enough to let us know precisely where your information had been obtained?' On her left Jane Wilson saw Sir Edward Boyd begin to rise in protest and, in the seconds available to her, delivered the final question. 'I suggest that your information came directly from Roddy Nailor himself.'

As he reached full height Sir Edward Boyd assumed an impressive appearance of indignation. '*Really*, I am very surprised at my learned friend. She knows the rules as well as anyone. The source of police information is the subject of public interest immunity. Unless a specific order is made, this witness cannot be asked to provide that information. Even I do not know the answer. Furthermore, I suspect the final question was based on pure speculation.'

Beside him on counsel's bench, John Wilkin also glowed with wrath and vigorously nodded his head.

Mr Justice Phillips remained calm. 'I imagine you would agree with this objection, Mr Wilkin?'

'I do indeed, my Lord. The question presupposes, of course, that my client had knowledge of precisely the crime with which he is now charged. If my learned friend was even to consider repeating that question before the jury, I would expect her to have the clearest possible evidence to support it.'

'Well,' said the judge, turning to Jane Wilson, 'you appear to have upset your colleagues at the bar, Miss Wilson, but I intend to deal with this in an orderly fashion. First, Chief Superintendent Wagner, may I take it that you do, indeed, object to answering these questions?'

'I do, my Lord, and I am afraid that I cannot divulge this information, even if ordered to do so. The identity of my informant is not even known to me. The information was received by telephone and the caller's number was withheld. The information that was provided, however, contained much detail which could only have been known to a person with real knowledge of this crime. In short, it contained information of which we were aware but which was a closely guarded secret, including the identity of Thomas Aylen.'

Jack Wagner paused slightly for effect and was gratified to notice the defeated expression on Jane Wilson's face. He continued, 'If I *was* asked that question before the jury then, I am afraid, that is the only answer which I could give. The call, incidentally, came to my mobile phone and incoming calls are not even logged.' Having firmly planted the knife, Jack Wagner allowed himself yet another short pause before twisting the blade. 'It appears that the information I was given was wholly accurate in every respect, save, unfortunately, for the details concerning the occupation of the house itself. That failure cost the life of one of my men, which I bitterly regret.'

Sitting behind his leader, Preston Lodge allowed himself a smile of admiration. 'This man is very good,' he thought, 'very good indeed. He is even better than Cole. Out of the same serpent's egg.'

Jane Wilson was defeated and she knew it. The box having been firmly closed, Mr Justice Phillips nailed down the lid. 'Do you really wish to pursue this, Miss Wilson? Would it not be better for us all if you pursued the main part of your objection based, I suspect, on the mental condition of your client?'

'As your Lordship pleases, I shall pursue this matter no more, at least at this stage. I will now turn, as your Lordship indicates, to the main point in issue.' Turning to the witness box, Jane Wilson continued, 'Chief Superintendent, when you began the interview with Thomas Aylen, you knew that he suffered from a mental illness?'

'I understand that it is called a syndrome.'

'Syndrome, illness, it is of no matter what it is called. It is, in fact, known as Menkies' Syndrome. You knew that, did you not?'

'I was aware of the medical background. Superintendent Cole had informed me and I had also seen the medical reports.'

'Were you aware that one of the effects of Menkies' Syndrome is to render the sufferer highly suggestible and to lessen his natural resistance to pressure and influence from others?'

'I was aware that was a *possible* interpretation. It is, however, a not uncommon defence: "obeying orders", "easily led". I have heard it before.'

Mr Justice Phillips intervened. 'Mr Wagner, please confine yourself to the question without comment. Were you aware that this man suffered from Menkies' Syndrome and that a possible effect was that described by Miss Wilson?'

'I accept both propositions.'

Jane Wilson seized the moment. 'In those circumstances, Mr Wagner, knowing that he was sick and knowing the nature of the sickness, why did you continue to subject him to interview?'

'An interview was necessary for Aylen's own benefit. He could have had an explanation. Also there could have been others involved and I wished to ascertain this fact as soon as possible. He refused, point blank, the services of a solicitor. I took the only course which I thought open to me and telephoned an eminent psychiatrist who had already advised on the case.'

'Is that Mr Barlow who I see sitting in court today?'

'It was, yes. I told him of all the circumstances and asked whether it would be safe to continue the interview. He told me that it would be safe provided that I was careful not to put pressure on Aylen or to make any kind of forceful suggestion as to his actions. I believe that we obeyed those rules.'

'You were able to do so because you had already, in the ambulance, told him what to say.'

'That, as I have already said, is simply totally untrue.'

The judge intervened, 'It is, I see, one o'clock, Miss Wilson. Do you have much more for this witness?'

'My Lord, I have entirely finished with Chief Superintendent Wagner. I do not, in the circumstances, require the attendance of Sergeant Derby who, I anticipate, will simply repeat the account given by the Chief Superintendent. We now move, I think, to the expert psychiatric evidence which may conveniently be heard at two o'clock.'

After the judge had left, John Wilkin turned to his colleague. 'Oh well,' he said, 'nice try, old girl, nice try.'

'Bugger off,' said Jane Wilson.

# Chapter 33

Thomas Aylen's defence team had assembled in the conference room on the second floor of the Old Bailey, together with Dr John Heathcliffe, chief psychiatrist at the Maudsley Hospital.

'Well, Frankenstein,' said Jane Wilson, without her usual levity. 'That was a bloody disaster.'

'Oh, I don't know,' said Gilbert Smith, 'it is not all wasted. At least we now know what *not* to ask this evil genius in front of the jury.'

'Thank you Gilbert,' said Jane Wilson, 'that is very comforting. Let us hope we do better on the medical evidence.'

As though on cue, John Heathcliffe gave an uncomfortable shrug. 'I am afraid,' he said, aware of the sudden heightened tension, 'that it may not be quite as simple as I thought.'

'What exactly does that mean?' said Jane Wilson in tones reminiscent of cracking granite. 'Are we contemplating jumping ship?'

'No, no, not exactly, it is just that I hadn't quite appreciated the nature of Barlow's advice on the telephone. If he really did give strict instructions not to suggest anything or exert any pressure on Aylen then I don't think it could be criticised.'

'But they told him what to say in the ambulance.'

John Heathcliffe gave an uncomfortable grimace. 'We don't actually appear to have any evidence of that.'

'We have got the evidence of our own client.'

'I appreciate that, but he is not exactly very reliable, is he?'

'Oh my God,' said Jane Wilson, 'there goes our medical evidence, bobbing away on the waves.'

'What do you mean, not calling any evidence?' demanded Edward Boyd. 'I have got his report. The judge has seen it.'

'I appreciate that,' said Jane Wilson, 'but it remains my choice whether I call him or not, and I am not going to call him to give evidence. That's the end of it.'

'Gone back on his report, has he? Jumped ship?'

'Certainly not. He is solid as a rock. I just feel like an early day.'

'I am still going to call Barlow.'

'Please yourself,' said Jane Wilson, 'call him any time you like.'

In the original building of the Old Bailey, few rooms are allocated for conferences between barristers and clients. The reason is simple. When this famous building was erected few of the accused were at liberty to enjoy the luxury of instructing their lawyers outside prison. For offences tried at Britain's most famous court, bail was rarely an option. In those more robust times, any contact between criminal and barrister was regarded as an unusual and undesirable event. Furthermore, in the days before the photocopying machine, barristers were largely unburdened by the vast weight of information now contained (in even the simplest cases) in vast numbers of folders and ring binders. Such conference rooms as existed were therefore constructed only to contain people without impedimenta and the average size is barely six feet square. Into one of these tiny places, shortly before the resumption of proceedings in Court One, Chief Superintendent Jack Wagner was sitting in close proximity to Alex Bentley, crime reporter of the *Evening News* and, on this occasion, purveyor of information and truth. Immediately after their arrival in the room, Jack Wagner had attempted to open the door in order to relieve the stifling reek of raw alcohol which exuded from the very pores of his informant.

'I wouldn't do that, if I were you,' said Alex Bentley; 'I know it is a bit close in here but what I have to tell you is highly confidential.'

Without speaking Jack Wagner resumed his seat, adopted an expression of polite interest and concentrated on shallow breathing.

'It is about the girl, Melanie Golding, the one with the bullet in the brain.'

Jack Wagner, despite his natural aversion, leaned forward. 'What about her?'

'She is making a statement, about her kidnapping, probably at this very moment.'

'That is impossible, the girl is in a coma. She cannot speak.'

'She *was* in a coma. She woke up this morning. She is making a statement now, ordered by Eddie Cole. It is being done deliberately without your knowledge. Don't ask me why.'

Jack Wagner advanced his face to within inches of Alex Bentley's purple nose. One focusing eye stared back at him in alarm. 'Precisely how do you know all this? Where is your source?'

'I am not at liberty to . . .'

The policeman interrupted, his voice as slow as lava. 'Mr Bentley, I will not even for one moment attempt to tell you the depths of the water in which you are treading. I will not begin to attempt to describe the nature of the beasts that lurk beneath this surface. You have been a hack for a long time and I dare say, in that time, you have heard of evil misdeeds and demonic power sufficient to crush the strongest of men but, I am telling you, you have not even got into the breaking surf on a fine day. Now I am going to give you precisely three seconds to tell me the source of this information.'

'I overheard Eddie Cole on the phone. He was talking to someone called Brendan. He told him to take a statement but make sure no one knew about it. He told him to make sure it was done under "expectation of death". He said it should be tape-recorded without any help or prompting. He said something about Nailor but I could not catch it. That's all. I was just trying to do my job. I am looking for the truth. I am a crime reporter.'

'And when precisely did this masterpiece of journalism take place?'

'This morning, when the court took a break. You had been in the witness box. I couldn't have told you earlier.'

'And who else knows about this interesting development?'

'No one, absolutely no one.'

Jack Wagner's pink hand stretched across the table, causing an extent of white cuff and gold cufflink to emerge from the blazer's sleeve. Alex Bentley, now shaking, watched as the hand fell from the side of the table and came to rest with exquisite gentleness on his upper thigh. There it remained, faintly pulsating, spread itself into a starfish and then began slowly to contract. 'You're lying.'

'No, I am not, not much, just a bit. Please stop it. Please.'

'Not much, I see. Now just how much is not much?'

'I told my editor, at the *Evening News*, he says he can't use it. Contempt of court and all that. Please stop.'

'So you told your *editor*, did you? On the *Evening News*, but he is not going to use it. Well well. Now, just suppose he changes his mind. Just suppose, tonight, this crap about Melanie Golding is all over fucking London. What are we going to do with you then.'

'He won't use it. If he says he won't use it, he won't use it. He used to work for the *Sunday Times*.'

'The *Sunday Times*? Well, well, well. Now, Mr Bentley, I am going to tell you what you are going to do. You are going to come with me and we are going to find a phone, a nice private telephone, and you are going to phone your editor on the *Evening News* – the one that used to work for the *Sunday Times* – and you are going to tell him that you have completely screwed up. You are going to tell him that you got the story all wrong. You are going to tell him that you have spoken to Eddie Cole and what you heard was a completely different case. That is what you are going to tell him.'

'I can't do it. I'll get the sack. Please stop. All right, all right, I'll do it.'

Five minutes later Alex Bentley spoke to Charlie McGrath, editor of the *Evening News*. Barely a hand's breadth on the far side of the receiver, the eyes of Jack Wagner watched him through narrow slits.

'I am sorry, Charlie. I am afraid I have cocked this up. Yes, the Golding story. I have spoken to Cole. What I heard is a completely different case. Something to do with animal rights. Someone got hit by a lorry-load of sheep. Very nasty. Anyway I thought I had better tell you at once, just in case you changed your mind and thought you might use it in the paper. Oh come on, Charlie, that's very unreasonable. Yes, I said sheep. Oh God, Charlie. No I haven't. Not since yesterday. Well, just one this morning. All right Charlie. All right, I'll be there.'

'There we are,' said Jack Wagner, 'that didn't hurt a bit did it?' The pink hand once again slipped from the blazer's sleeve and landed gently on the soiled lapel of Alex Bentley's jacket. 'Mr Bentley, I have known Superintendent Eddie Cole for thirty years. In case you did not know, he has been Head of the Serious Crime Squad for nearly a decade. He has destroyed men beside whom you would not appear as a speck of dust in the Himalayas. And if Eddie Cole is mighty then I am mightier still. When you listen to the voice of Eddie Cole, you listen to the voice of God. Eavesdropping on the Gods, Mr Bentley, is a very dangerous business. If you weren't such an ignorant pillock, I would remind you what happened to Prometheus. He was tied to a rock and every day, *every day*, a big bird came and pecked off his private bits. I know lots of little birds like that, Mr Bentley. Just think about it. *Every single day.* Just think how much Prometheus must have wished he had got the sack instead from someone who used to work for the *Sunday Times*.'

# Chapter 34

At 2.15 precisely on Friday, Jane Wilson waited patiently for the judge to assemble his papers before she said, 'My Lord, I thought I would tell your Lordship at this stage that I will not be calling Dr Heathcliffe to give evidence during this application. I may, of course, call him later in the trial to deal with the wider question of Mr Aylen's mental condition but on the question of the admissibility of the confession, I shall not call him to give evidence.'

Mr Justice Phillips narrowed his eyes. 'Miss Wilson, I am bound to say that I am surprised. Indeed I am very surprised. I have had his statement now for some weeks, together with that of Dr Barlow. In these circumstances will it be necessary for the prosecution to call Dr Barlow at all? His clear opinion is that Aylen was fit to be interviewed, notwithstanding the undoubted existence of Menkies' Syndrome.'

In the well of the court, Eddie Cole shifted restlessly.

In the event, Sir Edward Boyd interrupted to provide the answer. 'My Lord, the prosecution would rather call Dr Barlow. This is a sensitive and difficult matter and he was, after all, consulted at the very time that Aylen was interviewed. He is therefore something more than a mere expert. I propose to call him in any event.'

'Very well, Sir Edward, you are in charge of the case. Let us proceed. It may be that the afternoon will be rather shorter than we anticipated.'

At 2.35, Dr Alan Barlow mounted the steps to the witness box, studiously avoiding the fixed gaze of his friend, Superintendent Eddie Cole. The formalities were swiftly observed. Yes, he was Dr Alan Barlow, consultant psychiatrist, who had trained at Swansea University and had subsequently become, by examination, a member and then fellow of the Royal College of Psychiatrists. His particular field was forensic psychology and, as such, he had appeared, over thirty years, in very many criminal cases, particularly those involving criminal liability when associated with mental illness. In the present case, he had been called in at an early stage by Superintendent Eddie Cole, then in charge of the investigation. The purpose of this call was to assess the psychiatric background of the known or suspected participants in the crime and, thereby, to assess the degree of risk, both in relation to physical harm to Melanie Golding and the dangers of rescue attempts should they become feasible. He had carried out a certain amount of research at that time, in particular, in relation to Thomas Aylen, who had been treated for some months at the Ardingley Military Hospital for both his physical and mental disabilities. He had studied all the case notes made over a considerable period of time and was able to form a clear picture as to Mr Aylen's capacity and capabilities (or lack of them). He had advised accordingly.

Weeks later he had received a telephone call from Chief Superintendent Jack Wagner who, he understood, had assumed the ultimate charge of the operation. He was told that there had, indeed, been a rescue which had resulted in the arrest of Aylen who was, at that time, at Scotland Yard awaiting interview. On arrest Aylen was found to have two bone fractures, one to the leg and one to the arm. He, Dr Barlow, was not expressly consulted about these injuries. They were not strictly his field and, in any event, he understood that these injuries had been treated by St Mary's Hospital, who had released Aylen into police custody, having certified he was fit to be detained and interviewed following their treatment. The question raised by Chief Superintendent Wagner was whether Aylen, in his mental state, was capable of being interviewed in the absence of either a solicitor or a medical advisor. The question was relatively simple. Was someone such as Aylen, suffering from Menkies' Syndrome, capable of giving a clear and coherent and truthful account of events when under interrogation properly administered in a police station in accordance with the rules? At this point, Dr Barlow paused. The court became perfectly silent, embracing one of those moments already recorded when, by some chemistry unknown to modern science, a collective instinct perceives a moment of critical importance and potential danger. Sir Edward Boyd lifted his bloodhound eyes from the report which he had been following and observed his witness with mild surprise. Alan Barlow was normally perfectly capable of delivering his evidence in an unimpeded monologue containing a deadly mixture of apparent learning and popular prejudice. Concluding there must have been a momentary loss of concentration, Sir Edward attempted to assist. 'Did Chief Superintendent Wagner ask you, specifically, whether it would be safe to carry out an interview?'

'He did. He also provided me with some background.'

Sir Edward Boyd began to sense a problem. He scanned the report which lay on his lectern. 'What was the nature of this background?'

'He told me in brief terms the nature of the charges and allegations and the circumstances of the arrest. He also told me that it was extremely important that Aylen was interviewed as fast as possible in order to ascertain whether there were any other participants at large and potentially dangerous.'

Jane Wilson lifted her head, causing her wig to shift backwards across her gathered hair, the predatory jerk of the practised advocate sensing unexpected blood. 'Listen to this,' she hissed to Gilbert Smith behind her. 'I think he may be selling the pass.'

No such concern appeared on the professional features of Sir Edward Boyd. 'So he informed you that there was considerable urgency for the interview and asked whether it would be safe to proceed in view of Aylen's mental condition? And what did you say to him?'

In the witness box, for the first time, Alan Barlow allowed his grey eyes to fall upon Superintendent Eddie Cole. 'I cannot remember exactly what I said. I did not make any notes at the time, but the general nature of the answer was "maybe".'

'*Maybe?*'

'Yes, that would be the general gist. Generally speaking it would depend on the traumatic effect of the injuries and the arrest itself which, I gather, was a very violent affair, involving no less than four deaths and serious injury to Melanie Golding herself. Menkies' Syndrome is generally a constant state of affairs and it is, of course, incurable. But all of our mental states have a degree of constancy which can be affected, possibly grossly affected, by traumatic events. It may very well be that Aylen was fit to be examined but I do not remember being categorical.'

The voice of Sir Edward Boyd, always precise, assumed an edge which inspired the vision of bone and sinew being severed on a board. 'Where exactly, Dr Barlow, do we find this in your report?'

Rising to object, Jane Wilson was interrupted by the judge. 'Never mind the report, Sir Edward. I am sure you will not wish to cross-examine your own witness. I am interested in Dr Barlow's evidence. Reports often mislead. Dr Barlow, are you saying that the advice given to Mr Wagner was, in fact, only a qualified approval?'

'That may very well be. To be frank, I was concentrating in my report on Aylen's general mental condition, rather than the precise advice which I gave to Chief Superintendent Wagner. The conversation was very short and, like all conversations, subject to interpretation and misunderstanding. This is, of course, particularly likely to occur when there is obvious urgency and a strong motive to ascertain facts. Both I myself and Superintendent Wagner may well have been influenced by this state of affairs.'

Silence descended while Mr Justice Phillips made his detailed note. In the court the apostate witness stared fixedly at the panelling above the jury box. Sir Edward Boyd exuded melancholic resignation. John Wilkin, with some satisfaction, foresaw the shortening of the trial, Jane Wilson reflected on the wonders of chance and Eddie Cole contemplated the Sword of Justice suspended above the judicial bench.

Mr Justice Phillips concluded his writings and addressed himself to the leading counsel for the prosecution. 'In the light of what Dr Barlow has now frankly and candidly told us, can I possibly admit this confession into evidence? There is no doubt, is there, that this young man is mentally ill. There is no doubt that the illness is such that it is, at least, likely to render him suggestible. I could only allow in evidence a confession taken without either a solicitor or medical support if there were a clear and unequivocal expert view that the process was safe. Dr Barlow can provide no such evidence and, indeed, rather surprisingly, has come close to expressing the contrary. Do I need to trouble Miss Wilson? I appreciate that Mr Wilkin will be upset, but then in the technical and legal sense it does not concern his client at all, since it does not provide evidence either for or against him. That is the case, is it not?'

Recognising the inevitability of retreat Sir Edward Boyd executed the manoeuvre with the dignity of a field general. 'My Lord, the overwhelming consideration in this case, for your Lordship and for me, is one of fairness to the defendant. Your Lordship is right. I would not seek to maintain that this confession can be admitted. There is, of course, abundant further evidence against the accused, Aylen, but the jury must be content with what they have got.'

'On that point, Sir Edward, I have another matter which I want to raise. Dr Barlow's concession in relation to Aylen's state of mind may have rendered the confession inadmissable, but what does it do to the question of fitness to plead? If I find, as I do, that Aylen was unfit to withstand the rigours of interview, how can I, in all conscience, maintain that he is fit to conduct his trial or, in particular, to withstand cross-examination? I do not wish this matter to be argued now and I see that Miss Wilson has an energetic response. But I would like it to be fully considered on Monday morning.'

# Chapter 35

'I've got it, guv,' said Brendan O'Hara, 'I've got the whole thing, the whole statement clear as crystal. I asked her nothing and told her nothing. She simply dictated for half an hour without pause. I typed it up this afternoon myself. She has checked and signed two copies of the statement. Before you ask, I have also taken a copy of the tape. She is sleeping now. The hospital say her chances are good and improving. They have taken her off the drip and she is eating real food. She's a vegetarian, so she had some kind of cheese pancake . . .'

'Yes, yes, Brendan. Thank you,' said Eddie Cole, blowing cigarette smoke above the receiver of his office telephone. 'Never mind the diet. What is the gist? What did she say? Have we got Nailor or haven't we?'

'Guv, I am simply not, repeat not, going to read this over the telephone. I am on an open line at the hospital. Give me your fax number. There are fourteen pages with corrections.'

Eddie Cole stared at the machine in the corner of the room. 'I think it is still buggered. Try sending me one sheet, *not the statement*, anything will do. Try the hospital menu. I will give you two minutes.'

Replacing the receiver, Eddie Cole watched the rain falling against his window. The broken top vent, half open, allowed intermittent bursts of spray to fall upon a row of files stacked against the wall. Apart from this faint and irregular drumming nothing disturbed the profound silence of anticipation. 'The Truth,' thought Eddie Cole, gazing bitterly at his fax machine, 'I am waiting for the Truth and the oracle is completely buggered'.

As he lit a cigarette the fax machine rang, twice, and was silent. After two short coughs, the first sheet of the copying stack was sucked into the machine, whence it emerged seconds later bearing the day's menu at Ardingley Military Hospital. Two minutes later Eddie Cole spoke to Brendan O'Hara. 'Cereal, toast, prawn cocktail, steak and kidney pie, fruit salad, soup, ham salad, pear compote and coffee. The oracle is working, Brendan, send it through.'

For the next twenty minutes Eddie Cole sat beside the machine. From the black slit at its base the truth stuttered forth into his waiting hands. Above the rattle of the machine, truth was absorbed in silence, broken by the expletives of Cole and the inhalation of tobacco. 'Christ, Jesus Christ, Jesus wept. Well, well, well.'

After twenty minutes, the last page dropped and, with a gentle mechanical sigh, the machine returned once more to sleep.

The telephone rang. 'Did you get it, guv? Fifteen pages in all. Have you got it?'

'I have it, Brendan, I have it. How is she now?'

'Sleeping.'

'Can she give evidence?'

'In court or on commission?'

'What about a video link?'

'Christ, guv, I don't know. She is much better but she has only just come through. I can ask.'

'*Don't*, just don't ask, Brendan, for Christ's sake. If we ask it will go straight to the head boffin and he'll go to Wagner or Watson or both. No one must know about this. Not yet. As far as they are concerned the oracle is sleeping. Sleeping oracles stay alive and healthy. Now this is what I want you to do. Take one of the original statements and one original tape, stick them in one of those fluffy bags and post it by ordinary post to the following.' Eddie Cole carefully recited the working name and address of Anita Flynn. 'If you are reasonably tidy you can catch the last post. Keep the other original statement and tape in your own pocket and *give it to nobody*. Take five copies, send them to the following: Alan Farquharson QC, the Director of Public Prosections; George Fucking Fast Track Watson at Scotland Yard; Lord Justice Stoker at the Royal Courts of Justice in the Strand; Jane Wilson, QC, at her Chambers in the Temple, and Mr Justice Phillips at the Old Bailey. Send all of them today but *miss the post*. I want these birds to come home on Monday morning but not before. In the meantime we have a lot to do and I want Chief Superintendent Jack Wagner to remain in sublime and dark ignorance.'

At his end of the line, Brendan O'Hara's Irish voice fell an octave with shared conspiracy. 'Guv, I know you have read the statement, guv, and I don't suppose that you have missed this, but guv, there is *no mention of the newspaper*. Worse than that, she says, in terms, that she never received any communication from Nailor or about Nailor at any time prior to her kidnap. Whatever else this statement does, guv, it proves the paper was a plant. It puts the crushers on you. Are you sure that you want this sent?'

'Well now, Brendan, very nice of you to mention it and I appreciate the concern. As a Jesuit left-footer, I don't suppose you did much theology in your convent or whatever but you might just remember the old book about Samson and Delilah. You probably saw the film, Victor Mature and a woman with big tits. Big chap, Samson, powerful until the fatal hussy cut off his hair. You may remember that this made him just ever so slightly vulnerable, so they gave him a bit of a kicking and chained him up to the pillars of the temple. Unhappily for them, they forgot about employing a regular barber to keep him skinhead fashion. After a while his hair grew and he got quite back to his old self. And you know what he did, Brendan? You remember? He pushed it over. He pushed over the pillars. The whole fucking thing. Now either he was a pretty dim fucker from Donegal or it might just have occurred to him that he would end up like a cow pat with everyone else. Anyway, for whatever reason, he still did it. Now me, I'm a bald bugger. You may have noticed. I try and paste what's left over the top, but you see it is a futile waste of a narrow comb. But do you know, just now, just now, when you reminded me about the newspapers, I think I felt my hair beginning to grow.'

# Chapter 36

On Saturday morning, four fateful meetings occurred. At his flat in the Temple, Mr Justice Phillips entertained his old friend and fellow High Court judge, Roy Hadless. Simultaneously, a conference occurred between Roddy Nailor and his defence team at Wormwood Scrubs. Jane Wilson and Gilbert Smith assembled at the house of Mary Shelley on Clapham Common, and at Ardingley Military Hospital Eddie Cole, Brendan O'Hara and two members of the Serious Crime Squad worked together on the creation of Truth. Each meeting occurred in its own space, with its own preoccupations and in total ignorance of the other. As the symphony of crime and trial and punishment moved towards its resonant climax, the main players rehearsed in near-perfect discord.

Mr Justice Phillips opened the door to his fellow judge at 11.30 and offered him coffee which was declined in favour of a large gin. Both men settled on either side of the pine kitchen table and exchanged similar enquiries into the health of their respective families. The friendship between them was unusual at the Bar which tends, by its nature, to preclude close acquaintanceship between those who practise in widely different disciplines. Whereas Phillips had had little or no experiences in crime prior to his elevation to the Bench, Roy Hadless was steeped in it. At the Junior Bar, and at an early age, he had become Senior Treasury Counsel, responsible for the conduct of the most important and serious criminal trials of his day. After taking silk, he had turned almost exclusively to defence work, a gamekeeper/poacher transition actively encouraged by the system. He possessed a fierce intellect, unusual in the criminal Bar, and his advocacy was legendary. He had been persuaded, with considerable unwillingness, to accept a job as a High Court judge, thereby contributing immense skill and experience to the Bench and suffering a massive loss of personal income. He was widely liked and admired, had few enemies and a number of close, enduring friends, of whom Mr Justice Phillips was one. Formalities over, he came to the point of their meeting. 'You sounded worried on the phone. How can I help? Is it the trial or something personal?'

'It's the trial, of course. We have reached the critical stage. I think I know what I have to do and I do not want to do it.' Briefly the judge described the state of the evidence and the fact that he had excluded from the trial both the confession of Aylen and the assertion by Nailor that he had never had any contact, personal or by post, with Melanie Golding. Having refilled his friend's glass, he then said, 'There is one other thing about which I have told no one. I received an ... "approach" on behalf of Nailor.'

As his companion's frown deepened, he recounted the meeting at the Athenaeum. When he finished Roy Hadless blew a soft whistle across his raised glass.

'You are going to ask me whether I have ever had any experience of such a thing and, before you do, I can tell you that the answer is no. This is very serious. These waters are not just deep, they are unfathomable. When Nailor was being prosecuted ten years ago I did hear rumours that he was close to the Security Services, but that was all. Have you told absolutely no one else?'

'Absolutely no one.'

'Good, I think it must remain that way. I understand precisely what you are saying, but it is capable, of course, of immediate mis-representation. May I anticipate your concerns? Having been placed under this pressure you have no wish, whatsoever, either to succumb to it or *be seen to succumb to it*. However, the evidence against Nailor is now pitifully thin. You only have a newspaper said to be a plant. Without the denial by Nailor which excludes an innocent reason for those items to be in the girl's flat, the presence of the newspaper itself is not enough. Theoretically Aylen himself could have placed the newspaper in the flat for some reason, highly unlikely though that is.'

'That is precisely the problem, or, to be more accurate, that is the first problem.'

Roy Hadless placed a hand on his friend's arm. 'Let us take them one at a time. I have to say to you, bluntly, that there is insufficient evidence against Nailor for the trial to proceed beyond the end of the prosecution case. Also, bluntly, any other decision would be taken on the under-standable but wholly indefensible basis that the approach made to you on Nailor's behalf is some kind of evidence, which of course it is not. I am sorry to be pompous but that is it.'

'Precisely.'

'In those circumstances I do not think you have a choice.'

'Neither do I, but I wanted to hear you say so. Nailor must walk free on Monday. God knows what damage he will do, and his ghastly friends in high places will believe that they have won. It doesn't bear thinking about but I can see no other way.'

'Neither can I. Let us therefore bow to the unthinkable but inevitable. What is your second problem?'

'The second problem relates to Aylen. You know the police psychiatrist, Alan Barlow? I see that you do. He gave evidence for the prosecution in order, so it was thought, to support the admission of Aylen's confession in evidence. He appeared to retract his original report to a surprising degree. He expressed the view, contrary to that which he had previously reported, that Aylen may well be unable, in his mental condition, to withstand questioning. He was referring to police questioning but, in reality, there can be no difference between that and cross-examination. Indeed, Edward Boyd is a far more formidable interrogator than a Chief Superintendent from the Special Branch. How can I allow the trial to proceed in those circumstances? Aylen must be unfit to stand trial and Unfit to Plead.'

'It means the boy goes to Broadmoor.'

'I *know*. The condition is incurable, so it is a life sentence in the worst of conditions. If Nailor's friends are as powerful as it appears then even a more relaxed regime for Aylen is unlikely. His prospects are appalling. I am consigning him, without trial, to a living death. Let me get you another one of those.'

'Thank you. Have one yourself. I think you need it. Is there psychiatric evidence for the defence?'

'Yes, there is, but for some reason Jane Wilson did not call it.'

Roy Hadless received his drink and thought for a moment, staring at the top of the table. 'I think you must be right, but there is, is there not, one small consolation. If he continues to fight the case he can only do so on the basis that he committed the crime under duress by Nailor. Nailor is about to be acquitted on your direction. In these circumstances there is a near certainty of conviction, with overwhelming evidence on all counts, even without the confession. You could obtain a new jury who have not presided over Nailor's trial. Jane Wilson may ask you to do so. But in this case it helps not a jot. If convicted on charges of kidnap and rape, life in an "ordinary" prison is likely to be as bad, or worse than in Broadmoor. That is some consolation, small I know, but at least a little.'

'I know you are right, old friend, I wanted to hear it from you, but, in truth, I had already, I think, decided. I have done far less criminal work than you but these issues have a much wider landscape. I will always be haunted by the irony. I am the judge, I am Jove on Olympus. To do justice I would, without hesitation or regret, imprison Nailor for the rest of his life and release Aylen to the comfort and security of benign care. Because of the dictates of evidence and of circumstance, I will do precisely the reverse.'

'My friend,' said Roy Hadless, 'there is another consolation. This ghastly business, this terrible trial and the temptations and burdens which it creates, could not have been borne by a more decent man. No, it is true. Portia missed the point. To achieve a great right you cannot do a little wrong. Not you, not us. Gods we may be but we are Gods with a rule book. Let us have another and talk about my new house in the valley of the Lot.'

At 11.30 a.m. James Cameron and Preston Lodge sat on one side of a table in number 4 interview room at Wormwood Scrubs. They were awaiting the arrival of their client, Roddy Nailor, and also of John Wilkin, leading counsel, who was admitted at that very moment. 'Saturday morning,' he said, shaking his elegant head with disbelief. '*Saturday morning*. I simply do not understand what I am doing. Three wives and God knows how many children to support. Wall-to-wall school fees, vets' bills, endless subscriptions. Do you know what I get paid for this? Do you? I asked my clerk. It's his fault. He took this brief. I am going to have him suspended on piano wire. One hundred pounds! One hundred pounds! To come to Shepherd's Bush. I have never been to Shepherd's Bush. Have you seen it? A hundred pounds to come to Shepherd's Bush to listen to a psychopathic madman who believes he is Alexander the Great. Ah, hello, Mr Nailor.'

Ignoring him and taking his chair, Roddy Nailor spoke straight to James Cameron. 'You've heard, haven't you? You must have heard. I got the news yesterday evening. Never mind where from. The canary is awake and singing.'

John Wilkin intervened. 'Excuse me, what are we talking about precisely?'

'The girl, Sleeping Beauty. She is up and about and squaring up the dwarfs. God, doesn't anyone know anything? *You know*, don't you?' The accusing finger was thrust directly into James Cameron's face.

Unmoving, the solicitor replied, 'I have heard. I expect from the same source. We have not, as yet, received a formal notice of a statement. I have no idea what she is saying.'

'No, but I do. I know what the bitch is going to say. Dear God, she was supposed to be ga-ga. They said it was all right because she was a bloody vegetable. They said she could be left alone because she was a zombie.

Now she is apparently writing a book. What are they doing, for fuck's sake. What the hell . . .'

'Wait a minute.' John Wilkin's hand, palm upturned, rotated slowly in the air, and fell back to the table. 'Now this is a game we all need to play. I don't mind secrets, but I don't like not knowing about them. Now,' turning to James Cameron, 'who exactly are "they"?'

James Cameron's gaze shifted uncomfortably between his client and his counsel. 'Mr Nailor has sources of information close to the prosecution.'

'*Close to?*'

'I am afraid that I am not at liberty to say. However, I think I ought to say that I also have similar sources.'

John Wilkin spoke with exquisite softness into the silence which followed. 'Let me understand precisely what you are saying. You are telling me that we have, *have always had*, sources close to the prosecution but, presumably, unknown to prosecution counsel themselves?'

'I cannot answer that. I don't know what Edward Boyd and his junior know.'

John Wilkin's tone became softer and his gaze shifted between the eyes of James Cameron and Roddy Nailor. 'Let me explain something. I have known Edward Boyd for thirty years. We went to the same college at Oxford at the same time. We were called to the Bar together in the same Inn of Court and took silk within two years of each other. We are Benchers of the same Inn. He has fewer wives than I have, and far fewer children, but otherwise our lifestyles are very similar. We do not like each other much. If you want my candid view, he is a pompous, self-opinionated ass. I have not the slightest doubt he would say something very similar about me. He has a pedestrian intellect and an over-whelming desire to conform in a conformist society. He is about as corruptible as John the Baptist. If he knew that there were *sources close to the prosecution* which were dealing direct with one of the defendants in this case, then he would have told me. I do not know what your *sources* are, Mr Nailor, and I cannot require you to let me know. Perhaps it is best if I remain in total ignorance, but I will not be a party to corruption. Neither I nor Preston will be a party to corruption. Do I make myself absolutely clear? I will continue to act for you, Mr Nailor, at least until Monday and I will attempt to achieve your acquittal at the end of the prosecution case if it remains as it is now. I will do this because I do not believe the evidence against you is worth a row of jelly beans. But if there is another statement, if it is true that there is more evidence from the girl, then we may need a lot more evidence from you and, in those circumstances, I will require an undertaking in writing that these *sources* are not obtained by bribery or threat. Now Preston and I are going to leave. I suggest that you think very carefully about what I have said.'

Preston Lodge and John Wilkin rose together and effected a magisterial exit from the interview room. As they left the wicket gate and emerged from the prison into the dull midday of Shepherd's Bush, Preston Lodge said, 'I think you got that dead right. A very difficult ethical position. We need that undertaking if we are to carry on.'

John Wilkin paused and surveyed his junior with a gentle smile. 'My dear Preston, do you realise that on Monday morning, because of our client's little games, we may be released from the gloom and darkness of Legal Aid into the sunlit uplands of the freely negotiated fee? My dear Preston, ethics are the most wonderful things.'

In interview room 4, James Cameron said, 'That was very stupid. Very stupid indeed. We may just have lost our brief.'

'So fucking what? If that girl sings a happy song in court, I am back in Parkhurst, brief or no brief. If she has made a statement what will happen?'

'Then, if she can, she will give evidence.'

'If she can? What happens if she coughs it?'

'The statement, if there is one, will almost certainly have been taken under "expectation of death" rules. It can be admitted in evidence and, if it has been taken in that way, almost certainly would be. The jury would be told, of course, that she could not be there for cross-examination, but the damage will be done.'

'What if is she is alive and can't give evidence?'

'That is much more difficult. Theoretically the statement could still be read but questions would arise as to her mental capacity. If she was still alive then she could be examined. She has undoubtedly suffered a serious brain injury and we could argue that the statement was inherently unreliable. That would depend on expert evidence, neurologists, psychiatrists. That would be the best hope.'

Roddy Nailor tore at a fingernail and stared at his solicitor. 'Right, now you tell them. You know who I mean. You tell them I am not going down on my own. If I go back to Parkhurst then a lot of very respectable gentlemen are coming on the same trip.'

'Roddy,' said James Cameron with a slight grimace at the persuasive informality, 'for God's sake think. Is this wise? These are very powerful people.'

'Then let them do something about it if they are so fucking powerful. I did their work for them. Got paid fuck-all for it as well. When Buster

Cole stitched me up ten years ago I kept my mouth shut. But I am not going to do it again. I can't sort the girl out while I am stuck in this shit-hole but they can. I am in control of this. I've got it all, all the proof. I've kept it all these years. If I go, they go.'

'It will be the end of you too Roddy. You did the business for them.'

'Oh yeah, I know that. I've got O Levels, you know. Did you ever do R.E? Did you ever read the Bible? Do you remember the story about that Samson? Strong man. He brought the whole lot down on his head but he got all the bastards at the same time. Every fucking one of them. That's the power, you see, James. That's what makes us different. You tell them what I've said, James. You tell them to come and see me Sunday evening before we start this bloody charade again. You tell them to come and see me Sunday evening and tell me what they've done and, in the meantime, you tell them to look after the girl. If she goes back sleepy-byes but alive we are as good as out. You tell them that, James. You tell them Samson wants to see them in the temple.'

At 11.30 a.m. Mary Shelley poured herself a glass of wine. 'Anyone else?' she asked across her kitchen table in Clapham. 'Bit early but it is Saturday and we are working.'

'No thank you, Frankenstein,' said Jane Wilson, 'Gilbert will have one but I have to drive him home. Before you both lose your heads, let's take stock. I am very much afraid that Gilbert may have been right. We have got rid of our confession but buried our guy in the process. This judge is going to send him off to Broadmoor.'

'Nonsense,' said Mary Shelley, handing Gilbert Smith what appeared to be half a pint of wine. 'None of us could have foreseen this. We got Heathcliffe, gutless little bugger that he is, to tread the narrow line between unfit to interview and Unfit to Plead, but then the little gerbil got out of his wheel. Then Alan Barlow does his U-turn. Who knows what happened to him. Perhaps God spoke to him from a glass dog. Just when we least needed some compassion, we got it on a low loader. The judge must be right. Our guy can't fight the case and we can't call Heathcliffe, not now that we know he is about as reliable as a royal marriage. I am afraid that it all ends on Monday. Nailor walks and our guy's off to the funny farm, nightmare variety.'

'If only,' said Gilbert Smith, 'we had the girl.'

'If only,' said Mary Shelley.

'I'll have that wine now,' said Jane Wilson; 'we are down and out so let's go for skid row in a taxi. Anyway, even if we had the girl, even if she woke up with total recall and said everything that our guy tells us is the truth, she still couldn't get to court to give evidence. She's still got a bullet in the brain, for Christ's sake. The statement would have to be read. John Wilkin will go berserk. I can't see the judge letting it in. He has complete discretion and, frankly, I don't think he *should* exercise it in those circumstances. I wouldn't. Cheers.'

Into the gloom, Gilbert Smith asked the question from the grave. 'When do we tell his father?'

'We don't,' said Jane Wilson. 'He will be in court on Monday, he always is. He will see what happens. He will understand. We will fight it every inch of the way and, that, in truth, was all that he wanted. We did not run Unfit to Plead to cover guilt. We had it forced upon us. He will be content.'

'Until he visits him in Broadmoor.'

'Oh, *shut up*, Gilbert.' From Mary Shelley came a slow and rare anger. 'We did not invent this trial. We did not blow up our hero and take out half his brain. We did not breed and suckle Roddy Nailor and the lumpen bastards who do his will. We may have made mistakes. We probably have made mistakes. To err is human and we most certainly are not divine but we have done our best. We have done our best for that poor sick man and we could do nothing else.'

'Well said, Frankenstein,' said Jane Wilson. 'We have done our best. Now all we can do is sit and wait for the roof of the temple to fall in. Cheers.'

Colonel William Allen, consultant neurosurgeon at the Ardingley Military Hospital, watched Eddie Cole on the other side of his desk and wondered, as thousands have done before, whether his visitor was entirely normal.

'I do not accept this, Superintendent,' he said.

'I am telling you, sir. This girl is in danger. Very considerable danger.'

'I have listened to you very carefully, Superintendent. I have come into the hospital this morning specifically to do so. But I must tell you that I do not accept what you tell me.'

Eddie Cole removed a portable tape recorder from the briefcase at his feet and put it on the desk between them. 'Very well, sir. I wonder if you would be good enough to listen to this.' Eddie Cole switched on the machine and, after a very short time, the voice of Melanie Golding filled the room.

After twenty minutes the machine fell silent. The colonel stared at Eddie Cole. 'It is unbelievable.'

'But do you believe it?'

'Oh, I believe she is telling the truth. There is no doubt about that. What I find difficult to believe are the implications of it.'

'You see what I mean. She is in danger.'

'I see that she may very well be in danger. What do you want me to do?'

'Right,' said Eddie Cole, 'this is what we do. I have made all the arrangements but it needs your agreement and help.'

'Let me hear it.'

For the next two hours Eddie Cole went about his business, directing operations from the room of the chief matron. He did so with the help of Sergeant Brendan O'Hara and two members of the Serious Crime Squad, hand-picked and, in both cases, virtually hand-reared by Eddie Cole himself. These were part of the team that regarded their super- intendent with a reverence normally reserved for Zulu chiefs. These were the Impis of Eddie Cole. Given a convenient cliff in the region of Scotland Yard they would not have paused at its edge once the com- mand had been given. At two o'clock Eddie Cole and his team rose from their seats, packed their briefcases and walked into the corridor, where they collided with a similar, though larger, group of men led by Chief Superintendent Jack Wagner.

The two police officers regarded each other with silent malice.

'Well, well, Jack, now where are you off to? Out-patients? Dermatology?'

'Let's stop being silly, Eddie, shall we? I think you and I need a little chat on our own in there. If you will excuse us, gentlemen, we will be just one moment. Try to avoid cheerful conversation.'

Back in the matron's room, Jack Wagner began the conversation. 'Before you say anything Eddie, let me tell you that I have got the girl's statement.' From the inner pocket of his blazer Jack Wagner extracted a faxed copy of Melanie Golding's testimony and laid it on the desk. 'It's all there, the whole fairy tale. Better than Brothers Grimm, that is. You must have been busy.'

'There is a tape too, Jack. You haven't heard that but I think you'll like it. Not a pause, not a dramatic flicker, it's all there, Jack, my boy. The truth in all its glory. I am not surprised that you don't recognise it.'

'Now Eddie, let's just stop the wisecracks for a minute. I know you want to see Nailor's head on your pike and I know why. But just think, Eddie. Just think for a moment. Even if that statement got into evidence. Even if, what do you think it is going to do to you? What about the fucking newspaper?'

'Oh Jack, I think I am going to cry. Do you know, Jack, I have been in this game for nearly forty years. I came in when I was seventeen. When I joined I looked up the promotion ladder. Jacob's ladder, and at the top I didn't see the Commander or the Commissioner or the sweaty Chief Constables with their rhubarb hats. What I saw, Jack, was the Head of the Serious Crime Squad, sitting on the right hand of God and here I am. Ten years at the top of the mountain. There is no human depravity that I have not seen, Jack. None. What I have seen human beings do to each other would give the Marquis de Sade a serious feeling of inadequacy. It's made me hard, Jack, but I can still be touched, *moved*, when I see the hand of human kindness reaching out its tentative fingers, brother to brother, sister to sister. I am still moved, Jack, and that's how I feel now. Here's you, Jack, right in the middle of all this shit. Up to your fucking neck and standing on tip-toe and all you can think of is me. Jack, if I didn't know that regimental tie was a fake, I'd ask if I could dry my eyes on it.'

'You should write poetry Eddie, and read the *Guardian*. Of course the statement screws me up. So don't think for one minute, not for one single nanosecond that I am going to let it stand up. What I am doing is giving you a chance, Eddie. It's not too late to pull the bloody thing now. Forget about it. The girl's a headcase. Until last week she had a bullet in her fucking brain. Pull it.'

'As a matter of interest, where did you get that copy?'

'Your Mick sergeant, dear old Brendan, faxed you a copy, didn't he? Well, what he forgot, what *you* forgot, is that these fax machines have a memory. I've got my friends too, Eddie. I knew Sleeping Beauty was awake and chatting. Yes, I did. Do you want to know how? Alex Bentley told me, the hack from the *Evening News*. The Cyclops with the beer stains. He overheard you talking to Brendan. I knew Brendan would fax you anything he got, so I raided the hospital fax machine. Not me personally, of course, but I have friends too, Eddie, I have friends too.'

'So, by now, Nailor knows?'

'Don't push me Eddie. I don't like it. But it is not too late. Pull it now.'

'It happens to be the truth.'

'Fuck the truth. The truth is that you are a great copper. Probably the best there has ever been. That's the truth. If this statement ever saw a court, you would be the best ex-copper there has ever been.'

'I know that Jack. But there are some comforts. You will be coming with me. We may even share the same cell. Who knows, once we have run the gauntlet of the washrooms, we might go on the same course. Ever thought about reading philosophy, Jack? You'd like it. Full of moral imperatives.'

'Are you going to pull it?'

'No, Jack, it's too late. And, by the way, who's that little crowd of suits you have got with you?'

'I thought you would want to know that. Three of them are my people. One of them is a consultant neurologist. He's got a gong, *Sir Michael Spencer* to you. Said to be the best in the business. The other one's a consultant shrink called Bunkist or something. They are both out of the top drawer. Both often used by the Security Services for the odd sensitive job. They have come to look at our leftie lady.'

An expression close to admiration appeared to cross the face of Eddie Cole. 'Oh, I see, I see. Now just let me spell it out for you, Jack. Your little brain boys are going to have a good look at Melanie Golding and, do you know, I haven't got a degree to my name but I will tell you exactly what they are going to say. Sir Terribly Clever Neurologist is going to pronounce on only partial recovery. "Still clear evidence of brain injury . . . neurological deficit . . . nystagmus, bi-nystagmus, erasmus . . ." You name it, she'll have it. "Plainly in an agitated state . . . irrational impulses . . . Still requiring heavy sedation . . ." Meanwhile Mr Brain-Shrinking Bumkist adds his own little bit of learning: "Post-traumatic paranoia . . . post-traumatic illusions . . . danger of clinical psychosis . . . unreliable raconteur . . . agree broadly with neurological opinion . . . benefits of long sedation . . . et cetera, et cetera.' Then she gets a nice little injection and back she goes to sleepy-byes. Melanie Golding not available to give evidence . . . indefinite period of sedation required . . . imminent fear of death statement no good because she is *not dead*, only sleeping. Attempts to introduce statement under the Criminal Justice Act quite hopeless in the face of eminent psychiatric and neurological opinion. Even if her own consultant disagrees, who can tell? Benefit must go to the defendant. End of story. Melanie Golding may or may not wake up. Then what happens to the trial? On the present state of play, likely result already decided by judge. Nailor back with mummy in the East End and Thomas Aylen off to sunny Broadmoor for an indefinite spell in a straitjacket. I am right, aren't I Jack. Don't even bother to say anything. I can see it in your lovely face. Where do you get that suntan from, incidentally, at this time of year? Must be freak conditions on the Esher golf course. Or is it fake, Jack, like everything else? You know where those statements have gone, Jack, don't you? George Watson has got one. The Director has got one. The judge has got one. Sir Edward Boyd has gone one. Even Aylen's defence has got one. They will get them on Monday morning and there is nothing you can do to stop it.'

'No, they won't, Eddie. They will get them before that because I will fax them my copy. Don't you see now, it doesn't matter? It doesn't matter at all. It doesn't matter how many people see the truth, providing they don't believe it. You're right. When my little team have finished looking her over no one will believe it.'

As Jack Wagner watched, the face of his fellow detective appeared to change. He was later to reflect that he had never seen the features of Eddie Cole twist into such weary resignation. As with the eyes and jowls, the shoulders slumped. 'He's beaten,' thought Jack Wagner. 'Dear God, he's beaten.'

Aloud he said, 'Take it easy Eddie, take it easy. Let's forget the gratuitous insults for a minute, shall we? No statement, no planted newspaper, no arrest of Eddie Cole, no sentence of perverting the course of justice, no nasty accidents in the washroom. You never know, Eddie, they may even give you an MBE or some such crap. It is not a defeat, Eddie, it's victory. Victory for you, victory for me and victory for common sense.'

'What about Thomas Aylen?'

'Oh, it's not too bad. He will do a few years in Broadmoor, of course, but we won't forget him. When it's all died down, we will get him moved somewhere a bit less primitive. He's a victim, Eddie. There are always victims. Most of humanity are victims. They are the herd. If they are lucky they have collective instincts and television to tell them their collective instincts are right. If they are unlucky then their collective instincts tell them to accept the grinding shit-hole of poverty in which they live and to shag away to create an even bigger herd of beggars. But they are all victims, victims of the collective will. There are only a few of Us. You, me . . .'

'And Nailor?'

'Yes, and Nailor too. He's not quite as good as you and me. Witness ten years in the slammer. But he is a controller, Eddie, an Olympian. His own man.'

'He's controlling you, Jack.'

'No he's not. You think he is controlling me. You think he is controlling *them* who are controlling me. But he is not Eddie. Not really. He is actually controlling *you*. He is controlling you because you are obsessed with him. All that energy, Eddie, all that learning, all the genius. The greatest copper there has ever been, all come to this. The pitiless pursuit of Roddy Nailor. Forget him, Eddie, give it up. Resume control.'

Eddie Cole stood up on his side of the desk. Absently he moved aside a pile of medical documents relating to the illness and incapacity of others. 'Maybe you are right, Jack. Maybe you are right.'

Jack Wagner, also standing, also smiling, 'You know I am, Eddie. You know I am.' Then, apparently instinctively, Jack Wagner's pink hand was extended, pulling behind it inches of white cuff and a gold cufflink. With a small pause, it was met by the hand of Eddie Cole. 'Old times, Eddie. Old times.'

'Old times, Jack. Old times.'

Outside the matron's room, two groups of impatient men watched Eddie Cole and Jack Wagner leave the room and stiffened with anticipation.

'OK, Brendan, Donald, Phillip, let's go. Job done. Back to the Smoke.'

The eyes of Brendan O'Hara widened with disbelief. 'But guv, what about . . .'

'Shut up, Brendan,' said Eddie Cole pleasantly, 'we have done our job. It's time to go home. Cheers, Jack. See you Monday.'

Silently the team of Eddie Cole traversed the long corridor, their feet beating a rhythm on the polished lino and their backs closely observed by the forces of Wagner. Outside the main doors of the hospital, Eddie Cole led his Impis across the lawn to the car park on the far side. Seated in the back together with Brendan O'Hara, Eddie Cole said, 'Off we go, Phillip. Get round that green as fast as we can.'

The car moved forward over the gravel and began to accelerate around the long bend. In order to leave the car park at Ardingley it is necessary to follow the drive which brings vehicles immediately in front of the steps of the main building which they had just left. As the car made the first turn, the driver said, 'Fasten your belt, guv, I think we have got some company.'

Ahead of them, emerging from the hospital doors, Jack Wagner and four members of the Special Branch deployed themselves across the drive.

'What shall I do, guv?'

'Oh, draw up alongside, Phillip, let's have a chat.'

As the car came to a halt, Jack Wagner appeared at the window closest to Eddie Cole, which opened with an automatic hiss.

'All right, Eddie, game over. Where is she?'

'Oh, Jack, yes, I forgot to say, she's gone away for a bit of R and R. Not for long. Be back on Monday. Going straight to the Old Bailey, I gather.'

'Eddie, you cannot do this. I repeat *you cannot do this*. That girl is *sick*. Do you understand?'

'No, Jack, she's not sick. *You are sick*, Jack, and if you want me to garnish that a bit, you are sick and bent. Compared to you the girl is an Olympic pole-vaulter. You do worry about people, Jack. I am beginning to get quite moved again. But don't you worry, Jack, she is in a nice, safe place where she will get all the care that she needs. Now if you get back to where you bogeys live and start doing a bit of work for a change, then you will find that there are something in the order of four thousand medical establishments in the country capable of caring for the rehabilitation of brain injury. If you get going now, Jack, and employ everyone that you can, then you might just cover a few hundred of those by Monday morning and you might *just* get lucky. But I don't think you can do that, Jack, because the bogeys, your bogeys, aren't that good at that kind of police work. They like rolling around in combat jackets with automatic pistols firing at dummies. It makes them feel nice, doesn't it Jack? Gives them big erections. No, you need a proper police team to do that, Jack, and I am terribly sorry to say that the whole of the Serious Crime Squad is fully booked. You can ask George Watson to try and mobilise them which will be like a detailed request to a bowl of custard. These are my people and they are *terribly* busy.'

'Eddie, you have kidnapped that girl.'

'Oh no, I haven't, Jack. This is all authorised by her own consultant. Go and ask him. You will find him in his room. Room 401, I think it is. Indeed I have specifically asked him to wait to talk to you. I have played him the tape and shown him the statement. He knows the truth, Jack, and he recognises it. Oh, and just one other thing, you might like to know, before you speak to him, who he is. He is a colonel as well as a consultant neurologist, so he won't have any difficulty telling you to fuck off. But he is rather more than a colonel. He went into the Army Medical Service because he comes from a military family. *His* father was an officer in the Royal Marines. Indeed, I think he was the Commanding Officer of the Royal Marines. One of his fellow officers at staff college was Thomas Aylen's father. You see, Jack, a bit of conventional police work pays dividends. Our medical colonel knows all about this case, Jack, because he has discussed it with his dad who has discussed it with Thomas Aylen's dad. You can try to make him tell you where the girl has gone if you like, Jack. You can try as hard as you like. Because he is a colonel and a boffin, some of your more rigorous methods will be denied to you. You are not dealing with some cretinous Mick caught with an Armalite. Anyway, Jack, good luck.'

'Eddie, do you know what you are doing? Not to the girl, but to us?'

'Oh, Jack.' Eddie Cole was suddenly impatient. 'We have been through all that, Jack. I know where I am going and, who knows, we may be in the same cell. Things are a bit crowded now and we may be in the same cell as Roddy Nailor. Now, if you don't mind, I am going to go and enjoy the rest of the weekend. It may be the last enjoyable weekend I will have for a long time. I confidently expect that it will be. I would advise you to do the same for the same reasons. See if you can improve our handicap. It may have lapsed by the time you are able to use it but human endeavour is always worth while. Goodbye, Jack.'

As they left the gates of the hospital, Brendan O'Hara turned to his boss, 'Christ, guv, is there anything, *anything* that you can't do or won't do?'

'As a matter of fact Brendan, I cannot buy a drink. I came out this morning without a fucking sou and as we are going to break our journey at the first available pub, whatever it looks like, and may be there for some considerable time, you are going to have to do the honours. I am sorry, Phillip, you are driving so it may be rather a protracted and frustrating interlude.'

The driver looked at Eddie Cole in the centre mirror. 'Don't worry, guv, I would drive you to the end of the world if you wanted me to.'

'Nice of you, Phillip, but the Firkin and Gobble over there on the roundabout will do nicely.'

'Three pints, three large Bushmills and a lemonade and lime,' said Brendan O'Hara to the manager of the Firkin and Gobble at 4.45 p.m.

As the manager pulled the pints, he glanced over Brendan O'Hara's right shoulder. 'Well,' he said, 'I'll pull them off this time, but I don't think he ought to have any more.' The manager inclined his head briefly in the direction of Eddie Cole who had just missed the board with his third consecutive dart. 'I think he is getting a bit dangerous.'

Brendan O'Hara leaned across the bar until his broad face was within six inches of his host. 'Were you on the job?'

The manager's eyes widened with surprise. 'Fifteen years. I ended up as a DC in Croydon. Still shows, does it?'

'Written all over the boat race. Now do you know who he is? The little fellow to whom you are proposing to refuse a drink?'

'Surprise me.'

'That is Superintendent Eddie Cole.'

'Christ,' said the manager.

'Nearly,' said Brendan O'Hara.

'What's he doing down here then?'

'He is just having a little celebration before he goes away.'

'Going on holiday?'

'Sort of,' said Brendan O'Hara.

'Going away for long?'

'I think,' said Brendan O'Hara, 'that he is going to have a really long break. What do I owe you for that lot?'

'Nothing. Stay as long as you like. The rest is on me. Just tell him to be careful with those fucking arrows.'

As Brendan O'Hara returned to the table bearing a tray of drinks, the mobile phone rang in Eddie Cole's pocket.

'It's all right Brendan, I'll do it,' said Eddie Cole, punching uncertainly at the keyboard, 'it is probably the missus, hello darling, how are you?'

'It's Chief Superintendent George Watson, Eddie,' said the voice on the other end, 'is it all right to talk? You don't sound very well.'

'Sorry sir, certainly OK to talk. Not feeling one hundred per cent. Maybe it's haemorrhoids, don't know.'

'Good lord, Eddie, I'll come straight to the point. I gather from Jack Wagner that the girl, Melanie Goldsmith . . .'

'Golding.'

'Ah yes, Golding. I gather from Jack Wagner that she has woken up, come to. He's shown me a statement which she has apparently made to Brendan O'Hara. Is this right?'

'That's it, sir. Spot on. Did it all by herself into a tape recorder.'

'Yes, Jack Wagner told me there was a tape recording as well. Eddie, I gather the girl's not at Ardingley any more?'

'That's it. That's right.'

'I am also told that, for some reason, the doctors aren't telling us where she is. Eddie, Eddie, are you there?'

'Line's breaking up a bit. Me too actually.'

'Eddie, we really do need to see the girl. Have her examined. See how she is, whether she can give evidence, that sort of thing. Eddie, do you know where she is? Eddie, Eddie, are you there?'

'Very bad line here, sir. Only get snatches of what you say. Something about wanker?'

'Wagner, Eddie, Jack Wagner, Chief Superintendent Jack Wagner. Now, Eddie, *please*, if you know where she is, will you please tell me.'

'No good, sir. Nothing coming through at all. Just the odd word. Something about the telly.'

'Tell me, Eddie, tell me where the girl is. I am afraid that is an order.'

'No good, sir. This thing's completely buggered. I'll try and give you a ring later, sir. Bit busy at the moment.'

'Eddie, where are you?'

'Firkin and Gobble.'

'What did you say, Eddie?'

'That's it sir. You can't hear me and I can't hear you, sir. Complete breakdown of communication I am afraid. Also not feeling too good. Think I've got Monkey's Syndrome. Will try and phone you later sir.'

Eddie Cole passed the instrument to Brendan O'Hara. 'Turn that fucking thing off, Brendan, will you? Can't see the keyboard too well. Thank you. Now I think just a couple more for the road. Someone seems to have taken the darts.'

# Part III

## TRUTH

# Chapter 1

'This is getting a bit repetitive,' said Anita Flynn. 'This High Noon stuff is all very well, but Grace Kelly only had it once. Three times a week gets a girl down.'

'You can take it,' said Eddie Cole, considerately, his face illuminated in the darkness by the last draw on his cigarette. 'When are you going to get a bigger ashtray?'

'When I get some clients with some money. What's Jack Wagner doing with his spare time?'

'You can write him off. He's going away for a long time, like me. Can't see him on a rooftop protest myself. The Free Wagner campaign will not be a mass movement. The barman at the Cheam Golf Club. That's about it.'

'Be serious for a minute. How long do you think you'll get?'

'God knows. Seven, eight, be out in five if I haven't been wasted in the bogs first.'

'You have got friends inside, haven't you?'

'Oh yeah. Thousands. They just love it when you bang 'em up. I get letters all the time. "Without you, Mr Cole, I would never have had this lovely long rest and met such interesting friends." Every day. Hundreds of them.'

'What's going to happen tomorrow?'

'I'll bring the girl in early. They will be waiting for us, of course, but I know ways into the Old Bailey otherwise unknown to man. I've had to get some pretty difficult witnesses in before and I think I can do it with her. No one in the squad will give them any help so they will have to rely on the wankers in Special Branch and Security Services. Once I've got her safely in a room at the Bailey (she's all right on a wheelchair incidentally, for short periods) then I will present myself to the prosecution team and pray. Before I do, I'll have a word with one or two of the hacks. I might even give Alex Bentley the break of a lifetime before he explodes like a burst still. The judge has got the statement. I don't think they can avoid calling her. Then the temple comes down. Bye-bye Roddy Nailor, bye-bye Jack, bye-bye Buster. It may not work but, whatever way it goes, it is still bye-bye Buster. Got any more of that whisky?'

As she fetched the bottle, Anita Flynn said, 'I still haven't read the statement, you know. I never opened the letter. It's over there on the table.'

'No need to read. The tape's there as well. Got a recorder? We can listen to it now while I become tumescent.'

'Chance,' said Anita Flynn, 'is a many-splendored thing.'

# Chapter 2

'I, Melanie Golding, wish to make a statement. I am recording these words into a tape recorder I have been given by Sergeant Brendan O'Hara. The account which I shall give is the truth, the whole truth and nothing but the truth, and I know that I will be liable for prosecution if I have included anything in it which is false or which I do not believe to be true. I have received no prompting or suggestions prior to making this statement. I know that my life is at risk and I make this statement in contemplation of my possible death from my injuries. It is my wish, if I die before I am able to give this evidence on oath, that my statement should be read in criminal proceedings. I have recorded the beginning of my story on two occasions earlier on this tape. I have listened to those recordings again. What I said then was true. I had reached the point when I removed the balaclava helmet from the man I now know to be Thomas Aylen. I said what followed was "wonderful" and I want to explain what I meant. His face has now two different sides. They are remarkably divided almost exactly in the middle. His right side is by normal standards, as a result of his injuries, grotesque. The left side is quite beautiful. I find it difficult to describe the effect it had on me. Before removing the mask I had already felt compassion. When I saw his face it became a wave of feeling. It contained many things, warmth, strength, a desire to hold, to protect, and a quite extraordinary gentleness. I can remember distinctly gasping for air. I have had several lovers and I have believed myself to be in love but I have never experienced such a sensation. Even now, in this condition, it is still with me.

'As I have said, I felt no fear. None at all and I reacted by instinct. I touched his face, the broken side, and said, "What have they done to you?"

'At first he said nothing. Now I know why. It takes him time to assess demands of any kind, however benign. Also he has difficulties speaking, which causes him to reduce sentences to elementary meaning. Then he said, "A bomb in a car."

'"A car bomb? Was it in Ireland? Were you a soldier?"

'"A Marine, yes. Ireland."

' "What is your name?"

'Again, there was a long pause before he said, "Aylen. Thomas Aylen."

'It took me a moment before I could place him. Then I said, "I remember. It was widely reported, two years ago. But of course."

'There was a silence between us. The left side of his face still conveys a quite normal range of expression and I watched it change as he looked at me. Then I said, "Now that you have told me who you are, I think you should tell me why you are here."

'There was a very long pause, a suspension. I knew he was struggling, fighting something, reaching for normality. I had a clear sense that he was submerged, groping for the surface. He turned away from me and I made the question a demand.

' "You must tell me, Thomas Aylen, you must tell me why you are here."

'When he turned back there was a gun in his hand. It was not pointed at me. It was proffered, palm up, as an explanation.

' "I came to take you."

'Even then I was surprised, amazed at the absence of fear. I was possessed of a calmness, a type of clarity. I said, "You do not need that to take me with you, Thomas Aylen, unless it is somewhere we don't want to go."

'I do not know why I used the plural, it was an instinct, but the effect was obvious.

' "Not me," he said, "I have been sent. Told to."

'He put his right hand to his head and I noticed for the first time the glove grip. Then he began to strike his own forehead. It was the frustration of a child.

' "Stop it," I said, "stop it now." And he did. Almost immediately. I must have been encouraged. I also felt an immediate instinct to *command*. I said, "You do not have to do this, Thomas. You do not want to do it and *you are not going to do it*."

'As a result of speaking to him for many hours I now realise the importance of that command. He does realise, you know. It is very strange. He has been told about his illness and its effect. He knows all about Menkies' Syndrome, by name and symptom. His comprehension and his intelligence are almost untouched. He has, as the experts say, insight. He knows he is powerless to resist demands, orders. He is like a man recognising the onset of an epileptic fit. He can see himself act as in a drama or fiction but he cannot control the plot. It – sometimes *they* – control him. (I know that I am digressing and I know that time is short.)

'After my words, "You are not going to do it," he looked at me and smiled. *He can smile.* It is not pretty but it is there and it conveyed unmistakable relief. I held out my hand, "Give me the gun, Thomas." And he did. I have little experience of guns. I once stole some shotguns at school, not for any wicked purpose, but that was years ago. I have grasped the basics from popular fiction, and I looked at once for the safety catch. Seeing me do so he pointed to the small lever, "It is on."

'It was at that point that we both heard noises from the bedroom. Seconds later the door opened. In the bedroom were two men. Both had balaclava helmets. I now know their names – Alan and Terry Jones. I can remember standing by the desk. Thomas turned towards them and then immediately and with clear intent, took up a position in front of me.

'The first figure spoke from the bedroom door. "Well now, so what the fuck's going on then? Here we are waiting in the park and fucking nothing."

'He moved from the door. Thomas remained stationary.

' "Oh I see. That's the game soldier boy. Bottled it have we? Or gone soft more like. Pretty thing, isn't she? Far too pretty for a monster like you. Been talking to you has she? Telling you what to do? Never mind, we've got your dabs all over the place and that's the main thing. Just have to do the rest ourselves."

'As he came across the room I wrenched the receiver from the phone and tried to dial.

' "Don't worry about that sweetheart, that's as dead as mutton."

'Of course, he was right. It was only then, when I began to scream for help, that I realised, amazingly, that the Brahms was still playing. The radio is part of my music equipment and on a table by the bedroom door. Deliberately the second man, now in the room, moved to the set and increased it to full volume. The second said, "Scream away darling. We know all about this house. Two neighbours, one away, one stone deaf who gets meals on wheels. He won't even enjoy the nice music."

'Both of them then came across the room very fast. Impossibly, Thomas stopped them both. Despite his injuries he is, of course, a trained soldier. He threw his body into one and the other he delivered a blow by swinging his right arm. The prosthesis he wears is metal and, I now know, very heavy. By luck, or judgement, it hit the forehead. All three went down on the floor. They were behind the large chair and for a moment I could only hear the fighting.

'I could have made for the flat door. I did not do so. I then remember a mass of bodies fighting across the room, part standing, part rolling. The table was knocked violently backwards and they seemed to rebound towards the centre of the room. It was obvious that Thomas was losing, he had to, didn't he? The Jones brothers are both very strong. In a split second they had him pinned on the floor, his face pressed against the bottom of the wall. One, holding on to his feet, jerked upwards and I heard Thomas cry out.

'At that point I could clearly see both of the brothers between Thomas and myself. I raised the gun, moved the lever of the safety catch and shouted, "Stop it now."

'For a second, apart from the Brahms symphony, there was nothing. A suspension of time before one of them slowly got to his feet.

'"Well, well, what have we here? Annie fucking Oakley, large as life. That's his little shooter isn't it? Yes it is, I can see that. And you wouldn't have one anyway, would you Miss Jew-judge daughter? So why don't you just give it to me nice and quiet?"

'He came towards me. I pressed myself back on the desk, noticing, as I did so (it is extraordinary what one recollects), the pages of my work scattering on the floor. As he stepped across, I pulled the trigger. Nothing. I pulled again and again. By this time he was within an arm's length, menacing and smiling.

'"Now do you think, do you really think, we would give that fuckwit a loaded gun? Someone might have got badly hurt. *You* maybe. And our job is to take you in safe and sound."

'He moved forward and I brought the gun up with all my force under his chin. As I did so, I dropped it and ran for the door. I got there first, slipped the catch and ripped it open. Immediately outside there was a huge figure, also masked. I later learnt his name was Bedser.

'"Going somewhere?"

'There was only one other way out. I ran for the bedroom door and on to the balcony. There was no ladder. Someone held me from behind. I struggled back into the bedroom and grabbed the first thing, my alarm clock I think. It was immediately knocked from my hand. I fell on to the bed and something covered my face. After that I remember nothing until I woke in the cellar.

'There was one bulb above the cellar steps, otherwise it was in near darkness except when they came and went. In the gloom, I heard a quiet laboured breathing. I found, as you know, that I was chained to a pipe which ran near the bed. It caused me no pain or discomfort at this stage but it was difficult for me to turn. I knew it was Thomas. I called to him and he said nothing in reply. I heard him move across the floor to the side of the bed. He was not chained or tied and the reason was obvious. His left ankle was broken and his right leg is always nearly useless. The prosthesis in his right arm had been taken and he was, to all extents and purposes, crippled. The good side of his face was caked in blood from an injury to his forehead. With difficulty he sat on the floor beside the bed. He was to remain in that position for days. I had a violent headache and a terrible thirst but otherwise I was unharmed. I could not inspect my body but I knew that I was "intact".

'Time passed. Thomas told me about the cellar we were in. There was no water and no window. There is a vent. He said it had obviously been some kind of playroom and in the corner I could see a table-tennis table with bats and other games. I remember even then thinking it was bizarre furniture for a dungeon.

'After some time, hours perhaps, they came, all three of them without hoods. I found this alarming. Knowledge of identity presupposed eternal silence. They brought water, bread and cheese and some soup. They were obviously under instructions and said absolutely nothing. It was me who spoke.

'"How long are you keeping us for?"

'Silence.

'"Where are we?"

'Silence.

'"This man," I said, nodding towards Thomas, "is injured. He must have treatment."

'To this there was a reaction. One of the Jones brothers came to me and pointed to a cut on his own forehead. Having done so, he turned to Thomas and kicked him in the leg. I did not make the request again.

'The second time they came I demanded to be taken to the lavatory. One of the brothers shook his head but surprisingly the big man, Bedser, seemed to soften.

'"I'll take her upstairs," he said, "as for him, he can piss in his pants."

'I was released (as I was on a number of occasions after) and went with Bedser, filled with every dire premonition. I remained untouched. He looked at me but did nothing. But he did look. I told him that my clothes were soiled (they were) and I needed new ones. Without a word he brought me a man's shirt and I changed behind an open bathroom door. The house, I could see, was a neat suburban house, full of normal middle-class furniture. Parker Knoll chairs, bits of stripped pine. As I looked at the ephemera, I had a sense of total unreality.

'So it went on. Two days, three, four, I do not know. When alone we slept and talked. We rehearsed our lives, our tragedies, our hopes. We talked of plans, desires, disappointments. For hours we spoke of politics and philosophies and, yes, of course, do not ask. We fell in love.

'On the third day, fourth, fifth, does it matter? The cellar door opened, the lights came up and we knew immediately it was quite different. A new man came in with the others. I recognised him immediately from the press publicity. My father had sentenced him ten years before. For that reason we had all followed the case at school. Roddy Nailor. Even from my position one could feel the immense power he held over the others. It was a shock. Since the trial I had no knowledge of him or about him, absolutely nothing. He stood in the middle of the cellar and watched us. Then he spoke.

'"So, here we are. The judge's spawn and the War Hero, don't they look lovely? Quite a treat. I am sorry, I forgot the introductions. My name is Roddy Nailor, nothing special about me, not a judge, not a soldier, nothing fancy. One of nature's gentlemen from the Mile End Road. This is Bonkers Bedser from Manchester and these gentlemen are Alan and Terry Jones from Cardiff. Let's take a bow, boys, OK? One, two, three."

'And then, in a bizarre pantomime, they all did.

'"So that's our bow to you. Now what about your bow to us? Oh dear, Miss Golding can't because she is all twisted up in the plumbing. So let's have you, soldier boy, naughty, naughty soldier boy who disobeyed orders. Let's have you on your feet, just doing what you are told." He walked towards Thomas, bent down, and put his face within inches of Thomas's head. "Get up. Get up now. That is an order."

'I could see Thomas's face close to mine. I could read the confusion in his left eye. At first it radiated defiance but then, as the commands came, it dulled. Still he did not move. Nailor's eyes narrowed.

'"What's this? What's this? Not obeying orders again. Our Monkey Boy getting a mind of his own." Nailor stood back, loosened his jacket and from his waistband produced a gun. For the first time I noticed he was wearing gloves.

'"This is for disobeying orders, see. Where do we want the first shot?"

'Desperately I worked my face as close to Thomas as I could. "Get up Thomas," I said, "get up."

'He rose with immense difficulty. He had only one hand and a broken leg. With these he pulled himself to his feet and faced Nailor.

'"Ah, I see, taking orders all round? Now, last command. Here you are, *Captain* Aylen. Here's the gun, still got one good hand, haven't we? Don't worry, this one is loaded. Now you face Miss Golding, take the gun and shoot her. In the head. Oh, and just in case you felt like using it for any other purpose, Bonkers here will keep his gun at your head. If you do so much as twitch in his direction, he will blow *your* head off. Then he will do the same to her and his gun will be found in your hand.

The perfect murder and suicide by Mr Brain Dead. Now take the gun, that's it. Point it at her, that's it, now fire it. That is an order. Fire it. Now."

'I could see the barrel of the gun which grew to the size of a plate and behind it I could see Thomas's face and the single living eye. I said, "Do it, Thomas. They will kill me anyway. It's quicker like this and I would rather it was you."

'Lying there, I watched him start to shake. The tremor began with his hand and spread across his entire body. Great waves of movement racked him but the gun remained pointed straight at my head. Then suddenly he jerked it in the air and fired. The explosion was deafening in the cellar and plaster fell from the ceiling on to my bed. In one fast movement Nailor seized the gun and smashed it into the side of Thomas's head. Even before Thomas hit the ground, Nailor was over him, the gun jammed against his left eye. "You fucker," he said evenly, "you ugly little fucker. So we are going to have to wait, are we? Monkey Nuts Syndrome taking a day off, is it? Well, let's give you something to think about in the meantime."

He stood back and I remember shouting, "No, no, leave him alone," before he jumped with the full force of his body on to Thomas's left arm. There was no other sound but I heard the bone break.

'Nailor turned to me. "Now you fucking well shut up. What am I going to do with you? The answer to that is 'whatever I want'. I may get you to phone daddy tomorrow. I may send him bits of you. I may kill you or I may give you to Bonkers here who likes the daughters of Jew-judges. You just think about it. Come along gentlemen, let's leave them in peace."

'As the light dimmed, I heard Thomas cry out beside me. I heard him say, "I am sorry. I couldn't do it, even when you told me to."

'I said, "I know, my darling, I knew you wouldn't." It was a lie.

'A day passed, maybe two as before. Nailor was not seen. Then suddenly something happened. We both sensed it like an electric current. Our three jailers changed. Swaggering confidence became something close to panic. This expressed itself in anger towards us and, we could hear, to each other. Heated conversations in the room above, in part barely audible, gave us the news that Nailor had been arrested.

'Initial joy disappeared when we realised the inevitable consequence. It was a death sentence. As they left the cellar for the last time I said, "Thomas, I know you are not in the best of condition but do you think you could manage to get into this bed? I feel a strong need for close company. If necessary that is an order."

'He did so and we made love. It was not easy but in manacles, great pain and the imminent expectation of death we enjoyed a passion I had never known. Then we slept. We woke to an almighty crash and then there was firing. We heard the cellar door open. By this time Thomas had struggled across the floor. A figure emerged at the bottom of the steps wearing a blue combat suit. He also wore rimless glasses. My feelings of relief froze when I saw the expression on his face. He had a gun in each hand, one by the handle, and the other by the barrel. Thomas was half-lying on the floor beneath him and he said quietly, "Here we are, Aylen, take hold of this." Even as he placed the gun in Thomas's hand he kicked it away. He took a step back and pointed his own gun at Thomas's head. I screamed, "No, no." Then I remember quite clearly that he turned to me and said, quietly again, "Don't shout. Say your prayers." As he turned back to Thomas a second figure appeared at the foot of the cellar steps. I have no other recollection until waking here in the presence of Sergeant O'Hara who has been my friend and companion and has never attempted to suggest to me any facts or versions of events. This statement is the truth. I have made it of my own free will.'

# Chapter 3

At 8 a.m. on Monday, Eddie Cole paced Fleet Street, a quarter of a mile from the Old Bailey. As he moved he muttered, '*Come on Brendan, come on, where are you lad, you're late, she's late, we have got to get her into the fucking building. Come on boys, where are you?*'

In his pocket the mobile phone rang and, when activated, the voice of Brendan O'Hara spoke the words of doom. 'They've got her, guv, I am afraid. I'm sorry, guv. They came for her this morning at seven. Not the bogeys, not Special Branch, not Security Services. I don't know who they are but they are from up North. I think they are Six Regional Crime Squad, but I'm not sure. They say they are acting specifically under the directions of the Director of Public Prosecutions and they are under strict instructions to give no other information. One of them told me the Director has been to see your colonel doctor personally. They arrived at the nursing home last night, late, God knows what's going on guv. It looks as though we're fucked.'

Eddie Cole spoke quietly, barely audible to his sergeant above the noise of the London traffic. 'Don't worry, Brendan, we did our best. I don't know what's happening. I'm not in control any more. We did our best. You're in the clear, my son. I am going into the Bailey now. Go say some Hail Marys or whatever you Micks do before the hearse arrives.'

'Good luck, guv,' said Brendan O'Hara.

As Eddie Cole entered the police door of the Old Bailey two unknown men fell into close step with him.

'Superintendent Cole,' said one.

'Get it over with,' said Eddie Cole.

'Chief Inspector Moreton, Six Regional Crime Squad based in Sheffield. We met once, briefly, when you came to dinner.'

'I'm sorry,' said Eddie Cole, 'I never remember dinners very well.'

'Nor me usually, guv, but you were speaking.'

'God help you,' said Eddie Cole. 'What are you here for anyway?'

'Team of us came down. Quite a lot of weight, two superintendents. We're answering direct to the DPP. Other than that I don't know much.

The Director's here, by the way, he's got a room on the fourth floor. You've got an invitation to call in.'

'I wonder if I've got a choice?'

'Not much of one, guv, I should think. Not a job I enjoy, this.'

'Get on,' said Eddie Cole, 'best part of the job, knocking off the bosses. I tried it a long time ago. Didn't work then.'

'Jack Wagner's here as well.'

Eddie Cole turned to him and smiled. 'You have been doing your homework, Inspector Moreton. Congratulations. Unusual for Wagner to be first up the steps of the guillotine. But I'm going up smiling. It looks better in the basket.'

A surprising number of people turned to Eddie Cole as he entered the Director's room. Alan Farquharson, DPP for a little over a year, stood up from behind his desk. At the Bar he had been veteran of many prosecutions at the Old Bailey. The Head of the Serious Crime Squad was no stranger to him. On one occasion, after the Lurcher case, they had got drunk together at El Vino's.

'Good morning Eddie,' he said.

'Good morning, sir. Good morning, gentlemen, Miss Wilson, Miss Black.' As he spoke he nodded to the remaining occupants of the room who sat at the long table which stretched to the Director's desk: in addition to Antonia Black and Jane Wilson, there were Sir Edward Boyd, John Wilkin, Preston Lodge, Gilbert Smith, Jack Wagner, Lord Justice Stoker and Mr Justice Golding.

'Come and sit down, Superintendent,' Farquharson continued, 'you are the last to arrive but I suspect you have been waiting on a street corner. Come and sit close to me.'

'Thank you.'

'Now, Superintendent, as you are no doubt aware I have taken charge of this operation with the assistance of a team of officers from Six Regional Crime Squad. I have aquainted myself with the details of this case and have spent a considerable part of the weekend reading a transcript of the trial with which I have been thoughtfully provided. I have also read the statement of Miss Golding, of which we now all have a copy. I understand that there is also a tape recording which, I suspect, Superintendent, you have about your person. Perhaps you would give it to me. Thank you. Melanie Golding, for the benefit of any that do not know, is at the Farley Nursing Home, just outside Epsom. Five members of Six Regional Crime Squad are in attendance upon her.

'The statement which she has made is a remarkable document. It obviously comes from a remarkable young woman. It has, of course, put a wholly different complexion on many aspects of this case. It provides, of course, the clearest possible evidence against the defendant Nailor, which was previously almost non-existent. John Wilkin obviously agrees with that assessment.' The barrister nodded on cue. 'Simultaneously the statement exonerates Aylen on all counts, save for the technical possibility of proceeding on an attempt to kidnap based upon his early actions before the conversation with Miss Golding. That is a technicality which appeals to no one.'

At this point the Director paused, the level of his voice fell and the tempo slowed. 'It is also quite clear that the statement provides evidence relating to the arrest of Aylen and the existence, or non-existence of the famous newspaper. Of course, if Melanie Golding were to give evidence, she would be subject to cross-examination and some of this might be disbelieved. In the event, that will not be necessary. Perhaps that could be described as fortunate were it not for the gravity of the circumstances. Tragedy might even be a better word.'

In the short silence that followed, Eddie Cole's spirits sunk, through the dull ache of alcoholic depression. 'So that's it,' he thought, 'they have finished her. The Truth goes back to sleep.'

Sir Edward Boyd intervened. 'Grave, yes, but I must say, considering his crimes and background and what is contained in the girl's statement, I find it difficult to apply the word "tragedy". There is almost a poetic justice in this.'

Suddenly and painfully alert, Eddie Cole spoke straight to the Director. 'I wonder if I could be told what the nature of this tragedy or gravity is?'

Alan Farquharson raised his eyebrows, 'I had rather assumed, Eddie, that you would know. In my experience you know virtually everything before it happens. But then, of course, I forgot that you have been standing on a street corner since the early hours of this morning. Roddy Nailor hanged himself in his cell last night.'

A fierce wave began at the very extremities of Eddie Cole's misshapen body and rose, like a giant tide, towards his bald and pasted head. 'Hanged himself?'

The Director almost smiled. 'Yes, Eddie, hanged himself. It is a very unhappy business. Do you want to know what happened? There will, of course, have to be a full inquiry but the facts seem fairly clear. Nailor was aware somehow that the girl was awake and had made a statement. He must have been aware that not only did it make his position in this trial almost impossible but it also implicated him directly in the murder. At eight thirty last night he was found hanging behind the door of his cell.

All rope and cord and belts had, of course, been removed from him. The instrument he had used had obviously been smuggled to him. One suspects that the original purpose had been to enable him to carry out some ghastly assault, perhaps even an escape attempt. As it transpired, he used it to end his own life.'

'What did he use?'

The Director's eyes centred on Eddie Cole. 'Piano wire, a very unpleasant business. Not a pretty sight, I am afraid. He had done it at some time after seven p.m. which is the last occasion when he was seen alive. At the time that he was discovered he was only just dead. Piano wire apparently takes its time.'

Eddie Cole spoke without voluntary intention. 'I don't believe he would do this.'

'It is difficult, I know, but the facts appear to be incontrovertible. He had been seen at seven o'clock by two visitors who confirm that he was in a state of considerable depression. These gentlemen were both senior officers in the Security Services. Apparently, he had, in the dim and distant past, carried out some work for Mossad. For some extraordinary reason he thought that this factor might stand him in good stead. The officers told him in no uncertain terms that he could not benefit from such disclosure. They were the last to see him alive. Cells are unlocked at that hour in the remand wing and the officers had made their own departure. It was not until the warder arrived for lock-up at eight o'clock that the suicide was discovered. Now, Superintendent, I have already informed everyone here of the consequences of these seismic events. The decisions have already been taken and are not negotiable. Firstly, the existence of this statement makes any further proceedings against Aylen quite impossible. The only person who could have objected to Melanie Golding giving evidence was Roddy Nailor. There is no Roddy Nailor and no objection. Once this evidence is given, either by the girl or in writing, the acquittal of Aylen is obviously inevitable. Indeed I suspect it would be the fastest jury retirement on record. The Crown will, therefore, offer no further evidence against Aylen and he will be released. As to the other parts of the girl's statement, these will never be tested in evidence. Careful consideration has been given to the obvious implications but, when all is said and done, this is the evidence of a woman who has suffered severe brain injury. It is more than enough to secure an acquittal but whether it would be enough to mount a serious prosecution against long-standing and dedicated police officers is quite another. It has, therefore, already been decided that there will be no further action as a result of this information. I don't think that there is anything else to discuss. I will not be in court when the proceedings are concluded and Melanie Golding's statement will not be made public. There is no requirement to do so, and the less publicity that attends upon these unfortunate and injured people the better. Thank you, ladies, gentlemen, let us depart.'

In the corridor outside the Director's room, John Wilkin walked beside Jane Wilson.

'Thank God,' he said vehemently, 'thank God for that.'

'Hear, hear,' said Jane Wilson, 'that young man could have spent a lifetime in Broadmoor.'

'Oh *that*,' said John Wilkin, 'yes, yes, I suppose there is that. But Jane, just think, the nightmare of Legal Aid is now ended. My wives and my children may sleep in peace. Normal service is resumed.'

Behind the barrister's back, Jack Wagner walked with Eddie Cole.

'Lucky bastard,' he said.

'Snap,' said Eddie Cole, 'fucking snap.'

The transcript of the last day of the trial of Aylen and Nailor is a short document and is framed on the wall of the office of Superintendent Eddie Cole. This is it:

JUDGE  Good morning members of the jury. Yes, Sir Edward.

SIR EDWARD BOYD  It falls to me to tell your Lordship publicly that there have been, over the last weekend, quite momentous events which have affected this trial.

JUDGE  I am aware of at least some of them, Sir Edward. Perhaps you would be kind enough to give the court the details.

SIR EDWARD BOYD  My Lord, the two events are these. Firstly, I am delighted to tell your Lordship that Melanie Golding, the tragic victim in this case, has now made at least a partial recovery. She is conscious and articulate and has made a full statement to the police. The second grave event is this. On Sunday evening Roddy Nailor, the second defendant, was found dead in his cell.

JUDGE  Excuse me, Sir Edward, may I please issue a mild word of warning to the press and public galleries? I appreciate that these are sudden developments and that immediate noise reaction is understandable. However, it is important that these proceedings proceed, for I believe that they will shortly conclude, with some dignity and decorum. Thank you. Please continue, Sir Edward.

SIR EDWARD BOYD  There will undoubtedly be an inquiry into his death. But, at the moment, I must tell your Lordship that it appears that Mr Nailor took his own life. The consequences of these matters are twofold. First, for the most obvious reasons, the jury must be discharged from returning a verdict in his case. Second, the contents of Melanie Golding's statement (which are known to your Lordship) are such that the case against Thomas Aylen has become quite untenable. The Crown could not ask for a guilty verdict having regard to the contents of that statement and, in those circumstances, we would invite your Lordship to direct the jury to acquit Mr Aylen on all counts. I take this unusual course because Melanie Golding is, of course, still a patient at considerable risk and it would be a cruel imposition to require her to give evidence in court.

JUDGE  Thank you, Sir Edward, I agree with everything you have said and the courses which you propose. Does anyone else have any observations? No? Thank you. Very well, ladies and gentlemen of the jury, you have heard what has been said by Sir Edward. These developments will have come as a surprise to you and, I dare say, as a shock. I have, myself, had rather longer notice. Mr Nailor is dead and, in those circumstances, there can be no verdict and I will discharge you from giving one. In the case of Thomas Aylen, more difficulties arise. He is currently in your charge and the verdict must come from you. However, I can tell you that I have myself read the statement of Melanie Golding and I agree with everything that Sir Edward says. Were she to give evidence then an acquittal would be inevitable; indeed, I would not allow the case to proceed beyond the end of the prosecution case. Melanie Golding is, as you know, still unwell and it would be, as Sir Edward says, a cruel imposition to require her to give evidence. In those circumstances, I know you will agree that the best course is to provide, at this stage, a verdict of not guilty. I will ask my clerk to receive that verdict.

COURT CLERK  Will the foreman of the jury please rise. In the case of Roderick Nailor you are discharged, by his Lordship, from entering a verdict. In the case of Thomas Aylen, do you, Mr Foreman, find him not guilty of the offences for which he is charged?

FOREMAN  Not guilty on all charges.

JUDGE Mr Aylen, you are free to go. There is just one other matter which I would like to raise. I would like Detective Chief Superintendent Wagner and Superintendent Cole to stand, please. Gentleman, this case has come to a premature conclusion. Mr Nailor is dead and, in the case of Mr Aylen, it is quite clear that a potential miscarriage of justice has been avoided, perhaps at the last minute. I wish, however, to state publicly that the trial and the investigations which proceeded the trial demonstrated police work of the highest order. The injury to Melanie Golding resulted from a most tragic misadventure, but neither that injury nor the subsequent developments in this trial are the responsibility of police officers in this case. The two of you, who have borne joint responsibility for the investigation of this case, deserve commendation not only for your individual contribution but for the teamwork that you have inspired between yourselves and in others. It is my intention to pass this commendation to the Commissioner of Police and to the Home Secretary.

# Chapter 4

Six months later, Anita Flynn stared in astonishment at the profile of her lover rising above the pillow of her bed. 'What do you mean, giving up?'

'Well, it wasn't doing me any good. I wasn't too worried about lung cancer but it gives you a nasty dry skin. I've got enough problems without that. And you never got that ashtray. Kept on getting third degree burns, so this is my last one. I want to look my best when I go to the Palace.'

'Dear God, when is this?'

'Next Wednesday. I'm going with Jack fucking Wagner. His gong is worth more than mine but I gather they are doing us together for old time's sake.'

'How is he?'

'God knows. Taken early retirement. God help the Esher golf course.'

Anita Flynn turned and stared at the bald head of Eddie Cole. 'It came out all right in the end, didn't it?'

'Lovely. I've still got my balls and my job.'

'Not you, the others. What happened to Aylen in the end?'

'Went back to live with his father and his step-mother. I had a letter from his father the other day. I gather Melanie Golding sees him regularly. What will come of it, God knows. One thing for sure, he will do anything she tells him. Edward Boyd's been made a judge, Jane Wilson's still slugging it out in the Old Bailey, John Wilkin got divorced and Bob Phillips has gone to the Court of Appeal. It came out all right in the end. Oh bugger, I've burnt my bloody finger. What do the Arabs say about this bloody ashtray?'

'Arabs have impeccable manners. They do not smoke or swear in bed. They have other difficult habits but impeccable manners. Let me have a look at that hand. It's not much but I think you ought to put it in some cold water. Fill the basin.'

After a moment the boudoir of Anita Flynn was filled with half-light from the unit above the basin. She heard running water and the washing of hands.